Impetuous Desire

A severe beating was Elysia's first indication that she would have to battle alone to achieve her destiny. Young and beautiful, born into English nobility, Elysia was suddenly an orphan—and caught in the clutches of an aged, spiteful aunt whose brutality toward Elysia forced her to flee for her life!

Searing Passion

Alone and penniless, she embarked on a perilous journey through the English countryside,—only to encounter the man they called the Devil—Lord Alex Trevegne, with his jet-black hair, golden gypsy eyes, and enormous sensual appetites. Women meant but one thing to the arrogant Lord Alex—until he met Elysia . . .

Enduring Love

Thrown together by sinister forces into an alliance of hatred, Elysia and Alex soon felt stirrings of passion for each other—like none they'd ever felt. But pride kept them apart, until that one night when all the world seemed to explode—and the deep-seated rivers of emotion within Alex and Elysia burst into the white heat of desire and destiny!

**A RAPTUROUS TALE
OF SPLENDOROUS ROMANCE
AND BREATHTAKING EMOTION,
FROM THE PUBLISHERS OF
THE FLAME AND THE FLOWER**

Laurie McBain
Devil's Desire

AVON
PUBLISHERS OF BARD, CAMELOT, DISCUS, EQUINOX AND FLARE BOOKS

DEVIL'S DESIRE is an original publication of Avon Books.
This work has never before appeared in any form.

AVON BOOKS
A division of
The Hearst Corporation
959 Eighth Avenue
New York, New York 10019

ISBN: 0-380-00295-7

First Avon Printing, April, 1975.
Fifteenth Printing

AVON TRADEMARK REG. U.S. PAT. OFF. AND
FOREIGN COUNTRIES, REGISTERED TRADEMARK—
MARCA REGISTRADA, HECHO EN CHICAGO, U.S.A.

Printed in the U.S.A.

Tears, idle tears, I know not what they mean,
Tears from the depth of some divine despair,
Rise in the heart, and gather to the eyes,
In looking on the happy autumn-fields,
And thinking of the days that are no more.
                                    Tennyson

Chapter 1

High in a cloud-laden afternoon sky, a free-spirited skylark soared gracefully; its spread-winged shadow traveling swiftly over the colorful autumnal countryside below. Its song pierced the primeval silence of the forest below as the cheerful cry carried through the chill air; the clear notes penetrating beneath the thick canopy of branches, and reaching the soft, loam-covered forest floor, the sound was absorbed by the bright carpet of fallen leaves.

The woods seemed to come to life, humming with the chirpings and chatterings of busy forest creatures contentedly gathering food for the oncoming winter, until another sound intruded into the aimless animal-chatter and sent a hush over the clearing. An uneasy silence hung over it as the threatening sounds of baying hounds and pounding horses' hooves echoed in the distance.

The gossiping birds took wing and the bushy-tailed squirrels scurried into safe nests as a figure emerged from the trees, twigs snapping sharply as it moved into the clearing.

"Tally-ho!" Ribald laughter followed the cry of the hunt. "Where is that foxy wench? Damnation! Don't lose sight of her now, man!"

The excited voices drifted to a still figure, galvanizing it into action, and the raised voices became louder as the riders moved closer. Then the voices merged into one menacing sound as they intermingled with the snorting of their mounts.

As they came closer, Elysia could almost feel their hot breath against the back of her neck, as she held up her skirts and hurriedly climbed over a fallen tree. She stopped, pausing to catch her breath, panting heavily as she leaned against another tree for support. She could hear the raised voices of the men as they searched about the undergrowth, not far off, beating it back to find her hiding place. She shivered as she heard the throaty yelping of the dogs, and saw movement through the trees as the horsemen pressed on toward her; each passing second bringing them closer.

She stood still, frozen with fear, her eyes darting about like those of a trapped animal seeking safety. Suddenly, she noticed the hollowed out trunk of the fallen tree, the opening partially concealed by the full-fronded ferns and wild weeds that grew about the gaping mouth. She moved quickly into the cool, concealing darkness. Crawling past the thick ferns, she pulled them back into order as she stretched out full length on the rotted and damp bottom. She shivered as she felt the little crawling inhabitants of the decayed tree about her. Elysia's breath caught painfully in her throat as she heard the pounding of the horses' hooves coming straight towards her; shaking the earth beneath her body until she thought she would be trampled to death beneath them.

"Bloody fool! You've let her flee!" said a petulant voice, startling Elysia by its closeness.

"Damn it all, it's you who slowed me up—thought you saw her in a dozen different places," another voice complained.

"First decent bit o' muslin I've seen in this damned county, and what happens?" demanded the first voice, self-pityingly. "She gets away. Did you see that glorious hair! A real little fox she was—and those long legs! By God, I'll not be cheated out of my prize after going to the trouble of giving chase!"

Elysia heard the creaking of his saddle as the rider shifted impatiently, and the ominous snapping sound of a riding crop being tapped angrily against gloved hands.

"Where are those cursed hounds? We'd have had her flushed out by now if those hounds were on her scent. Could've sworn I saw something over here."

"Sounds like they've caught scent of something over that way," the other man spoke as the distant sound of raised voices and barking reached them.

"Damn! It'd better be the wench! I'll beat their hides off if they've cornered a bloody hare. I'm going to have that maid to warm my bed this eve. It's too damned cold in this blasted place to sleep alone." He sighed in exasperation. "We'd better find her soon, because I'm played out; too damned tired to even breathe, much less enjoy the wench. Wish I were back in London—don't have to hunt for my pleasures there. Plenty of high-steppers just begging for my favors," he boasted.

"You're getting soft, my friend. The hunt adds spice to the victory, but we'd best be off, or you'll only have your old housekeeper to warm your bones this eve," his friend snickered.

"I'll be warming myself against that red-haired wench. You can have my housekeeper, or one of the scullions—more your style," he said laughing loudly.

"You don't have her yet, and who knows, she might prefer me after she's caught a glimpse of you."

"Damned if she will!" he answered rising to the bait. "I'll wager my team of blacks she begs me to take her back to London before the night's out."

Elysia heard their laughter, and then trembled as

she felt the fragile walls of her sanctuary shake as the riders urged their mounts over the fallen tree, and moved off into the trees toward the excited barking of the hounds.

Elysia waited, scarcely breathing as she listened to the retreating hoof beats. Breathlessly, she peered out between the lacy, interwoven fronds, seeing only emptiness in the clearing beyond. At last, they were gone.

Slowly, like a hunted animal, she crawled from the safety of her hole and paused, as if sniffing the air for the scent of an enemy, poised for flight at the first sign of danger. As she made her way through the trees Elysia felt tears of rage and fright well up in her eyes.

Her lips quivered as she thought of herself like some animal being hunted for pleasure. No wonder the villagers kept their young daughters close to their sides when the wild bloods, the fancy London gentlemen, paid their irregular visits to their estates in the country. Attired in their finely-cut coats and lacy cravats, jewels glittering from their long white fingers, they demanded, and expected, anything they wanted, causing havoc the few days they took up residence on their country estates. They abused their landlordly rights by browbeating their tenants, and seducing their daughters. From upstairs maid to milk maid—not one comely face was safe from their lust.

And now she, Elysia Dèmarice, daughter of aristocratic parents, was humiliated and reduced to cowering like a frightened beast, afraid for her life. She had to suffer the indignity of being pursued by fun-seeking young bloods from London, out to satisfy their carnal desires. Were she still under the protection of her father's house, they would not dare to approach her; she was their equal—in name and position. Possessing beauty was a liability when one did not have the protection of one's family.

But a far greater outrage, Elysia thought, was her aunt's perfidy. She had sent her out here to the north end of the property, well aware that young Lord Tanner was visiting with a party of his disreputable friends. The possibility of their paths crossing while she innocently searched for acorns, had probably wriggled in the back of Aunt Agatha's mind like a worm in a rotting apple.

Aunt Agatha seemed to derive some sadistic pleasure in reducing her to the lowest level of human existence. What sin had she committed? What gods had she angered to deserve such a fate, Elysia wondered despondently? If only she could turn back the clock and return to happier days. The happier times, the innocence of her childhood—those were the things of which she dreamed.

Elysia slowed her pace, feeling safe as she skirted a field of dumbly grazing sheep, unaware of the burrs and mud clinging to the hem of her dress. She wandered down the stony path, her mind far too preoccupied by other thoughts to see the dark storm clouds gathering to the north, or to feel the wind gaining strength and threatening the colorful autumn leaves on the trees.

The wind whipped the hair framing her face into curls of wild disorder and brought color to her pale white cheeks. Elysia clutched her shawl closer about her shoulders as it grew chillier and the cold penetrated her light woolen dress.

Jumping as agilely as a cat onto the wet and slippery stones bridging the gurgling brook, Elysia landed sure-footedly on the bank opposite. She looked towards the large house in the distance. A small copse of sturdy oak partially hid it from her view, but she knew by heart every line of its unwelcoming outline. She had memorized each ugly, gray stone in its walls, every shuttered window and locked door— each was indelibly imprinted upon her mind.

Elysia wished that she could travel on past the old house, passing without a glance of recognition at its unfriendly appearance; but she couldn't. She had lived at Graystone Manor, her aunt's house, since the death of her parents.

How different her life had been before that fateful day! She could never forget the image of her father's sleek new phaeton as it overturned on a sharp curve of the road near their home. The panicked horses raced wildly down the road, dragging the overturned carriage with her helpless parents trapped beneath it.

Their death had left Elysia alone in the world. Without a guardian she had been unable to deal with the affairs of their estate as the army of solicitors and tradesmen descended down upon her like vultures smelling death.

Her father, Charles Demarice, blithely unaware of

his fate, had left no will. With his death went the last of the income they had been living on from day to day—money won in gambling. This, added to the inheritance left to her father by his grandmother, had allowed them to live comfortably, if not extravagantly. But now Elysia found, to her dismay, all that was left of that gradually depleted inheritance were the debts to be paid.

Her home would have to be sold, along with the furnishings, and their stable of horses. It would be difficult to leave Rose Arbor, the manor house she had known since she had been born; but the thought of parting with her treasured stallion Ariel was too much to bear.

She and her brother Ian had learned how to ride at an early age, and Elysia could mount and ride a horse with a skill few men could equal. She had been taught by her father and Gentle Jims, the family's groom, who seemed to read a horse's mind and had a hand as gentle as a baby's upon the reins. Riding was Elysia's existence, the breath of life to her and she rode like a wild and free spirit of the moors. Ariel was a pure Arabian stallion, sleek and white, his slender tapered legs barely touching the ground as he galloped through the misty mornings with Elysia joyously astride him.

Elysia had known that she had caused considerable talk among the villagers with her escapades. She had heard the gossiping about her, but it was of little concern to her; in fact it had amused her to hear what they had said, especially the self-ap-

pointed matriarch of the village, the Widow Mac-
Pherson.

"T'isn't natural the way her rides that horse. You
wouldn't believe me if I was to tell ye that she talks
to that beastie, aye, and by all that is Holy, if he
don't understand her too!" she had raved. "I see
dark clouds over the horizon. She be a heathen, that
one." But Elysia had only laughed as she had listened to the Widow's rantings to a wide-eyed audience of avid listeners.

The Widow MacPherson had cautioned the villagers with this ominous prediction during the years
that the Demarices had lived in their manor near
the village. The villagers began to believe her
prophesies when Elysia's brother, an officer in the
British Navy, was lost at sea only a day after the
tragic death of their parents. The villagers cowered
behind closed doors as Elysia rode madly through
the village at midnight after hearing the news, her
long hair streaking behind her, Ariel a white flash of
light against the darkness of the night.

That had been the last time Elysia had ridden
Ariel. Within the week a relative she had never met
arrived at Rose Arbor claiming to be her mother's
stepsister. Elysia vaguely remembered her mother
telling her that she had lived with a stepsister when
she was a young girl. That was all she would tell
her. What was in the past was best forgotten, her
mother had said sadly, with a look of remembered
pain darkening her blue eyes, and it had been the

only time Elysia remembered seeing her so un-
happy.

Agatha Penwick, a tall, thin woman in her fifties,
had taken command of Rose Arbor and all business
and financial matters with authoritative efficiency.
Her plain, gaunt face, with its long, narrow nose
and small, colorless eyes had a speculative, calculat-
ing look as she inspected the house; assessing the
value of everything down to the last shilling.

"I am your mother's only living relative, and I believe your father had no one who could take on the
responsibility of raising you now," she had said
coldly, without a trace of warmth or commiseration
in her voice for Elysia's loss. "The proceeds, if any
are left after paying off your parents' debts, will
serve as payment to me for taking you into a proper
home."

Agatha had then proceeded to have auctioned off
the family's possessions, pleasing the Demarices'
creditors and solicitors. Everyone had been pleased
with the results except Elysia, whose wishes had
been ruthlessly dismissed as sentimental rubbish.

Elysia had been heartbroken as Agatha coldly
dismissed all of the Demarice's faithful servants,
most of them having served the family for over
thirty years.

"They will have to find new employment. I have
no use for them, and furthermore, they are past
their prime. Do me no good," as she curtly answered Elysia's plea to take them with her to Graystone Manor.

Elysia had tried to reassure them; promising to find them all new positions as soon as she could. But she doubted whether the older servants could find new employers—or would want to. They were ready to retire—only having stayed with the Demarices out of loyalty and love.

The night before she had left Rose Arbor, Bridget, her old nanny, had sat brushing Elysia's long, silky hair as she had done each night since Elysia had been a little girl, a tearful smile on her wrinkled face as she tried to comfort her young charge. "You just take care Miss Elysia, and don't you fret your pretty little head about me. If you need me—well, you know where I'll be, and even though my niece's place isn't very big, and it's way out in Wales, you'd still be welcomed. You just wait and see, we'll all be together again, little one, just like before, and some day I'll be burping your wee ones like I did you and Ian, God rest his soul."

Elysia had smiled, agreeing with her, but somehow she knew that nothing would ever be the same again.

Her eyes still filled with tears as she thought of Ariel. Her aunt had sent him to London to be sold at a higher price than they would have gotten in the Northern counties. Elysia had pleaded tearfully with her aunt to allow her to keep him, but she had brushed Elysia's pleas aside contemptuously, saying that she would have little time for riding or playing where she was going.

Elysia's only consolation had been that Gentle

Jims had gone to London, where he would seek new employment, and would personally handle Ariel until he was sold. She knew Jims would take care of Ariel, who with the exception of herself and Jims, would allow no one else near him. Elysia had worried about this—afraid that as a one-master horse he would be useless to anyone else. She could only hope that whoever purchased him would be gentle with him and give him the chance to adjust to a new master. It was too much to hope for—that Jims might be able to stay with him and remain his trainer. But Elysia knew that she could never stop worrying about Ariel; nor would she ever be able to forget him.

Graystone Manor was as gloomy and gray as its name implied, Elysia thought, as they drove up the circular drive to the austere entrance of the house. She felt depressed and subdued after the day's journey in silence with her aunt.

That had been two years ago. Elysia's thoughts came back to the present as she stood again, staring up at the gray house that never seemed to change.

With a deep sigh she walked steadily up the slope towards it, passing through the grove of oaks, strong and invincible, withstanding the winds and rains which beat down upon them year after year, only to seem more unconquerable each new spring. If only she had some of their strength and durability, she thought with mounting despair as she skirted around to the side of the house. Elysia walked to the servants' entrance and quietly pushed open the heavy wooden door, anxious not to attract attention. She climbed slowly up the back stairs to the first landing, then through a narrow door to another flight of stairs concealed behind it—the uncarpeted steps leading to the servants' quarters, in which she had a room, but separated even further by another, and narrower flight of steps that led to the attic. There Elysia had a bed and cast-off chair of faded chintz, a threadbare rug, and a small chest-of-drawers to keep her meager belongings in. Her few pitiful dresses hung on a rod fixed in the corner, and seemed to rebuke her for their sad appearance.

Elysia stared at her clothes with disgust. They hung limply like the rags they were; the elbows mended time and again, the cuffs frayed and color-worn. It pained her to think of the sachet-scented closet full of brightly-colored satin and velvet dresses she had once worn; the matching shoes peeking out saucily beneath the row of dresses. Elysia turned away, her heavily-clad feet in their wooden clogs noisily raking the floor; practical shoes that carried one through the sodden fields and muddy lanes, repulsing the wetness as thinly-soled satin and leather slippers never would.

Elysia shivered in her damp dress, which now felt clammy against her chilled skin. She was beginning to unbutton her bodice when a knock sounded on the door. She watched silently as the doorknob was turned experimentally but the lock that she had placed on the door held the unannounced visitor at bay. The knocking came again, but more impatiently this time.

" 'Ere, answer up. Oi knows ye be in ther. Oi've a message fer ye from the Mistress."

Elysia opened the door reluctantly, dreading the scene that would follow as she faced the burly footman standing insolently before her, a sneering smile on his thick lips.

"Well now, that be better," he said as his eyes roved over her rosy cheeks and disarrayed red-gold curls.

"What is the message?" Elysia asked coldly.

" 'Ere now that's not whats Oi calls friendly. Ye knows Oi could make yer lot a bit easier if ye was te be a bit more friendly with me." He put out his big calloused hand, the nails dirty and broken, to touch a button that Elysia had missed re-fastening in her haste.

She slapped his hand away, glaring at him in warning. "Don't you dare touch me!"

He only laughed, but his eyes were as cold and deadly as a snake's watching its prey squirm before it pounces.

"The fine lady, eh? Thought that'd have been worked out of ye by now—but no, ye still be te good fer the likes o' me. Well, we'll see, my fine 'un." He grinned unpleasantly, leering into Elysia's face. "Oi'll have ye yet, my pretty, and ask any o' the maids if Oi don't treats 'em good—real good."

He flicked the latch on the door with a contemptuous finger. "And don't be thinkin' that little bit o' metal's going to keep me out."

"You ought to be flogged, and if you continue with these insults, I'll—"

"Ye'll what?" he said in an ugly voice. "Go tells yer auntie. Ha! That be a good 'un. If she be so interested in yer well-being then why are ye up here and working more than a scullery maid? No, Oi'll not be ascared o' the Mistress on that account." He smiled triumphantly, knowing Elysia could not deny his accusations.

"No, maybe she would not interfere," Elysia agreed softly, "but I'll put a hole through that thick skull of yours if you ever dare to lay a hand on me." Elysia narrowed her eyes, smiling slightly as she continued quietly, "I am a very keen shot—in fact, I rarely miss when I take aim between some vermin's eyes."

She made no idle threat, for she had her father's pistol neatly tucked away under her mattress; originally kept as a memento, it was now used for a very different purpose.

The footman's grin faded, and he eyed the young girl who stood before him—threatening him—with a new and guarded look in his shifty eyes.

"Reckon ye just might at that. Quality does strange things, heard tell. Why ye should wanta shoot me when Oi was just offering ye a little bit o' fun," he whined placatingly, shrugging his heavy shoulders, but watching her with a sly, cunning look.

"What is the message from my aunt?" Elysia asked once more, feeling more sure of herself.

"Wants ye downstairs in the Salon," he told her sullenly. Then he stomped down the wooden steps with ill-contained anger.

Elysia followed him down, wondering what her aunt would want of her this time—to complain that the floors were not scrubbed clean enough; or the windows needed washing; or the linen needed airing? There was inevitably some small detail that Elysia had missed, but which had not escaped her aunt's critical eye.

She crossed the entrance hall, forever in shadow, the dark wood-paneling absorbing whatever light seeped in through the two narrow windows. Elysia knocked, and then entered the Salon to stand in seemingly respectful silence before the cold stare of her aunt.

"I see you have been out." She looked at Elysia disapprovingly. "I suppose you forgot the acorns? I did ask you to fetch me some, but you always think of your own pleasures first. You did go to the North field to look, didn't you?" Aunt Agatha's colorless eyes brightened as she anticipated the answer.

Elysia bit her lip, trying to control the anger and hatred she felt surging within her against this cruel woman.

"I am sorry that I forgot the acorns," Elysia finally replied shortly. She knew what her aunt expected to hear, but she would say nothing to satisfy her twisted curiosity.

"Forgot! Ha! From the looks of you, it was the furthest thing from your mind," Agatha hissed, noticing the dirt and stains on Elysia's dress. "Thought you'd sneak into my house like some common scullery maid after a night of rolling in the hay. Well, miss? Maybe you weren't out 'picking flowers' all of the time," Agatha said meaningfully, looking at the late-blooming wildflowers Elysia had tucked into the pocket of her half-apron. "Maybe you got deflowered yourself? Did some stable-boy steal a few sweet kisses from you down under the trees?" she added crudely, a look of malice in her eyes.

Her cruel remarks made Elysia flinch, and her shoulders slumped almost unconsciously with defeat. She had suffered humiliation and indignity, and she was chilled to the bone, and so tired of all of this that she did not know how much longer she could endure it. She assumed her aunt had finished with her, having called her in only to assess the damage her malicious errand might have caused. All Elysia wanted now was to warm herself before the fire in the big kitchen, and pour a cup of strong, hot tea. But Agatha put a detaining hand on Elysia's wrist as she turned to leave.

"I want to speak with you."

"Yes, Aunt Agatha, but I would like to change first and get a cup of—"

"Later," Agatha interrupted rudely. "You can just stay in those damp things until I am finished. It is what you deserve for flouting my wishes."

And punishment for returning unscathed, Elysia

thought dryly as she glanced about the drab Salon with its green and gray-patterned wallpaper, olive-green, striped, satin sofa and chairs and brownish-green carpet. The cold-looking marble-topped tables and stern-visaged family portraits were all reflected over and over again in the ornately carved gilt mirror above the fireplace, where a small fire was burning, sending out an aura of warmth to which Elysia automatically moved.

"Sit over there," her aunt said imperiously, indicating one of the hard-backed chairs near the window. Elysia sat down slowly, trying to get comfortable on the hard cushion. She shivered, feeling a cold draft seeping in through the window frame.

Aunt Agatha settled herself carefully on the striped satin cushions of the sofa which sat greedily before the fire, swallowing up all of the warmth put out by the struggling flames. Agatha smoothed back an imaginary piece of loose hair. Elysia had never seen a piece escape yet from the tight little bun at the nape of her aunt's neck. Never had Elysia seen her aunt's face alight with joy, humor, or love. Her whole appearance was severe.

During the two years that Elysia had lived at Graystone Manor she had never heard Agatha speak a kind word to her—or to anyone—but she seemed to be the butt of her aunt's enmity more than the others. Agatha had not acquired a niece when she had taken Elysia into her home, but a maid-of-all-work, with the added advantage of not having to pay her wages in return for her labors.

Elysia had left the Salon confused and bewildered. She had been raised as a lady; the protected and sheltered daughter of aristocratic parents who had provided for her every need, and had been fully educated by tutors to use her intellect. To find that she had been reduced to the lowest of menials, and in her own aunt's household had been a severe blow. It was not that she was lazy, for she had always been anxious to help and athletic, despite it being not proper behavior for a girl of her class.

Had her family been poor, she would gladly have helped her parents in any way that she could have; even if it meant getting down on her hands and knees to scrub the floors. It would have been a sacrifice she would have borne proudly to help her family. She would never have felt any degradation or humiliation.

But here at Graystone Manor, Agatha had no need to subject her to this position. Her own aunt had forced her to become a scullery maid, not even allowed the freedom of the lowliest of servants, with no standing in the household, existing in a barren no-man's-land; cut off from everything and everyone. The other servants, knowing her to be Quality, and the niece of their Mistress, kept to themselves, ostracizing her from their circle. They knew Agatha would not raise a hand to help Elysia, so they delegated her more work than three maids could manage. Elysia felt as if she were in the workhouse. She never seemed to have an idle moment—no thought or time to call her own. She was constantly busy cleaning the manor, rubbing beeswax into the aged wood, scrubbing floors until immaculate, airing the bedrooms, mending linen, until her brow dripped beads of perspiration, and sweat drenched her dress.

And Agatha was always behind her watching, directing, ordering, yet never lifting a finger herself. She sometimes throught Agatha would have enjoyed having a whip to crack over her head as she bent doing some endless chore.

Elysia remembered bitterly how she had hated the idea of becoming a burden and inconvenience to her aunt, but she knew now how incorrect an assumption that had been. Aunt Agatha's household was run frugally, with no excess in any form, and Elysia's small share of food, in comparison to the back-breaking work she did in the house, more than compensated for any possible strain she had put on the household budget—or debt that she owed Agatha.

All this at a time in Elysia's life when she needed love and understanding more than ever before; when she had been left an orphan, and cut off from all that she had loved and known. Hungry, with only memories to fill the ache within her when she thought she would starve for a friendly smile or kind word. She received only hate and abuse from those around her.

Elysia constantly felt Agatha's colorless eyes watching her. She antagonized Elysia; goaded her into doing something foolish, and then seemed to derive some personal satisfaction out of punishing her for it. She knew Aunt Agatha was waiting patiently for her to break down—but she wouldn't. She would fight her—if not outwardly in a verbal battle, then silently in her mind and heart. She still had some small vestige of pride left in her.

At the end of the day when Agatha's taunting became unendurable, and her body ached with fatigue, Elysia would climb the flights of stairs to her attic bedchamber—a cold and bare room up under the eaves. How many times had she stood looking out of the dormer windows at the distant horizon, wishing so many things that could never be, remembering distant times when she had been innocent of cruelty and malice, loneliness and grief!

Her dreams were her only comfort when she went to bed at night. She would put on a thin nightdress, slip between the cold sheets of the bed, shivering. Then she would fall asleep listening to the mice scurrying in the walls.

Once in awhile she could escape outside when Agatha had some errand for her to run, sending her to the village or nearby farms for numerous items her aunt suddenly found she needed. Elysia had to hide the excitement and pleasure in her eyes as she pretended to wearily accept another chore. Had Agatha but known how eagerly she looked forward to these excursions she would have forbidden her to set foot out of doors; so intent was she on denying Elysia any pleasures.

Elysia would rush outside, beyond the stifling

walls of Graystone Manor, down through the trees
to the little babbling brook of clear sparkling water.
She would lie there enjoying the lazy summer days
under the trees, staring up through their green leafy
branches at odd shaped portions of blue sky, sometimes dappled with fluffy white clouds. But even on
cold winter days she would rejoice in her small
flight of freedom; forgetting the circumstances that
had thrown her to the mercy of Aunt Agatha, and
remembering the smiling faces that were now as in-
substantial as ghosts.

How could she not compare the silent and grim
Graystone Manor with the smaller house of her parents; echoing with laughter, gaiety, and love. Her
parents were so full of love and the breath of life—
Charles Demarice, tall and straight, lean as a younger man of twenty, silver threading through his
once raven-black hair; his strangely green eyes still
as bright and deep with color as ever, despite his
fifty years—the sweet memory of her mother's grace-
ful figure, crowned by her glorious red-gold hair,
shining with the sun's rays above her twinkling blue
eyes, as she picked flowers in the garden.

If only they were still here with her, Elysia
thought despondently; but they were gone—as well
at Ian.

Elysia looked out of the window of the Salon, not
listening to Agatha's words, wondering how she had
managed to survive these last two years of living—
no, existing—under Agatha's roof. Why Agatha felt
animosity towards her was still an unanswered

question. She felt that Aunt Agatha had hated her before they'd ever met, so it couldn't have been something she had personally done. The only possible explanation was that something had occurred to cause a rift between Agatha and her own family, back when her mother had lived at Graystone Manor with Agatha. Her mother's reluctance to discuss that time of her life, and her father's similar silence led her to believe that something unpleasant had happened; but she had no idea as to what, nor would she probably ever know.

Elysia's straying thoughts came back to the present, the chilly Salon and Agatha's harshly grating voice as cold as the draft seeping in from the window.

"... and so, naturally I was surprised when I met Squire Masters this afternoon on my way to the village, and what he had to relate to me," her aunt was saying.

Squire Masters. The mere thought of him made Elysia shudder. She had never met a more repulsive man than the squire, and she fervently hoped that she would never meet him again. She had been introduced to the middle-aged widower and his three daughters for the first time a fortnight ago when they had been invited over to dine one evening at Graystone Manor.

It had come as a shock, when Agatha told her they would be having guests to dine that evening— and that she, Elysia, was to join in the festivities.

Elysia usually ate in solitude in a corner of the

kitchen, or as she preferred, on a tray in the privacy of her room, away from the servants' curious eyes and gossip. Not that mealtimes were to be looked forward to with delicious hot dishes to entice one's appetite; what they served was only to keep your body going one more endless day. Agatha had lectured her one evening when she had been a few minutes late, warning Elysia that if she continued to be tardy for meals, then she would have to learn to go without. Elysia had refrained from telling her aunt that missing a meal was no real hardship, her thoughts on the unappetizing and poorly prepared food, and the small amount allowed as her portion. The thin slice of coarse, brown bread—white flour being too expensive to serve the servants—and mushy, overcooked vegetables with occasional meat or fish ended up in pies over and over again until gone. Breakfast consisted of even less—tea and tasteless gruel, usually lumpy and cold. Bread and cheese served as luncheon. But in summer, when the fruit from the orchard was ripe and sweet, Elysia would secretly pick handfuls of the sun-ripened fruit to hide away in her room. When hunger rumbled in her stomach in the middle of the night, keeping her from sleep, she would feast on the delicious stolen fruit.

Agatha seemed uncommonly excited about the Masters' visit. She ordered the cook to prepare a variety of assorted savories and pastries. Pork, lamb, and beef were sent from a nearby farm along with fancy vegetables and fruits which far surpassed the meager results from Agatha's own garden.

The best china and silver was polished until it shone and sparkled among the beautiful crystal. Fragrant mouth-watering aromas drifted throughout the house, bringing back memories of delicacies which Elysia had not tasted in years.

But there was a feeling of unease throughout the house, as if something were not quite right.

Elysia puzzled over the invitation as she soaked in a tub of warm water, washing away the dirt and grime of her day's work. She had heated and carried her own bath water up the long flights of stairs; but it was worth the effort to relax in the soapy water, her tense muscles soothed by the heat.

Her surprise at being included in the party was only exceeded by her amazement at finding a beautifully-made, brand-new, evening gown hanging on the rod in the corner of her room. It made the other dresses look like poor relations, in contrast.

Only Agatha could have purchased such a gown. But why? What motive could her aunt have this time? Agatha was not the type to do something without a purpose. Why should she suddenly include Elysia as a guest at a dinner party she was hostessing? Was this another sadistic plot of hers, or was she planning to embarrass her, subject her to ridicule?

All of these questions repeated themselves in Elysia's mind as she made her way downstairs, aware of the curious stares of the servants. She could well imagine their curiosity. Hadn't she been one of them just that afternoon?

Elysia's memory of the evening was vivid, lingering in her mind like the aftertaste of a horrible nightmare. The images became distorted and grotesque, the scenes moving through her mind as if she were drugged.

How could she forget the sight of her aunt in a mustard-colored evening gown that made her face look like a death mask; her long arms outstretched to welcome her guests, Squire Masters and his daughters: Hope, Delight, and Charmian. She tried to politely engage them in conversation, but they either banded together and talked among themselves, excluding her; or they asked her personal questions, ridiculing her answers with laughter and scorn when she ventured to give an opinion. She only wished that their father were as scornful, but he acted no such way. Elysia felt his protruding, bovine-like eyes watching her slightest gesture.

She felt ill-at-ease in the thin muslin gown that Agatha had purchased for her. It was beautiful indeed, but the décolletage of the gown seemed indecent for a young unmarried girl—her shoulders bare above the delicate lace that barely covered the soft curves of her breasts. It was one of the new Empire gowns that had become the rage of London fashion; a style popularized by Napoleon's wife, the Empress Josephine.

The Masters sisters were also dressed in this new style of Empire gown that fitted snugly under the breasts before falling in smooth, straight lines to the floor. But where Elysia's dress seemed to float about her, hinting at the curves beneath, the Masters' created the impression of stuffed sausages. The daughters had unfortunately inherited their figures from the Squire, who was large and stout, and they also had the same round, brown eyes as their father.

With each breath that she took, Elysia felt the Squire's brown eyes on her breasts as they rose and fell beneath the pale-green muslin of her gown. She saw his eyes rove slowly and appreciatively over her body as they were introduced, and as she looked into his eyes, she perceived a hungry, lustful glint. Elysia looked away in embarrassment, only to see a satisfied and pleased expression on her aunt's face as she watched the Squire's obvious admiration.

After dining they retired to the Salon to hear Delight entertain them with her semi-trained, nasal voice, accompanied by her inexpertise on the pianoforte. Hope and Charmian giggled and snickered constantly throughout their sister's singing and playing, but she finally finished her performance, after hitting every off-key note possible.

Elysia was seated next to Squire Masters on the settee; her aunt upon entering the Salon selected the lone chair by the window. The Squire sat a little too close for Elysia's comfort, his knee and thigh pressing intimately against hers, and he constantly leaned closer to whisper some inane remark into her ear while breathing in of her fragrance and feasting his eyes on the white, alabaster flesh revealed by the low-cut gown.

But she remained puzzled as to the reasons for her inclusion in the party; she could see no reason for it. Unless it was the intention of her aunt to show her of what she was no longer a part; that as a servant she had no place in polite society. It would be like her aunt to give her an evening of pleasure, a new dress, and then the very next day reduce her to her servant's position again.

She bade her aunt a quiet good night and hastened to the haven of her room. The next day began as though the previous evening had never taken place, and Elysia's days went on as before. The new dress disappeared as mysteriously as it had appeared.

"I'm talking to you, miss!" Aunt Agatha's voice interrupted Elysia's thoughts of that evening with the Masters. "Always dreaming; and about things a decent girl shouldn't, I'll wager. Well, you can listen to me now, and be glad I've taken an interest in your welfare; not that you deserve it, mind you, but you are my dear stepsister's child, and I owe it to her to fix you up proper."

Agatha's tone was gloating, and there was a watchful look in her eyes as a spot of bright color dotted each cheekbone.

"I do not understand," Elysia spoke haltingly, puzzled by her aunt's odd statement. "Have you found me a position of some sort?"

"Oh, yes, indeed I have. One you should find

most interesting—and rewarding," her aunt crooned. "You do remember that I said I met Squire Masters on my way to the village?"

"What has he to do with it?" Elysia asked, thinking that maybe she had misjudged Aunt Agatha after all. Then a sudden thought struck her, and she asked anxiously, "It is not a position with the Squire, is it?"

"Oh, no, my dear Elysia," her aunt chuckled gleefully, showing the first hint of humor Elysia had ever seen on her face. "It is not some lowly position in the Squire's household that I have accepted on your behalf, but—" she paused dramatically, an inner light brightening her eyes, "—the envied position as the wife of Squire Masters."

Can I forget the dismal night that gave
My soul's best part forever to the grave?
                                    Gray

Chapter 2

"Well, can't you speak? Aren't you going to thank your dear Aunt Agatha for securing you a respectable future?" She watched Elysia's flushed cheeks blanch, leaving her face pale and drawn-looking; her eyes dark pools of despair as her lips began to tremble.

Elysia sat dumbfounded as Agatha's face became contorted and her harsh laughter rang through the room. Agatha's head was thrown back as she shook with deranged mirth, her thin chest shaking uncontrollably.

"We decided it, the Squire and myself, this afternoon on the road to the village," Agatha said breathlessly. "He was most anxious to come to an arrangement. You will find him to be a most attentive bridegroom, my dear. And being such a healthy young girl, you should provide Squire Masters with the sons he has longed for."

Agatha stared at Elysia as her hand nervously smoothed her hair in the tight bun and she added almost to herself, "You're such a beautiful girl, too—just like your mother was. I remember the first day that I saw her; she was just a child, but so beautiful—even then."

Elysia stared in horror at Aunt Agatha. She finally gained control of herself, but her voice sounded strained; the words coming jerkily from between her thin lips.

"I cannot possibly marry the Squire," Elysia said clearly to her aunt, despite her pounding heart. This could not be happening to her, she thought in desperation. Squire Masters! Never! She would rather die than be married to him.

"You have no choice, my dear Elysia. It has all been arranged."

"I will not marry him, and you cannot make me! Don't you understand that I can't stand him. I'm repulsed by him—to be married to him would be torture."

Elysia rose from her chair, and the words tumbled out emotionally as she pleaded with her aunt. But her aunt was unyielding.

"Your feelings do not enter into this at all. You

should be thankful to have this opportunity for marriage. Your prospects are not good, but Squire Masters has agreed to overlook your poverty, and forget the usually expected dowry," Agatha said impatiently, her previous good humor forgotten in the face of Elysia's defiance.

"I am afraid that you will have to send my regrets to the Squire, because it is out of the question that I could, or would, ever marry him. You never even consulted me as to my wishes—why, the Squire is old enough to be my father!"

Elysia looked at her aunt curiously. "This is what you have wanted all along ... to humiliate me. Well, you won't succeed this time, Aunt Agatha, just as you didn't succeed this afternoon when you purposely sent me to the North field."

Agatha rose and faced Elysia, digging her hard fingers into Elysia's shoulders as she glared viciously at her.

"Do you think I will let the likes of you ruin all my plans!" Agatha shrieked. "I have finally realized my greatest wish—and you will not interfere. Do you hear me?" She shook Elysia until her red-gold hair tumbled in thick waves about her shoulders.

"I will not marry him! I will not! I—I would rather die first!" Elysia cried.

Agatha released her shoulders from her death-like grip, and lifting her hand slapped Elysia hard across the face. Elysia managed to jerk away, putting her shaking hands to her smarting cheeks, she stared at her aunt with a wounded, puzzled look in her eyes.

"No, you won't die—yet. Maybe after a year's marriage to that lecherous old fool you will desire to; but marry him you will—and next week. He can hardly wait to get you into his bed, my dear," Agatha added tauntingly. She laughed aloud again; another wild, uncontrolled laugh—but this time full of triumph.

"Oh, sweet, sweet revenge! I knew if I waited long enough that one day I would taste it. Beautiful Elysia, just like your mother and grandmother. I told you that your mother was beautiful? Well, so was your grandmother—my stepmother. Father was bewitched by her and brought her home as his wife. Here! To my house—to take over as the new mistress of Graystone Manor. Fool—to think that anyone could take my place.

"We had always been so happy, Father and I, here at Graystone, even though Mother had died years before. Then *she* came. She had no right to come here and to bring that little brat with her. I can remember them standing there in the hall." Agatha stared towards the hall; her eyes glazed as her mind moved back through the years to an earlier time.

"They wore fine lace and velvet, and little plumed hats. The sun was shining down on that strange red-gold hair, turning it into living flames of fire. Their smiles were as false as their hearts. They came here; taking my house, my father, expecting me to be friends. Well, I pretended as they pretended, to be friends, but whenever I had the chance, I let your mother, the darling little Elizabeth, know where her true place was.

"When your grandmother finally died, I took over the running of the house—as I should have from the beginning. Father was fit for nothing after she died. She ruined him!"

Agatha paused, momentarily perplexed by her thought, a frown marring her forehead. Her hands were clenched tightly and her breathing was ragged as she glanced about wildly. Beads of perspiration were dotting her upper lip as she put her hand nervously to her temple, pressing it as if the pain were unbearable. "I think I was about nineteen or twenty; your mother was only about eleven years old. But I was old enough to assume the responsibility of running the Manor—and I managed it better than your grandmother had.

"I told your mother, the darling Elizabeth, the things she would be expected to do just as I have told you your duties. Father was not around much; and when he was, he was so drunk he didn't recognize anyone or anything. Elizabeth soon found her proper place in *my* Manor. Ha! The little upstart—trying to worm her way into Graystone with that sweet, sly smile of hers. Well, she got what she deserved!"

A smile of remembrance broke on Agatha's face, her eyes glinting evilly. "Father died not long after that—in fact, it's a miracle he lasted as long as he did. I didn't miss him—he only interfered; spent too much money on whiskey anyway."

"Do you know how he died? It's rather amusing," Agatha said looking directly at Elysia, and seeming to see her for the first time. "He thought he saw your grandmother at the foot of the stairs. He came stumbling down them and tripped over the loose sash of his robe. He fell hard—right at my feet— breaking his neck. I had no idea that he would mistake her for me. I was only wearing her dressing gown to do some of the dusting in—I didn't want to spoil my dress, of course," she added indifferently.

"Father was a weak, drunken fool; his mind not only besotted by her, but by drink as well. After his death the Manor became mine. I was finally rightful mistress of Graystone, the legal owner by law. The Courts also saw fit to make me your mother's legal guardian, a guardianship which I am sure she hated. She never even thanked me for providing her with a home when I could have thrown her out; which is what I should have done. The day I let that cheap, deceitful, little hoyden stay under my roof—"

"That is not true! She was not—" Elysia interrupted, anger loosening her tongue, which had been frozen in silence by Agatha's wild disclosures.

"You shut up and listen to the real truth about your precious mother, not the lies that she has told you," Agatha snarled. "Your mother was living under *my* roof, accepting *my* charity, not doing half the work I ordered her to do for her keep—a lazy chit just like you. And how did she repay me? She snuck behind my back and stole what was rightfully mine!"

Agatha began to speak quickly, almost breathlessly, as she remembered the past; the bottled-up words tumbling out in a torrent of hate.

"There was to be a grand ball at a neighboring estate, and I received an invitation. It was the event of the year. I had to send your mother's regrets, of course. She had nothing proper to wear, and she really was too young; she hadn't even had a season in London yet. But then it would have been too expensive, and besides, I'd already had mine, and one season in London in a family is enough, don't you agree?

"That night is still so vivid in my mind. It was even more elaborate than some of the balls I'd attended in London. There were a thousand or more candles lighting up the ballroom where the ladies, elegant in jewels and feathers, danced around and around. There was champagne, laughing faces, music—and Captain Demarice. He was so handsome, so debonair—like a prince. He was a cavalry officer, a brilliant horseman—one of the best in the country— and so full of adventure and daring. He was the younger son of a lord, and didn't have a fortune, or any expectations of gaining an estate. But he was so extraordinary, it didn't matter that he was not rich. He was tall, and had thick, black hair and strange, green eyes that slanted upwards at their corners."

Agatha's glance rested momentarily on Elysia's

upturned face. She paled visibly as she stared into Elysia's eyes.

"You've got his eyes! Damn you! Every time I look at you I see him standing there looking at me with contempt, the smile I cherished wiped from his face. He said things to me that I can never forget; his voice haunts me at night in my dreams. I can't escape from it even in my sleep—it's always there."

Agatha's thin fingers pulled nervously at the neatly pinned hair, until several gray-streaked strands hung loosely about her face.

"I came home from the ball feeling like I had never felt before. Why, I actually felt frivolous and gay; I felt like a different person. I knew that Captain Demarice would come calling; I just knew it. But I waited, and waited and waited. And while I waited, Elizabeth met Captain Demarice in the woods down by the brook. An accidental meeting they said—ha! I knew her deceitful ways. She knew that I wanted him; she always wanted what was mine—even when we were small. He would have asked me to become his wife, if she hadn't connived her way into his affections, like her mother had into my father's. She played the innocent maiden, meeting him secretly behind my back whenever she could.

"He finally accepted my invitation to tea; but with an ulterior motive, I was soon to find out. How could I know that he had met Elizabeth? I had let her go out more often, certain to have her out of the way when Captain Demarice called; but he never did until that day. We were seated in here, in the salon, just beginning to get acquainted when he asked me about Elizabeth. I told him that I had a stepsister. 'She's a young and lazy chit of a girl,' I said. He raised his eyebrow slightly, and with a glance invited me to continue; encouraging my confidences. I knew that I would have to blacken her name before he saw her and was blinded by her false beauty. She would trick him, having learned her evil ways from her mother; so I told him all about her hoydenish ways and the deceitful acts that made her the little slut that she was.

"He said, after I had finished, he already had the pleasure of meeting of Miss Elizabeth, and had found her to be a sweet, gentle, and honest young lady. I couldn't believe what I was hearing. He had already met Elizabeth? Where? When? How could it have happened? She didn't have access to the homes where he would be entertained.

"He was deaf to my words. He had been blinded by Elizabeth's treachery already. He stood up tall and straight, and told me in a cold voice, that cut me like a knife, that I was speaking of the woman he hoped to marry. He had made inquiries, he said, and found out how I had been treating Elizabeth.

"'Lies, lies!' I screamed at him. 'What has that she-devil told you?' I demanded. 'None of it is true. She twists everything around to her advantage—she has lied to you.' I told him that I would make a better wife than Elizabeth. I remember the shocked look on his face as I declared my love for him; evidently he had never realized my feelings, nor could he return that love and desire. I told him that I had everything to offer him; money, Graystone Manor, land. Elizabeth had nothing to give him—nothing!

" 'For your information, Elizabeth has never said a word against you, yet how she has managed to keep her silence about one such as you, I shall never comprehend. But then she is innocent of the evil in this house. She offers me her love; and that is all I desire, not money, nor an estate. But I doubt whether you are capable of understanding that, for in your wretchedness you can see nothing decent in anyone. You are a cruel and selfish woman whose own bitterness and hatred will destroy you. *You* are the only evil in this house.'

"He said those things to me! I can remember every word as if it were yesterday. He stared at me with such loathing and contempt I couldn't bear it. And then Elizabeth came in, timidly standing in the doorway, pretending she had not known that we were there. She glanced back and forth between us; looking so worried and concerned that I felt enraged at the very sight of her angelic face masking such evil and deceit, and I rushed at her to claw it off and reveal the truth to him. But he moved as quickly as a cat and shielded her from me. I screamed at them both. Told them I never wanted to see either of them again as long as I lived, and told him to take his little whore and get out.

"They left and I never saw Charles again. He took Elizabeth that day, and they stayed with friends until they could marry. I heard that they moved away to the North after they'd wed, where he had inherited some small property.

"I dreamt all these years of seeing them again, and getting my revenge by showing them that I was better than either of them. Graystone Manor was mine. Elizabeth always coveted what was mine—my father, my house, Charles. Well she'd never get Graystone. It's mine—all mine!"

Elysia stared at Agatha in terror, and began to back slowly towards the door as she saw the insane look contorting her aunt's face.

"Don't go, Elysia," Agatha said suddenly. "I've much more to tell you. Don't you want to know how pleased I was to have you placed in my hands? I told your solicitor how my beloved stepsister's daughter would be as welcome here in my home as her mother had been. He was more than relieved, as your other high-born relatives would have nothing to do with you.

"It's been a joy to have you here—working some of that Demarice arrogance out of you, humiliating you, having you at my beck and call—you the fine lady, reduced to a scullery maid.

"Oh, if only Charles and Elizabeth could see me now," Agatha sighed ecstatically, "with their precious, beloved daughter Elysia, in my house that they had scorned, awaiting her coming nuptials with—dare I say it—anticipation?"

Elysia gasped, feeling a sickness rise within her.

Agatha's eyes focused on Elysia with unyielding intensity.

"Why, you look quite pale, my dear. Do go up and rest in your room for awhile. I do believe the news has been too much for you; and such a great honor too. So very seldom do we receive what we truly deserve in life, but *you* shall, Elysia—*you* shall!"

Elysia gave a sob and ran from the room, tears streaking her face as she made her way up the stairs to the attic; hearing Agatha's loud, insane laughter echoing after her.

Elysia paced back and forth in the small space of the attic, her head brushing against the slope of the roof as her steps guided her aimlessly to and fro. She must be a madwoman, Elysia thought. No one could carry such feelings of hatred for so long and not become deranged by it. Oh dear God, what was she to do? Where could she go? She had no one left in the world to turn to. She would rather go to the workhouse than do what Agatha commanded her to do—marry into the Masters family.

She couldn't stay in this oppressive house any longer. It pressed down upon her—trying to break her will—stripping her of her dignity and freedom. She moved toward the window where she could look out at the woodlands and hills in the distance to the south. A sudden gust of wind blew a fallen leaf up into the air, holding it for a moment, tantalizing her with its freedom, before floating away into the fading light.

Elysia made up her mind suddenly, resolutely; she would leave Graystone and travel to London, where she would seek employment of some kind. There was no other alternative. She couldn't consider marriage to Squire Masters, nor could she remain under Agatha's roof when that woman hated her, and would keep trying to force her into marriage with the Squire. No, there was no other course open to her but to flee.

Elysia suddenly felt completely exhausted. She was drained of all emotion as she stumbled wearily to her bed. She flung herself down upon it, resting her head against the pillow. There was nothing she could accomplish until darkness fell, so ... Slowly her eyes closed, sleep creeping over her.

Elysia awoke to a darkened room, illuminated only by a pale shaft of moonlight, streaking through the window onto her bed, spreading its searching fingers across her face.

She sat up abruptly, her heart pounding. What time was it? She glanced out of the window at the silvery moon, peeking out behind slowly drifting clouds. It wasn't too high in the sky yet, so it couldn't be very late. She was relieved to see that the storm had temporarily abated. It would make it easier for her to travel across the fields and through the woods if she did not have to battle the storm in a rain-soaked cape.

She leapt quietly to her feet, her plan of action foremost in her mind, clearing it of the haziness of sleep. She went around her room quickly gathering up her few belongings—her dresses, a nightdress, a warm shawl, and her mother's silver brush and comb set, which she had kept hidden from Agatha. She reached into the far corner of the dresser drawer and withdrew a small phial of scent—the jasmine and roses her mother had loved so much, then retrieved the pistol which was tucked into a corner of the large, woven straw bag.

Kneeling down and reaching under her bed, Elysia carefully pulled out a wrapped bundle. Unwinding an old, faded, blue shawl she lifted out her most cherished possession—a delicate porcelain doll. Its little pointed face with its brightly-painted blue eyes and small, pink, rose bud mouth stared up at her. Elysia's hands lovingly smoothed out the wrinkles in the delicate lace dress adorned with rows of blue velvet bows. Her hands strayed to the plump round golden curls as she thought back to the day her father had returned from a month in London, his arms full of packages and presents as he regaled her with amusing stories of his adventures. He had placed the little doll in her small chubby hands, watching with enjoyment as she had crooned over it in a motherly fashion, her eyes as bright as stars.

Elysia smiled sweetly as she re-wrapped the little doll, and placed it on top of her dresses, under the thick shawl in the straw bag. She had kept these most precious possessions from her past life carefully hidden, guarding them from Agatha's watchful eyes, knowing that she would have thrown them out—as she had done with other mementos Elysia had been unable to hide away.

Elysia looked quickly about the room while swinging her heavy cloak over her shoulders. It was an ugly room, this servant's room, and she felt glad to leave it. She picked up her bag and reached for the door, quietly turning the knob.

It wouldn't open! Elysia turned it the other way, but no movement. The door was locked. Agatha had not trusted her, and she had locked her in. She was trapped!

Elysia's heart was pounding so loudly she thought the whole house would surely hear its deafening beats. She must not panic, she told herself. She must keep her wits about her, even though she felt her head swimming from the blood being pumped by her frantic heart. She hurried over to the window and peered down at the ground beneath. It seemed miles to the firm earth below. Elysia opened the window slowly, praying that it wouldn't squeak in protest. She would have to slide over the shingled roof to the edge, the dormer window giving her a platform to sit on as she climbed out.

There was a large sturdy vine of ivy that had been growing unrestrained on the side of the house for years. The branches were thick and hard, and if she were careful, it would see her safely to the ground below.

She reached for her straw bag, and yanking the cord from the curtains that hung limply beside the window, tied it to the handle, and lowered it over the window sill, past the edge of the roof and slowly down the side of the house until the cord would reach no further. She reluctantly let it drop into the darkness below, where it landed with a muffled thud as it hit the damp earth.

Elysia climbed through the window casement and sat on the sill looking down as an uninvited and insidious thought came to her—what if she should slip and fall. . . ! Well, it had to be risked, and besides she really wasn't too worried, she reassured herself staunchly as she continued to look down at the ground. After all, hadn't she done quite a bit of climbing of trees and walls with Ian when she was a child? She always had perfect balance—what was there to fear?

She climbed from the window, and slid across the roof to the edge, making as little noise as possible. She grasped a large vine, seeking a foothold as she leaned over the edge, and with a swift movement, swung out, putting her full weight on the vine. It held. She breathed a sigh of relief as she carefully searched for other secure spots to place her feet as she slowly lowered herself to the ground.

Feeling a sense of exultation as she felt the soft firmness of turf beneath her feet, Elysia quickly untied the cord from her bag and hurried to the back of the house. She held her breath as she turned the knob of the kitchen door, knowing that the cook often forgot to lock it.

Elysia felt the door open a bit, creaking softly. Squeezing in through the crack, she moved silently about the large kitchen; taking a loaf of bread, cheese, a few slices of cold beef and ham, and two freshly-baked turnovers filled with sweetened fruit. She seldom had sweets, and these were for Agatha's early morning tea. She smiled as she thought of Agatha's face when she discovered the theft of the turnovers. But her smile quickly faded as the thought of being caught by her aunt chilled her to the bone.

Wrapping the stolen food in a large checkered cloth she stuffed it in her straw bag, then moved over to a shelf where the kitchen money was kept to pay any deliveries ordered for the kitchen. There wasn't very much, Elysia thought in disappointment, but there should be enough to see her to London.

The moon had risen higher, casting a silver light over the fields and woods as Elysia left the kitchen as quietly as she had entered, moments before. She slipped wraith-like across the wide unprotected stretch of ground between the house and woodlands.

Elysia cast no last look over her shoulder at Graystone Manor as she reached the wood, but kept going at a steady pace until deep within the trees. Taking a deep breath, she mentally shed the shackles that had held her in captivity. She must keep going and put as much distance between herself and Agatha as possible. She wanted no part of Agatha's rage when she found that her quarry had fled the trap.

She wouldn't be able to return there ever, nor would she want to. Since she was homeless, she had no choice but to go to London. Agatha would probably expect her to run home, to the familiar places that she knew, and she was not going to chance Agatha finding her. She could seek employment as a governess or companion; after all, she had been decently educated and brought up as a lady. She would not allow any self-doubts or nervousness to dissuade her from her decided course of action.

She traveled as quickly as she could in the light from the moon, stumbling into thorny bushes, their sharp thorns catching at her cloak, holding her secure, until she ripped and tugged her release, her hands scratched and bleeding. She continued onward, putting more distance between herself and Graystone Manor. She hoped to reach the edge of the woods before dawn, and be across the road and open pastures to the safety of another belt of woodland, before the farmers started traveling with their produce on their way to market. She didn't want to be seen, for rumor traveled through the marketplace, from farmer to servant to master, within the space of a couple of hours.

Elysia broke through the last part of the woods, and felt the hard-packed dirt of the lane beneath her feet, as the first light of dawn was beginning to break to the east. From behind her the sweet, melodious notes of a nightingale drifted into the fresh morning air, its nighttime revery hushed by the golden rays of the sun.

Elysia calculated that Graystone Manor was hours and miles behind her as she dashed across the lane, her feet barely touching, glancing about as she crawled into the thick hedge running along the far side of the lane.

She would have to hurry if she wanted to safely reach the cover of the trees in the distance, before the sun rose, bringing with it its revealing light.

Edging her way through the thick branches, Elysia was about to stand up and make a run across the field, when she froze. In the distance she heard the sound of wagon wheels, and the steady clop, clop, clop, of horses' hooves. Her heart pounded painfully as Elysia paused in indecision. It would be light any minute now and she must get across that field, but she couldn't risk being seen dashing madly across it be some local farmer who might know her.

Elysia raised herself up slightly, and peeked through a leafy branch of shrubbery. A few yards away, coming down the lane, was an old horse pulling a loaded cart full of protesting pigs. A young boy prodded the old mare to no avail. She kept her leisurely pace, paying no attention to the impatient driver. Elysia recognized him as Tom, the son of a farmer who was a tenant of the Squire's. She couldn't reveal herself to him, of all people. But he was so slow! Time was running out. A faint glow of pink was beginning to appear in the sky as the loaded cart passed by her hiding place in the hedge. She allowed him to get a little further down the road, then hurried out from under the hedge and ran wildly towards the woods, hoping Tom wouldn't look back.

Her lungs felt as if they were going to burst, and her sides ached as she reached the first concealing trees of the forest. Elysia leaned thankfully back against the trunk of a large oak as she gazed back to enjoy the beauty of a glorious sunrise. The light flooded across the fields, turning them from gray to green, the sky a prism of changing pinks and oranges, fading into a vivid blue. She was safe!

She smiled grimly as she thought of her wild rush across the field. When she'd been a little girl she had run gaily through the fields, never dreaming that one day she would be running in earnest for her freedom.

By mid-morning Elysia's legs ached with fatigue, and she felt light-headed with hunger. She heard a stream gurgling nearby, and following a path to its bank, she knelt down on the edge and drank thirstily of its clear sparkling water, her cupped hands dripping water down her forearms, wetting the long sleeves of her dress.

Climbing up to a mossy bank overhanging the stream, she took out the red and white checked cloth wrapped around her small cache of stolen food, and unfolding it, spreading it out on her lap. Elysia broke off a piece of the bread, put a hunk of cheese on it and took a hungry bite. Elysia added some of the sweet-tasting pink ham, and then nibbled at the fragrant turnover, savoring each mouthful of the fresh fruit filling. The hungry growling of her stomach began to stop as she finished the turn-over, and thought to herself that never had any meal tasted so good.

Elysia began to hum a tune beneath her breath, snatches of verse from a long forgotten song coming to mind. The lines of the old gypsy ballad rang in her ears, capturing her mood as she relaxed back against the slope of the creek, staring down into the crystal effervescence of the water.

> I be a-wanderer, a-wanderer, no ties to keep
> me still
> a silver moon above me head, the ground
> beneath me back
> I be a-wanderer, a-wanderer, between the val-
> ley and hill
> fair colleens by the dozen I've seen, they call
> me Gypsy Jack.

Elysia sang softly, lingering over the words of the song. Free to wander. Yes she was free. Free to follow whatever path she chose; not a direction of her own choosing, perhaps, but she would make the best of it—now that she had nothing to return to.

She allowed herself a few more minutes of rest then wearily rose and walked along the stream searching for an easy place to cross before heading deeper into the woods. The sun appeared, disappeared, and then reappeared from behind the clouds which had built up gradually throughout the day. A cool wind rose from the north, whipping

Elysia's cape around her as she walked under the canopy of branches. By late afternoon she felt that she had gained enough distance to stop for the night.

The small bit of warmth fled as the sun's feeble rays faded and the shadows lengthened, bringing a cool crispness to the air. Elysia saw a large tree in the fading light and hurried over to it, feeling the ground beneath it soft with a covering of ferns. She sat down and took out her food, eating sparingly, not knowing how much longer she would have to make it last. She didn't believe she had much further to go; sometime during the following morning she should reach the main road.

Elysia pulled out her warm shawl, and taking off her cloak wrapped the shawl over her shoulders and head, then pulled her cloak back on over it, feeling warm and snug against the cold she knew would soon engulf her with the coming of night. She only hoped that the storm which had been brewing all day would not decide to break in the middle of the night.

She curled up, hugging her knees to her chest, and rested her cheek on her arm. She slept instantly, oblivious to the cold creeping in, or to the sounds of the small forest animals as they foraged for food among the trees.

Elysia awoke to a light drizzle falling from the leaden skies and, shivering from the cold and dampness, struggled to her feet. Her body was stiff and sore from running the day before, and the cold ground during the long hours of the night.

She ate the rest of her food while a weak light spread across the cloudy skies, changing them from black to dark gray, and thunder rumbled threateningly in the distance. She re-packed her bag and began to walk slowly through the trees until she came to her destination; the road cutting through the trees in a straight line toward London. She could see in the distance a crossroads, and hurried toward it as the rain began to fall in cold sheets against her face.

Dear, damned, distracting town, farewell!
  Thy fools no more I'll tease
This year in peace, ye critics dwell,
  Ye harlots, sleep at ease!

                                        Pope

Chapter 3

Sunlight streamed through the long window onto the green baize table where the last card had been played, and the victor was collecting his winnings.

"Well, that lets me out. I'm an out-and-out beggar after that hand," one of the younger gentlemen declared, laughing dejectedly, trying not to show his remorse at having lost more than he could comfortably afford. He straightened the soft velvet of his new coat and wondered how he was going to pay for it. Charles hated to ask his father for another advance on his allowance, and besides, he seriously doubted whether that stern gentleman would agree to yet another demand for funds.

"You've had quite a run of luck tonight, Trevegne, but then you always do," Lord Danvers declared loudly, taking a large swig of brandy and downing it in one gulp. "Heard rumors you played with the Devil and I'm beginning to believe it now," he grumbled while making a mental note of his losses.

He leaned back in the small gilt chair as he surveyed the others, his cravet crumpled and askew, his blue brocade vest unbuttoned to allow his ample stomach room to escape and relax as it overhung the tight waist of his breeches. "How about one more hand?" he inquired eagerly, his fever for play overriding his empty pockets.

"I'm more than willing to allow you to win back your losses, gentlemen," Lord Trevegne replied in a bored voice, straightening the lacy cuffs of his sleeve with an experienced flick of his wrist. He glanced slowly at each player in thoughtful silence, a hint of amusement gleaming in his tawny eyes.

The youngest gentleman nervously looked around the table, shifting slightly in his chair, trying to get up enough courage to admit that he was broke. He finally ended up murmuring softly to no one in particular, "Too tired," and relaxed back in his chair with relief at having made so difficult a decision.

"Are you really, dear Charles? Such a pity," Lord

Trevegne said sympathetically, a cynical twist on his sensual lips.

Charles Lackton flushed red to his fiery-colored hair, and turned resentful blue eyes on His Lordship's lounging figure, feeling both anger and admiration for the man. He had admired Lord Trevegne for as long as he could remember, the stories of Trevegne's escapades having fired his imagination, until Trevegne had become a legend to him.

Charles was startled out of his thoughts by the shuffle of the cards, the gentlemen having decided on one last hand. He watched in fascination as the cards were dealt swiftly and expertly by Lord Trevegne's long, narrow fingers, the odd, gold ring that he wore on his little finger glowing mystically up into Charles' somewhat bemused periwinkle-blue eyes; eyes as guileless as a child's. He continued to stare at His Lordship's unconcerned expression as he played his hand, apparently uncaring whether he lost or won, even though the stakes made Charles draw in his breath, thankful he was not in on the last hand. This whole game was a little rich for his blood. He had gamed for lesser stakes in most of the clubs, and had only received an invitation for private play at Trevegne's because of his friendship with His Lordship's younger brother Peter. He had thoroughly enjoyed the evening even though his pockets were empty.

The room was now quiet except for the breathing of the two men sitting comfortably in two leather chairs by the fireplace. The fire was cold, the cards spread in careless abandon upon the table, and empty glasses scattered with ashes and cigar butts throughout the room were the only sign of the night's play.

"You've the luck of the Devil, Alex," the older of the two men stated emphatically, but with good humor. "Sure you haven't made a pact with him? You certainly had Danvers' pockets to let last night, and he's not one to like losing," he chuckled in remembrance of Danvers' red, perspiration-streaked face.

"It just wasn't your evening, George. Next time try to keep that twinkle out of your eye when you think you've got a winning hand," Lord Trevegne laughed as he rose and stretched his long, lean body, running a negligent hand through his raven-black hair.

"I've always thought you were part hawk with those sharp eyes of yours. See a damned sight too much for a mortal man," George complained.

"Don't tell me you've been listening to those stories doing the rounds of St. James? I had thought better of you, George," he inquired casually, pouring two brandies. He handed Lord Denet one as he resettled himself in the large chair.

"I know you're no Lucifer, or devil incarnate, as some seem fond of calling you, your brother among them, but sometimes your luck is uncanny," replied the older man.

"I may have a lucky star, but I prefer to think it's my skill that enables me to win, not Lady Luck. As with most females, she is fickle, and not to be trusted. No thank you. I shall continue to rely on my own devices, rather than to play into the lovely, but quicksilver hands of Lady Luck." He took a sip of brandy, and smilingly added, "And as for Peter, he's just a young cub following the pack, like young Lackton. He'll soon find his feet. He's just miffed because I won't advance him his allowance. Spend it before I can even get it out of my pocket." He loosened his cravat and settled deeper into the chair.

"I can see that you're tired, Alex, and hinting that I should take my leave, but I've one other subject to discuss first," said Lord Denet, getting to his feet, and planting them firmly, as if in preparation for an attack upon his person.

"I was not hinting that you should take your leave. Why, George, how could I allow you to think me so lax a host as to show my guest the door? Even though it is rather late—or early—whichever you prefer. I was merely attempting to make myself more comfortable." He smiled up at his old friend.

"Well, no offense taken, but I'll say my piece and then leave. I'll say no more upon the matter, this I promise, but—" He hesitated, reluctant now that he had his host's attention.

"Do continue, George, this is beginning to interest me. I gather that you've some advice to impart to me?" Lord Trevegne asked helpfully in a quiet voice.

Lord Denet had known Alexander Trevegne since he had been in short pants, and knew that the quiet, languid voice was deceiving to those who were not aware that it masked a will of iron and a fierce temper. Lord Trevegne's quiet tones were soft and ominous, and more deadly than a man who raged like a bull. Alex, when angered, struck quickly and quietly. He had seen Alex cut a man to pieces with his sharp sarcastic tongue, reducing him to a quivering animal ready to turn tail and run. Few men cared—or dared—to cross words, or weapons with Lord Trevegne, the Marquis of St. Fleur. He was a deadly shot with pistols, and even deadlier at reducing some annoying acquaintance into looking the fool with his notorious set downs and snubs.

George mentally gathered up his courage and plunged straight on. "I think you ought to consider marrying, Alex. I only say this because I feel that I owe it to your dead parents, who, as you know, were close friends of mine."

Lord Trevegne gave a harsh laugh. "You're a fine one to be lecturing me, George. You happen to be a bachelor still, or are you planning on joining your friends in wedded bliss?"

"That's not the point, and anyway, I have four brothers who are quite capable of keeping the nurseries full, and I'm too old now to set up housekeeping with one woman." He frowned as if the thought were too painful to contemplate. "But I have acted responsibly and discreetly with my liaisons, which I might add, you have not. In fact, I believe you purposely enjoy causing gossip. You aren't satisfied with one ladybird. No, you have to have half a dozen fighting for your favors; flaunting your presents in every gaming hall from London to Paris. But even that doesn't satisfy you, for then you entertain certain Ladies of Quality whom you treat as casually as your other paramours. There are rumors, after this last affair of yours with Lady Mariana, of kicking you out of Almack's. Now you can't allow that!" George expostulated heatedly.

"I don't give a damn about those clucking hens at Almack's," Lord Trevegne spoke in disgust.

"And how about Peter? What kind of an example are you setting for him?"

"You know, George, if you weren't such an old friend I'd call you out for the liberties you have taken this morn. No one has ever dared to speak to me thusly." His voice had hardened with his meaning, the golden eyes darkened.

"I'm only doing what I consider to be my duty." George said a trifle too heartily, then cast a look of speculation on the Marquis as he added, "And maybe it is about time that someone began to talk back to you. Do you a bit of good to be given a dressing down."

The Marquis laughed in genuine amusement. "You think so, George? I've yet to meet the man."

"Maybe it won't be a man ..." George hinted obliquely. "Maybe you'll meet your match in a feminine devil in skirts, who'll humble you with a look from provocative eyes that only have disdain in them for you. And if you aren't careful you'll lose her—the only time in your life when you'll desire something that you won't be able to buy or win,"

George concluded, turning red as he gave Lord Trevegne an embarrassed look, surprised by his own vehemence.

"Well, well, I had no idea that you had turned into a crystal-gazer, George. So, you believe I shall meet a paragon—no," Lord Trevegne paused, a sneer on his lips, "a she-devil if she's to be my mate—who will give me a royal setdown." He laughed again, his black head thrown back. "I hope I've not long to wait for this confrontation. If what you predict is true, then I shall look forward to it with anticipation. It promises to be a fiery affair—be sure to keep a safe distance, George, or the sparks that fly will no doubt set you alight."

George guffawed loudly, unable to repress the smile that hovered upon his lips as he threw up his hands in defeat. "You're a devil, Alex. You mock everything—nothing is sacred to you. But listen, if you were married and settled down, then people would be appeased. A wife will add respectability to even the most roguish of blackguards."

"If I ever get married, it certainly won't be to satisfy a bunch of snoopy busybodies, sticking their pointed noses into others' affairs," Lord Trevegne answered, a twisted smile on his lips as he continued in mock offense, "and to think you hold me in such low esteem—a roguish blackguard, indeed! Would you have me do penance in sackcloth and ashes, prostrating myself on a marriage bed in atonement for my plunge into dissipation?"

"Certainly not!" George disclaimed, shaken. "I

certainly do not hold you in low esteem, Alex. Why, you're a gentleman of the highest order. Your name is certainly not to be held in derision by anyone—in fact I have never heard a slur cast upon the name of Trevegne. There is no one more honorable than you, Alex, but—well, you have a damnable reputation for being a libertine; for seeking your amusements to the exclusion of all else. Not that there is anything wrong in that—but must you always succeed? It's the envy and jealousy of other, less fortunate roués who have been grumbling about your extraordinary successes that have set Almack's to talking."

"I cannot control what others will say, nor can I let gossip rule my life. My God, I'd have to sit home with a prayer book if I did."

"Well if you won't consider marriage, then at least try to be less conspicuous about flaunting your mistresses, especially when they're Quality. Everyone knew about Lady Mariana, even when you threw her over. I must say, I did rather think she might manage to become your Marchioness. Had me worried, that. Never been one of my favorites, the Lady Mariana. Granted she's a beauty, but too damned uppity for my likes. Hear she's after higher stakes, now. The Duke of Linville. Won't be getting much in His Grace, I can tell you. Laughing Lin ain't got much to recommend him except his title and well-lined pockets. Never did meet a more obnoxious character; even if he is a Duke. Knew him as a boy, disliked him then, dislike him now. Got the damndest laugh I ever heard," Lord Denet said disgustedly. "You were too young of course, but—"

"Enough reminiscences, George, please," Lord Trevegne pleaded, holding up his hands placatingly. "I think I have made my position on marriage quite clear, and to set your over-active imagination at rest, I will tell you that I never entertained the thought of marrying Lady Mariana, beautiful as she is, but then she didn't expect marriage either. I've never dallied with young innocents who would misunderstand my intentions—or lack of them, nor do I deceive any woman into thinking that I have intended more than just a casual liaison." Lord Trevegne's voice hardened as he continued coldly, "And only occasionally will some lady try to extend what had been an enjoyable affair into something more permanent. But it's never worked." The Marquis took a swallow of brandy, and glancing at the silent George added with cynical amusement, "I hope that allays any doubts you have harbored concerning my welfare, and by the way, I shall be leaving London shortly." He covered a yawn with his hand gracefully.

"Leaving London!" George exclaimed as if leaving London was something unheard of. "But, I don't understand? Leaving London?"

"Yes, leaving London. Please, George, you have us sounding like parrots," the Marquis laughed as George repeated his words once again. "I've business to attend to, and I'm anxious for a bit of hunting. Now satisfied? Let us drop the subject, because I've become exceedingly bored by it all. All these questions and answers—I shall have to take counsel under this catechism." Alex feigned another yawn, looking up at George, an innocent expression on his handsome face.

"By God! I do believe I'm boring you to sleep. You are a demon, Alex. Nothing seems to affect you except to bore you. If you are so bored, then why are you leaving town? There's plenty to do here to keep you busy. Your estate agent can handle all your business affairs, so surely there's no need to go gallivanting across the countryside, is there? Cursed uncomfortable if you ask me."

"You've answered that one yourself, George."

"Eh, what?" George bent a confused look upon the relaxed Marquis.

"Boredom, George." Alex returned his look with jaded golden eyes. "As plain and simple as that. I would rather be down by the sea, in the fresh air, doing some hunting, than closed up in balls and assemblies. It will serve as a trip with twofold purpose—relaxation and business, to be carried out at my leisure. And I can promise you that I've no seventh mistress tucked away on my estate, nor do I have designs on my estate manager's wife. However . . ." he added devilishly, "I might have a bride safely secured, eagerly awaiting my pleasure, in the master bedroom."

The Marquis laughed, and rising as if in preparation to retire, successfully ended the conversation. "Listen, George, come down to Westerly when you tire of London. You're welcome any time."

"Well, thank you, Alex. Glad to know you don't hold what I've said against me, even if I do wish you had a bride hidden away somewhere," he answered gruffly, feeling genuine affection for the Marquis, who he looked upon almost as a son. "I'll be off then, and see you soon, I suspect. Dashed dull around here without your devilish tongue, Alex."

Lord Denet left the room, his footsteps echoing down the stairs until Lord Trevegne finally heard voices and the slamming of a door. He poured himself another brandy and stared morosely at the floral pattern on the Aubusson carpet beneath his feet. His mouth was set in a grim line, his body as tense as a tightly-coiled spring. He would leave the following morning for the coast, and travel at his leisure. He was in no hurry—except maybe to leave London.

He had told George most of the truth. He was bored with London and the endless rounds of clubs and parties and balls, the same silly chatter and expressionless faces night after night. He felt the need to clear his mind of the fogginess caused by late nights of heavy drinking and gambling, to set himself free from the clinging, destructive tentacles of London society. He felt restless, as if something was missing from his life. He felt as if he were searching for something; but he wasn't quite sure what it was. Hell, all he really needed was to sort out his mind— he was just drunk on the gay life here. What he needed was fresh and clean spring water to wash away the bitterness.

He could achieve this out in the country where the unexpected could happen, challenging him to his fullest capabilities. He needed something to whet his appetite from the monotonous routine of town life.

Alex could feel his blood begin to surge as he thought of open country, the moors and jagged coastline of Cornwall, and Sheik, his big black Arabian stallion beneath him as they raced like the wind across the countryside.

"You're up shockingly early, old boy," a voice drawled from the doorway.

"I could say the same of you, Peter," Lord Trevegne answered, casting a disapproving look over his young brother, who had quietly entered the room. "Where the blazes have you come from this early in the morning, looking like Hell itself?" Alex demanded as he watched his brother pour out a large brandy from his quickly depleting decanter.

Peter settled himself casually in an armchair, trying to appear calm, but failing to conceal his excitement from those golden eyes across the room.

"You might as well tell me, Peter, for I shall probably hear about it soon enough," he sighed in resignation.

"You'll never guess, Alex, but I beat Teddie's time by three minutes!" he exclaimed, unable to contain his excitement.

"Really," Alex drawled, "pray tell me at what? I'm no gypsy fortune teller."

"His time from Vauxhall Gardens to Regent's Park—and during the crush too! His blacks were no match for my bays. All he saw was my dust the whole distance. Never saw a madder look on a fellow's face. Of course he lost a bundle, I can tell you!" he stated smugly, smiling to himself as he took a large swig of his brandy, choking as it went down the wrong way, tears streaming from his eyes as he coughed.

Lord Trevegne slapped his brother hard on the back and smothered a grin as Peter straightened, wiping furtively at his eyes.

"There is no record to beat in finishing that brandy, my lad. And, it happens to be one of my finest, so do go easy on it, if not for your own sake, then for my injured senses as a gentleman, who deplores seeing his fine brandy tossed off like a tankard of ale."

"Your pardon, Alex, but I had a damnable thirst to quench and wasn't quite thinking." Peter said contritely, taking a small sip from the snifter as he tried to regain his composure. He stood up and walked over to the window and stared out at the park across the street. The sunlight filtering in played on his black hair, bringing out red highlights among the raven strands. He turned back and grinned mischievously before saying casually, "I'd like to borrow your team of blacks. Nothing can beat them." His blue eyes twinkled irrepressibly as he

DEVIL'S DESIRE

watched the frown settle on his brother's face, then the golden eyes caught the imp of mischief in the blue eyes.

Alex's lips parted in an answering smile. "If I had thought you were serious I would have guessed that you'd driven your team while standing on your head. But I'm glad that you've decided to pay me a visit. I had imagined myself having to cross the Channel in search of you on one of your crazy antics. But seeing how Napoleon wishes to win this war, he would waste little time in dispatching you speedily back to England."

"Oh, come now, Alex, I'm not as bad as that. Just having a little fun," he complained happily.

"Well, just don't get yourself thrown out of Almack's," Alex warned, forgetting that he himself was in danger of that very happening, and of his own scoffing attitude.

"You've come pretty close yourself, and if rumor has it, then—"

"—then you will be careful and remember that I've warned you," Alex interrupted his brother's rebuttal.

"Well, what did you want to see me about? Not about that, I'll wager," Peter replied, a trifle put out.

"I'm leaving for Westerly tomorrow," Alex answered succinctly.

"Leaving London! You can't possibly be serious, Alex. Why, whatever will you do down there?" Peter demanded increduously.

"This is beginning to sound like a Shakespearean

71

comedy! Does no one leave London these days?" he sighed, then turning a hard golden-eyed stare at Peter, said, "I might add that I'll be seeing to the estate that keeps your pockets well-lined."

Peter had the grace to look slightly ashamed at that remark, but puzzlement still showed in his eyes as Alex continued.

"London is full of mincing fops, unlicked cubs and needle-witted mamas shoving their daughters into the highest bidder's bed and I'm sick of the lot of them," he declared with contempt in his voice.

"Sure it's not Mariana that's made you turn tail?"

"I don't believe I heard you correctly, Peter. Would you care to repeat that remark?" Lord Trevegne asked in a tone so quiet and menacing it made Peter's blood run cold. He feared he had pushed his brother's temper too far this time, and felt sick as he thought of the other men who had also learned too late of Lord Trevegne's deadly temper and were now laid to rest in the bowels of the earth.

"I'm sorry, Alex. Please forget I ever said that. I know you'd never run from anything. I'm just a beef-head sometimes, but it's just that I know how much you loved her, and she did last longer than anyone else. I never did understand why you dropped her. She's a real beauty, and now they say she's got old Linville almost at the altar, so I thought maybe you minded even though you've said you were through with her," he stammered.

Lord Trevegne gave a sigh of exasperation, his

patience beginning to become frayed about the edges by this well-intentioned, yet aggravating interest in his welfare.

"You play with fire, Peter. I know you well enough not to take half of what you say seriously, knowing how impetuous you are, but others do not realize that you often say things you find yourself regretting later. So take care Peter, or you shall find yourself in very deep waters," Alex reprimanded him coldly. "But to answer your question. I was never in love with Mariana, nor have I ever been in love with any woman. At least not enough to ask her to marry me. I should be bored with her before the honeymoon was over. I'm tired of having them fall at my feet, or more aptly, into my bed, either because they think they're in love with me, or because of my title and estates—which I believe they love even more," he said cynically. "Mariana and I enjoyed a brief *affaire de coeur*, and now it's over— maybe a little sooner than it would have been, but that was merely precipitated by a disagreement which could not be eradicated. So we had a parting of the ways, and whoever she becomes entangled with next is of no interest to me," he said with a strange smile lurking in his eyes. "I'm only discussing this with you to end, once and for all, this speculation, which, it would seem the whole of London is concerned with. I do not make it a practice of mine to discuss my personal affairs with anyone—even you. But it would seem that most of my private life is common knowledge, and of exaggerated interest in every drawing-room and tavern. I would at least like to have the story straight in your mind before you inadvertently add to the gossip out of your own imagination—or while you're in your cups."

"I say, Alex, I'm no long-tongued chatterer telling tales about my own brother!" Peter exclaimed in a grievous tone, adding indignantly, "And I can hold my liquor as well as any man. Trevegne blood's thicker than wine anyway."

"I beg your pardon." Alex bowed slightly. "I know that you would not say anything injurious to me on purpose—but you might be goaded to in anger."

Peter finished off his brandy with a careless flourish of his hand, draining it to the last drop, then laughed suddenly. "Damned if I'll get in a duel over somebody else's ladybird. She may be a beauty, but I've always thought her a bit above herself. Won't even give me the time of day and hasn't got a sense of humor, either. Nor will I challenge every man in the street over some tittle-tattle at a tea-party! Should be over something more important than a windbag, eh?"

Alex threw back his head and laughed, joining Peter in his mirth, both men standing tall and proud, bearing a marked family resemblance to each other in their aristocratic faces and arrogantly tilted square jaws, their hawk-visaged features softened by their laughter. The fifteen years difference in their ages disappeared as they laughed together in boyish abandon.

Alex looked fondly at his brother's slighter figure, feeling the full weight of responsibility for Peter on his shoulders; broad shoulders that were accustomed to bearing responsibility. Watching Peter, he wondered whether he had ever been that young and carefree? Innocent of worries, and unaware of how very lonely the world really was? It seemed like an eternity since he had felt the warmth of an unselfish love surrounding him; a love that could warm like a welcoming fire on a cold night, seeming to penetrate to the very depths of one's body. He had enjoyed love these past years, but it was not the same kind of love. It was an unsatisfying love that consumed and devoured, leaving only regrets in its stead. But he had come to expect nothing else. That other type of love was something that no longer existed for him.

Lord of the Manor at fifteen, he'd been a very young and inexperienced heir to the enormous estates and holdings of the Trevegnes. Lord Denet had been his guardian, and had become a good friend while helping him bear up under his new and heavy responsibility. With the help of trusted estate agents and lawyers, he had learned to manage Westerly; proving himself a very capable young Lord of the Manor.

But it was no easy victory, and there were many battles along the way. A young and inexperienced Marquis was considered easy game by crooked estate agents who cared for nothing except to fill their own pockets, and by the supposedly close friends of his father who claimed they had been owed a debt by the deceased—nothing written, of course, just sealed with a handshake. And then there was the friendly advice from his father's friends, most of whom had young daughters and impoverished estates, who hinted at a secret agreement of a marriage contract that had been made years previously; the young Marquis' assets making him an excellent son-in-law.

But Lord Denet was nobody's fool; and armed with his staff of lawyers he managed to keep the vultures at bay until the new Marquis could stand on his own.

So the young Marquis had grown up; and hardened into iron along the way. That he never had the opportunity of being carefree and gay, lines of worry etched into his face before he was twenty, did not seem to bother him. He made up for the earlier years of his manhood that he missed by living every moment to the fullest these last years in London and on the continent.

No one could have guessed how far-reaching the death of his father had been. He was killed in a duel shortly before the birth of his second son—murdered by an adversary who had fired early. Alex remembered his father as a man of action who loved parties, gaming, and even more, the hunt. He thoroughly enjoyed life, but he had little business acumen. He'd let the estate run itself and the holdings go unchecked for years. Westerly, however, had been kept up, partly due to the efforts of his mother, and was still a magnificent manor house.

But Lady Trevegne had not lived to enjoy it—nor had she lived long enough to see her second son. A birth and a death—nature equalizing itself.

Alex bitterly resented the fact that Peter had never known her. There would never be another woman like her. She was the only woman he had ever trusted. He remembered her bright blue eyes— Peter's eyes—laughing, teasing, letting him pull her golden curls out of place, hugging him tightly when she put him to bed. She had made each day seem a gay holiday; each night in front of the grand fireplace, a make-believe world of fairies and elves, blood-thirsty pirates and brave knights—filling his world with a love and security lost forever with her death. He had felt cheated by it, but at least he had his memories. Peter had nothing.

Gradually he settled down to his way of life and accepted it. He seldom went to London, and then only on affairs dealing with business and the estate. As he got older, he missed at first the closeness of his friends and the gaiety and pleasures that life in London could give a young man. But as the time passed, he matured faster than his friends, living an easy and frivolous London life. His healthy country life turned him into a virile man, his hands strong, lean and brown, not the lily-white hands of the town gentleman. Even when he had returned to London after years of exile, he couldn't completely forget his other way of life. His muscles remained firm and rock-hard, and he was capable of great endurance and strength—enjoying boxing and fencing, riding hard, unable to feign fatigue as many of his contemporaries seemed fond of doing after a light canter.

He became a member of the Corinthian set and of the Four-in-Hand Club, with his unparalleled expertise at the reins. He was invited to many a rout, party, and week-end outing, but his cynical nature only gained in strength as he participated in the social whirl of London life. Over the years, rumors began to surround his handsome and haughty figure. As he withdrew further into himself with his cynicism—presenting an inscrutable mien to the world—the stories grew about him. He was an unknown entity. His wild escapades, some true, some not, began to gain him fame throughout London, and combined with a certain mysterious aura that surrounded him, fired people's imaginations. Nothing is so intriguing as a mystery—a puzzle. And the Marquis of St. Fleur presented one. His luck with chance, beating the odds, was uncanny. He never seemed to lose; whether it be at cards, or with the ladies.

When he entered a room, dressed totally in black, as he seemed fond of doing, he could set feminine hearts fluttering from a mere glance of his golden eyes. He was indifferent, arrogant, and at times insultingly rude even to the most beautiful women, but that only added to his devil-may-care figure. And the thought of his estates, money and the famous Trevegne jewels made him more desirable yet.

"You don't mind if I stay in London for awhile, do you?" inquired Peter hopefully.

"No, stay as long as you wish, but do try to act with a little decorum for a change."

"You needn't worry. I won't do anything that you yourself wouldn't do," Peter promised rashly, a twinkle in his eyes.

"That's precisely what has me worried," replied Lord Trevegne seriously as he walked to the door with his brother, cuffing his ear fondly as he warned, "Be careful, Peter. Remember I won't be here to help you out of a difficult time."

"Don't worry, old boy," Peter grinned, but with serious eyes for once. "I shall be a model of society, and do you proud," he said in farewell, leaping down the stairs two at a time, his promise already forgotten.

Alex stood shaking his head, a frown of worry on his forehead as he turned towards his bedchamber, and the sleep long awaited. He wanted Peter to have what he had missed in his youth, but maybe he was too lenient with him at times. He didn't want Peter to feel deprived of anything. He deserved everything that he could give him—small comfort for never having known either of his parents.

"Very well, Your Lordship," Dawson, Lord Trevegne's secretary answered, clearing the large, mahogany desk of the accounts and orders they had just been through for the last hour. "Will there be anything else, M'Lord?"

"No, just continue as usual, and no advances to Peter, unless I approve them. And if anything urgent should arise send me a missive immediately," Alex answered, straightening his lacy, white cravat before the mirror. "Otherwise, I leave you in charge, Dawson. I've complete confidence in your ability."

"Thank you, Your Lordship," Dawson answered, flustered by the compliment.

"You do me a great honor, and may I wish you a pleasant journey—although it promises rain before evening. It shall be a wet and gloomy morning for your trip tomorrow. Are you sure you wish to ride on ahead of the carriage, Your Lordship?" he asked worriedly.

Lord Trevegne looked at the small, gray-haired man with his stooped shoulders and squinting eyes. He trusted Dawson implicitly, as he could few other men. Dawson had taken over management of his estates for him many years ago, and Dawson knew as much, if not more, about his financial affairs than he did himself. He told Dawson the truth when he stated he had complete confidence in him.

"No need to worry, Dawson. I shall—" Lord Trevegne began to answer, when there was a knock on the door. It was opened by a footman announcing stiffly:

"Lady Mariana Woodley, Your Lordship."

He stepped aside as Lady Mariana swept regally

into the room in a bright-red, velvet walking dress and matching fur-trimmed mantle and bonnet, her hands tucked into a large, dark, fur muff; her exotic perfume reaching out to the two men standing in the middle of the room as she moved toward them.

Dawson made his way to the door unnoticed. He never liked Lady Mariana, and personally speaking, was glad that His Lordship was finished with her; he only wished that he could send her on her way without so much as a by your leave. In fact, His Lordship would have been surprised to learn this was the concensus of most of his household.

"Alex, darling," she murmured softly. "You have been very impolite by not coming to see me since I've returned from the country." She pouted prettily.

Lord Trevegne watched through narrowed eyes as she moved towards him, her long, narrow hands now outstretched gracefully. She was indeed a beautiful woman, her dark-brown hair superbly coiffed to reveal a long, slender neck, beautifully arched like a swan's.

He looked down into her liquid, brown eyes and long artificially-darkened lashes, her lips raised, inviting his kiss, a kiss that he knew could be long and deep; fully reciprocated by her. He did not desire her as he once had, but he could still feel admiration, and something more, as he continued to stare at her. His eyes wandered slowly over her rounded, white breasts, barely concealed by the low-cut, red velvet of her dress and his memory filled in the rest of her curvaceous body—the feel of her warm and naked, lying pressed against his own bare flesh.

He turned abruptly away. "What do you want, Mariana?" he asked impatiently as he walked over to his desk, selecting a thin cheroot from a carved wooden box. He lighted it, and turning around, exhaled smoke which masked his expression, the aroma of the fine tobacco engulfing her heady perfume. "It's not proper, my dear, for an unescorted lady to call at a gentleman's home during the day."

"And when have either you or I ever done what is considered proper?" she countered.

"I really didn't believe that we had anything further to say to one another. We've both made our decisions, and I intend to keep to mine. From what I've heard, you have been doing the same—unless, of course, they're only rumors," he added tauntingly.

"They are not rumors!" Lady Mariana answered angrily, her dark-brown eyes flashing.

"Well then, what have we further to say to one another?" Lord Trevegne replied coldly.

"We've everything to talk about, Alex." She moved closer to stand directly in front of him, her eyes looking beseechingly up into his hard, golden ones.

"Can you actually stand here, before me now, and say you do not desire me? That you don't wish we were upstairs—"

"Don't, Mariana," he said harshly, gripping her

soft arms with hard, biting fingers. "You're just cheapening yourself by going on this way."

"Cheapening myself!" Mariana cried shrilly. "I'm merely stating the truth—the bare facts. We're in love with one another. At least I admit it!"

"No, Mariana. We desired each other, that's all, nothing more. We both knew that it would end someday and you just ended it sooner by your threats. No one threatens me, or tries to blackmail me, my dear." He pushed her away from him in disgust, and looked away from her angry, white face and heaving breasts.

"I only threatened to leave you for the Duke—unless you married me—to try and force you to admit to yourself that you loved me and wanted to marry me. You can't stand the thought of some other man making love to me, can you?"

"My dear Mariana, I don't give a damn whose bed you warm. What we had is through. You finished it yourself, although I must admit it would have ended shortly as the heat of desire became cold ashes," he said indifferently.

"I don't believe you. You're mad about me. I'm in your blood, just as you're in mine," she spoke passionately. "I could have had Linville over a year ago, but no, I decided to let becoming a Duchess take second place to my love for you."

"Ah, yes, the Duke. That really has been your supreme goal in life; Lady Mariana, the Duchess. Don't blind yourself to your real motive with me, my dear. You may have desired me, but you also desired all that I hold, including the diamonds and emeralds and other fabulous trinkets which will drape the next Lady Trevegne, Marchioness of St. Fleur.

"You knew that I never thought of marriage when our affair began, but you didn't seem to mind. You even told me once you enjoyed your widowhood—free to sample all the delights without having a jealous husband to worry about, I believe you said. Why the sudden change of face, my dear, or was it a charade all along—get me in bed with you, in love with you, then legally tied to you?"

"You beast!" Lady Mariana spoke, trying to regain her composure, her nostrils flared, her pupils dilated in anger at his revelation of the truth which she could not deny. She threatened leaving him and promised to marry the Duke if he wouldn't marry her. She was so sure of her control over him that she thought he would plead with her to stay and marry him immediately, but instead he told her to do as she wished, he didn't care. She thought his pride was merely injured and that he would soon come after her, but he didn't. He ignored her and even cut her in front of people at Almack's, giving her that contemptuous look that she had seen him give to the hangers-on who tried to flatter him and seek his favors. The whole plan got far out of control and she was desperate to put things back in their proper order once more.

"Can't we forget what has happened, Alex? We

can go back to the way it was before we had this little quarrel. I'm here now, offering you—"

"No, it's no use, Mariana. Neither of us has changed, and I think I know you well enough now to know that you're unable to alter your ways. Besides, the fire has died; I no longer want you. I didn't want to be so blunt, but these conversations do neither of us any good."

Lady Mariana stood silent; a confused look on her beautiful face. She had always had her way, always received what she wanted. She was the only daughter of elderly parents; spoiled and petted, expecting constant attention and pampering from her admirers. Being raised on a country estate, she grew up craving the excitement and gaiety which she sampled occasionally in London. Praised as a nonpareil in her first season in London, she quickly made an advantageous match with young Lord Woodley in order not to have to return to the country and her elderly parents, who could not face the rigor of hectic London and the constant entertaining. And she was now a member of the peerage, no longer just Miss Mariana Greene; but the Lady Mariana Woodley. They enjoyed themselves in her first years in London, living wildly and extravagantly; living for fun rather than for each other and she was not broken-hearted when he died in a drunken stupor beneath the wheels of his overturned curricle, for there was one less person to spend the money now, and she could pursue her own desires first.

She was called The Wild Widow Woodley around London, and she wholeheartedly enjoyed living up to that name. Then, after years of casual, light-hearted affairs she met Lord Trevegne and fell in love for the first time in her life. He had been in London when she first made her debut, and she could remember how his dark, virile looks had excited her, but then he disappeared. He was traveling around the world, she heard. She forgot about him until one evening when they met again, and she knew that she had not forgotten, as the desire flared between them.

From then on, she laid her plans carefully, for this was the man she wanted. Her only regret was that he was only a Marquis, and not a Duke. But she allowed her ambition to be drowned by the tide of his desire, thinking she would have to settle on becoming a mere Marchioness. And at least there were the Trevegne jewels, worth a King's ransom, to salve her disappointment. She knew of his reluctance to become married, the rumors circulating that she wouldn't last a month, but she was so sure of his love and desire for her and of her own powers over men, that it never entered her head that he wouldn't ask her to become his wife. She pretended to be in horror of a second marriage, and as anxious as he to keep her freedom. She did not want to scare him off, after all, she had plenty of time, and she was not about to do something she might regret later.

She knew that he had other mistresses, but they

posed no threat to her plans for a more permanent association, but as time went on and he never mentioned marriage she decided to scare him by threatening to leave him for another. Only he had not reacted as she had anticipated.

It must still be his stubborn pride that was keeping him from coming around to her wishes. She had forgotten how proud he was. She glanced at his handsome face, the firm, sensual lips and felt panic at the thought of losing him. She just couldn't lose Alex; the only man she had ever fallen in love with. She had had dozens of lovers—just as handsome as Alex—but there was a difference in Alex. Maybe it was his indifference at times, or his arrogance, that never let her forget that he was a man. He never crawled to her, he never let her have the upper hand; yet she thought she had a hold over him. He was an ardent lover, making her senses swim, making her feel like a complete woman. She felt lost while with him, and dead without him. To feel his arms around her slim body now, his lips pressing against hers ...

"I am sure you must have some appointment which you are late for, Lady Mariana, so do not let me detain you any longer. It wouldn't do to have your carriage seen outside my door," Lord Trevegne said politely, his voice cold and impersonal as he watched the conflicting emotions chase across her face. "You would not want your reputation tarnished."

Lady Mariana glanced up at him in indecision, chewing nervously on her lower lip, and finally found a solution, a seductive smile curving her lips.

"As a matter of fact, Linny is waiting for me right now, so I must leave, but can we meet tomorrow if I can find the time? You know how possessive Linny is, so I will have to see if I can manage to spare a few minutes," she said airily, still trying to make him jealous of the Duke.

"I'm afraid, Lady Mariana, that I will not be here tomorrow."

"Oh, where will you be?" she asked curiously, pulling on her red, kid gloves casually, her mind already devising a way of luring him into her bed-chamber.

"I shall be out of London."

"But you mustn't leave London—you can't leave me here!" she exclaimed, shock in her eyes. "You're running away," Mariana said dramatically, "but it's all so unnecessary! If only you would forget your stupid pride, and—"

"Lady Woodley, what I do is no longer of any concern to you, and never have I had to explain my actions to anyone—which it seems I have begun to do since deciding to leave London," he said in exasperation.

"I won't let you leave!" Mariana cried, fear in her voice. She knew that if he left she would lose him forever. He would not be jealous of what he could not see or hear about, and he might find someone else while he was gone.

She threw her arms around his neck, pressing her body close to his, and kissed him hungrily, her mouth trying to part his firm lips, receiving no response from him until he wrenched her arms from around his neck and backed away from her hot, clinging body. He wanted to convince her, once and for all, that he felt nothing for her any longer, and said the first thing that came to his mind as a possible deterrent to her hopes.

"I shall probably be a married man by the next time I see you, and I doubt whether my wife would approve of our little liaison," he said hiding his amusement at the startled look on her pretty face. He felt no pity for a woman who would use her body to blackmail a man. Maybe he would get married after all. It would certainly settle a lot of problems he seemed to be accumulating recently. He thought of the young daughter of Squire Blackmore's, his nearest neighbor at Westerly. He had not seen her in a while, in fact he could not even remember what she looked like, but he thought she would be about the right age, and the Squire was always hinting at such an alliance. Yes, some little nonentity, someone who would give him no trouble, and not play on his affections.

"Married! You?" Mariana laughed harshly, thinking it a bluff. "To whom, pray tell? Not to one of those mealy-mouthed chits foisted on you by their frantic mamas. You might try Bradshaw's daughter, let me see"—she paused reflectively—"what is her name? Mary, yes Mary I believe, but of course she does look rather horsey. Or there is Caroline something-or-other, who has a stupendous fortune but, poor dear, she stutters and squints horribly—however, if you are determined to tie the knot ..." She finished in a speculative voice, biting the tip of her slender finger, as if trying to remember other eligible girls for him to choose from, when he startled her by saying in a cold and hard voice:

"I'm afraid you haven't had the pleasure of meeting the future Lady Trevegne, my dear, she happens to live out of London."

"You can't be serious!" she gasped. "You are planning to be married?" She looked at his face, grim and austere, giving nothing away. "What, may I ask, happened to your pledge to remain a bachelor?" she asked acidly. "This seems so sudden after all those years of confirmed bachelorhood, that you will forgive me if I have my doubts." She smiled unpleasantly. "I'll believe that nursery tale when I have the—pleasure—of meeting this paragon who has finally managed to get your ring on her finger—and not until then!"

Alex walked slowly over to his desk and opened a drawer, pulling out several papers and sorting them while Mariana watched him in puzzlement.

"My special license to marry, my dear," he told her, casually looking up into her shocked face. She hurried over to the desk, grabbing the piece of paper out of his hands, glancing at it briefly before throwing it down again, as if it burned her fingers.

Lady Woodley flounced to the door, leaving behind her a trail of heavy clinging perfume. Turning at the door she warned Lord Trevegne as he stood leaning casually against the desk, taking a deep draw off his cheroot, exhaling the smoke slowly, a cynical smile on his lips:

"Don't do anything we will both be sorry for later. And I don't take that nonsensical slip of paper seriously; it's not worth a brass farthing!" she said confidently before turning a haughty shoulder into his face, her curls bouncing provocatively.

Alex stood staring at the closed door for several minutes after Mariana left, and sighed when he heard her carriage pull away from in front of the house. How he had remembered the marriage license he wasn't sure; but it had suddenly come to him as the inspiration to convince her of his seriousness. That he had taken it away from Peter the day before when he had threatened to run away and marry the actress that he was currently enamored of, unless given an advance on his allowance—Mariana need never know.

Acting quickly and impulsively, he called for his valet and made arrangements to leave right away—not waiting until morning as he had previously planned. He had Dawson cancel his engagements for the evening, and quickly changed clothes.

He instructed a flustered and upset valet to meet him at the Wayfarer's Rest sometime on the morrow with his coach, and an hour later he was riding swiftly out of London.

He glanced about him at the fields of the open countryside and at the dark clouds gathering over his head. As he breathed deeply of the cool, pine-scented air, he felt it caress his face while Sheik streaked through the afternoon, sending a cloud of dust flying up behind them from his hooves.

"Slow down, boy," he spoke softly, pulling gently upon the reins, "we don't want to scare the Devil himself."

He laughed aloud, a deep resonant sound, full of mirth and tinged with abandon. He hadn't a care in the world; nothing to stop him. Giving Sheik his head, they sped wildly up the road, racing the wind and clouds, his many-tiered greatcoat billowing out behind him.

O villainy! Ho! let the door be lock'd:
Treachery! seek it out.

Shakespeare

Chapter 4

The wind had been blowing since daybreak, scattering the leaves from the surrounding trees against the walls of the inn, then hurling them on to disappear towards the dark, distant hills, bleak in the fading light of evening. The drizzle that had started at noon had gradually become a heavy downpour.

To Tibbitts, the owner and proprietor of the inn, Wayfarer's Rest, it merely caused annoyance. Bad weather was no blessing for his business; just extra work for him. Too many neglected cracks and holes in the roof were made evident by the rain, finding its way through onto his floors, or God forbid, onto one of his customers. His inn was situated at the crossroads intersecting the northern and coastal roads to London, and received all the traffic from each direction, including the mail coaches which stopped regularly to let off passengers changing coaches, or to rest and change the tired horses before continuing on.

"Come back 'ere, brat!" roared Tibbitts, as a small, thin boy ran past him down the narrow hall. He stretched out a long hairy arm and grabbed the youth by the back of his neck. "What are ye up to, eh? Didn't Oi tells yer to clean up the gentleman's room?" Tibbitts yelled as he gave the boy a firm shake.

"Oi'd 'ave done it, but the gent, 'e tells me to be about me business, and 'e 'ad a mean look in his eye, that 'e did. So Oi tells meself to git movin' and so Oi did," the boy said sullenly, trying to squirm loose.

"Ye tellin' me the truth, brat? If yer playin' me false, Oi'll 'ave yer scruffy 'ead for it. Oi'll 'ave no double-tongued brat gettin' me in bad with the gentry. Oi've seen 'em when they gets in a rage an Oi'll not care to sees it agin. T'ain't a pretty sight whats they can do when they be worked up into a passion. Oi remembers the time when some ladyship, a guest o' mine, stood right where yer a-standing, gnashing 'er teeth she be so mad, an all because Oi wouldn't give me best cut o' beef to 'er ladyship's little dog. Kept 'im with 'er always—never saw it out of 'er sight. She even rapped me knuckles over that cursed yappin' piece o' fur. So Oi'll not 'ave ye, a no-account, good fer nothin' gettin' me in bad, ye 'ere?" Tibbitts growled at the cowering boy.

"Oi ain't tellin' no fibs!" he cried as Tibbitts' hold tightened painfully.

"All right, brat, get into the back, an' Oi'll not be hearin' a word from ye, or else . . ." he said pushing the boy on down the hall before turning to make his way into the main room of the inn.

He watched with a critical eye as the serving maid laid the table for the evening meal. It was set for several customers, his private dining-room being occupied presently by a Dowager Duchess of formidable appearance. The two rich-looking London gentlemen, who were already occupying two of his best rooms, would have to share each other's company over their dinner this evening, and perhaps with the arrival of the mail coach he would have more customers to serve, but in this weather it could be delayed hours behind schedule. He had already had several rooms prepared for any passengers who would have to change coaches and—of necessity—stay overnight before catching another. He smiled to himself, mentally rubbing his palms together in anticipation of the large tips he knew he would be receiving.

Not too bad a night's work, Tibbitts thought, as he added more wood to the fire burning brightly in the hearth. The flames shot up, lighting the shadows in the room, throwing into contrast the low, oak-beamed ceiling; the beams soot-blackened from the countless fires burned in the large fireplace. The multi-assorted pewter flagons and tankards gleamed dully from shelves, and thick candles dripped grease that spit as it touched the cool metal of the brass candlesticks.

A broad toothy grin split Tibbitt's face again as he thought of more gold guineas filling his pockets; but now he would be satisfied with a hot meal to fill his belly.

Sir Jason Beckingham, to the contrary, was not smiling as he gazed moodily out of the rain-spattered windows of the room directly above Tibbitts.

He felt enraged! Here, under the same roof, in a room down the hall, was his most bitter and devastating enemy, Lord Alex Trevegne. How he hated the mere mention of that devil's name! He couldn't believe his eyes when he saw Trevegne ride into the yard of the inn a little while ago, his big, black horse pawing the mud impatiently while Trevegne dismounted, then walked briskly out of the rain as the stableboys led his horse away.

Lord Trevegne ... the name was more ominous-sounding to him than the deafening thunder outside. Ever since that demon entered his life his luck had changed. Before that he congratulated himself upon having won quite a large sum in a streak of lucky wagers. Also, his winnings from numerous late-night card games enabled him, for the first time in a long while, to sit comfortably without the worry of his creditors banging on his doors, demanding payment.

He'd been out of pocket for far too long to be satisfied with his temporarily enrichened state of being. He knew only too well how quickly expenses ate a hole in one's purse and he had no intention of returning to his previous state of poverty and near-degradation. His somewhat straightened circumstances of the past had caused him a great many embarrassments, and had reduced him at times to a hanger-on, a toad-eating toff; not only despised by those basking in his insincere flatteries, but, worst of all, by himself. To lose one's own self-respect was the worst possible treachery to befall a gentleman.

After all, he only wanted what he felt he deserved, and was his hereditary right. He was born a gentleman and that, by God, was how he should live. Instead, he had to resort to chicanery; becoming an accomplished slyboots. He had become quite adept at maneuvering people, and evading any unpleasant issue at hand. He actually believed that he could talk himself out of any situation, so well-versed in the art had he become out of necessity and a need for self-preservation. He defended himself—it really was not because of any fault of his own that he had to resort to such practices.

His loving parents, between them, gambled away his inheritance; and he was left with their extravagant debts when they died.

He learned early that he would have to fight hard and rough if he intended to stay among the ton, the elite of London, and take his proper place in society. His parents were known as the "royal couple," the King and Queen of Diamonds. They were always found at a game of chance; challenging the cards, rather than their opponents, with their skill.

Sir Jason did not inherit his parents' fanatical obsession for gambling, merely their expertise, to help him profit by other's misfortunes—and it was not beneath him, at times, to stack the deck in his favor. And he too, acquired a nickname from the cards—the Joker.

One could always count upon Beckingham, the Joker, to liven up a party. No one ever knew quite what to expect from him, or when he would pop up in the most unexpected place, just when the going was dull and one needed to see a new face, with some juicy gossip to impart.

But the Joker's real, true face, was hidden from all who looked at him, and they gaily went along accepting the face he chose to wear; jester, banterer, wit, snapper—a zany mad-cap that sent everyone into hilarity. The real Sir Jason wanted wealth and power at any cost. He never again would degrade himself by playing the flunky to some rich, past-her-prime duchess, or escorting some pock-marked, cow-faced chit, because of her rich dowry.

There was seldom an exception where his desires and necessity were not at odds, but Catherine Bellington was that exception. That beauty and wealth should come together so neatly in one package was too good to be true.

He should have remembered that one's luck would

run out, that the odds run against you, but he felt so sure that this time nothing on earth could stop him from achieving his goal, marriage to Catherine and acquiring her fortune. He didn't blame himself for the loss of his chance. All the gods of ancient Eygpt could not have prevented his failure. The cards were stacked against him and not by the hand of a mortal. The Devil had interfered with his plans, the Devil, disguised as Catherine's guardian—Lord Trevegne.

All that could have been his by marriage to Catherine was now beyond his reach. Still young, in her first season in London, she had been so naïve and easy to flatter.

He really never loved Catherine, but he found her attractive, and she had amused him at times. They would have dealt quite well with each other, he thought, until a certain devil with his all-seeing, amber eyes had appeared—almost magically—to whisk away Catherine, and her fortune, into the lap of another gentleman.

Catherine, his golden opportunity, was married to some suitable country gentleman. No doubt a florid, pompous, windbag; bow-legged with a pot-belly and bulbous, red nose from imbibing too freely with Sir John Barleycorn, he thought maliciously, turning to stare into the wall mirror at his own handsome and dapper figure. She would have been far better off with a Beckingham than with some country bumpkin, he thought conceitedly.

But that Trevegne stepped in to destroy everything, leaving him the laughing stock of London. He was warned that Catherine Bellington was Lord Trevegne's ward, and that he had complete authority over her and her estates until she married—and that only with his approval. Other fortune-hunting friends of his ominously predicted that it would be to little or no purpose to waste precious funds on such a Herculean task; and the devil to pay if you angered Trevegne in the process.

They had good reason to fear; for Lord Trevegne's reputation wasn't based on exaggeration or hearsay. Sir Jason had seen him tooling his black and gold high-perch phaeton, with its perfectly-matched Arabian stallions, with unequalled skill, in fact, Lord Trevegne was supposed to have some Arabian blood in him, which might explain why he had such an affinity with his horses—as if they were soul-mates.

Lord Trevegne's close friends called him Lucifer to his face, and he would only laugh and agree. Sir Jason heard others say that Lord Trevegne wasn't human, and was called the Prince of the Devil because he had beaten unbelievable odds. Few men Sir Jason knew would gamble or wager against him because he never lost. Onlookers to a game would swear that His Lordship had mesmerized the cards, that the strange twisted gold ring on his little finger was a magic ring investing him with mystical powers.

He believed that Trevegne had caused his luck to fall under an evil star; and now he felt the ground crumbling under his feet, and nothing he could do seemed to change his luck. Things were not supposed to have gone this way. He even went to see a gypsy when his luck was running in his favor, just to confirm his ascending star. The gypsy caravan was camped outside the city when he rode out to have his fortune told by some foul-smelling, toothless old hag. The thieving gypsy had cost enough, but she told him his future looked bright; that Lady Luck was riding with him. She had predicted a woman like the reflection of fire before his triumph, and then some gibberish about a looming, black cloud and some dire disaster. He didn't believe that shadowy business about death and disaster because he'd been on a winning streak, and he had yet to meet the woman who was a reflection of fire. But there was no triumph either, only misfortunes, and certainly nothing approaching the magnitude of death, although he had to admit that at times like these, he almost welcomed it.

Lord Trevegne. Always having the upper hand, always triumphant. Sir Jason could not recall a time that Trevegne had not succeeded, and won, whether at cards, or with a woman. He had caused many women to lose their hearts in vain to him. Sir Jason knew many ladies of high quality who would have leapt at the chance to share a bed with him, given the opportunity.

He captivated the most sought after young women of London and Europe, but once he knew they would capitulate, he lost interest, and soon became bored with their protestations of love. He remained a bachelor, turning his broad-shouldered back on them all only to leave them wanting him more than ever. Why

Trevegne didn't succumb to the beauty and wealth of some of those women, he could not comprehend. If he had been in Trevegne's place he would now have a fortune in his keeping; along with maybe a castle or chateau from marriage with one of those foreign princesses or baronesses.

By God, Trevegne wasn't human to turn his back on that. If only there were some way of defeating Trevegne—without doing an injury to himself, of course, for he had no intention of being challenged by Trevegne who was a deadly shot with pistols. No, he did not want him to know that he had a mortal enemy in Sir Jason Beckingham; better to let the noble Marquis think that the Joker held nothing against him. Ah, revenge would taste as sweet as honey in his mouth should he contrive some punishment for the almighty Lord Trevegne.

A knock at the door broke into Sir Jason's thoughts as he stood gazing blindly out of the window.

"Yes, yes, do enter!" Sir Jason commanded, turning around at the interruption.

"If Sir Beckingham would be so kind as to come downstairs, 'is dinner be prepared and awaitin' 'im," Tibbitts announced heartily.

"Very well. I shall be down shortly, and by the way, has Lord Trevegne dined yet?" he asked Tibbitts in a casually bored tone.

"No, 'e just went down," Tibbitts replied. Tibbitts gladly made his way down the narrow, rickety stairs, thinking that the brat was right, that buck had a mean look in his eye, all right. Bet he would be a nasty customer to cross. He shivered as he remembered the cold look in Sir Jason's eyes. His eyes roved over the big, rough plank table set for their dinner, and rested on his other guest standing meditatively before the big roaring fire, availing himself of its heat.

Now there was another gentleman that he would hate to displease, Lord Trevegne, who often stopped at his inn when traveling the long distance to his estates in Cornwall. Aye, he had heard some things about His Lordship all right, and it boded nothing good to anyone who annoyed him. But then what could you expect from one of those foreigners from that inhospitable Cornish coast—a real no-man's-land from what he had heard.

"Damned drafts," grumbled Tibbitts, as he tried to secure the windows more snugly, unsuccessfully cutting off the cool drafts blowing in to disturb his guests.

" 'Ere ye are, Sir Beckingham." Tibbitts quickly pulled out a chair for Sir Jason, who had just entered the room, resplendent in a pink velvet coat and yellow breeches, orange and yellow striped vest, and white lacy cravat, stiffly starched to stand high, and intricately tied in rows and rows of ruffles.

Lord Trevegne slowly turned from his contemplation of the fire to look at the other guest as he entered, arching a dark brow as he recognized him.

"Evening, Beckingham," Lord Trevegne drawled as he took the seat across from Sir Jason at the table.

"Am I to have the . . . pleasure of your company for this hearty repast we are about to indulge in?"

"Lord Trevegne," Sir Jason acknowledged smoothly, conquering the panic he had felt as he had walked through the door, knowing he would come face to face with the Marquis. "It will be my pleasure to share your companionship, M'Lord," he said ingratiatingly, while wishing to plunge his dinner knife through Trevegne's black heart.

He gave Lord Trevegne a curious look and asked conversationally, "You're a hell of a way from London on such a beastly night." He neatly speared a small boiled potato into his mouth, and began to cut a piece of the thick beef, rare and juicy, that filled his plate.

"As it happens, I'm on my way to St. Fleur. But you happen to be out in it also."

St. Fleur, the Sainted Flower. Now that was a misnomer for the home of Lord Trevegne, Sir Jason thought in amusement. Why not name it St. Demon in honor of its master? "I'm here for the cockfights at Brown's Mill. Supposed to be some tough ones fighting—heard Rawsley had a real killer sent down from York," he explained, watching Trevegne take a thick slice of ham from the platter put down by the serving maid. Her low cut blouse revealed plump shoulders and breasts as she gave Trevegne an inviting look from her dimpled face, before collecting his empty tankard of ale to be refilled.

"I didn't notice your coach out in the yard," Sir Jason inquired. "Surely you aren't traveling all the way to the coast on horseback in this weather?" he demanded, his face mirroring disbelief.

Sir Jason shifted uncomfortably, wondering what he had said to cause the flicker of amusement on the Marquis's face.

"I rode on ahead from London, and my coach and valet will follow at a more leisurely pace. They should be here at the inn tomorrow morning," Lord Trevegne answered uncommunicatively as he finished his meal off with a dish of creamy custard sprinkled with cinnamon.

They continued to talk as the evening passed. Tibbitts poured out two big snifters of his best smuggled-in brandy, and presented them to the two men sitting in the big chairs before the fire, and added another log before leaving the room.

They talked trivialities for a good part of an hour, discussing the merits of cockfighting, and who was the best pugilist in London and whether Napoleon would invade the sacred shores of England, until Sir Jason said suddenly, tired of the banalities:

"I would have imagined that you would go up North with your ward, Catherine Bellington." Sir Jason paused for a moment as if in thought. ". . . No, it is not Bellington anymore is it? I do believe I heard somewhere that she had recently married, but I'm afraid I didn't quite catch the name of the fortunate bridegroom."

"Yes, Catherine is now married, and I am not with her because I rather doubt whether the fortunate bridegroom would enjoy having me along on their honeymoon."

"I had no idea that she was betrothed when she was in London. She is quite young, after all. We had an engagement to attend a theatre party when I was suddenly informed that she would be unable to attend because she had left London. No explanation, or reasons given. Leaving rather abruptly, almost spirited away, one might say," Sir Jason continued persistently, some demon driving him to say something he knew he would regret.

"She was in some danger, not from the spirit world, but rather, from the fortune-grabbing outsiders who latch onto society," Trevegne said bluntly, taking a sip of brandy, his golden eyes narrowed and watchful as he stared at Sir Jason. "I merely removed a temptation from their reach. In reality it was quite unnecessary, because whoever might marry Catherine without my consent, would never set eyes upon her fortune—and that would have defeated his purpose—also he would have had to deal with me—a guardian who takes his title quite seriously."

"And what of Catherine, shouldn't she have been allowed to choose her own husband? What if she had loved some man in London, and he had loved her? It would not be only her fortune that a man would be attracted to. She happens to be a very lovely young woman."

"And what makes you think that Catherine did not choose the man she wanted to marry?" Lord Trevegne asked, surprising a stunned look on Sir Jason's face. "She has been in love with her husband since they were both in the school-room, and both were very anxious to wed. Catherine merely wanted a taste of London life before settling down in the country, and 'becoming a staid matron,' to quote her own words. Undeniably she is attractive, but I think we all know the names of those who would profit from such an alliance, and of their past records and reputations for trying to latch onto any heiress available. However, I fail to see what the conversation is about, since Catherine was never available, and certainly is not now that she has a husband."

"As you wish, but hypothetically speaking, what if she did not want to marry this man; if she were in love with someone else? Would you have forced her into marriage, even if the man were repugnant to her?"

"Had Catherine not wished to marry, then I would not have forced her to. However, the young man, Beardsley, was acceptable to me and to her, and lives on the neighboring estate, bringing the two estates together nicely into one property. It happens to be fortunate that they are in love, for eventually I would have selected some suitable young man for her future husband, had she not engaged her attentions elsewhere, and with my approval. But why your insistence upon love in the marriage? Few people of my acquaintance—and I imagine yours—have ever married for it; in fact, I seriously doubt if they even consider it, or know what it means," Lord Trevegne sneered.

"You mean that you would never marry for love?" Sir Jason accused the Marquis.

"What I mean is that I doubt whether such a thing as love exists. When I marry it will be to acquire an heir; not because I am in love with the woman."

"Then you would marry a woman for what she could provide for you!" Beckingham said triumphantly, defending his own reasons for marriage.

"No, not in the sense that I'm quite sure you are implying, Beckingham. I would marry a woman for the one thing she could provide me with that I, by myself, would be incapable of having—an heir to my name and estates. I would be able to provide all else. She could, in fact, come to me as naked as the day she was born. But I should not delude her into thinking that I was in love with her—that is where we differ, I believe. Deception is not my forte."

The Marquis raised his glass in a silent toast to the red-faced Sir Jason, who sat uncomfortably across from him, and then turned his attention to the fire, a scowl settling upon his hawk-like features.

Sir Jason continued to stare at the Marquis' profile, hatred burning in his pale eyes. He's in a foul mood, Sir Jason speculated, tapping his ringed fingers nervously as he searched his mind for some suitable end for the Marquis—there was always murder . . .

Elysia could feel the rush of cold air through her woolen cloak as she pushed open the heavy oak door of the posting inn. Rain poured through the small space the opened door made, as if seeking shelter from the malevolence of the storm outside.

"Pull shut that damned door, or is it your intention to drown us all?" came a threatening voice from a high-backed chair in front of a large, brightly burning fire.

Elysia hastily struggled to close the heavy door against the gale-like wind, but her efforts were to no avail against the tempest raging outside the inn. The door broke from her grasp and swung freely against the wall, allowing another sheet of icy, wet rain to enter the room.

"Hell and damnation! Are you just a fool, or are you trying to freeze us for your own sadistic pleasure? And where is that innkeeper?" the voice threatened again.

A tall form rose from the depths of one of the chairs before the fire, and came menacingly towards Elysia as she stood struggling with the door. She could feel her strength ebbing away. She had been riding on the mail coach since catching it earlier that morning, and she was exhausted.

It had seemed an endless ride across the bleak countryside in the swaying coach; their progress slowed by the muddy roads and torrential rains. She was wedged in between a fat farmer's wife with the odor of the barnyard clinging to her clothing, and a very merry vicar who made his sacraments at the shrine of Bacchus. Between his constant belching, followed by sly apologetic giggles, and the snores of the farmer's wife, she felt she had neared the end of her endurance, but now was confronted by an angry gentleman.

"My dear young woman, would you be so kind as to remove yourself from the doorway so I can secure the door, or would you prefer to stand here in this hellish draft until we both perish from exposure?"

Elysia felt two strong hands grip her elbows as she was propelled aside, and the offending door was swung shut with a slam.

Without awaiting his further displeasure, Elysia moved on into the room toward the area from whence the disagreeable figure had emerged, and stood in front of the crackling fire, stretching out her cold, slender hands to the warmth. The hood of her cape concealed her face from the view of the garishly-clad gentleman in the other chair she had observed as she'd entered. A London dandy, no doubt, she thought disparagingly. She heard the other gentleman return to his chair, and without turning her head to acknowledge him, she continued to warm herself gratefully by the fire.

Tibbitts came bustling in, having been detained in the cellars searching for his best rum, when the coach had arrived. He saw the lone figure, cloaked in a dark blue cape, standing before the fire, the steam rising up from the wet material as it dried, and hurried towards her.

"Welcome to Wayfarer's Rest," he beamed as the cloaked figure turned. "May Oi be of service to ye, miss?" he asked in his best innkeeper's voice, thinking her cloak looked a little threadbare, and he wouldn't be getting much of a tip from her.

"Yes, I should like lodging for the night, as I am taking the London coach in the morning," Elysia answered as she lowered her hood from about her head, and the concealing cloak from her shoulders.

Both Sir Jason and Lord Trevegne had been sitting staring into the flames, ignoring the cloaked figure, until the low and husky notes of a very feminine voice startled them from their thoughts. She spoke in a cultured manner that had an unconscious seductiveness about it. They both looked up as she removed her cloak to reveal a perfect profile with a straight, narrow nose and a well-proportioned mouth. But their eyes were attracted, like a moth to flame, by her bright red-gold curls glowing richly from the light of the fire.

Sir Jason quickly stood up, bowing slightly as he said in his most charming voice, "If you could possibly forgive my rudeness in allowing you to stand, I would gladly offer you my chair, and introduce myself. Sir Jason Beckingham, at your service."

"Thank you," Elysia replied coolly, taking his chair in front of the fire, "I am quite fatigued and chilled to the bone." She shivered slightly, giving Sir Jason an inquiring look from brilliant green eyes as he continued to stand by her chair, staring down at her in a bemused fashion.

"Tibbitts," Sir Jason commanded, "fetch this young lady something warm to drink, and then dinner. Hurry up, man!" He waved away Tibbitts, who had

111

stood silent, his assessment of his latest guest changing rapidly as he saw her face. She might not be too rich in the pocket from the look of her clothes, but she was gentry, that was for sure, and would be expecting better than he'd planned originally. Especially if the gentleman was paying for it. Besides, she just might be one of those eccentric aristocrats who dressed up like a servant just for the fun of it. Hadn't a pack of young bucks, dressed up as coachmen and driving a mail coach come through his inn just last week? They drank all night long, and then nearly overturned the coach with its passengers the following morning before it had even gone halfway down the road. No, he was taking no chances with this one. He'd treat her proper.

Sir Jason had pulled up another chair for himself, and was about to sit down when he stopped, apparently aghast. "How remiss of me," he groaned as if filled with remorse, "what will you think of my manners? Allow me to introduce," he apologized as he indicated the man who had acted so abominably to Elysia, and who had been sitting quietly watching, throughout their exchange, "Lord Trevegne, the Marquis of St. Fleur, and you are Miss. . . ?"

"Miss Elysia Demarice," she extended her hand with its long tapering fingers to Sir Jason, and then to Lord Trevegne, who had risen lazily to his feet at the introduction.

"Miss Demarice," he drawled, taking her hand and bowing elegantly over it. Elysia suddenly pulled her hand free, feeling a shock run through her at the

112

touch of his strong fingers. They could be cruel hands, she thought, as she gazed hypnotically at the strange gold ring on his little finger that reflected the gold of his eyes—odd eyes under heavy lids, that seemed to penetrate her mind, reading her innermost thoughts.

" 'Ere you are Miss, a nice 'ot toddy to warm ye up nicely," Tibbitts interrupted, breaking the spell that seemed to hold Elysia. He put the steaming mug into Elysia's hands and looked around, a frown on his florid face. " 'Aven't ye any baggage, Miss?"

"No, I have not, with the exception of that straw bag," Elysia said indicating it sitting forlornly by itself near the door. "I'm traveling light," she added, a small smile tugging at the corners of her mouth as she thought of all her earthly possessions tucked neatly away in that bag. Tibbitts shrugged, and went out carrying her bag with him.

"You are traveling so lightly, Miss Demarice, and in such foul weather," the Marquis said softly, "that one is tempted to wonder why? You aren't by any chance, one of these tiresome females running away from home to elope, a pack of hysterical relations in hot pursuit? I shudder at the thought of being confronted here in the inn and accused of being an accomplice— or even the prospective groom, heaven forbid," he said derisively, taking a pinch of snuff.

"That, M'Lord, happens to be my private business, and of concern only to myself," Elysia answered shortly, "but, if it will set you at rest, then I will reassure you that I am not fleeing my home to elope. I should indeed hate to cause you any nervousness on that account, nor could I imagine a more unlikely candidate as the prospective groom, M'Lord," Elysia added acidly. She felt dismayed at how close he had come to the truth, as two spots of bright color stained her high cheekbones.

Lord Trevegne looked at her with narrowed eyes that had a gleam in them as Elysia stared back defiantly. Finally, a crooked smile appeared on his harsh face.

"Demarice? That name sounds familiar." Sir Jason was looking at Elysia as if trying to recognize something about her face which alluded him, when a look of revelation cleared it. "Charles Demarice! That's it," he exclaimed. "He's your father, isn't he? But of course, he would have to be with those eyes of yours. You know he's nicknamed Cat Demarice because his eyes slant upwards just like a cat's—and by God, so do yours. It's like looking at a cat."

Elysia blushed with embarrassment as both men stared openly at her face, and then she felt the Marquis' eyes slowly appraising the rest of her appearance, making her feel plain and dowdy in comparison to his elegant coat of satin and velvet, and his spotlessly clean linen. She could see the puzzlement in their eyes, they must be wondering what Charles Demarice's daughter was doing dressed in rags.

"Where is he? I haven't seen him in London in years. Almost forgotten all about him, been so long," Sir Jason asked curiously.

"My father died over two years ago, as did my

mother. They were both killed when their phaeton overturned," Elysia said quietly, a shadow of grief entering her eyes, darkening them as she remembered her agony when given the news.

"I say, I'm awfully sorry," Sir Jason apologized contritely. "I hadn't the faintest idea of your loss. Please accept my condolences on so great a misfortune."

"I sometimes think that it was kinder that they died together, as they did, for I doubt whether they could have survived without each other, so much in love were they."

"How extraordinary! One seldom finds such devotion between man and wife, in fact, Lord Trevegne here, doesn't even believe in love—especially in marriage. Am I not correct, M'Lord?" Sir Jason asked the bored-looking Marquis pointedly.

"Quite correct. Love exists only in the minds of impoverished poets catering to the fantasies of adolescents and old maids," Lord Trevegne answered sarcastically, a sneer on his lips.

"You show your ignorance of the finer things with a statement like that, M'Lord—but then I would expect little else from a London gentleman," Elysia refuted angrily.

"Really, and I suppose you have experienced this state of bliss to be envied by mortals and gods alike?" he taunted.

"No, I have not, but—"

"Then you know nothing about it, or if I am not mistaken—passion either. You know only what you have seen, or read about. I find most women fit into two categories; either they are romantic sentimentalists, with tears for every occasion, or mercenary opportunists, out to get what they can." Lord Trevegne looked at Elysia questioningly. "Now which are you, I wonder?" His long lips curled slightly as he added to the insult. "But with your looks, you shouldn't have any trouble having your every little wish granted by some poor besotted fool."

"I am neither, M'Lord," Elysia replied clearly and coldly, looking directly into the Marquis' golden eyes. "I am a realist. One who knows that most men are inhuman beasts, intent on their own selfish desires, without a thought as to the feelings of others around them—especially, if one is unfortunate enough to be the wife of one of those overgrown schoolboys," Elysia said contemptuously, warming to her subject as she continued, her small, rounded chin thrust forward arrogantly. "I indeed pity your wife, M'Lord, if that is the opinion you hold of the female sex. But then, as I stated once before, I would expect little else from one of your set. The London gentleman—ha! Gentleman, indeed! Your knavery is only exceeded by your narcissism, and I for one think women far better off without your egotistical presence and should hold your whole sex in contempt."

Elysia stopped breathlessly, scandalized by her own behavior, and a trifle confused by her diatribe to the rather astonished-looking Marquis. He almost looked disconcerted, something she doubted he ever was. But she refused to apologize for only defending herself from his insults.

"Touché," Sir Jason said amusedly, having enjoyed the exchange immensely. He clapped his hands in appreciation, causing a blush to appear on Elysia's cheeks in mortification. "Well, well, you certainly gave the Marquis a dressing down, which is something that no one has ever done I'll wager, eh, M'Lord?" Sir Jason smiled. "You will forgive me, Miss Demarice, for being one of that odious sex you so despise, and allow me to continue to enjoy your delightful company," Sir Jason pleaded, a twinkle softening his blue eyes. "Did you ever meet Miss Demarice's parents, Trevegne?" he asked conversationally, turning to the Marquis as the tension died down.

"I had the pleasure of meeting your parents once or twice, if memory serves me correctly. They very seldom came to London, I believe." Lord Trevegne paused. "But I can remember your mother vividly. You have the same color hair she had."

The Marquis stared rudely at her, making Elysia feel that it was a crime to have her color hair. She fingered a bright curl lovingly, and thought that she couldn't care less if that odious man approved of her or not.

She thankfully excused herself as Tibbitts brought in her dinner and placed it down on the large table. Elysia sat down and hungrily began to eat the plump pigeon pie, and slice of beef and fresh green peas, sweet and tasty, set before her. It seemed a feast to her, so used was she to the plain unappetizing meals at Aunt Agatha's.

Aunt Agatha. She wondered what she was doing right now? Probably cursing her with every breath in her thin, bony body, Elysia thought wryly. But her amusement faded as she remembered the strength of those long, thin fingers as they had shaken her shoulder in a merciless grip, and of the punishment Agatha would enjoy giving her should she ever find her.

She stared down at the piping hot pigeon pie, nervously biting her lip as she wondered if she had done the right thing? If she could possibly succeed in finding a job in London, if . . .

"Isn't it good?" an amused voice asked, and Elysia glanced up into the smiling face of Sir Jason. She supposed he really was quite nice, in spite of his airs and brightly-colored clothes. As much as she detested the arrogant Marquis, she had to admit that he was dressed more to her liking in a fawn-colored riding coat, and pale buckskins that accentuated his muscular thighs above his highly-polished black Hessian boots. No one could mistake him for a dandy she thought. His clothes and his rude manner belied that.

"Mmmm, it's quite delicious," Elysia said breathing deeply, "and I know I'm not being very ladylike eating all of it, but I'm just famished."

Sir Jason sat staring at Elysia as if seeing a ghost, or vision of something extraordinary, a meditative look in his light-blue eyes.

"Surely you are not alone in the world, now that

your parents are dead?" Sir Jason asked. "You must have other relatives with whom you've been staying and who would be upset to have you traveling alone?"

"Yes, I have relatives," Elysia answered noncommittally as she finished off the pie, beginning to wish Sir Jason was not quite so friendly and inquisitive, for the less said about Aunt Agatha the better. But Sir Jason seemed satisfied by her answers, and stood up excusing himself, saying mysteriously:

"My dear Miss Demarice, tonight a certain prophesy told to me by a gypsy has come true, and I am extremely grateful to you."

Elysia smiled at his somewhat cryptic remark, not understanding him at all, but too tired to question him. She rose quietly from the table after finishing her dinner, and left the room, not disturbing the two gentlemen as they sat at a smaller table absorbed in their game of cards. As Elysia climbed up the rough wooden stairs, she heard the door at the entrance of the inn open. Glancing back over her shoulder she saw a rotund gentleman enter, throwing his rain-splattered coat down upon a narrow bench set against the wall as he yelled for the innkeeper, then made his way over to where the other two gentlemen were sitting.

Elysia went on down the dark hall, past several doors to her own, where Tibbitts had told her he had put her bag, and entered, closing the door softly behind her. She felt so tired, so drained of all emotion as she removed her dress, pulled on her nightdress, and sank gratefully down on the bed.

She hadn't planned to stay overnight at an inn, thinking the mail coach would travel straight to London. She took out her precious horde of money, which was quickly diminishing in size. She'd had to pay close to five pence a mile, plus tips to the coachman and guard who rode along to guard the mail from highwaymen. She would have to pay for her meal and room, and the rest of the journey tomorrow. She had hoped her money would last until she reached London, but doubted now that she would even have enough to rent a room until acquiring a position. Well, she would have to worry about that when she got there.

Elysia was about to climb into bed when there was a knock on the door, and opening it a crack she saw Tibbitts standing there with a small mug of some steaming liquid in his hands.

"Compliments of the gentleman, Sir Jason, miss," he said handing it to her. "To 'elp ye keep warm and get a good night's sleep 'e says to tell ye."

"Thank you," Elysia murmured accepting the hot drink gratefully, "and will you please extend my warmest 'thank you' to Sir Jason."

She closed the door and, warming her hands on the mug, thought that maybe she had been hasty. Maybe all London gentlemen were not rogues to be feared. Elysia drank down all of the delicious rum-flavored brew, feeling it spread throughout her chilled body. She felt a little fuzzy as she got into bed and slipped under the covers. It must be the rum she thought foggily. She just wasn't used to spirits; but she did feel so warm and nice now. Elysia snuggled down further into the bed, and drifted off into a deep sleep.

I met a Lady in the Meads
Full beautiful, a faery's child,
Her hair was long, her foot was light
And her eyes were wild.

Keats

Chapter 5

Elysia felt all upside down. Hazy mists drifted
through her mind in lazy swirls.

> Curly locks, Curly locks,
> Wilt thou be mine?
> Thou shalt not wash dishes
> Nor yet feed the swine.
> But sit on a cushion
> And sew a fine seam,
> And feed upon strawberries,
> Sugar and cream.

Strawberries? They were out of season now, but she did like them with sugar and cream. She giggled,

> Little Polly Flinders
> Sat among the cinders,
> Warming her pretty little toes
> Her mother came and caught her,
> And whipped her little daughter
> For spoiling her nice new clothes.

What nice new clothes? She hadn't had any nice new clothes in a long time. It would be nice to eat strawberries and cream in nice new clothes. Oooh . . . her head ached. What was wrong with her? She was too old for these school-room and nursery rhymes. She could hear rain beating against the windowpane; she wouldn't be able to go out and play,

> Rain, rain, go away,
> Come again another day.

The rain beating against the glass became louder, and Elysia opened her eyes sleepily, staring at the crystal-like rivulets of water as they ran down the pane, like tiny elfin streams. Elysia closed her eyes and tried to recapture her dream, but it was too elusive to remember, and she felt herself drifting along, as if on a cloud, and smiled complacently. She should open her eyes and wake up, but she felt so warm and rested, her eyelids so heavy and weighed down, that she seriously doubted whether she could open them. It was too bleak and cold a morning to be out of bed anyway.

She rolled sideways, hugging her pillow, and heard the steady beating of her heart. It sounded as if it were in her ear. And now she could hear two hearts beating. What foolishness was this? She didn't have two hearts she thought drowsily, her mind clouded by an odd thickness.

Elysia struggled to re-open her eyes, the lids flickering slowly as she tried to focus. Everything looked indistinct. She stared down at the pillow beneath her cheek in confusion. It looked like a man's chest.

Elysia gave a gasp and looked up into the sleeping face of a man. The Marquis! Her eyes widened as she became aware that she was lying curled up against him with her leg intimately wedged in between his legs as he lay on his back; her arm draped across his hairy, muscular chest.

She cautiously moved over, trying to sit up, but felt light-headed as she stared about the room. What was he doing in her room? But no, it was not her room. She was in a strange room! Elysia felt panic race within her—how could this be? Last night she had been in her own room—that she knew for a certainty—so what was she doing in here with a strange man in bed with her? Oh, God, what had happened? How could she and the Marquis be sharing a bed?

Elysia threw back her side of the quilt and stretched out her legs to jump from the bed and realized that they were bare! She looked down in shock at her long slender thighs, and yanked them back under the cover, trembling at the discovery.

She was naked! Where was her nightdress? She looked frantically around the room while cowering beneath the covers, but could see no sign of it anywhere. She bit her fingernail nervously, giving the sleeping Marquis a suspicious look. Could he have done this? No, he had taken a violent dislike to her when they first met. And for some reason, she instinctively knew that he did not seem the type to play this sort of game, or whatever it was. But she knew that she must get out of the room before he awoke and . . . and then what? For if he was innocent of this deed, then he would no doubt believe the worst—that she had come into his room . . . and into his bed. Oh, dear! What was she to do?

Elysia heard him give a deep sigh, and stretch, feeling deepening terror at the thought of his waking and finding her here. In her panic she jumped up and started to race for the door, then gave a terrified shriek as she felt hard hands reach out and pull her back onto the big bed before she could take more than a step. She fought like a wild cat, her hands and feet flying, trying to scratch and kick at him, but he was too quick and strong for her, and Elysia found herself pinned beneath his hard body, her arms stretched above her head in a vise-like grip, her legs held down by his—her unclad body pressed intimately to his naked one. They were both breathing heavily, her shocked green eyes, wide and dilated, staring into his surprised golden ones—neither of them speaking—their eyes locked together.

She watched as a crooked smile began to appear on his face and his eyes wandered over her frightened face with its parted and quivering lips and flared nostrils. They moved on to her hair, loose and flowing about her like a red-gold veil, and finally she saw them narrow and darken as he looked down at her breasts as they heaved uncontrollably beneath him.

"Well, well," he drawled. "I must say I haven't had such a pleasant surprise in years. To awaken and find Aphrodite had slipped into one's bed during the night, and so suitably dressed," he paused, one hand moving down over her naked body insultingly, "or should I say, so suitably undressed? It is indeed unexpected. But that she should not have awakened me—now that was unpardonable of her."

"Please, please listen to me," Elysia begged him as she felt his lips traveling slowly up her neck, and felt him nibble with his teeth on the soft lobe of her ear, causing shivers to run up her spine.

He was apparently just as surprised as she to find them together in his bed. She had guessed correctly when she thought that the Marquis would not be a party to this, but she must now try to convince him that neither would she.

"I don't know how I came to be here in your bed. I—I was as surprised and as shocked as you were to find myself here, but please you must be—" she tried to tell him, but his mouth came down on her mouth cruelly, cutting off any explanations she might have made. She felt his hard lips parting her softer ones, his tongue finding hers, shocking her with its touch, and its intimate searching of her mouth.

Elysia was gasping for breath as his lips lifted from hers, having explored and plundered their softness. His lips were moving down her throat in quick, hard kisses, and she could feel his hand searching out the curves of her body, exploring them with each persuasive caress. She struggled helplessly against the hand which still held her bound, his mouth teasing a pink-tipped breast until it tautened.

What was he doing to her? She had never felt this way before, had never experienced a man's kisses or a lover's caresses. She was frightened. But a liquid fire was burning through her blood—an odd excitement flaring deep inside her—equal to her fright.

"You've bewitched me," he murmured thickly, in between kisses, "made me dizzy with desire. My head feels as if it would explode!"

His lips moved along her temples to her wild eyes, closing them with his kisses until finally his mouth settled possessively upon her reddened lips.

"My icy, green-eyed witch, so disdainful with her flaming hair—I'll make you come alive with passion, Elysia," Lord Trevegne whispered almost incoherently, her name sounding like a caress on his lips.

His mouth pressed against hers, hurting her as he smothered her protests and moans with his hungry kisses that became deeper and rougher as the endless minutes passed. Elysia felt him searching, then the feeling of something hard and alien to her feminine body touching her intimately. She felt terrified, and renewed her struggles with a new-found strength, but she knew she was fighting a losing battle. And then she heard the noise.

The door to the room was swung open, and voices

seemed to fill Elysia's ears, and she felt the hard weight of Lord Trevegne's muscular body lifted.

"Here we are, Terry," a familiar voice said, and then abruptly stopped. "I say, I'm awfully sorry! I must have mistaken this for my room."

Sir Jason's voice sounded shocked and apologetic. Lord Trevegne, who had rolled off Elysia at the first sound of voices, was now sitting up, staring with a deadly look on his face, at the two confused-looking gentlemen standing nervously in the doorway.

"If you will excuse us, Trevegne ..." Sir Jason paused delicately, his eyes wandering over Elysia's disarrayed hair and bare shoulders as she huddled under the sheet, ". . . and, Miss Demarice, please accept our deepest apologies."

The other gentleman's face was suffused with a bright red color as he nervously looked at Lord Trevegne, and the murderous expression in those golden eyes, and then, unable to control himself, at the delectable-looking creature with the wild, red hair and huge, green eyes lying next to the Marquis on the bed.

"Uh, yes, yes, please accept my, uh, apologies," he mumbled, making a quick retreat from those two pairs of disturbing eyes; and the blackening temper of the Marquis—a man he would not care to anger.

Sir Jason followed a little more slowly, looking over his shoulder as he closed the door, a wide triumphant grin tinged with undeniable malice upon his face, which neither Lord Trevegne, nor Elysia, could possibly have missed.

Lord Trevegne put his face into his hands and gave himself a shake as if trying to clear his mind of cloudiness. Then he turned his head and gave Elysia a devilish look, his eyes penetrating and steady, still darkened—but now with anger, not passion. "I am afraid that I was in no mood to listen to your explanations earlier, but now I want the truth, and no fabrications," he added menacingly, "for I believe we have just been witness to quite a performance by Sir Beckingham, and if that entrance was by accident, then I'll sell all my horses to the first country bumpkin I meet for a damned shilling!"

"You, M'Lord, have the nerve, after trying to rape me, to sit there and swear in a rage at me, demanding that *I* should be the one to give the explanation, when it should be me demanding one from you!" Elysia began in indignation, having at last found her tongue, only to be interrupted by his snarled oath.

"Hell and damnation, you don't really want me to stand and bow, and present myself most gentlemanly, begging your pardon?" he demanded making a threatening movement to leave the bed. "We've gone a little beyond Court manners, I believe."

Elysia gasped. "Of course not!" she conceded quickly, not unaware of his nakedness.

"Now, how did you come to be in my bed, my dear?" he drawled casually, his golden eyes alert as she answered.

"I really don't know. After I left your company, and Sir Jason's, I went directly to my room which is the last one at the end of the corridor. Why, I don't even know where this one is!" Elysia looked wide-eyed at the Marquis' thoughtful stare.

"It is at the opposite end of the hall from yours, opposite the staircase. I happened to see Sir Jason enter his room at the end of the hall last night—probably the room across from yours—that is why I doubt very seriously whether he could have mistakenly entered my room thinking it his," Lord Trevegne answered, his eyes narrowing. "Proceed. You went to your room and . . ."

"I was tired from the day's journey, and I was preparing for bed when the innkeeper brought me a hot drink, rum I believe, because I remember feeling drowsy afterwards because of its potency. It had been sent up by Sir Jason, and that is all that I remember before I fell asleep. You must believe me, M'Lord. That is the truth, I swear to you," Elysia added as she noticed the fierce look that had settled on his face.

"So Sir Jason ordered you up a hot rum toddy," he speculated softly. "As it so happens, he also insisted that I join him in one before retiring. I would hazard to guess, my dear Miss Demarice, that we were drugged insensible last night by those infamous rum toddies and while senseless—Sir Jason was up to mischief."

"But if what you say is true, then what was the purpose? Sir Jason has no reason to feel ill will towards me," Elysia asked in puzzlement.

"Ah, but he feels that he has a legitimate grievance against me, I daresay, and you, my dear young woman, unsuspectingly became his pawn of revenge against me."

"I am afraid that I still fail to see how this can be revenge against you? It has been an insult, and an indignity to me—but revenge on you. . . ?"

"Yes, revenge. Sir Jason hoped to entrap me in a position that I would find most difficult to extricate myself from—that of being found compromising an innocent young lady of quality. One does not seduce, and then desert the daughter of one's peers—if one is a gentleman," he looked at her mockingly, "and if the young lady in question has vengeful relatives, who will no doubt, hear about this escapade. It will, of course, be the talk of all London by tomorrow evening how Trevegne and a lovely woman were found locked in an embrace and . . . You do get the idea? I need not elaborate further?"

"Well, it will not work, for Sir Jason's plan has gone awry," Elysia stated firmly, "for I have no relatives who would either demand satisfaction or would force you into marrying me to save my good name. My God, aren't you married?"

"My dear Miss Demarice," Lord Trevegne said softly, leaning over her, forcing Elysia back onto the pillows, and placing a hand on each side of her shoulders, "no one forces me to do anything that I do not wish to do. I am answerable to no one, do you understand? And—I am not married."

"Yes, I understand, but wouldn't Sir Jason also be aware of this? If you are so impregnable, then why are you so upset by Sir Jason's treachery. He can not harm you—his plan has failed."

"No one makes a fool of a Trevegne!" the Marquis said angrily, staring down into Elysia's face as if pondering something of interest to him.

"Then it is just your injured pride that causes your indignation," she said scornfully, gasping in pain as his hard fingers closed over her soft shoulders in warning.

"Well, I cannot be forced into a marriage either! You, M'Lord, are not the only one who will not be blackmailed into something distasteful to him."

"Oh, you would find marriage to me distasteful would you?"

"Yes, but then since the fact of a marriage between us does not arise, it does not signify how I feel."

"Hmmm," he replied noncommittally. "Surely there is someone who cares about your welfare?"

"No, Lord Trevegne, I have no one who would care if I were found drowned, and floating in the Thames; merely an inconvenience for having to send to London to fetch my body," Elysia spoke bitterly. "You said I have been used as a pawn, well I can tell you, M'Lord, that it is not the first time I have been callously taken advantage of to further a revenge. My aunt would have me married off to a fat, lecherous, old squire against my will, because of some grievance against my parents, which she has nurtured for over thirty years."

"This aunt of yours, surely she would be upset to hear of this occurrence?" he asked curiously.

"My aunt would be overjoyed to know of my predicament, and furthermore loathes the very sight of me. And if you would allow me to get up, I will leave the room and not further complicate your life, M'Lord," Elysia told him, trying to push him away, but he resisted her efforts easily, and continued to stare at her, a gleam of amusement entering his eyes.

"I am afraid that I cannot allow you to leave, Miss Demarice," he said decidedly, having come to a decision.

Elysia looked at him wide-eyed. "You can't keep me here against my will!" she cried, fearful he might be planning to resume where he had left off before being so timely interrupted by Sir Jason and friend.

"Are you daring me, Miss Demarice?" Lord Trevegne asked her meaningfully, pressing down on her shoulders with his hard fingers.

"You know very well that I don't have half your strength; it would be foolhardy of me to try. But I fail to see any reason for you to keep me here. The damage is done, and as a gentleman, I know you won't . . ." Elysia paused in embarrassment, trying to select her words carefully.

"I won't continue to make love to you—no matter how enjoyable it was—if that is what you wanted me to say?" He looked amused at her confusion, his lip curling slightly. "Did you run away from home, Elysia?" he asked, giving her a slight shake as he watched the mutinous look on her face, compelling her to look into his eyes. "Is that why you are traveling without a maid, or proper chaperone? And with-

133

out an excess of baggage? Traveling light, I believe you said."

"Yes, I was," Elysia told him honestly, defiance in her voice, "it was no longer possible for me to live with my aunt. I had to leave. She was quite insane, I believe," she whispered brokenly, thinking of her aunt's contorted features as she had raged at her in fury.

"Then you have no home—no place to go?"

"No, I have no home, but I am going to London."

"What were you planning to do in London? Seek employment?" he asked doubtfully.

"Yes, I shall look for a position as a governess, or possibly as a companion."

"You won't, you know," Lord Trevegne stated baldly. "You are going to marry me."

Elysia felt as if the breath had been knocked out of her. She looked at him as if he were crazed. "But that is absurd!" she cried. "You have just told me that no one could force you into marriage, and I don't want to marry you anyway."

"No one is forcing me into marriage," Lord Trevegne answered silkily. "I have been thinking of acquiring a wife, and you happen to be here, and available. I am merely taking advantage of the situation. You also have several points in your favor, the most inviting being your lack of relatives, for I should hate to have a bossy, interfering mother-in-law troubling me all the time. You also look as though you could bear me several fine sons," he laughed at Elysia's outraged expression, "and you happen to be a damned fine-looking woman." He dropped a light kiss on her nose, thoroughly enjoying himself.

"I will not marry you!" Elysia told him angrily, her eyes glinting greenly. "I have no intention of agreeing to your proposals. I shall continue to London as planned and seek employment," she stated firmly, staring him in the eye. "You insult me, M'Lord. Proposing to me as if you were purchasing a mare—going over my finer points, indeed!"

"Do you actually imagine that any woman would hire you to be a governess for her children, or as a companion to herself? Have you no awareness of yourself as a woman?" he disbelievingly demanded. "I've never yet met a woman who was not vain about her looks, and you are certainly a beauty, and bound to be a distraction to any man—especially if you're sleeping under his roof. I can't believe that a wife would willingly put you within sight of her husband's eye. Nor would some dowager enjoy seeing you everyday—a constant reminder of her lost youth and beauty, which she will never recapture again."

Elysia stared up at him, dismay written across her face by his words, spoken in obvious truthfulness.

"And furthermore," he continued relentlessly, "your reputation will have preceded you to London. Do you actually believe that any decent woman would hire you to look after her children?" he asked incredulously.

"And don't doubt for a moment that Sir Jason will waste any time in telling his tale, without his own duplicity of course, and if not Beckingham, then that thick-headed friend of his, Twillington. He arrived late last night. I don't believe you had the pleasure of meeting him until this morning. Of all the men I know, he must be the biggest windbag in all of London. His tongue runs on wheels, so you may be assured that the clubs of St. James will echo with this story. No doubt he will have lavishly embroidered it in exaggeration, so we will indeed, my dear, be painted black. That is, if it is possible for my reputation to be made blacker," he laughed deeply. "But you, my dear, will become notorious, for having been found in bed with me, and I would not give your chances of finding employment—decent employment, that is—as much of a chance as a snowball in Hell has."

"You don't feel regretful or embarrassed about my predicament at all!" Elysia said in rising indignation. "I don't believe you have a shred of decency."

"No, I doubt if I do, but would you have me believe that you would rather work in some ungratifying and degrading job than marry a wealthy and titled gentleman, and have your every wish granted?"

"If that gentleman be you, then yes, I would! I would hire out as a scullery maid before accepting your name! You are no gentleman, M'Lord," Elysia declared hotly.

"By birth, yes. By reputation. . . ?" he shrugged doubtfully. "But you sound quite the affronted and scorned female—well, if that is how you feel . . ." He released her shoulders, and leapt easily from the bed, ripping the covers from Elysia's naked body. He picked her up in one swoop, deposited her on the cold wooden floor squarely in the middle of the room, and then stood back and leisurely allowed his eyes to rove over her body. Elysia stood rigidly with her long hair rippling down below her hips. Her breasts were firm and round above a small waist and slender hips, her skin as smooth and white as alabaster. She could feel the flush of embarrassment heat her body as she tried ineffectually to shield herself with her hands.

"That's quite unnecessary, my dear, for I've already seen your charms—and sampled a few," he said cruelly, not sparing her from his ridicule. She kept her eyes averted from his bare body as he stood there unashamedly, with his broad muscular chest, its black curly hairs tapering down to lean narrow hips and long, firmly-muscled thighs, his obvious maleness flaunted before her shocked eyes. She had never seen a man's naked body before, and he was making her feel uncomfortable, very much aware of herself as a woman—and the difference between them.

"Now if you really are the well brought-up young lady you would have me believe, why aren't you making plans to drown yourself in some deep and murky pool, your honor saved? Of course, you could always wait until you reached London, and then jump from a bridge into the Thames. Much more dramatic, my dear, and society would love it. You, of course, would be pitied, becoming a martyr for young womanhood betrayed. After all, you have spent the night with the notorious rake of London society—

Lord Trevegne, and taken the only possible, and indeed, honorable way out."

Elysia felt tears swell in her eyes at his sneering and ridiculing remarks; her eyes large and luminous beneath her arched brows. She hung her head in dejection, tears of despair running down her pale cheeks. She tried valiantly but in vain to stifle her sobs as she felt all defiance drain out of her.

Something soft and warm was placed around her shoulders, and through her tears she saw that it was Lord Trevegne's coat. He guided her over to his bed, helping her in and covering her with a warm blanket. He stood staring down at her as she stared up into his face with watery, green eyes.

"You see, my dear, you really have no choice in the matter," he said not unkindly for once, "and I might add, that it would be criminal of me to allow so lovely a child to fling herself into the cold arms of Death, when mine are much warmer."

With that last jibe, he turned and proceeded to quickly dress. While pulling on his tall Hessians, he said shortly, "You stay where you are, and I'll fetch your belongings. You may dress yourself in here. My carriage should be arriving momentarily, and then we will leave. But first I'll have some breakfast sent up to you."

Elysia glanced at him as he left the room, his tall, broad form blocking the doorway, then disappearing as he closed the door behind him. She stared unseeingly up at the ceiling. Maybe she should try to drown herself, or even hang herself from the rafters, but that would give the inn a bad name, and that was hardly fair to the friendly innkeeper, she thought practically. She really should feel like killing herself—but the horrible thing was that she didn't feel in the least like taking her life. It was true that she had nobody left in the world to love, but some spark, some will to live was too strong in her to succumb to the death wish. But what would life be like married to Lord Trevegne, a roué and a knave, who admitted to his own blackened reputation?

Maybe she could run away? She must escape the Marquis. She was thinking of several possibilities when the Marquis opened the door and came in, putting her straw bag on the bed, along with her cloak and dress.

"I will have my coat now," he said, coming over to her side. She reluctantly struggled out of it and handed it to him, pulling the covers up securely around her shoulders as she peered up at him in uncertainty.

"My coach has arrived, so hurry and dress. We will depart in less than a half hour. And don't try to leave me by slipping out the back way, for I have made up my mind to marry you, and I shall, and I would find you Elysia," he threatened her coldly. "Also, I have confiscated this dangerous weapon of yours that I found concealed in your clothes," he said, holding it gingerly in his large hands.

Elysia bit her lip in vexation. She had not forgotten the weapon, and had planned to use it to aid her escape.

"A very fine duelling pistol," he added expertly, fingering the smoothly curved grip of the pistol, the long barrel glinting with inlaid silver. He looked at Elysia in speculation. "You would not have been tempted to use this on me, would you?"

Elysia shrugged indifferently, masking her fear with flippancy. "I would not regret putting a hole in your arrogant chest, only it would be deflected when it hit that piece of rock you call a heart."

He laughed, apparently amused by her vitriolic reply. "You are very fortunate you did not try, my dear, for I deal harshly with attackers."

He left without a backward glance, and Elysia got slowly out of the bed and moved to her bag, checking to see if everything was still there. She found her nightdress stuffed in a wrinkled wad in the corner of it, and blushed in shame as she thought of how Sir Jason must have removed her gown and carried her naked to place her in the Marquis' bed.

Her mortification was replaced by anger and hatred as she thought of the indignity and humiliation Sir Jason had caused her. Lord Trevegne, she didn't doubt, deserved it however.

Elysia was dressed and re-packing her bag when the tavern maid entered carrying a tray with hot chocolate, a thick piece of ham, hot, savory-smelling muffins filled with melting butter, and a small pot of golden honey. She placed it on the small table by the window and left hurriedly, giving Elysia a friendly wink; a knowing look on her freckled face as she closed the door with a giggle.

Of all the impudence, thought Elysia, chagrined at

what the maid must think, and bit hungrily into the warm muffin dripping honey.

She had just finished eating as the Marquis entered the room resplendent in total black, with the exception of a gold brocade waistcoat and startling white cravat.

"You could have had the good manners to knock before entering," Elysia said disagreeably, feeling beggarly in her old, faded, wool dress. "We are not man and wife yet."

"No we aren't—yet," he retorted mockingly, "but then prospective brides are not supposed to sleep, or dress in their future husbands' rooms either." He laughed as she blushed a vivid pink, angry with herself for giving him the opportunity to mock her.

"Come, my dear, we must be off." He picked up her bag and draped her cape over her shoulders caressingly, smiling his crooked smile as he said softly into her ear, his breath tickling it intimately, "Smile, you're about to become a bride, not a widow."

As they descended the stairs Elysia glanced about apprehensively, afraid she might see Sir Jason's amused, blue eyes, and be forced to suffer his rudeness once again.

"No, my dear, Sir Jason is long gone from here, probably halfway to London by now," Lord Trevegne said softly, interpreting her nervous glances. "He would be dead now, however, should he have had the effrontery to stay within range of my pistol," he continued in a deadly tone, "but he is a cur who would do his knavery like a thief in the night, and then turn tail and run by day."

They continued out of the inn into the yard where a large black and gold coach stood waiting for them, drawn by four, big, black horses; their black and silver harnesses jingling expectantly. The liveried coachman sat atop the box, the reins held loosely in his gloved hands, and next to him another man sat huddled in his coat, and a third stood holding the spirited horses' heads, while a fourth held open the door to the coach. They were all dressed totally in black with gold buttons and stockings, gold buckles gleaming on their shoes, and crimson-lined greatcoats protecting them from the cold.

Elysia was helped into the coach, past the door with the Marquis' crest emblazoned on it, and settled on the soft, velvet cushions within. The door closed snugly behind her, and she looked out of the window and saw with relief that Lord Trevegne was mounted on a big black stallion, rather than in the coach with her. She glanced up at the angry clouds, gathering strength to unleash another downpour upon the unfortunate traveler, and wondered how long she would have the privacy of the coach before the weather drove Lord Trevegne to take shelter.

The sky became darker as they traveled along the hard-packed dirt road, the strong, healthy horses eating up the distance as easily as a bag of oats, their hooves pounding effortlessly through the puddles. She remembered the constant swaying and jolting of the mail coach, which only yesterday had been conveying her to London. How different His Lordship's well-sprung coach made traveling the long uncomfortable miles over the pot-holed road, Elysia thought, as she leaned gratefully back against the softly-cushioned seat.

She must have dozed off for awhile, because suddenly the coach was still and she could hear the rain pattering against the windows. The door was jerked open, and a caped figure jumped in as the coach began to move again.

Lord Trevegne brushed the raindrops from his coat and settled back against the seat eyeing Elysia sardonically. "I'm sure you would have preferred that I remain outside, but out of necessity I have been forced inside with you. You would not have me catch a chill—or would you, my dear?"

"How long until we reach your home, M'Lord?" Elysia asked, ignoring his jibe, her voice sounding small and child-like with her nervousness.

"Sometime in the early hours of the morning, I should imagine. We will have to make a change of teams. I live in Cornwall, and I also think it is about time that you called me by my first name, Elysia. It is Alex."

"That far!" Elysia gasped in surprise, a sick feeling in her stomach at the thought of being so far from all that she had previously known. Her plans to escape to London were futile if she were in the far reaches of Cornwall. But she shouldn't be surprised; it seemed appropriate that the Marquis should live on

that rocky coast. "I had no idea that you lived there
..." Elysia finally said weakly.

"There is no reason why you should have, my dear.
Would you have contemplated escape had you realized we would be so far into the wilds?" He leaned
forward to look into her eyes. "Oh, I see. You had already been devising some means to escape from me.
You would have tamely entered my home as my
guest and fiancée, and then absconded during the
night while the household slept, thinking yourself
close to London. My, my, you *are* a determined little
devil."

He removed a thin cheroot from a slender silver
and gold case and lit it, the sweet aroma floating to
Elysia's nostrils. "Well, I'm afraid that plan of yours
would have come to naught. For you see, my dear,
we are making a brief stop in a short while—a very
necessary stop—to get married."

Elysia looked at him, wild-eyed with dismay, her
lips partially open in bewilderment. "Married?
Tonight? But how can that be? You've not had time
to post the banns, or secure a license. A—and we can't
get married so soon," she ended lamely, her voice
quivering as a feeling of finality engulfed her. She
felt as if she was taking an irrevocable step into
something beyond her control. Elysia gazed at the
Marquis, her eyes unconsciously pleading for more
time, but he was looking out of the window, his dark
head turned away.

"I've a special license to marry and we shall be
stopping momentarily with an acquaintance of mine

who is a Bishop, and he will perform the ceremony. It will probably be the triumph of his rather elongated life to see me married, and by his hand. That should assure you of its validity, my dear. So never think of leaving me with the idea that we were not legally married, for we shall be, and forever—or until one of us should die," he said indifferently.

"You have it all worked out," Elysia said resentfully. "You think you have me neatly tied up? Well, we shall see."

"You will learn Elysia, that I am a very thorough man, and very careful and watchful over those things that belong to me," he said quietly, a thread of iron in his voice.

The coach came to a sudden halt, and Lord Trevegne jumped down, holding out his arms for Elysia to alight. Her eyes turned toward the pale yellow lights shining from the house, in resignation and submission to her fate.

> . . . A hawk clutched with his talons a
> gaily-colored nightingale and bore her
> aloft into the clouds when she wailed
> piteously, pierced by the crooked claws, the
> hawk said arrogantly: "Wretch! Why do
> you shriek? One much stronger now holds
> you and you must go wherever I take you,
> singer though you are."
>
> Hesiod

Chapter 6

Sir Jason whipped his horses to a faster pace as
they raced through the rain-slick streets of London.
The rain had temporarily halted, and through a
break in the clouds he could see the moon shining
mistily above.

He wondered what Lord Trevegne was doing at
this moment and grinned widely with unholy
amusement as he thought of the possibilities. He felt

absolutely elated at his triumph over the invincible Lord Trevegne—oh, if only he could relate to all of London how he had maneuvered the great Marquis into his power; but of course, he could never tell that part of the story, and still be accepted at Almack's and his other clubs.

He was no fool, and he knew that if Lord Trevegne ever suspected, or had proof of what he had done, his life wouldn't be worth a farthing. He shuddered at the thought of Trevegne's deadly aim with pistols. Oh no, he would never admit to his crime—or accomplishment as he preferred to call it. At least not to Trevegne, although he could think of someone else he would relish relating it to. He wasn't finished with the almighty Marquis yet.

Sir Jason thought of how already, between himself and Twillington, everyone at White's and Watier's had heard the story. Twillington. Now that had been an unexpected, if not miraculous piece of luck. To have that twittering tattler Twillington show up at the inn, just at the opportune moment. Why, he could hardly have planned it better himself.

He had vaguely entertained the idea of using Miss Demarice as he sat talking to her over dinner, but hadn't quite figured in what way. She didn't look too well dressed, so she might accept money to help him ensnare Lord Trevegne, but unfortunately she didn't seem the type. He had even thought of killing her, and then blaming it on His Lordship, but that could get rather messy. He sat puzzling over this when Twillington started jabbering about some General's family, in a flap and demanding reparation for their daughter, who had been seduced by a town gentleman.

That was when the idea crystallized in his mind. He must somehow involve Lord Trevegne with the virtuous Miss Demarice. It was a shame she was such a beauty, for he would love to have the irresistible Lord Trevegne involved with a mawkish-looking old maid.

Drugging their rum toddies was no problem. He simply took the bottle of laudanum which he kept for use when he had trouble sleeping, and after ordering hot rum toddies for everyone, intercepted Tibbitts with the tray of drinks. He sent him back to get another one for himself, and quickly put the drug in two of the mugs. He then handed one of them to Tibbitts to take to Miss Demarice, with his compliments, while he took in the rest of the drinks himself.

It was almost too easy. Lord Trevegne retired, his eyelids weighing heavily. Sir Jason remained downstairs, seated before the fire, until he was certain Lord Trevegne would be deep asleep. Then Sir Jason entered Miss Demarice's darkened room and crept over to the bed to hear her breathing deeply, the drug having worked perfectly. He lighted a candle and carefully undressed the sleeping figure, pausing briefly to stare admiringly at her naked body. He picked up her limp form and carried her quietly and quickly down the hall to Lord Trevegne's room, and laid her down on the bed next to the Marquis. He then disrobed the sleeping man, feeling momentarily alarmed at his success thus far, but shrugged, thinking it another indication of his brilliance and ingenuity.

He would never forget the surge of excitement he felt as he and Twillington entered the room to see the two bodies locked in an embrace. He hadn't quite expected that, especially after the way Miss Demarice and the Marquis had reacted to each other the night before. However, the Marquis was a man, and to find a beautiful and naked woman in bed with him was too good an opportunity not to take advantage of. Miss Demarice would have a great deal of explaining to do, and he did not envy her one bit.

Sir Jason wondered suddenly what she was thinking. She had certainly looked flustered and confused this morning, and very appealing. Poor Miss Demarice, to find herself at the mercy of a man she had spurned was ironic, and probably most uncomfortable.

He wouldn't be at all surprised if the Marquis just up and left her, refusing to marry her despite the gossip. No, the Marquis had an eye for beauty—he just might make her his mistress, especially after what he had seen this morning of His Lordship's desire for the disdainful Miss Demarice.

Well, it did not really matter if Lord Trevegne married her or not, his reputation would be so blackened that even the husband-hunting mamas would think twice before wanting to become his mother-in-law. And Sir Jason doubted if Lord Trevegne would be able ever to find a suitable and acceptable wife now. Especially if he got thrown out of Almack's as the rumor had it.

But his superb triumph had been in tricking Lord Trevegne. Having him at his mercy, under his power. Why, he could have plunged a knife through his chest as he slept if he had wanted. But it was better to see him squirm—forced to either marry against his will or face disgrace. He might already have a black reputation, but even the Marquis could go only so far before facing the consequences.

Sir Jason almost hoped that Trevegne threw Miss Demarice out. He would find her then, and offer his protection—make her *his* mistress. She was lovely, he thought, remembering her body gleaming eerily in the candlelight. Yes, he must see what he could do about that, and then he chuckled as he again wondered what was happening with Trevegne?

Elysia stared down at her hands in the darkness, unable to see the twisted gold ring, taken from Lord Trevegne's little finger and placed on her third, but putting her hand over it she could feel its contorted shape. It felt heavy and strange upon her finger, marking her as a belonging, for less than an hour ago, she had pledged to love and obey this stranger sitting silently across from her in the carriage.

What manner of man was he, this man that she

had married, she wondered, as she risked a furtive glance at his harsh profile—shown briefly by a flash of lightning that illuminated the inside of the coach. He was lounging back carelessly against the cushion, his long legs stretched out onto the empty seat opposite.

She was now his wife—Lady Trevegne—and she could not even bear to call him by his Christian name. She had always dreamed of someday falling in love, and marrying to raise a family which she would cherish and love—a very foolhardy and naïve assumption. She couldn't believe how vulnerable she had allowed herself to become.

Elysia thought nostalgically of her parents, and wondered what they would have been thinking now. They had differed with the rest of society in their condemnation of arranged marriages. Their own marriage was a love-match, an unparalleled success, consequently they believed in marriage for love only. They would never have allowed her to be sacrificed in a loveless marriage to further her position, or theirs, and yet here she sat, married to a disreputable member of the ton; wealthy, handsome, and completely ruthless where his own desires were concerned, not caring a damn about her.

Why had he insisted upon marriage to her? He admitted, very succinctly, that no one could force him to do something he did not desire, and he apparently already had a black reputation, so one further act of debauchery would not amount to much. He said that he wanted an heir. Well, there were plenty of women around who would no doubt consider it a privilege to bear his children. But she was not among that elite group, and if he thought she was going to bear those children, then he was badly mistaken. He did not love her, nor she him, but she knew he desired her. And vowed she would have nothing to do with him.

She still could not understand it. If he merely desired her, then he could have taken what he wanted this morning as she had lain helplessly within his power, unable to fight against his greater strength. He had no reason to marry her—he was not the type to be troubled by her soiled reputation.

Elysia shivered in memory of what nearly had happened to her this morning, feeling chilled by her near-escape.

"Cold?" Lord Trevegne asked out of the darkness of the coach. Not waiting for a reply, he leaned over and pulled Elysia across his lap, wrapping his coat around her shivering body, and holding her close within his arms.

"Better?" he murmured, his breath warm against her neck.

"Yes, thank you, but I was quite comfortable where I was," Elysia spoke breathlessly, trying to release herself, but his arms only tightened.

"Be quiet," he growled softly, his lips moving caressingly behind her ear.

"Please," she begged, feeling a new shiver spread through her body at the touch of his lips.

"Please what, my dear ... wife?" the Marquis

laughed silently, his lips closing down completely upon hers. He kissed her long and deeply, his mouth parting hers as he relentlessly pressed kiss upon hard kiss onto her soft and unresisting lips. She could feel his hands moving, searching, until they found the small buttons of her bodice, smoothly unbuttoning them, his hand sliding underneath to caress her soft, warm skin. His lips lifted from her mouth to move down the length of her neck, his arms tightening as he pressed his face against her breasts, breathing deeply of her scent.

"You smell like a garden of jasmine and roses," Lord Trevegne whispered hoarsely, his lips returning to her mouth once more as he kissed her wildly, passionately, until Elysia thought she would suffocate from lack of breath.

Finally, his lips moved from her throbbing mouth, and he rained light, soft kisses upon her face, hugging her closer as he put back his head, one hard hand cupping one of her breasts possessively. He closed his eyes, a smile of triumph on his firm masculine lips.

After a while Elysia felt his even breathing beneath her ear where her head rested on his chest. He was a demon she thought tearfully, feeling confused by the emotions he had aroused within her. She should despise him—yes, she did—but he made her feel so faint and hot, so unlike herself. It was wrong, this strange feeling inside of her—when she hated him. Elysia closed her eyes, thinking of his kisses, and fell asleep with her cheek pressed against his heart.

Elysia awakened as the coach jolted to a halt. She glanced about sleepily, then sat up in surprise, she was back on her own side of the seat. She put her hands quickly to her opened bodice—it was buttoned securely.

Had it all been a dream—his hard demanding kisses? She nervously ran her tongue over her lips feeling them tender to her touch. Elysia looked inquiringly to Lord Trevegne who sat watching her, an amused look in his golden eyes that were gleaming brightly from a light shining in through the opened door of the coach. No, it had not been a dream she read embarrassingly from his eyes, a blush spreading up her neck to her face.

"Come, my dear wife," the Marquis said, leaping down and holding out his arms, "we are home at last."

The rain was falling steadily as Elysia and Lord Trevegne hurried inside the arched entrance to the Hall, past the enormously thick, wooden doors with their elaborately carved panels set between strips of golden metal.

Elysia could hear the big doors closing behind her as they continued into the long, wide hall, its ceiling stretching upwards into a sloping roof, the stained glass clerestory windows reflecting the flashes of lightning in radiant blues, greens and reds. A gallery with iron castings clung to the sides of the great hall, held aloft by thick, fluted columns reaching sturdily down to the Spanish-tiled floor.

Elysia stood silently as Lord Trevegne sent for the housekeeper, his face shadowed by the flickering lights from the wall sconces being hurriedly lit. Most of the hall was in darkness, the tables and chests taking on distorted shapes like creatures from the Underworld.

A door opened from a corner of the hall beneath the gallery, and a beam of light appeared, floating closer until a wrinkled face with twinkling eyes came into focus above the flame of the candle being held by a gnarled hand.

"Lord Alex," the old man said, surprise shaking his voice, "we had no idea to expect you, until just moments before when your outrider arrived with the news." He glanced curiously at Elysia wrapped in her cape, as he directed the quickly-appearing footmen to take up their luggage, some of them still half-dressed as they scurried about.

"We shall want the master suite," he corrected the butler, who had instructed Elysia's bag to a guest room. Shock was evident upon his parchment-like face at the Marquis' words. He bid the footmen do as ordered, a disapproving look in his eyes.

"Don't look so scandalized, Browne," Lord Trevegne laughed. "May I present to you my wife, Lady Trevegne." He pulled Elysia forward, to stand beside him, his arm lying heavy across her shoulders.

"Your wife!" Browne croaked. The shock on his

face giving way to pleasure as he bowed, and, recovering, said, "It is an honor, Lady Trevegne, to welcome you to Westerly."

"Thank you, Browne," Lord Trevegne said, smiling warmly at the old man, leaving Elysia staring at him in surprise, having thought him incapable of any warmth or kindness.

"Browne has been with the family for half a century, practically runs us—or at least he tries to," he added, giving the man a long-suffering look.

"And since when have you ever listened to me, Lord Alex?" he answered back with the audacity of an old and trusted servant.

"I have gotten myself a wife now, haven't I? I seem to remember you, and—" he was interrupted by a wail coming from somewhere above them, and then a hurrying little figure could be seen coming down the center of the grand staircase at the end of the hall.

"Lord Alex," she demanded, "what ye be coming here in the middle of the night like this? You always was the one for upsetting the household, even as a boy," she chuckled, delighted to see him no matter what the hour.

"Elysia, my dear, I want you to meet Mrs. Danfield, my old nanny, and housekeeper at Westerly since I no longer need her devoted ministrations in the nursery. Dany, this is my wife, Lady Elysia Trevenge."

Elysia looked down into her kind, berry-brown eyes, and smiled a lovely, tentative smile, unconsciously asking for reassurance, feeling lost and tired in her new surroundings.

"Lady Trevegne," Mrs. Danfield curtsied, giving a reproachful glance to His Lordship. "Ye've gone and got yesel' married, without letting me know. What will yer bride be thinkin', with the house all dark and cold, no welcomin' feast or greetins from the staff." Her eyes were skimming over Elysia's figure, taking in her old cloak and mended gloves, the strain evident on her young face.

"We had not expected any such frivolity," Lord Trevegne said shortly. "My bride and I prefer things to proceed as usual," he commanded sternly.

"Well, now," Mrs. Danfield said bristling, giving them a puzzled look, "it's not every day you bring home a bride, and I was beginning to wonder that you ever would. How did you manage to find such a lovely and unspoiled child?" she asked, giving Elysia a friendly smile which Elysia returned. No fancy, snooty town miss here, Mrs. Danfield thought in relief. "I didn't think any decent mamas would let you within a mile of their daughters." She frowned disapprovingly at him, well aware of his bad reputation.

"Oh, there was nothing on earth that could separate us, Dany," Lord Trevegne explained, hesitating briefly before continuing. "You might say we both opened our eyes one morning and saw the light of our mutual love. It was quite a revelation, almost as if we'd awakened from a drugged sleep." He grinned wickedly at Elysia's shocked look, daring her to add to it. "Now Dany, show Lady Trevegne to her room. I am sure she grows fatigued standing here while you appease your curiosity." He turned and disappeared into one of the many doors opening off the hall, while Browne, who had been listening avidly to Lord Trevegne's explanation, hurried as fast as his rheumatic legs would carry him after His Lordship.

Mrs. Danfield hustled Elysia up the wide, marble stairs, sending orders over her shoulder to the maids below as Elysia hurried after her small trotting figure. They walked along the gallery until they entered another wing of the great house, and moved along a wide corridor. Ancestral faces stared down at them out of the flickering light of Mrs. Danfield's candles as they passed beneath.

At the end of the corridor, she threw open a delicately-carved pair of double doors. Preceding Elysia into the room she lighted the tall tapers throughout, the contents of the room springing to life.

Elysia stared about her in awe. Everything in the room was crimson, gold, or black. There was a crimson and gold satin settee, black- and gold-painted chairs with gold, velvet cushions, black-lacquered commodes and dwarf bookcases, and dominating the room, a large red and black silk screen painted with beautiful Chinese motifs, while a large Oriental carpet covered the floor in a blaze of colors.

"It's beautiful," Elysia finally uttered in a reverent voice.

"Aye, 'tis a lovely room," Mrs. Danfield said,

pleased with Elysia's reaction, and appreciation. "These be the Trevegne colors; black for vengeance, crimson for blood, and gold for glory. They were a fierce lot, those first Trevegnes."

Elysia shuddered, thinking they still were.

"Now this over here be yer room, M'Lady," she said indicating a gold-panelled door, "and that one over there be His Lordship's."

The two doors were separated by a long chiffonier displaying delicate porcelain vases and exquisite jade figures. Mrs. Danfield opened the door of Elysia's new room and proceeded to light more tapers as Elysia followed her into the room. Her eyes feasted upon the huge canopied bed with its crimson velvet hangings, and she remembered her own small, hard bed at Aunt Agatha's, with its faded, blue coverlet. In comparison, this looked like a queen's bed.

"Now, dear, wouldn't you like a nice hot bath to rest in and ease your aches and pains after all of that traveling?" Mrs. Danfield asked, taking Elysia's cloak from about her shoulders and hanging it up in the enormous wardrobe with its many doors and sliding trays to hold all of a lady's requirements and possessions.

"Is your maid to be coming later?" she inquired, frowning slightly at the unconventionality of Lady Trevegne traveling without the assistance of a lady's maid, and with only a small, straw bag.

"I haven't a lady's maid, Mrs. Danfield," Elysia said stiffly, expecting a horrified look from the housekeeper, but she was surprised by the little woman's nod of satisfaction.

"Well, it's just as well, for I've plenty of bright girls here who will make yer Ladyship a good maid, and far better than one of those London pieces of baggage," she said disgustedly. "Ye can't trust the likes of them, gone before you know it, and without a word of warning. So don't ye worry, we'll be getting ye one. And yer clothes?" she asked looking doubtfully at Elysia's straw bag, and the dull and worn dress she was wearing. "Ye'll be having them arrive soon?"

"No, I am afraid that all that I own in the world you see before you," Elysia answered softly, but proudly, her chin held high. "I am an orphan, but at least no one can accuse Lord Trevegne of having married me for my fortune; just the opposite, for I fear that I shall be labelled the adventuress."

"Now, now, no one in their right mind would be believin' that of ye, seein' what a lady ye are, and how pretty. Why, anyone would know why Lord Alex married ye!" she said sympathetically with a motherly smile, her heart going out to this brave child standing so proudly before her. "Ye don't be worrying that pretty little head of yours with nonsense now."

"Thank you Mrs. Danfield," Elysia said humbly, her eyes shining with tears caused by the first kindness she had received in years.

"And ye call me Dany, like Lord Alex; none of

this Mrs. Danfield." She paused uncertainly. "It would please me so, Ye Ladyship."

"Thank you again, Dany. I would be honored. And would you call me Elysia?" she asked shyly.

Dany flushed with pleasure at her compliment and hurried to the door, turning as she said with a shake of her silver head:

"I just don't know how he manages to win the prize so many times. As much as I love Lord Alex, I believe he's got himself a lady too good for him. Ye be the angel to his devil, I be thinkin', and God help us," she added prophetically as she left the room to arrange for Elysia's needs.

Elysia smiled to herself as she walked around her bedchamber. She had felt so nervous in anticipation of her introduction to Lord Trevegne's household. She had imagined their resentment at having to accept a new mistress and taking a dislike to her, yet she found a friend, one she knew she could trust and love. She suddenly felt as if a weight had been lifted from her shoulders.

Elysia glanced about the gold and crimson room, not a sign of black visible. A gilt dressing table stood along a wall and a gold, satin-cushioned couch with a shell back sat before a crimson-curtained window. A delicate-legged writing desk, and several gilt- and crimson-painted cane chairs and occasional tables made up the rest of the furniture, plus a beautiful gold and white marble fireplace.

Another door stood partly open and, opening it further, Elysia saw that it was another bedchamber, but decorated in black and gold only, and very masculine. Her eyes traveled over the long, golden drapes and a large, four-poster bed, the black lacquered commode, and, covering the floor, a large black- and gold-flowered carpet; the twin to hers of crimson and gold flowers. An Egyptian couch with black leather upholstery sat before a fireplace of black and gold swirled marble. From the opened doors of the closet Elysia could see rows of velvet and satin coats, and the many-tiered riding coat that Lord Trevegne had been wearing earlier. She quickly closed the connecting door between their bedrooms, noticing there was no lock on the door.

An ornate tub mysteriously appeared before the fireplace, and two young maids were in the process of carrying steaming pails of water to fill it. They glanced shyly at Elysia before leaving the room. Elysia sunk gratefully down into the tub. She rubbed herself with the little bar of fragrant, French soap. She stretched out a slender leg and lathered her thigh, then scooping up handfuls of water, let it cascade caressingly down her leg, washing away the bubbles. She sat up and was running her soapy hands over her shoulders and breasts, when she caught the aroma of tobacco, the same brand Lord Trevegne had been smoking in the coach. Her nostrils twitched in warning. She turned, startled to see the connecting door close sharply. How long had he been standing there, silently watching her bathe? Elysia was embarrassed and flustered as she rose from the tub, wrapping a large, warm towel about

162

her wet body and quickly drying herself. She put on the lacy nightdress Dany had brought to her, the fine lawn material feeling soft and smooth against her skin, and wondered with feminine curiosity to whom it belonged.

Elysia jumped nervously into bed as she heard footsteps approaching, but the main door to her bedchamber opened, and Dany entered carrying a tray with a little china pot of tea and a plate with thinly-sliced bread and butter, and small, delicate cakes. Elysia sighed in relief, and began to get out of bed, when Dany ordered her unceremoniously to stay put.

"A cup of tea is just what you need to help you sleep, dear, so just stay where you are in your warm bed," she said placing the tray across Elysia's lap, and looked approvingly at her in the bed.

"It's a lovely nightdress, Dany," Elysia said sipping her tea, glad to see it wasn't a rum toddy. "I hope no one will mind my borrowing it?"

"Aye, you look lovely in it too, but no one will be minding. It belonged to Lord Alex's mother; she always liked pretty things," Dany replied, beginning to unpack Elysia's bag. She pulled out the carefully wrapped doll and unwound it, placing the doll on a small table near the bed.

"This be the prettiest little china doll I've ever seen," she exclaimed in admiration, carefully straightening the long full skirt.

"My father gave it to me when I was just a small child, but I've always cared for it, even when I had grubby little hands. I suppose I knew even then that I would treasure it always. And those belonged to my mother before she died," Elysia said as Dany took out the silver brush and comb and placed them upon the dressing table where they seemed to belong.

"Ye've not much to remember them by, have ye dear?" Dany asked, pity in her kind eyes.

"No, not material possessions, but I have my memories, Dany, and they are precious to me, no one can ever take those from me, like they did my other possessions—the house, and stables—my horse—practically everything had to be sold. There is a trunk of my father's things, and a few other family articles that my old Nanny is keeping for me. They will be safe with her, and only because they would not have brought much profit do I still own them. They would have been for my brother, Ian, but he died at sea, somewhere in the Mediterranean in a battle with Napoleon's forces. I received a letter from the Naval Department the day after my parents died," Elysia glanced away, biting her trembling lips.

"Oh, my poor little dear," Dany cried softly, putting her arms protectively around Elysia. "Ye've had a hard time of it, haven't ye? Well ye not to worry anymore. Ye be home now, and Dany'll take care of ye. Ye just remember all of the good and happy times with ye family and don't think of the sadness. Try to think that they be away visitin', and will be back soon."

"I'll try Dany. I'm being so silly—I guess I'm just tired," Elysia smiled.

"And ye've a right to be—travelin' all through the night without a break—I never," Dany said in disapproval. "Now, lie down and close ye eyes, and go to sleep," she ordered, tucking Elysia in like a small child, "and be good. T'is what I used to tell the boys."

She snuffed out the candles and picked up the tray, bidding Elysia a good night as she left the room. Elysia turned on her side and stared into the darkness, hearing the chiming of a clock on one of the tables.

Would he come? He now had the right to sleep in her bed, and do with her as he wished. She hoped that he would not come, but there was very little she could do to stop him if he wanted to.

And now she had placed herself in his hands, a man whom she had disliked on sight, and had known no longer than a day. She knew little to nothing about him, or his family, except for the few things Dany had said. She knew that both his parents were dead, and Dany had said "the boys" when talking about putting them to bed, so maybe Lord Trevegne had brothers and sisters, Elysia thought hopefully. Maybe a sister who was her own age, and would befriend her. But then she might be like Lord Trevegne, tall and dark and overbearing. That would be worse, Elysia thought sleepily, closing her eyes as sleep overcame her tired body.

Lord Trevegne sat moodily staring into the flames of the fire in the big fireplace in his study. He was twirling the brandy in his glass, warming it against his palm as he thought about the girl on the floor above in the master suite—his wife!

He laughed aloud, a harsh cruel sound that rang about the room. Marriage, he sneered, thinking of his friends' marriages. A signed contract to bed a woman and plant your seed with the best wishes of society and the Church, and if you happened to acquire a fortune in the process, well then, all the better, and an added congratulation for being such an enterprising fellow, especially if you managed to keep several mistresses on the side.

And the bride, he mustn't forget the charming bride, who gained a household to run, and more money to spend; a man to manage, and, if a virgin, rescue from becoming an old maid, or if already some man's mistress, respectability. Yes, all parties profited nicely.

Well, he was a married man now, and no one could accuse him of marrying his wife for her dowry. She had come to him with only the clothes on her back, not even that, if the truth be known. He suddenly remembered how he had told Beckingham that his 'wife could come to him as naked as the day she was born,' and by God, so she had! If he didn't hate Beckingham so, he would have to commend him on his masterful touch of having taken him at his word, and place her naked in bed with him. He had to admit that Beckingham had outdone himself this time.

His thoughts raced on to Beckingham drugging them and stripping them like a graverobber robbing the dead, and he felt a sudden rage rise in him. Yes, he would have to find a suitable way of dealing with Sir Jason Beckingham, he thought grimly.

The Marquis stared into his brandy glass, seeing long slender legs, one outstretched and lathered in soap, red-gold hair piled up on her head curling riotously from the steam of the bath, her white shoulders and firmly-rounded breasts flushed pinkly from the warmth of the bath water, and glow from the fire.

She was a beauty, he thought, as he remembered the feel of her soft body beneath his, and her sweet-tasting mouth. At least Sir Jason hadn't bedded him with a simpering, long-faced chit, crying for her mama. If he wanted to really punish Beckingham, he would thank him for helping him to find such a perfect wife.

He suddenly felt an uncontrollable, hot anger surge through him at the thought of Beckingham seeing Elysia naked, touching her as he had undressed her. He could not explain it, but he felt murderous towards Beckingham. Elysia belonged to him now, and no one but he had the right touch to her.

Elysia. Yes, she was his now, and he wanted her. He had felt attracted to her the moment he laid eyes on her as she stood warming herself before the fire at the inn. She was the first woman who had ever taken a dislike to him, which was something of a novelty. Most women, he thought without conceit, would have desired a liaison with him, but not the lovely Miss Demarice, who had looked at him disdainfully and coolly, a note of censure in her husky voice—and then had fought like a wild creature in his bed. He hadn't felt like charming her, or any female, after that scene with Mariana. In fact, he had felt distinctly antagonistic towards all women, venting his disgust and cynicism upon the first one he met. A flame-haired, green-eyed witch, who had captivated him against his will, and destroyed his misanthropic intentions by the sway of her hips.

She might need handling with that fiery temper of hers, but he would hate to have been tied to a milksop. Rather a vixen, he thought with an anticipatory gleam in his golden eyes, than that.

He drank off the last of his brandy, and left the room, taking the stairs two at a time, heading down the long corridor to the master suite, his long strides measuring off the distance in less than a minute.

He entered Elysia's room and walked toward the bed, standing quietly beside it. He looked down upon the sleeping figure in the big bed as the lighted candle held in his hand sent a golden glow across her face.

Elysia's hair spilled about the covers, red in the glowing light. Her thin hand was lying outside the cover, his gold ring looking foreign against her pale white skin—a visible mark of his domination and hold upon her.

He bent down, careful not to drip the hot, melting wax onto her exposed hand, and looked hungrily at her lips, the full lower lip slightly parted, her thick, dark lashes shuttering the eyes he wanted to look into, to lose himself in. The hollow at the base of her throat caught his eye, and lowering his head he placed a soft kiss in the space fashioned for his lips, while he entwined a piece of long hair through his fingers, soft and silky to his touch.

She was murmuring softly in her sleep, and he saw a tear slip out of the corner of her eye and run slowly down her cheek. He put a finger out and caught it, curiously feeling its moisture on the tips of his fingers.

He felt the heat in his body ebb away, and turning abruptly away from the bed, he left the room. He was no better than a dog after some bitch in heat. He was damned if he was going to act like some animal over that red-haired wench in the other room. To hell with her, he thought savagely, as he stripped and got into bed alone.

Her skirt was of the grass-green silk,
  Her mantle of the velvet fine,
At ilka tett of her horse's mane
  Hung fifty silver bells and nine.
                    15th Century Ballad

Chapter 7

Elysia sat staring out of the large, mullioned windows at the choppy, gray sea below, its angry waves crashing heavily against the rocks at the base of the cliff. White sprays of foam were shooting high into the air like giant uncontrolled fountains. The rain which had been continuous since the night of her arrival over a week ago had finally ceased, giving way to sullen overcast skies.

Elysia shivered and stood up, hugging her shawl closer about her shoulders as she moved to sit in a green and blue-striped satin chair before the hissing fire. The logs were shooting orange sparks as they burned brightly in the hearth.

Of Lord Trevegne, she had seen little, except at dinner when she was allowed the privilege of his company—a privilege she wished she could forego. Those few hours with him became either unbearable with his biting sarcasms and cruel remarks, or completely unnerving to her with his cold penetrating stares—she didn't know which was worse.

Unfortunately, it was always just the two of them, no sister or other members of his family whom she could become friends with, only a younger brother in London, who was probably just like Lord Trevegne—and she could hardly cope with him, much less another just like him. Why couldn't he have had a large, warm family? She could have lost herself among their chatter, and been protected from his constant displeasure. He would hardly single her out in a family gathering as he did with just the two of them dining at that long banqueting table with the crystal and silver gleaming under the sparkling candelabras.

What had she done to displease him? She never saw him long enough to do anything to cause him annoyance. He prowled around the great house like a caged bear, growling at anyone who made the mistake of addressing him. Even Dany was not immune from his foul temper.

Elysia sighed dispiritedly and looked down at her old woolen gown. She hated the sight of it, but her

171

other two dresses were in just as poor condition—if not worse—and hopelessly out of style. No wonder Lord Trevegne could hardly bear the sight of her, averting his eyes after only a glance at her, as if she made him physically ill. She had caught his golden eyes brooding on her several times however, with a speculative gleam in them until he noticed her look, and scowling heavily, dared her to speak.

Elysia cringed at the thought of asking him for new clothes, or even the money to buy material so she could make something for herself to wear, but even as she gathered up her courage she thought of his unpredictable temper and remained silent.

Dany had been kind, tactfully ignoring her impoverished appearance, sensing Elysia would not accept pity or charity, but she could see the curious stares of the servants, and knew what they were whispering and gossiping about in the servants' quarters. Most of the servants were better dressed than the mistress of Westerly, so what could they be expected to think of her? Lord Trevegne's destitute bride.

Elysia stood up in vexation, walking around the big room in boredom. She couldn't help but remember the long, almost never-ending days of tedious work at Aunt Agatha's, but she had to admit she had never been bored—she'd always been too busy, or too tired. It would seem she was never to be happy. What was wrong with her? Was she never to find an in-between state of being? Either she was worked to death or bored to death. She should be able to enjoy her leisure—but there was something missing—companionship?

Elysia had found that Westerly was run as smoothly as the intricate workings of a clock—efficiently and orderly—as it had for centuries. As the Marchioness, she was expected to do little more than select flower arrangements and approve menus—menus that were faultlessly prepared by Lord Trevegne's French chef. And she never had been able to sit hours on end enjoying the lady-like arts of embroidery and petit-point; her mind always seeming to wander in various directions—along with her stitches. She might not have strenuous labor to do at Westerly, but she still existed in that no-man's-land of not being a part of, or belonging to something. Dany had befriended her, but she was busy with the endless duties she had to perform to run the large mansion she had managed for almost twenty years. And with a household as large as Westerly, with its army of servants, Elysia was content to let Dany continue to run it—although Dany respected her as the new mistress, and consulted her about any major problem or decision. Elysia could see why Lord Trevegne loved the little woman; she was indeed a gem.

But no, she would not allow herself to mope. She was happy here. Who wouldn't be in this beautiful mansion? And the sea—the strangely alluring, but brutal sea that lulled her to sleep each night with its pounding lullaby. Lying awake each night, hearing her husband move about in his room, wondering if that night would be the night he would come to her, demanding his rights. That was really what was bothering her, worrying her. If it hadn't been for that constant fear—then she would truly be happy here at Westerly.

Elysia picked up a small delicately-formed vase sprouting a bouquet of flowers and buds formed of small pink and white seashells. The whole salon, in fact, seemed to be an extension of the sea, with its dominant greens and blues of varying shades, intermingling with the gilt furniture. On a bright summer day the room would be beautiful and airy with the light streaming in from the large expanse of floor-length windows facing onto the sea. She could just imagine the room bathed in the rays of the setting sun, the Oriental carpets enrichened into deep reds and blues and golds, the tapestries hanging on the walls coming to life and gaining depth and the illusion of movement. But today, with the darkening shadows of oncoming winter and her despondent mind, it seemed cold and austere.

But every room in Westerly was just as magnificently furnished. Built on the ruins of an old Norman fort that had once guarded the conquered land from further invaders, Elysia had been given a tour of inspection by Dany, and been surprised by the size and the splendor of this ancient home. She'd had no idea that Lord Trevegne was so wealthy. She had indeed suspected that he was not living in penury by the fine clothes he wore, the elegant coach and horseflesh he sported, and his habit of traveling with a full entourage of liveried servants. He was also too commanding a figure not to have riches, his air of *hauteur* and arrogance signified wealth.

Elysia had seen the Gold Salon with its golden elegance and Queen Anne furnishings, the Red Drawing-room like a seductive lady bedecked in rubies—the dark reds glowing richly against the old, highly-polished mahogany. There was the dining-room in colors of champagne and pink; the table long enough to seat a hundred, and seeming insignificant next to the banqueting hall that could, no doubt, seat five hundred hungry guests—but it was seldom, if ever used now.

But one of her favorite rooms was the morning-room, facing east to enjoy the rising sun that warmed the room on clear days, the creamy-yellow, satin cushions and drapes a reflection of the sunbeams as they entered the room, making Elysia think of butter and honey pouring from the walls.

She'd lost count of the many drawing-rooms and bedrooms in the different wings of the house. Each room was carefully and elegantly furnished so each guest would feel privileged to sleep beneath a silk, canopied bed or delicately-painted ceiling.

Even the servants' quarters were well-kept and properly heated and ventilated for winter and summer, a far cry from the dingy and overcrowded servants' rooms at Graystone Manor.

But throughout all her explorations from cellars to attics, west wing to east wing, seeing every magnificent room and climbing countless staircases in the enormous house dating back before the reign of Queen Elizabeth, nothing could compare to Lord Trevegne's well-stocked library with its wall-to-wall shelves and spiralling staircase, which twisted up to a small loft with its large comfortable chairs. A wide window stretched down to the floor below and provided ample light to read by. Elysia had found this treasure trove only a few days before and now spent most of her time reading from the handsomely-covered volumes which she had filched from its shelves. She would read in bed in the early hours of the morning until her breakfast was brought to her, for she still rose early, unaccustomed, after her years with Agatha, to lounging lazily in bed. Or later in the day she would sit quietly up in the loft, carefully out of sight from overly-observant eyes— golden ones in particular.

Elysia had missed the luxury of reading almost as much as she had missed horseback riding. Reading was the only inactive pastime she truly enjoyed, something that if she'd had the opportunity at Agatha's to enjoy, would have been forbidden. It was Agatha's contention that books were evil, and a waste of time—giving people foolish ideas above their station in life.

But now she could enjoy reading all of the books that she desired. Never had she seen such a large selection of books, covering such a wide assortment of subjects, many of which would be considered unsuitable reading for a young girl. But Elysia had been educated far beyond the average female's approved academic curriculum, having shared a tutor with her brother Ian; she had read not only the Greek classics, but many of the popular eighteenth-century novels like *Robinson Crusoe* and *Gulliver's Travels*, and even Fielding's *Tom Jones*.

Lord Trevegne's library had all of her favorites, including the complete works of Shakespeare, and the young modern Romanticists; Byron, Coleridge, Keats and Shelly, who were just receiving their first taste of public approbation. She had been excited and surprised to find these romantics in Lord Trevegne's library, being a self-admitted cynic, but then Elysia supposed that even he would make some sacrifices to have a complete library. Also they were all acquaintances of his, and it was the least he could do to honor their friendship—especially since the volumes were personally inscribed by the authors to the Marquis.

Elysia leant her forehead against the cold pane, wondering where Lord Trevegne was this morning? Shrugging her shoulders she picked up a slim volume of love sonnets by Shakespeare and sat down before the fire, beginning to read, when the door was opened by Dany, who sailed in with the household keys jingling at her plump waist.

"Now here ye are, Lady Elysia," she said disapprovingly. "Ye didn't touch ye breakfast this mornin', and here I was thinkin' we were puttin' some flesh back on those bones again."

"I was not especially hungry this morning, Dany,"

Elysia answered, closing her book without a glance at the printed words.

"Well, we'll just have to prepare ye a good appetizing lunch, eh?" Dany said coaxingly, scrutinizing her young mistress's pale face with concern.

"Have you seen Lord Trevegne?" Elysia asked, pretending disinterest as she smoothed a crease in her dress and missed the relieved look that came to Dany's eyes as she realized what was amiss with Elysia—at least it was nothing physical.

"Oh, yes, early this morning, and growling like a bear to be let out, he was," she said clucking her tongue disapprovingly, while running her finger along the mantel shelf checking for dust. "And glad I was to see him leave."

"Where did he go?" Elysia asked in surprise.

"Out on the estate somewhere on that big, black brute of his."

"He's gone out riding, then?" Elysia said enviously, wishing she could have ridden out into the cool air on a horse as powerful as Lord Trevegne's black.

"Aye, and a more vicious animal I've never seen! The Lord's had mercy on us that he's not been killed by that devil-horse!" Dany said in denunciation of the big horse.

"Oh, Dany," Elysia said chuckling, "he's a beautiful horse. And I should, for once, love to be with Lord Trevegne who is out riding that horse right now," she added gaily, blushing as she realized the indiscretion of her words when she saw the odd look on Dany's face.

The door to the salon was opened by a footman announcing the delivery of Lady Trevegne's trunks and baggage from London. Elysia looked startled at the news, and looked at Dany in a perplexed fashion.

"But, I've no trunks, Dany. Surely there is some mistake."

"Well, now. We best go and see, hadn't we?" the older woman said matter of factly, leading a protesting Elysia up to her room.

There were three large trunks and several boxes and bags crowded together in her room as she and Dany entered.

"Oh, Dany! There must be an error; these must have been sent for *Lord* Trevegne—not *Lady* Trevegne," Elysia said nervously, trying to stop the trembling excitement she was feeling at the sight of the very feminine-looking trunks of pale blue, and the lacy-edged hat boxes. Maybe they were for her, but how could they possibly be, since she had not had measurements taken, or been fitted by a seamstress for any new clothes?

Lucy, the lady's maid that Dany had provided for Elysia, was already opening the big trunks, and giving an excited screech as the door of one swung open to reveal a row of beautiful, gauzy dresses in a rainbow of colors.

"Oooh! Your Ladyship!" Lucy exclaimed in awe, as she drew out a cobweb-fine, white lace gown, its train floating about Lucy like a cloud as she lifted it carefully from the confines of the trunk.

"It's exquisite," Elysia breathed as she lightly touched its gossamer fineness, "but can it really be for me?" She turned to look at Dany almost beseechingly.

"Aye, they be for ye my dear," Dany said opening up another trunk to reveal satins and velvets crowded together. She reached in and pulled out a bottle-green mantle, high-waisted and trimmed in fiery fox fur, and a matching muff and bonnet with a wide brim, trimmed with the same.

"But how can these clothes be for me? I was never fitted for them, so how can they possibly fit?" Elysia asked worriedly, taking off the borrowed slippers Dany had somehow managed to secure for her. Her old clogs shocked Dany to the core of her being when she'd seen Elysia wearing them in the salon. Elysia slipped her narrow foot into a jade green leather slipper which fit perfectly. Lucy began to hang the dresses up in the closet. Her other two dresses, resting in a neglected and crumpled heap on the floor, were ousted from the closet by Lucy with a contemptuous sniff of her pert little nose.

"Everything will fit just perfectly," Dany commented as she watched Elysia admire the green slipper, "because I took your measurements from one of your old gowns and your shoes."

"Dany—you did this? You got all of these things for *me*?" Elysia ran to the little woman and impulsively hugged her, crushing the powder-blue, velvet robe Dany was shaking out, between them.

"Well now, I only got your measurements for them. T'was your husband, Lord Alex, who ordered them for you—and very explicit he was in what he wanted from London. 'Bright colors,' he says, 'in greens and golds. Get her everything she needs for a complete wardrobe.' Oh, yes, Lord Alex knew what he wanted. And only the *best* for his bride." Dany was smiling proudly up in Elysia's astonished face, beaming like a cherubic magician pleased with his tricks of magic.

"Lord Trevegne ordered these for me from London!" Elysia exclaimed, dropping a filmy white nightdress as if it burned her fingers. He had gotten all of these clothes for her, and in so short a space of time! He must have had every seamstress in London working until midnight to complete her wardrobe—and how expensive it must have been, Elysia thought, as she looked at all of the dresses strewn across the room. Morning dresses, afternoon dresses, walking dresses, with shoes and bonnets to match each, with cloaks and robes, and the finest undergarments and lawn nightdresses. Lany opened another trunk to reveal, in glorious colors, a ball gown with a flounce of turquoise satin, and a sea-green gown sprinkled liberally with *diamanté* stars. She could see the skirts of other gowns peeking out from behind, in a kaleidoscope of colors and fabrics.

Elysia looked down at all the beautiful dresses spread over the bed, unable to decide, now that she had a choice, what to wear. Suddenly, she spied a deep-green, velvet dress. Elysia reached for it quickly, holding it up against herself in excitement.

"Now, what will you wear, Lady Elysia?" Dany asked, selecting a lovely violet, flowered, muslin morning dress with long narrow sleeves and rows of ruffles at the hem. "T'is a lovely dress, here."

"No. I'll wear this," Elysia said positively, making up her mind as she held out the riding outfit. "I'm going riding!"

"Lady Elysia!" Dany looked momentarily taken aback. "Ye can't go out riding on one of Lord Alex's horses. He doesn't allow anyone but Peter, or some of his closest friends, to ride them," she said, scandalized by the thought.

"I can ride as well, if not better than any man, and I am Lady Trevegne. I have the right," Elysia said stubbornly, thankful for the first time that she was Lady Trevegne, and could demand her pleasure for a change. "What can Lord Trevegne possibly do to me anyway? I am his wife, aren't I?" she demanded arrogantly, seeking confirmation from the two silent women who stood staring at her in awe, a hint of concern in their faces.

"Help me into it, Dany," Elysia requested, starting to unbutton her dress. "Please," she added entreatingly, a dimple peeping out of the corner of her mouth.

"Very well, Lady Elysia. I can't deny ye when ye look at me like that. Ye'd charm the devil himself— and maybe ye be at it now," she added portentously, helping Elysia into the superbly-cut riding dress which fit her snugly across the shoulder. Elysia gave a squeal of delight when Dany unearthed a pair of riding boots from the depths of one of the trunks. "Do you think they'll fit?" she asked, as she fell back onto the bed in an undignified position. She struggled into them, exclaiming triumphantly as she paraded across the room, an impish smile on her face. "Perfect!"

"And here's ye hat." A smile tugged at the corner of Dany's mouth as she placed the ridiculous little bit of hat with its lavender-plumed feather, saucily over one of Elysia's arched brows. "There ye are. Ye be all set, but for what, I'd rather not know." Dany declared in resignation, for she felt Elysia was bound for disaster.

Elysia stared at herself in the large dressing table mirror, looking critically at her reflection, but unable to find anything at fault in the tall, slender figure dressed in dark green velvet staring back at her. The small beaver hat and feather and her half-boots laced with green complimented the outfit. She hardly recognized herself out of her rags. Elysia couldn't suppress a satisfied smile curving her lips as she turned to see the admiration of Dany and Lucy, standing amidst the colorful dresses that were scattered about the room like a field of spring flowers.

"I'm off," she declared, giving a giggle as she tripped over the edge of one of the trunks reaching for a pair of gloves. Elysia's tinkling laugh echoed in the room after she had left and Lucy and Dany stood staring at each other in nervousness at their young mistress's precipitous actions—neither of them voicing their fears.

Elysia hurried down the grand staircase, breezily pushing through the large double doors at the entrance much to the consternation of Browne, who was hobbling across the hall with a tray of freshly-shined and sparkling crystal. Elysia gave him a cheery hello as she disappeared, her bobbing lavender plume the last thing Browne saw of her as he stood shaking his white head.

She took a deep breath of the tangy salt breeze blowing off the ocean. Elysia could still see the pounding waves as she walked toward the stables, and drawing nearer she could hear the muffled whinnies of the horses beyond the broad stable doors. She quickened her pace in anticipation.

Elysia entered, and stood silently watching the bustling activity of the busy stableboys and grooms, noticing how spotless a stable it was, even with many stalls. Since it was such a big stable, she should surely be able to find one horse that Lord Trevegne would not object to her riding. She was glancing about, hoping to spot the head groom, when she saw a short, wiry figure standing squarely in the middle of an empty stall. He was issuing orders to several stableboys standing attentively by. Elysia walked purposefully toward the man, her chin set firmly forward.

"Excuse me, but I should like a mount," she said in an arrogant voice, deciding a show of authority would be her best attitude to adopt—although she was shaking within. The short man turned around in surprise at the sound of a feminine voice behind him.

Elysia stepped back in shock, her mouth soundlessly opening several times before she finally, almost inaudibly uttered, "Jims!"

The grizzle-haired man rubbed the back of his hands over his eyes, and stared up at the green-clad figure in disbelief. "Miss Elysia?"

"Oh, Jims, is it really you?" Elysia asked, her eyes hanging onto his small figure as if afraid he was a mirage.

"Miss Elysia. T'is good to see ye," he spoke in a choked voice, his eyes suspiciously bright. "I'd thought never to lay eyes on ye again."

Elysia smiled tremulously. "What are you doing here, Jims?"

"Why, I work here, Miss Elysia. I'm the head groom, and a finer stable ye'll not find in all of England," he said proudly.

"With you running it, that would indeed be doubtful," Elysia said, looking about her with admiration.

"Well, it's His Lordship that's got the eye for bloodlines. Never seen a finer eye for stock—except maybe for yer Papa, Miss Elysia," he added reverently, still loyal to his first employer and friend. "But what are ye doing here? His Lordship be just recently married, and a surprise to us all it was, us thinkin' him a bachelor fer life. Ye be a'visitin' here then?"

"No, Jims. I live here now—you see, *I* am the new Lady Trevegne."

Jims looked stunned by Elysia's news. "Ye be married to His Lordship, Miss Elysia?" A frown appeared on his weathered brow. He knew His Lordship's reputation, and was pretty sure that this marriage would not have met with approval from Miss Elysia's parents—even though he was of the opinion that His Lordship was on the square, and played the game fair.

"Yes, Jims, I am," Elysia answered, surprised that Jims did not seem overly concerned at finding her married to the Marquis.

"Well, I be glad ye've left *that* woman's house, anyway," he said, spitting as he shifted the wad of tobacco he was chewing to the other side of his mouth. "No disrespect meant, Miss Elysia, but I never did like the looks of her. She treat ye all right, didn't she?" Jims asked, looking fierce at the thought of anyone mistreating his Miss Elysia.

"It's all over now, Jims, and I shall never see her again," Elysia answered, reluctant to explain more of what she had lived through.

"I can't believe it, that I be workin' fer ye agin. It be fate that ye be here now, Miss Elysia." He cast a glance over at the boys busily scrubbing down the stall, and then added hesitantly, "His Lordship ain't exactly like your father, Miss Elysia, but I'll tell ye that he be a good man deep down inside. Treats his horses good; never takes the whip to them. Anyone who loves horses can't be all bad," he said, giving a somewhat qualified approval to her marriage. "He be a strange man at times, but he be honest."

Elysia silently agreed with him. She was indeed married to a strange man, but whether it was fate—or just bad luck—that had caused it, she didn't know. It was too late now to change anything, and she was beginning to feel the truth of the fact, she was Lady Elysia Trevegne, the wife of Lord Trevegne, and never again would she be plain Elysia Demarice. There was no escaping that fact—and she would have to live with it.

"So, ye be wantin' to ride, eh, Miss Elysia?" Jims said happily, pleased to have his favorite *protégée* back under his care again. "Aye, I can see th' sparkle in yer eye," he said chuckling.

"If you only knew how long I've waited and longed to ride once again, Jims. It's like a fever with me," she said following him along the row of stalls.

"So, ye've not had a good ride in a long while? No decent mounts for ye to ride, eh?" Jims commented with understanding, knowing no other stable could meet his standards of horseflesh—nor Miss Elysia's.

Elysia laughed. "Finding a decent mount was the least of my troubles, Jims. In fact, there were no saddle horses. Only a couple of old nags to pull an out-of-date carriage."

"You've not ridden at all!" Jims croaked in astonishment. "Lord help that woman—not to be lettin' ye ride. Aye, she be a mean 'un, all right," he grumbled, muttering curses on Agatha's head.

Elysia smiled. If he only knew half of what Agatha had done to her . . .

"Now, did the Marquis say ye was to have any particular horse?" he asked, eyeing her carefully.

"No, the truth is—I haven't asked His Lordship's permission to ride," Elysia told Jims truthfully.

"Ye haven't, eh?" he said, rubbing his chin. "Well, I don't likely know if I should let ye then, Miss, er, Lady Elysia. He be a real cool 'un about who's to ride his bloods."

"Jims!" Elysia said reproachfully. "You, above all people, know that I can ride better than any man. Between you and Father, I've had the best teachers in the country," she added matter-of-factly.

"Aye, that you have," Jims agreed with pride, well aware of her expertise, for which he had partially been responsible.

"I want to ride now, Jims. I just can't wait, and besides Lord Trevegne is out somewhere on the estate. By the time he returns it might be noontime, or later. Oh, please, Jims," she spoke beseechingly. "I'll even ride an old mare if that is all that is available," Elysia added desperately—and a trifle too innocently.

Jims pulled himself up to his full five feet, looking affronted. "Now, Miss—er, Lady Elysia," he corrected, unable to adjust to her new title, "ye knows better than to think that I would ever mount ye on anything but the very best."

"I know you would not like to . . . but if that is all that is available—then you know I would prefer that to causing you any trouble, Jims," Elysia answered placatingly.

"Let's see what we can find for ye," he said, inspecting several satin-coated horses, which Elysia would have loved to have ridden, without stopping. Her husband certainly did know how to pick fine horseflesh, she had to admit, as they passed champion- after champion-caliber horse. Surely Jims could find something for her to mount, she thought worriedly as they came to the last stall—one set apart from the others.

"Well, I don't know if ye'll be likin' this 'un, but ye can give it a try if ye like," Jims told her with a doubtful look on his face.

Elysia looked into the stall, curious as to what Jims finally had selected for her, and gave an indrawn breath as she saw the sleek, muscular, white flanks.

"Ariel!" Elysia cried, opening the gate and rushing in as the big horse turned at the sound of her voice. Remembering her, he neighed softly, putting his head against her neck and snorting hotly.

"Oh, Ariel, Ariel," she murmured as the tears cascaded down her cheeks. She rubbed his velvety nose and hugged his muscular neck with outstretched arms.

"Well, I see ye've not forgotten each other," Jims finally broke in, his voice muffled by emotion.

Elysia released her hold on Ariel, and turned to

look at the little man, a warmth of undying gratitude in her green eyes. She impulsively hugged him, planting a kiss on his leathery cheek, unable to express her feelings in words. Ariel nudged her back, neighing for her attention again, and she turned back to him, murmuring softly into his cocked ear.

"Aye, the two of ye belong together, and no one else would he allow on his back, not even His Lordship, who has a way with horses that I've seldom seen. But ol' Ariel wouldn't let him on—for two years now. Even so, the Marquis wouldn't have him destroyed, or sold—said he was too beautiful an animal to send out of this world, even if he was apparently a one-master horse. And seein' how I knows him, and could care for him, he lets the beastie have his way. We been breedin' him. Have a couple of nice young 'uns about the place now, and His Lordship be real proud of them."

"I can't believe it, Jims," Elysia tearfully managed to say, "that I should see both of you again, when I had come to believe that the past was indeed dead, and inhabited by mere ghosts of the people and things that I had loved." Elysia sighed deeply. "If you only knew how many times I thought of you, and Ariel; wondering what had happened to you, and if Ariel's new owner would be kind to him. And now here he is—my Ariel. It just seems too utterly fantastic to believe."

"Not so fantastic—after all, the Marquis has the best stables in England, so it's not strange that he'd want Ariel—seein' how he's such a fine horse," Jims explained. "But I have to admit I'd been a might worried that day we left fer London. Oh, we got down easily enough, but t'was the auction that had me feelin' between hawk and buzzard. Didn't care to part with him that I didn't, what with all them young bucks too eager to use the whip eyeing him over, and seein' how he wasn't likely to let any of 'em on his back. But then His Lordship shows up, and buys him right off. He'd watched me working with Ariel before the auction and liked my style, so before I knows it, I be workin' fer him, and takin' Ariel down to his estate fer him. I'd told him I couldn't get no references, seein' how my last employer had died, but he says all he needed to know was what he'd seen me do with the horse."

"So you and Ariel have been here—safe, all of this time. I'm so relieved." Elysia turned back to the big horse and planted a kiss on his nose. "Does Lord Trevegne know that Ariel is my horse—was my horse?" Elysia asked Jims.

"Well now, when Ariel wouldn't let him ride him, he did ask who had owned him before, but when I said it was a woman—well, he smiled crookedly and sorta sneered like, and said, 'Then it doesn't surprise me that he's so difficult.' Although he was a bit surprised to think that a woman could handle such a big stallion. Remember he said it must have been some fierce Amazon. Whatever that be. And then he didn't ask any more questions."

"An Amazon, did he say?" Elysia demanded, feeling oddly put out. She shrugged away the feeling—

what did she care what he thought of her. "Shall we go for a romp, Ariel? I'll bet you've longed for one as much as I have in my exile. All right, Jims?" Elysia looked for permission.

"Aye, Miss Elysia, we'll get him saddled up."

They stopped at a closed stall, and opening it, Jims showed Elysia a new-born foal, its coat ruffled and damp as it wobbled on unsteady legs. Ariel snorted behind Elysia's shoulder, and the mare standing protectively by her new-born foal neighed softly in answer. Elysia looked at the little foal with new interest.

"You'll have to be using a firm hand on Ariel, what with him strutting about playing the proud sire," Jims chuckled.

"So this is one of Ariel's," Elysia breathed softly, having fallen in love immediately with the precariously-balanced foal.

Elysia felt mixed emotions as they led the frisky Ariel out into the stable yard. Outwardly, they were the same—but time had changed them. Ariel and she did not belong to each other as they had before. They'd been carefree and one as they'd raced across the fields, but now Ariel had a mate—and she, Elysia, belonged to the Marquis.

Jims saddled him up while the stableboys and grooms stood about, gawking at the sight of the big, white stallion that no one could go near, nuzzling gently the face of the beautiful lady in green.

Jims helped Elysia mount, and cautioned her, "Go easy, Miss Elysia. Ye've both got plenty 'o time to catch up and no hurry to do it in, so don't try to race the wind."

Elysia waved as she and Ariel cantered sedately out of the yard, not fooling Jims, who knew they'd be flying as soon as they cleared the yard.

Elysia headed eastward, racing down the road which connected Westerly with the village of St. Fleur and the major road further inland. She halted on a rise, trying to decide which way to ride, and looked back at the huge H-shaped house, the Great Hall forming the bar of the H. Westerly seemed to loom above the sea, as it sat on a promontory of rocks. The Marquis' flag waved in the breeze, proclaiming his residence—the crimson, black and gold crest brightening the sky.

Giving a last glance to the sea, Elysia headed inland, galloping wildly across the moorland paths, feeling the cool air caressing her cheeks. The golden oranges and yellows of the autumn landscape merged into one blur of color as it flashed past the galloping hooves.

They jumped a stone wall in one fluid motion, Ariel's hooves clearing it by feet as they sped on across the rolling expanse of ground, mud flying upwards by the heavy hooves. She felt so free—so safe, to be riding on the familiar back of the big, white horse, and knowing her dear Jims was back at the stable. She could so easily have been back at her home, out for an early morning canter, her brother riding hard to catch up with her, scolding her with a smile for her fool-hardiness.

Elysia could almost hear the hooves pounding furiously behind her, and involuntarily she looked over her shoulder, only to see a rider closing the distance between them. For a brief moment she thought her dream had merged into reality as she watched the familiar figure, then she recognized the big black horse, and knew that it was not her brother—but the Marquis—who was trying to intercept her. Elysia felt a spark of defiance and excitement race through her veins as she urged Ariel to a faster pace, his mane flying backwards as they increased the distance. But Lord Trevegne was still gaining upon them, until finally, he was even with them. He reached across and pulled up on Ariel's reins, slowing them down until they both stopped abreast of each other.

"Hell and damnation! What the devil—" Lord Trevegne began, only to stop abruptly when he saw who the rider was. "Elysia!" he said incredulously, his eyes blazing in his white face. "What the devil are you doing on this horse? No one rides him. He's dangerous." He reached across and tried to draw Elysia from her saddle and into his arms, but she jerked the reins and backed Ariel up, moving out of his reach and allowing the horse to rear up, his hooves pawing the air threateningly.

"Obviously you are mistaken, M'Lord, for as you can plainly see I am on his back," Elysia said, enjoying herself immensely at Lord Trevegne's expense.

"Yes, I can plainly see that, but how the devil you managed it is a mystery. You could be lying out there with a broken neck!" he said tersely, making an obvious effort to control himself. His black horse nervously pawed the ground as he sensed his master's anger.

"It's no mystery, Lord Trevegne, for you did call me a witch one time—if I recollect accurately, so I am merely utilizing my powers," Elysia couldn't resist taunting.

"I did not think that you would have forgotten *that* occasion, Elysia," he retorted, both of them well aware of his inference. He always did manage to get in the last word, Elysia thought resentfully.

"How did you get him out of the stables? I've strict orders that no one is to go near him," he said severely, yet puzzled by her feat.

"I took full responsibility when I ordered the mount of my choosing," she explained quickly in defense of Jims, should he be blamed.

"Damn, you've no right to go over my authority. My word is law. That Jims would have allowed you to take Ariel out, knowing the danger and that I forbade it, he must be crazed—and I'll have his—"

"There was no danger, and Jims knew that."

"No danger! Good Lord, if anyone knows that horse, Jims does. Granted you kept your seat, but he *is* dangerous. Jims is a fool to have let you mount him. My God, he trained the brute and—"

"—and I owned him," Elysia admitted quietly, watching the surprise enter his eyes as the heavy lids momentarily lifted to give her the full effect of those golden eyes.

"*You* owned him?" he demanded in disbelief.

The Marquis looked at her as if she had sprouted horns, Elysia thought in amusement. "Yes. Ariel was mine, until I was forced to sell him at auction, along with all else that my family possessed, to pay the debts when my parents died."

The Marquis stared at Elysia, his eyes narrowed in thought as he sat contemplating her defiant face. "So, you were the owner of Ariel. I now know why he acted so prickly and stubborn. He takes after his mistress when he refuses to be ridden," he added softly.

Elysia gasped at his crude comparison, her eyes roving over him in derision as she said acidly, "We both happen to be very discriminating in our likes."

"What a tragic circumstance for you, Lady Trevegne, since *I* happen to be your *loving* husband," he told her menacingly as he made a quick lunge and lifted Elysia from her saddle in one smooth sweep. He held her tightly in his arms, hurting her with his strength.

Elysia struggled ineffectively, staring up fearfully into his angry face, afraid she had taunted him too far this time.

"So, you do not care for my caresses, my kisses," he whispered in a hard voice before his mouth closed down upon her lips, pressing hard against them in his anger, bruising them beneath his. The painful pressure lessened as his lips softened on hers, persuasively moving against them—parting them and invading their softness. This altered and gentle attack was far more devastating than his previous brutality. She was crushed against his hard chest as he continued to kiss her determinedly, until he felt her body relax against him, and Elysia gave a small sigh of surrender.

"Are you sure you do not desire my kisses, Elysia?" he demanded against her softly trembling mouth. She kept her eyes closed, refusing to look into his golden eyes—knowing she would find them mocking her. "Look at me, Elysia," he persisted, giving her a little shake.

Elysia opened her eyes at last, and stared up into his, which reflected her hatred of him in their darkened golden depths.

"You shall admit your true feelings one day, Elysia—I shall make you," he said arrogantly, his proud, dark head held high as he stared hypnotically into her flushed face.

He rode over to where Ariel had grazed and lifted Elysia back onto her saddle, giving a deep, almost violent laugh at her obvious relief at being out of his arms. Elysia shot him a murderous look, and turned Ariel, urging him into a gallop as they headed towards the house. The Marquis followed, easily keeping pace with Elysia.

"Ariel is fast, Elysia, but Sheik is faster. You could not outrun me, you know." He grinned at her stubbornly-set jaw, yet Elysia heard the warning in his voice.

Still, she was able to answer him casually. "Sheik it a beautiful horse, and more than likely he is faster than Ariel. Ariel has stamina—can you say the same of him?" she asked.

"I can push him hard, but very seldom will he lather up, or become winded. He can hold his own, never fear. I see you have been taught well how to ride. Jims was your family's groom since you were a child, no doubt. In truth, I must admit that I have seldom seen a better seat on a horse than you have, my dear," he was forced into acknowledging as he watched Elysia ride—a hint of admiration in his voice.

"Yes, Jims was a superb teacher, as was my father. But thank you, M'Lord, for the compliment," Elysia replied, flustered by his praise, and added reluctantly, "you handle Sheik extremely well, I have also noticed."

The Marquis laughed loudly, in genuine amusement. "That is the first compliment my wife has paid me. This is indeed a historic occasion—not only do I find that my wife can nearly outride me, and on a horse that no one else can mount, but also that her acerb tongue has a light coating of sweetness when she so desires."

Elysia sent him a scowling look under drawn-together brows, but he continued to laugh deeply, ignoring her lifted chin and pouting mouth. They rode on towards the big house in the distance, its mullioned windows reflecting the light from the pale morning sun as it struggled valiantly to dominate the cloudy sky.

Elysia breathed in awe as she stared down at

Westerly, unaware of Lord Trevegne's scrutiny until he asked with interest, "Do you really approve of my home? Most claim it to be too isolated and desolate to visit for long—let alone to live here."

"It is isolated, but then I have always lived in the country, and in less populated places than the Home Counties. I enjoy the wide open spaces in preference to crowded, and noisy town life."

"There are certain advantages, like amusements, which are offered only by life in London."

"Yes, I am sure *you* have availed yourself of all the 'amusements', M'Lord." Elysia paused delicately over the word. "However, if one can afford but one way of life ... then I would much prefer life in the country than an existence in London. Those who have access to both ways of life can travel between the two when ennui sets in, which is indeed to be envied, for then you have the best of both worlds."

"My wife will envy no one," Lord Trevegne said arrogantly, "for I have many estates, and a townhouse in London which we shall make use of during the year."

"I shall miss Westerly," Elysia confessed, a trifle begrudgingly. She felt reluctant to admit a liking for anything belonging to him. "It is an interesting house, especially the Great Hall, with its Spanish tiles and ornaments."

Lord Trevegne smiled at her praise. "One could almost call the hall our trophy room. My ancestors enjoyed these *objets d'art* with an added enthusiasm—plunder from the sixteenth century. It was also rather daring to decorate one's hall with Spanish possessions and architecture when England was at war with Spain. One of my ancestors told Queen Elizabeth that he enjoyed feasting his eyes upon the bounties from the vanquished—rewards of a successful freebooter. I do believe he actually admired and cherished these Spanish trophies—recognizing some of them as priceless pieces of art," the Marquis elaborated with relish as he noticed Elysia's look of distaste as he described his ancestors. "I wonder how my ancestors would have treated such a spirited wench as you, my dear? I rather doubt that you would have enjoyed it. Although I have heard that my ancestors were quite charming at Court, rivaling perhaps even Sir Walter Raleigh in gentlemanly courtesies."

"Apparently in that aspect you inherited very little, and too much perhaps of their pirate instincts," Elysia said sarcastically.

"I knew it was too good to last—this false sweetness of yours. I shall have to prescribe a spoonful of honey each morning to help sweeten that sour disposition of yours," Lord Trevegne told Elysia warningly, "for I am not accustomed to being talked back to in such a disrespectful manner. You will have to show a little more affection when in company, my dear. Try to act like the loving wife, and I shall pretend to be your devoted slave."

Elysia was saved from her angry retort by their entrance into the stable yard where Lord Trevegne dismounted quickly and lifted Elysia down before she could protest. His hands felt hard and cruel about her small waist as he held her close for a moment, and they stared into each other's eyes like protagonists. He flicked her lavender plume with a careless finger, and set her free as he sent a quelling glance to Jims who had been standing quietly, and apprehensively, in the doorway to the stables.

"Had I not known beforehand how bewitching my wife could be, Jims, you would now be on your way from Westerly, and all of Cornwall, for disobeying my orders. Elysia has a way of twisting a man about her little finger to get her way, and I would imagine she has had years of practice with you. But I shall expect my wishes to come first from now on. You answer to me, Jims."

Jims came forward, relief written across his face. "Aye, Yer Lordship, but I didn't think ye'd be mindin' her ridin' Ariel, seein' how Miss Elysia raised him from a colt. And they both looked as if they could use the exercise," he answered, smiling at Elysia. "Did ye and Ariel enjoy ye ride?"

"I can answer that for you," Lord Trevegne said grimly. "I saw her and that damn horse racing madly across the moor, and could scarcely believe my eyes—and I had a damnable time catching them. In future, you will go out with a groom or myself—but never alone. And if I might inquire, why was she alone, Jims?" he asked softly, turning to Jims with a frown on his face.

"Didn't see any sense in it, Yer Lordship, seein' how Miss Elysia would've lost him," Jims answered practically.

"Sensible as always, Jims, but *Lady* Elysia, is now my wife and she will take a groom in future—or not at all," he warned them both.

Jims chuckled, shaking his head as he watched them walk toward the house, making a striking-looking couple. The Demarices may not have desired the Marquis as a husband for their daughter, but he was beginning to think that His Lordship had just what Miss Elysia needed—a good firm hand to guide her. He might be a bit wild and have a bad reputation, but he was a cut above the rest, thought Jims, even though he was not the jovial sort of bloke that liked to joke around. He'd been surprised to hear of His Lordship's marriage, but since it had been to Miss Elysia he could understand His Lordship giving up being a bachelor. There was no one as lovely as his Miss Elyisa. Must have been love at first sight, for he knew as well as anyone that Miss Elysia had no money, and His Lordship was as rich as can be—anyway you could tell by the way he looked at her that he was crazy about her. Miss Elysia was a very lucky young lady, he thought happily whistling a tune as he entered the stables.

Elysia shuddered as they entered the Great Hall with its obvious glories of war and bloodshed, and some of the beauty, which she had admired before, faded before her eyes as she glanced about.

As if divining her thoughts Lord Trevegne said, "It was a long time ago, and no ghosts linger within these walls."

"I know, but it still saddens me to think of these things having been taken from others," she commented, indicating a row of gold chalices encrusted with jewels, gleaming brightly in display, on a marble-topped, pier table against one of the walls.

"There is always a victor—and a vanquished in any confrontation. You of all people should realize that," he said, taking her elbow firmly as he guided her up the broad staircase.

As they entered their salon, Elysia remembered that she had not thanked him for her new wardrobe from London, and she turned abruptly to face him, a shy smile curving her lips.

"I had forgotten, in my excitement at riding Ariel, to thank you for the clothes you had made for me so quickly in London. It was very kind of you," she added hesitantly.

"Kind? Hardly that, my dear. I merely did not want you to shame me in front of my friends, looking little better than a servant. In fact, my staff was better dressed than you, and they find enough to gossip about as it is," he explained in a bored voice.

"Oh, you insufferable cad! I think I hate you more than ever!" Elysia exclaimed, the color flaming uncomfortably into her cheeks. "You shall never hear of me thanking you for anything again, *Your Lordship*," she spat at him as she ran from the room, slamming the door behind her, leaving Lord Trevegne standing speechless where he was.

Elysia pulled her hat from her head and threw herself onto the bed, burying her head in her folded arms on the pillow. The beast, she thought angrily. Would she never understand him? One minute he jokes with her, then the next he kisses her, and then snaps her head off the following minute. Life was certainly not easy, she thought in dismay, as she remembered his passionate kisses on the moor. He was right, Elysia thought with disgust. She *did* want to be kissed by him—at least sometimes she felt this strange need for him, but most of the time she felt as if she could have callously murdered him—feeling no regrets.

Elysia rubbed her forehead wearily and stood up. How could she possibly want to be kissed by someone so cruel? she thought in exasperation. She despised herself for her weakness. She ought to put on one of her old woolens, and see what His Lordship would have to say to that, she thought defiantly. Elysia looked through the rows of dresses, but couldn't find them among the peacock colors, nor could she find her old shoes or cloak. Dany must have thrown them out when they put away her new ones.

Oh, well, she did not really want to wear them again, even if it would anger him. She was struggling with her boots when Lucy appeared with a couple of chambermaids, carrying a tub and pails of hot water.

"Mrs. Danfield thought ye'd be wantin' to freshen up after ye ride, Lady Elysia," she said timidly, staring at Elysia as if she were a ghost.

"Thank you, and would you help me off with my boots?" she asked Lucy as the girl slowly came forward, looking frightened.

"What is the matter?" Elysia demanded as the two chambermaids stared goggle-eyed.

"Oh nothing, Lady Elysia," Lucy mumbled, helping Elysia unlace her boots with shaking fingers.

"Tell me, Lucy," Elysia persisted, seeing the girl shake at the contact with Elysia's ankle.

"Oh, Yer Ladyship! Ye rode the horse. The one even His Lordship can't ride and he be almost like the devil himself!" She rolled her eyes nervously.

"Listen, Lucy, and both of you too. I won't have you go telling tales around the house," Elysia said to the other two who stood cowering together. "That horse before he came here, belonged to me. I raised him from a baby with wobbly legs and downy-like coat. He has only known me, and will only allow me to ride him," she explained patiently, watching the relief come to the three faces, "and you know Jims, you trust him?" They nodded their capped heads. "Well he has known me since I was a baby, and can vouch for my lack of any mystical powers." Elysia held her hands out in supplication.

The three girls smiled and giggled as they began to prepare her bath, Lucy helping efficiently when Elysia dressed afterwards.

If only she really did have mystical powers, then she would find a way out of this situation she was in, taking care of His Lordship once and for all in the process, Elysia thought with relish, as she walked slowly downstairs. She wore a white, muslin dress embroidered with green and blue flowers and tied with green velvet ribbons beneath her breasts. The ends trailed down her back to the hem, with similar bandings around the ruffled cuffs of the long sleeves and high neck. Her hair had been dressed high on her head á la Grecque, the thick red-gold curls cascading about her shoulder. Odd how new clothes could give one a feeling of confidence and self-respect. She need no longer feel ashamed of her appearance—nor need anyone else!

Elysia walked soundlessly across the tiled floor of the Great Hall in her green, kid slippers. A footman opened the door of the salon, and upon entering, Elysia saw the Marquis in conversation with a thick-set gentleman sitting comfortably in one of the chairs before the fire. They stood up as Elysia entered, Lord Trevegne's golden eyes going over her figure with approval as she came forward.

"My wife, Lady Trevegne," the Marquis said with what almost sounded like pride in his voice. But she knew better than to believe that. "Elysia, may I introduce you to our nearest neighbor, Squire Blackmore."

The Squire took Elysia's hand and bowed awkwardly. "A pleasure, Lady Trevegne, and may I commend you, Lord Trevegne, on your wife's beauty!"

The Marquis nodded his head arrogantly in acceptance of the compliment, while Elysia wondered what he had to do with her looks. She sat down demurely with a serene smile on her lips, listening to the garrulous Squire Blackmore's ramblings.

"I could scarcely believe my ears when I heard in London that you had finally been caught, Trevegne. Louisa will be heartbroken," he expostulated loudly as if he still found it hard to believe.

"And how did you come to hear the news?" Lord Trevegne asked curiously.

"Well, it was in the Gazette, but I heard about it first in the shops," he said baldly.

"In the shops!" Lord Trevegne ejaculated in surprise, and then laughed.

"Well, you did order quite a trousseau for your bride, and wanted it in an uncommon hurry, so I've heard. It's bound to get around," he explained apologetically to Elysia, who was glaring at the Marquis' amused expression.

"You heard nothing else—except that I had wed?" he suddenly asked quietly.

Squire Blackmore looked ill at ease for a moment, his close-set eyes darting about the room nervously. "Well, not much really. You know how there is always some rumor going the rounds about Your Lordship." He laughed immoderately, sending Elysia another apologetic glance.

"Still can't believe it," he said to Elysia, "had hopes for a match with His Lordship and my daughter Louisa. Crazy about him, she is. Of course, I perfectly understand why he married Your Ladyship, yes indeed."

He stood up quickly as if he had suddenly thought of something. "Well, I must take my leave, however I wanted to wish you my felicitations and ask you to dine with us one evening. I just arrived from London a few hours ago, along with several guests who are now resting from the long journey. Please come, although we shall understand if you prefer to be alone," he said ingratiatingly, bowing flamboyantly. "Lady Trevegne, a pleasure—Lord Trevegne."

They watched him scurry off, leaving the room before the footman Lord Trevegne had rung for could see him to the door.

"It certainly did not take long for it to reach London," he commented as he lighted a cheroot. "However I really had expected the good Squire before now. I am rather disappointed."

"Why had you expected Squire Blackmore?"

"Because, my dear wife, the Squire has had hopes of marrying his daughter—Louisa, I believe he called her—off to me for the past few years. In fact, had I not met you so . . . unexpectedly, then I might have considered the girl. She had a few good points in her favor, if I remember her correctly? Very quiet, and unassuming, in fact one would hardly know she was around. Quite the opposite of you, my dear; but the only drawback of course would be to find myself related to the Squire—too much to contemplate, even in conjecture."

"What a pity I have no intention of obliging you, and turning amenable," Elysia smiled sweetly up at him, the smile not reaching her green eyes.

"Never fear that you have disappointed me, my dear, for I seldom play long odds, and only then if it is a sure thing. With you, my dear, I am never sure of anything," he smiled crookedly. "Although I must say, the Squire acted rather well at masking what must have been a shattering disappointment, considering his ambitions have been ruined by your existence."

"I do believe you enjoy seeing the hopes of others destroyed."

"No, not really. But the Squire has made rather a nuisance of himself, trying to foister off his daughter on me, merely to achieve his own desires of having a titled son-in-law, and adding my money and estates to his. Unfortunately for him, my estates are willed to my heirs—he would not be able to touch them."

"I cannot understand you. You have wealth, looks, and your health. Yet you despise everyone. Why is it? Maybe it is really that you despise yourself and what you have become," Elysia told him boldly, staring into those flaming golden eyes.

He grabbed her arms in a tight grip, almost snarling as he said, "Do not push me too far, Elysia, for you are, after all, married to that thing that I've become." He pushed her away and stalked out of the room, leaving her standing alone and shaken.

"*A cruel man and impious thou art*
Sweet lady, let her pray, and sleep,
*   and dream*
Alone with her good angels, far apart
From wicked men like thee. Go, go!—I deem
Keats

Chapter 8

Elysia paced restlessly to and fro in front of a large, gray boulder, kicking aimlessly at any small stone in her path. The weak sun had failed to assert itself and was retreating back behind the distant hills, taking its pale light with it. The wind whipped up the hem of her dress as it blew coldly around her, feeling like a cool balm on her flushed cheeks and disquieted nerves.

Luncheon had been a disaster, with Lord Trevegne glowering and taunting her in his anger-which had smouldered dangerously since she had dared to give her opinion of his character. Finally, unable to take his abuse any longer, she had stormed out of the dining room, leaving her food uneaten, not caring about Lord Trevegne's look of offended outrage, and the servants' surprised faces at her abrupt departure. Elysia had rushed up to the sanctuary of her room only to find the walls of the room closing in upon her as she sat brooding—full of self-pity. Finally, she changed into her riding habit and quickly and quietly made her escape from the tense and uneasy atmosphere of the house—leaving without a word to anyone. She saddled Ariel herself, Jims luckily absent from the stables, and rode triumphantly and defiantly off into the storm-threatened afternoon.

Elysia had no idea how long she had been wandering about the outcropping of rock watching Ariel grazing peacefully, when she heard the sound of approaching hoofbeats, and turned expecting to see His Lordship's thunderous brow. Instead, she saw a dainty, chestnut mare with a blue-clad rider come prancing towards her.

"Good afternoon," the girl said as she came closer to Elysia, who was now halted in her tracks and watching the approaching rider curiously. The girl was slight with light-brown hair and smoky-gray eyes. Her cheeks were rosy from her ride in the cool air.

"I am Louisa Blackmore," she said in a small, sweet voice, "and I live at Blackmore Hall—a few miles from here. I am being rude by introducing myself this way, but we very seldom see strangers in these parts. So I just could not pass by without inquiring as to who you are, and if in fact, you might be lost?" She looked at Elysia with concern.

"No, I am not lost, merely enjoying a ride before this storm breaks, which I fear shall happen soon. I am Elysia Dem—Trevegne," Elysia answered, smiling at the other girl.

"Trevegne!" Louisa Blackmore looked nonplussed for a moment, and then recovering, exclaimed, "Then you are Lady Trevegne, Lord Trevegne's new wife?"

"Yes I am, and you are Squire Blackmore's daughter. I made his acquaintance earlier today."

"Oh, it is indeed a pleasure to meet you, Lady Trevegne," Louisa said extending her gloved hand eagerly. "I do not feel that I have committed a *faux pas* and been too forward now—I'm always being scolded for that—but since you have heard of me, and I am not a complete stranger to you, then all is well."

She smiled in genuine friendliness at Elysia. Hardly heartbroken, thought Elysia, as she smiled back at Louisa's cheery face, and remembered Squire Blackmore's evaluation of his daughter's state of mind upon hearing of the new Lady Trevegne.

"Thank you," Elysia answered politely, "and it is a pleasure to make your acquaintance also." She was puzzled by Louisa Blackmore's obvious delight in finding that she was Lady Trevegne.

A loud clap of thunder rumbled overhead, causing the horses to shy nervously.

"I think I should remount before this storm comes down upon us and soaks us completely," Elysia remarked apprehensively, gathering Ariel's reins and leading him over to the rock where she could climb up to mount.

"We can talk on our way back to the road, I go the opposite way, once there," Louisa said as they began to canter side by side. "I cannot believe that you are actually riding that horse," she continued in awe, with a hint of fear in her voice, "for I should die of fright even to touch him. He is the horse that no one can ride. I mean, even Lord Trevegne cannot mount him, yet here you are riding him, and without a groom to accompany you. My groom is waiting on the road up ahead, a constant shadow—but it does make me feel safer. And here you are riding out alone, and on that wild horse." She gave a delicate shudder at the thought.

Elysia laughed with the first genuine amusement she had felt in years. "I seem to be creating a rather distorted image of myself. I suddenly find that I am endowed with strange mystical powers because I am riding a horse that supposedly cannot be ridden. When the plain truth of the matter is, I raised this horse, and trained him until I was forced to sell him. So you see, I am a mere mortal, with no extraordinary powers of persuasion."

"Well, that is a relief. I'm sure I thought you were a witch," Louisa said jokingly, "but you do ride so well, and I can scarcely control little Dove when she gets frisky, that I feel ashamed to ride with you," she complimented Elysia, patting Dove's satiny neck affectionately.

"You ride quite well, considering you are so tiny. It would indeed be foolish, and dangerous to mount you on a big unpredictable horse," Elysia told her. Adding as she watched the small child-like hands control the reins, "Why, you make me feel as though I were some muscular Amazon—my spear and shield at hand to repel an attack."

Louisa gave a giggle, and threw Elysia an incredulous look. "But that can't be true, you are so beautiful. I should love to have your red-gold hair. It's such a glorious color compared to my plain, brown curls," she sighed. "Papa calls me a little mouse—which I fear he might be right in believing, for I appear to be shockingly lacking in courage and robustness."

"That makes you sound as if you should be a blacksmith or miller," Elysia laughed. "You are merely delicate and petite, and I do envy you. Shall we trade places?"

"Oh, goodness no! That would never do, for I would never be able to be the wife of the Marquis. He strikes absolute terror into me," she said, her eyes growing round. She put a small hand to her mouth in embarrassment. "Oh, what will you think of me for saying such a thing about your husband? It is just that you are so nice that I forgot you were a Marchioness."

"I shall think that you are completely honest, and have reason to feel so, for the Marquis can be absolutely beastly at times," Elysia replied matter-of-factly.

Louisa looked at her in admiration. "I'm so glad that I've met you, for you are so nice, and not at all what I imagined you would be like. I thought you would be snobbish and supercilious like those ladies from London who occasionally visit Blackmore. They make me feel so gauche—as if I were still in the schoolroom," she declared in an indignant voice.

"Well, you need not expect any airs from me, for I have never been a la-dee-da-type London lady. I much prefer the simplicity of the country," Elysia stated firmly, although she could hardly call Westerly simple.

"Does that mean that you shall be spending a great deal of time down here?" Louisa asked excitedly. "I do hope so. I have been so lonely. There is no one to talk to, and Papa and Mama are often in London. Since I am too young to have a season yet, I have had to stay here to finish my studies. I wish so often for a friend—and I hope you will be mine, Lady Trevegne?"

"Please, call me Elysia. I too have longed for a friend to talk with." Elysia glanced at Louisa's small-framed figure and added in a teasing tone, "I have need of a good, strong shoulder to lean upon at times."

Louisa laughed delightedly. "This is truly wonderful, for I think that we shall become dear friends. You seem so nice and amusing, and now Papa shall no longer be able to berate me for not winning Lord Trevegne's admiration. If you only knew how terrified I was at the thought, or even the possibility of Lord Trevegne having noticed me," she said paling visibly.

"Your father actually desired a match between you and Lord Trevegne?" Elysia found it hard to believe that anyone would wish to marry off his daughter to one such as her husband.

"Yes, he had quite set his mind upon it, and was very upset this morning when he told us that the Marquis had wed. I am afraid he really believed that His Lordship would have married me—which is ridiculous really, I'm not his type at all."

They had almost reached the road, when a light drizzle began to fall and they quickened their pace.

"I hope you've not a long way to go, Louisa. Why don't you stay at Westerly until a carriage can be arranged to take you home?"

"No, I've not far to ride, really. And if I hurry I shall make it. Will I see you soon?" Louisa asked hopefully.

"Possibly tomorrow night. We have been invited to dine."

"Oh I do hope so. I feel so ill-at-ease with Papa's friends from London," Louisa said worriedly, "and several carriages of them arrived this morning from London, it would seem for an indefinite stay." Louisa smiled half-heartedly and waved as she turned her little mare in the opposite direction, the groom close behind her as they headed down the road.

Elysia waved back and hurried faster toward the house, standing mistily in the rain in the distance. She felt happy. She had actually found a friend, someone with whom she could talk and share things. Elysia was smiling and humming a little tune as she rode into the stable yard. She was glad she'd decided to ride. She'd only ridden a short way this morning before being forced to return, and she had thoroughly enjoyed giving Ariel his head. It had also helped her to clear the cobwebs from her mind and relieve some of the restlessness she was feeling. But her smile faded, and the tune she was humming abruptly stopped as Elysia noticed Lord Trevegne preparing to mount Sheik, and Jims looking up with relief as he heard the hooves approaching.

Elysia was helped down by Jims, Lord Trevegne making no move to assist her. She risked a glance at his scowling face—he actually looked as if he would like to strangle her, so murderous was his expression.

"Ye should'na have gone out without tellin' no one, Miss Elysia," Jims scolded her.

"I am sorry, Jims, but there was no one here, and I felt like a ride," Elysia explained nervously as she felt Lord Trevegne's hard fingers grip her arm as he came up to her.

"Shall we go in, Elysia. I am sure you will want to change," he said in a very soft and quiet voice. Elysia glanced at him in surprise, he didn't sound angry, even though she had disobeyed him—despite his tightened lips and quivering nostrils.

"Yes, that is precisely what I had in mind," Elysia said waving to Jims, who was staring at her unconcerned face in bewilderment. His Lordship was in a foul temper, and Miss Elysia was in for a real tongue-lashing—if not more. He had never seen Lord Trevegne looking quite so put out, his eyes glowing darkly when he found out Miss Elysia had ridden by herself. The only obvious sign of his anger, however, was the clenching of his fists. His Lordship wasn't used to being crossed, and Miss Elysia being the high-spirited little filly that she was, was certainly heading for trouble. He wondered if the Marquis would be able to handle her? Miss Elysia always gave as good as she got. Ah, well . . . they'd work it out.

Elysia tried to pull her arm from the Marquis' tight grasp as they walked briskly toward the big double doors, but he only tightened it painfully.

"You are hurting my arm," Elysia gasped out between gritted teeth. But he ignored her protest, dragging her with him into his study, a room she had not been into yet, anxious not to disturb the lion in his den.

It was a warm-looking room with dark, wine-colored drapes, Oriental carpets, and big, red, leather chairs. A large, mahogany desk sat squarely before the French windows. On its smooth, highly polished surface was a gold hawk with a sharp beak weighing down a pile of papers. A fire was burning brightly in the grate—crackling noisily.

Without warning, Lord Trevegne took Elysia's other arm and shook her until she thought her head would roll off. Elysia stared up at him with tearful eyes when his anger had abated, her lips quivering uncontrollably.

"If you ever disobey my orders again, Elysia, I'll thrash you within an inch of your life," he ground out in a hoarse voice.

"You wouldn't dare!" Elysia squeaked in a shocked voice, a pulse in her throat beating wildly.

"I will dare anything. Don't push me too far, for I am nearing the end of my tether. I gave specific orders that you were not to ride unaccompanied. It was not a whim, nor an idle wish. You do not know this country, the moors can be dangerous—along with other unexpected hazards. We live on the coast, we are at war with France. Smugglers and spies, and God only knows what else may lurk in coves and estuaries throughout this area."

Elysia stared at him in dismay, feeling guilty. After all, he had only forbidden her to ride alone for her own protection. "I am sorry, Lord . . . uh, M'Lord," Elysia hesitated confusedly, feeling unable to call him by his first name.

"My name is Alex. A-L-E-X, and by God you shall use it. Say it. Say my name now." He gave her another threatening shake.

"A—Alex," Elysia mumbled softly, staring into the fire.

"Yes, Alex. That was not so difficult, now was it?"
He dropped his hands from Elysia's shoulders and
turned away.

"I am truly sorry, but I have always ridden alone,
and I am not used to having a groom trail me," she
tried to explain.

"Not here you shan't ride alone. You shall do as
I say, and not question my wishes."

"If you had told me the reason why I should not
ride alone, then I would have followed your
advice," Elysia told him in exasperation, forgetting
her previous submissiveness.

"I do not need to explain myself to you, my dear.
You will do my bidding, regardless," the Marquis
said arrogantly, flicking her a look of challenge.

"In other words, I'm your slave—your chattel.
Well, I shall not be! I've a mind and feelings, which
come before your bidding!" Elysia declared
heatedly.

Lord Trevegne looked at her with narrowed eyes,
his hands clenched. "Were I not a gentleman I
would strike you, my dear, but I should not like to
mark your pretty face."

"Oh, no, go ahead and beat me. That is all you
ever do—threaten me with abuse. You have longed
to do some physical violence to my person since first
we met," she challenged him.

"My dear, if you only knew what I really have
longed to do since first we met, then you would not
stand there so provocatively daring me to prove my
masculinity by physical force. You would not care

221

for the methods I would use to subdue you," he told her scornfully, his golden eyes running over her tense figure, the fire a reflection in his eyes.

Elysia backed up a step in retreat, suddenly afraid of what he was implying. "I am not challenging you, but you will find that I am not a spineless wife who will mindlessly do her husband's bidding without consideration for my own desires. And, I shall continue to feel this way regardless of how you may try to order me about."

"Will you really, my dear? My, my, I had no idea I had become married to a libertarian. This is a most revealing conversation. I am quite shattered, and what will my friends think?" he continued mockingly, sitting down in one of the red, leather, wing-back chairs. "Here I was under the misconception that you were a docile and thoroughly tractable female, who welcomed me as her husband and master—with open arms."

"You mock everything," Elysia said furiously. Striding to the door she turned and glared at him with brilliant green eyes, "so let this be the mock marriage that it is, with neither of us demanding—or expecting—anything from the other."

Elysia stormed out of the room heedless of his angry and imperious calling of her name.

Elysia rolled onto her back and stared up into the blackness of the canopy over her bed. She had been tossing and turning for hours. It was no use, she could not get to sleep. She sat up hugging her knees, resting her chin on her crossed forearms, and thought about another endless dinner she had suffered through, unaware of what she had been eating as dish after dish, course after course, had been removed and replaced by another. She was glad of the long length of the great dining table between her and the Marquis, who sat glaring at her from his end of the table. She doubted whether they had ever enjoyed a meal together. Poor Antoine, His Lordship's temperamental French chef, must be near to tears at the thought of his unappreciated culinary triumphs being served to the footmen and maids.

How long could either of them hold out in this continuous atmosphere of warfare? It seemed to Elysia's tired eyes that Lord Trevegne thrived upon it. She, on the other hand, felt tense and nervous, wondering when the next remark would come and how she would parry it, her mental faculties put to their utmost in defense.

She felt uneasy—as if on the edge of a precipice, and one false step would send her plunging into depths from which she would not be able to escape. Although she was not too well-versed in His Lordship's character, Elysia knew instinctively that he was seething, and seemed to turn more demoniacal with each passing hour. She apparently had the power to try his patience beyond what he was accustomed to. Well, the arrogant Marquis had indeed met his match in her, Elysia smiled to herself in satisfaction, thoroughly enjoying being the thorn in his side. She would play her cards carefully—and the Marquis would see who held the winning hand in this game of wits. But she certainly had no intention of endangering her own and rather precarious position, by taunting him too far, once too often. She had certainly caused his blood to boil today—and she had received a glimpse of those tightly leashed passions which he usually held in rein. Yes, she had cause to fear. So now she would tread lightly. She valued her skin too much to play recklessly with the Marquis.

Elysia threw back the covers and slipped from the bed, her feet searching for the dainty, little, turquoise-blue slippers that matched her velvet robe. She welcomed its warmth as she slipped it over the thin lawn nightdress with its high gathered waist held up by two thin velvet ribbons.

She tied the sash at her waist snugly, and lit a candle from the fire that was burning low in the fireplace, and then made her way down the corridor that was quiet except for the muffled sound of the sea in the distance. Elysia walked slowly, trying not to glance into the dark corners and alcoves as her candle spread a wavering light ahead of her. She protected the flame carefully with her cupped hand, from the drafts that would have carelessly snuffed it out.

As she left the stairs she heard the grandfather clock in the hall chime two, its bell-like notes echoing. Elysia glanced furtively toward Lord Trevegne's study. No light appeared beneath the bottom of the door; he must finally have gone to bed. He had taken a bottle of port from the side board and left the dining-room immediately after the last course, foregoing dessert. Then he closeted himself in his study, and was still there when she retired a few hours later.

Elysia held her candle up along the row of books, its light revealing the titles as she moved down in front of one of the shelves in the Library, trying to decide upon a selection. Surely one of these would help her to sleep. Elysia was reaching for a thick volume of Latin when she felt that she was not alone, and turned around quickly.

Lord Trevegne stood in the doorway that connected his study to the library. He was leaning against the door jamb, minus his coat and cravat, the light from the fire playing over his figure, the half-empty glass in his hand.

"Well, well, what have we here?" he said coming forward into the room, "a midnight raid upon my library?"

"I thought you had gone to bed," Elysia said clutching the thick book to her breasts protectingly, afraid of the strange glint in his eyes.

He took the shaking candle from her hand and held it up in front of her, his eyes going over her slowly, lingering on her unbound hair as it shimmered from the glow of the flame. "The door was open, and I thought I heard a noise, so I came to investigate—and what do I find? My blue-stocking wife," he sneered. "Couldn't you sleep? Too bad, but in a *mock* marriage you have only your books to comfort you in the wee hours of the morning."

"It is sufficient enough. You think men are the only ones who should be educated? Well, women have just as much right to use their minds—"

"They have no need to cultivate their minds, my dear," he interrupted, "for all they need use to get what they desire is their bodies."

Elysia gasped, the color flooding into her cheeks. "That's a lie!" she told him hotly, stepping closer in her anger, "for it is you men who would keep us ignorant, and used purely for your pleasures. Your wife to obey your commands, bear your children and manage your home, your mistress to obey and satisfy your desires. Oh, yes, you would keep us ignorant—for once educated, with rights of our own, we would have no need for you!"

Lord Trevegne stood silently staring down into Elysia's white face, her eyes blazing green fire in her anger and her breasts heaving from her outburst. He threw his now-empty glass into the fireplace where it shattered into a thousand splintering shards.

Elysia flinched at the sound of the breaking glass, and the violence of the gesture that reflected his feelings. He snuffed out the candle he had taken from her with his fingers and dropped it to the floor as he reached for Elysia, grabbing her shoulders with his big hands.

"So you would not need men?" he said ominously, his eyes smouldering into her frightened face. "It is

time I taught you just how much you do need us—
me to be precise, for you shall never know another
man, now that you are mine. I have waited far too
long to teach you a few lessons—putting up with
your vixenish ways, allowing your insults to go un-
punished, suffering what I would never have allowed another to do—and live." He laughed cruelly.
"A mock marriage you would have! I am going to
show you, my snow queen, how very real it can
be—and will be."

The Marquis pulled her into his arms before Elysia could make a move to protest, his lips coming
down hard on hers. She felt him pressing her soft
body against his, molding her to him. His muscular
thighs were pressed tightly against her legs, his
hands roving caressingly over her back and down to
her hips, pressing her still closer. Elysia tried to
struggle from his iron-like grip, but he only tightened it until she felt like a part of him. His opened
mouth parted her lips with demand, while one of
his hands moved over her shoulder and down to the
neck of her robe, sliding beneath to the edge of her
nightdress—the flimsy material of little protection
from his searching fingers, as they found and
caressed the soft, warm flesh of her breast.

He stopped abruptly, and picking Elysia up into
his arms, strode from the Library, carrying her
across the Great Hall and up the wide staircase.
Elysia fought frantically with him, aware now of
the full impact of his intentions. She knew that
nothing could stop him from succeeding this time.

"Put me down! Or I'll scream this house down about your damned head!" Elysia threatened as they neared the top of the stairs.

"Go ahead! No one would dare to interfere. I am sole master here—and, master of you, my wife. I have a legal and moral right to do with you as I please." He laughed, sounding diabolical to Elysia's terrified mind.

Elysia beat at his chest and shoulders, striking a hard slap across his face before he shifted her in his arms, securing her flaying arms beneath his—where they remained impotently pinned.

The Marquis' swashbuckling ancestors seemed to look down approvingly as he passed with the struggling girl in his arms; his devilish look matching theirs.

"You beast! Would you rape me? For that is what it will be," she told him in a voice shrill with fear. "Would you force your attentions on an unwilling woman, who would find them repulsive?"

"No, it shall not be rape, Elysia," he said grimly as he freed his hand to open the door to his bedroom, "for I shall make you desire my kisses and caresses until you beg me to take you and make you mine; and by God you shall want me!"

The last thing Elysia saw before he closed the door was the Chinese screen; its lacquered faces staring down grotesquely into her frightened eyes. The thin red lips painted forever into vacuous smiles, and black, slanted eyes staring coldly and expressionlessly into space, the richly-colored Oriental dresses mocking the death-mask faces.

The Marquis threw Elysia down upon the bed and began to strip himself of his pantaloons and shirt. "Don't try it, Elysia," he warned as she made a sudden move to leave the bed, "for there is no escape for you now."

Elysia stared up at his naked body in panic, feeling a terror so deep that her body began to shake uncontrollably. She rolled off the bed, making a run for her bedchamber, but Lord Trevegne moved quickly, grabbing a handful of her long hair as it flew out behind her. Giving it a painful yank, he jerked her back into his arms. "Afraid, my dear? Can't you take the dare—afraid I am right?" he asked quietly as he pulled her out of her robe, the semi-transparent nightdress masking her body until he ripped it from her with one rendering sweep of his long fingers.

He picked her up and threw her onto the bed, following her down, his long lean body pressing hers into the softness of the mattress. Elysia turned her head away from his seeking lips, moving it back and forth on the pillow, until finally, he held it still with his hands while his mouth settled possessively upon her lips.

Elysia felt an engulfing blackness descending down into her consciousness, and the wetness of tears on her cheeks. She was expecting to be hurt and bruised by the punishing force of his kisses—but she wasn't. She felt soft and light nibbles against her vulnerable mouth, tender from his earlier, angry kisses. The pressure deepened—not painfully—but persuasively. Her breathing became his as he continued to kiss her, exploring slowly her mouth, opened to his searching tongue.

She could feel his hands moving down over her body, caressing her flesh in a hypnotic fashion—touching her intimately, and making her body turn traitor to her mind as she felt strange sensations spreading throughout, as he buried his face in her soft hair, entwining it about his neck and shoulders, binding them together. Alex continued his slow, but determined attack on her senses, exploring her until she moaned softly. Elysia felt beyond herself—she no longer had control of her emotions. He was like a master puppeteer, pulling the strings that controlled her every movement, as she involuntarily put her limp arms around his strong neck hugging him closer, moving invitingly beneath him, her movements coming naturally to her in her desire to feel the ultimate pleasure and satisfaction from his lovemaking.

The Marquis gave a deep laugh, full of triumph, as his lips closed down on her parted mouth hungrily, and as she finally kissed him back, giving him eagerly all the sweetness of her mouth.

"Do you want me, Elysia?" he asked thickly, smothering her face in kisses, and waiting for her answer almost breathlessly.

Elysia turned her head, this time she was seeking his lips—to give him his answer as she surrendered her mouth to his deep kiss, which became deeper and deeper until he jerked his mouth away and demanded hoarsely, "Tell me you desire me—want me. Shall I leave you?"

"No," Elysia finally managed to whisper brokenly. "*I want you . . . Alex.*"

Her words seemed to inflame him. "Ah, you shall soon be mine—truly M'Lady, in fact, as well as in name. I've melted that iciness you hide behind. Do you think you could fool me when your hair seems to blaze, and your eyes dare me to make you mine? Oh, M'Lady, you shall soon reap the rewards of your beauty."

"You're a devil," Elysia whispered, aware that she had lost the battle.

"Aye, M'Lady—and I've a devil's desire for you."

He moved then, pressing down upon her as he parted her thighs and entered her, gently, tentatively, until she felt a sharp pain and a building pressure within. He seemed to have no control over himself after he'd merged with her body, only an all-consuming need to satisfy himself.

Elysia lay still. The sound of his breathing next to her matched to her own. His arm moved to encircle her, and pull her beneath him again. She gave a token resistance to his embrace, but he would not be denied.

"This time, M'Lady, you shall equal my desire."

She felt once again the now familiar pressure within her, and his hard body pressing into hers. But this time as he moved against her he created sensations that spread through her body like wild-fire, until she gasped aloud as everything exploded from deep inside her, taking her into a world of such delight and exhilaration that she almost fainted with the excitement of it. He seemed propelled by demons as he loved her into the night and morning—becoming more of her body and soul than she herself. Elysia felt drained of all energy and emotion—as if Alex had absorbed her life force into his body. She felt as if she were dying when he left her.

She lay breathing heavily, tears streaking her face. Elysia turned her head and moved it gently and shyly to lie against his chest. Alex looked down into her face and pulled her closer against his side, smoothing her tangled hair from about her face with a gentle hand. Elysia closed her heavy lids and sighed deeply, feeling oddly comforted. She felt safe, as her hand curled about his neck, she slept.

All the world's a stage,
And all the men and women merely players:
They all have their exits and entrances;
                                    Shakespeare

Chapter 9

Elysia heard the clinking of china and cutlery and burrowed her head into the soft, feather pillow, smothering a yawn.

The chambermaid pulled open the heavy drapes and a shaft of sunlight penetrated into the shadowy room. "It's past eleven, Your Ladyship," Lucy told her, taking the laden breakfast tray from the maid.

Elysia jerked up in dismay. Past eleven! It couldn't be. She looked at the little clock ticking away on the mantel and shook her head in disbelief.

She must have slept like one of the dead. Never before had she slumbered so deeply. Elysia moved to sit up, but shrank back down beneath the coverlet as she became aware of her nakedness. She flushed brightly as she saw her gown draped over a small gilt chair, her robe trailing onto the rug, where it had been dropped by a careless hand.

Lucy intercepted her embarrassed glance, and putting the tray down reached for a frilly, white, bed jacket, tactfully commenting that it was chilly and she might welcome its added warmth. Elysia gratefully slipped into it, and devoted an uncommon amount of attention to her breakfast, forcing herself to eat several mouthfuls of fluffy omelette, until she heard Lucy leave. She looked at the closed door between her room and Alex's. Had she really been in his room last night? Alex—she could now say his name without hesitating and stumbling over it.

Elysia felt a warm blush cover her body as she thought of what had happened last night between them, during that bewitching midnight hour that had seemed to stretch into eternity. She ought to hate him—but she couldn't. He had told her he wouldn't be forcing her to submit to him, and she hadn't. She had willingly given in to his desires—almost equalling them. She could not honestly blame him for what had happened. He would have left her, had she only told him to do so—but she hadn't—she had wanted him to stay. He had sworn he would make her want him, and she had—until she ached. She hadn't thought a woman could feel this way. Maybe it was wrong, this desire she was feeling so deeply inside of her? It couldn't be love— love was different. It was companionship and warmth, and friendship. If they were in love with each other they would have laughed together, and talked until they knew everything about each other. What did she know about her husband? Nothing really. He was rich, he had a brother, was an orphan, and admitted to an unsavory reputation. He could be cruel, sarcastic, cynical and blazingly angry. This was not the kind of man she had always dreamed of falling in love with—and marrying. She felt so confused with these new, and conflicting emotions.

Elysia picked up the delicate, china teacup and took a sip, grimacing as she put the cup of cold hot chocolate back down on the tray. She got out of bed and removed the bedjacket, staring at her slim naked body in the large full-length mirror. She still looked the same—except maybe for a few bluish-purple bruises on her shoulders and breasts. She felt muscles she had not known existed as she moved about the room. She found her gaze constantly drifting to the closed door. Vaguely, she remembered being lifted up and carried in the cool morning air, grumbling because she had been disturbed from her warm bed only to be placed in another one that was not half so warm. She was thankful now, that Alex had returned her to her own bed.

She rang for Lucy, and securely wrapping herself in her robe, walked over to the window and stood staring at the sea—still choppy and unsettled from the storm. Large swells tossed the small fishing boats from the village like toys.

How could she face Alex? What would he be thinking . . . now? She veered away from the intimate details of the evening before. She could envision that derisive smile of his, already—that triumphant gleam in his eyes. She couldn't bear it if he said anything that would degrade what had happened between them.

Elysia looked worriedly into the distance, wondering how she could successfully carry off their ultimate meeting. Should she feign indifference—cool disdain—coolness over something that had shattered her life—changed her for all time? She was no longer an innocent girl. She was a woman—Alex's woman—and he was a very demanding lover.

Elysia's attention was caught by a movement on the road in the distance. A bright yellow and red curricle was racing uncontrollably up the road, pulled by a pair of very high-stepping bays, and tooled by a very busy gentleman trying to stop them as they hurled into the courtyard below. In the distance, Elysia could see another conveyance, traveling more sedately as it made its way slowly along the rutted road. The first gentleman, of the flashy curricle, had managed to stop his pair with the help of the stableboys, and was now looking about nervously, while pacing back and forth in apparent indecision.

Elysia quickly went to her wardrobe and grabbed

the first dress she saw and hurriedly began to dress, anxious to know what was going on outside. With Lucy's expert help and efficient hands, and her own impatient proddings, Elysia was dressed and on her way downstairs within ten minutes or so, her hair pulled back into curls and tied with a yellow, gauze ribbon that matched the yellow, muslin dress and slippers, and the flowered, silk shawl draped carelessly over her shoulders.

There was a flurry of activity in the Great Hall below. Elysia called to Browne, his usual calmness having deserted him as he hurried past with his white hair ruffled and standing up in tufts, his mouth working soundlessly in agitation.

Something dreadful must have happened to cause Browne to lose control—a control he had probably kept for over fifty years without ever losing. Only one thing could cause it to disintegrate—and that was if something had happened to the Marquis. Alex must be injured, or in some difficulty, Elysia thought in panic. She hurried to the big double doors, and forgetting her previous decision of indifference, flew out the doors like a small whirlwind, her fringed shawl floating about her.

Charles Lackton turned at the sound of approaching footsteps, and stood spellbound as he stared at the flying figure. He had been prepared to face Lord Trevegne, but not this extraordinary yellow-clad figure that seemed to be about to attack him. He took a hasty step backwards in retreat.

The figure halted in front of him and he found his

sleeve clutched in two shaking hands. He stared increduously down into a white face with luminous green eyes.

"What has happened? Is it Alex—he's not hurt?" Elysia choked, staring up imploringly at this young gentleman with the bright red hair and somewhat frightened look on his face.

"Lord Trevegne?" Charles asked in puzzlement. Was he ill too? And who was this woman? he thought in wonder. He noticed her beauty for the first time—now that he was safe from attack. "As far as I know he is just—"

"Fine," came a deep voice from behind, and turning, Elysia saw her husband standing next to them, giving her a searching look, mingled with surprise.

"I had no idea you cared, M'Lady," he whispered for her ears alone, but his golden eyes seemed to soften as they stared down into her worried ones. "Charles, what brings you here?" Lord Trevegne demanded, not at all anxious for house guests.

"It's—" he began, but was interrupted by the arrival of the other coach entering the courtyard, and pulling up next to where they were standing.

"What the devil!" Alex said, recognizing his own coach. "I'll have a few answers, Charles, if you please," he added in a dangerous tone, only to stare in dismay as the door of the coach opened to reveal a head with curly black hair, and a gaunt white face with feverish, bright, blue eyes. "Peter!" Alex shouted in surprise, his eyes quickly taking in his brother's unhealthy pallor and empty sleeve. He reached the lurching figure before it fell, and yelling to Lackton for assistance, managed to carry Peter's limp form into the Great Hall.

Elysia followed the three men—temporarily forgotten. So this was Alex's brother, Peter. He didn't look at all well. She hurried after them into the hall, and stood silently as two footmen and Lord Trevegne carried Peter Trevegne up the long flight of stairs, leaving a bemused Charles Lackton standing at the foot, helplessly.

"Is there anything I can do to help?" Elysia asked as Dany hurried by carrying a loaded tray, full of bandages and medicinal-looking dark bottles.

"Ach, no, I've cared for these two when they be in worse scrapes, and they be tougher than leather," she said confidently, even though there was a worried look in her brown eyes. "Ye might help the young gentleman here, Lady Elysia. For I don't rightly think he'll make it," she added giving a professional look at Charles' grayish face, and the beads of perspiration dotting his upper lip, before continuing up the stairs to Peter's room with her doctoring skills.

"Please, will you come into the salon and have a cup of tea—or a drink," Elysia added wisely, smiling at the bewildered young man, "for I am quite certain that you could do with something bracing."

He followed her like a lost puppy into the salon where they sat in an uneasy silence, each with his own thoughts to keep him company. Charles gulped down the brandy Elysia ordered for him, while she sat quietly sipping her own cup of fragrant tea.

"How seriously is he injured?" Elysia finally asked when the young man seemed to have regained his composure—half of which he must have lost while tooling the curricle and wild bays. And from what Elysia had seen from her window, he had been sadly out of control most of the time—no wonder he was badly shaken.

"Pretty bad—a hole that big, I'll wager," he answered shaping his hands into a small circle.

"A hole?" Elysia looked confused—not understanding this fiery-headed, young gentleman in his bright, canary-yellow- and turquoise-striped waistcoat and plum colored cutaway coat. She watched hypnotically the elaborate tassels swinging to and fro on his Hessians, as he swung his legs distractingly.

"In his shoulder—just missed his heart—lucky to be alive at all. Doctor had to dig the shot out—took a hell of a long time doing it too," he stopped abruptly, and looking embarrassed apologized, "Please forgive me. Didn't mean to swear." He continued to look at her wonderingly, and then blurted, "I do beg your pardon, but, who are you?"

Elysia smiled in amusement. "I am Lady Trevegne, and I'm afraid that I do not know who you are either, so you have nothing to apologize for."

He stood up quickly, looking like a flustered schoolboy. "Your pardon, Lady Trevegne," he said as if he couldn't believe his eyes. "I'm Charles Lackton—a friend of the family, and it is an honor to make your acquaintance." He bowed elegantly over her hand, a lock of bright red hair dangling over his forehead.

"Forgot about that—quite a jolt to hear of His Lordship's marriage—surprised all of London. Couldn't believe it."

"Yes, it was quite a surprise to everyone," Elysia agreed, not adding herself included. "How did Peter wound himself? Was it a hunting accident?"

"Wasn't an accident—a duel."

"A duel!" Elysia repeated horrified.

"Yes, Peter did himself and Lord Trevegne proud. Honor to be his friend," Charles spoke proudly.

"But why? What caused this—duel?" Elysia asked curiously.

"Well, you see ... ah," Charles hedged uncomfortably, "it's not really something one can tell a lady about. But it was a point of honor that had to be satisfied. I was Peter's second."

"And what happened to the man he challenged?"

"Dead."

"Peter killed him?" Elysia asked in disbelief.

"Had to—Beckingham cheated—fired before the end of the count," Charles said with obvious disgust.

"Beckingham? You did say Beckingham?" Elysia asked faintly. "Not Sir Jason Beckingham."

"Yes, that's the one—a real outsider, and a coward. Good riddance I say!" Charles spoke vehemently, a look of distaste on his handsome and open face.

Elysia carefully placed her cup down on the tea caddy, her hand shaking almost uncontrollably. So Sir Jason was dead. She had hated him—but she had not wished him dead. She had indeed been worried about his knowledge of the circumstances of their marriage, and what an unscrupulous person like Sir Jason could do with the information to cause further embarrassment to them. However, she believed Alex would certainly have dealt effectively with him—or would he have? After all this young man, Charles Lackton, had said that Sir Jason had cheated and fired first. Alex could very easily have been killed—or wounded like his brother. Yes, it was just as well— God forgive her—that Sir Jason was no longer a danger to them.

"If Sir Jason fired before the end of the count, I believe you said, then how did Peter manage to shoot him?" Elysia now asked Charles who had been sitting silently, staring at Elysia with a moon-struck look on his boyish face, and he blushed a dull red as Elysia caught him out.

"Well, Sir Jason had a somewhat unsavory reputation concerning several duels he had won under rather odd circumstances. So we were expecting something underhanded, and I told Peter to watch me and if I noticed anything odd, I would signal him. So when Beckingham turned before the end of the count, I could scarcely believe it—even though I was expecting it!" Charles looked shamefacedly at

Elysia. "So . . . I was a little slow in signalling and Beckingham got his shot off, but Peter had already turned at my warning, and it only caught him in the shoulder—instead of through the heart as Beckingham had intended. Peter got his shot off anyway, and it killed Beckingham instantly. But you know, it was strange. He had a smile on his face even in death," Charles said shuddering as if someone had walked over his grave.

Peter controlled the shudder of pain that shot through him as Alex and the footmen carefully lowered him onto the bed.

"Are you all right, Peter?" Alex asked worriedly. critically running his eye over his brother's shirt which was beginning to show a seepage of bright red blood where his wound had opened again.

Peter gave a pitiful attempt at a smile which was little more than a grimace. "I'm not dead yet—take more than a coward's hand and these ham-fisted footmen to finish me off."

He was interrupted by an involuntary groan as Dany cut away his shirt and bandage, exposing the wound—raw and angry-looking, but clean in his shoulder.

"Now, Dany, what are you poking around at?" he demanded as Dany probed his wound. "The doctor took care of it. I should know—it hurt enough," he complained.

"And I'll have no bairn of mine not properly

cared for. Them London doctors haven't a lick of
sense. So ye just let Dany take care of this, and
we'll see who knows what's best for ye," she said
huffily, applying an evil-smelling concoction and
re-wrapping his shoulder with clean strips of cloth.

"You should know better by now than to argue
with Dany, Peter," Alex laughed, and then wrinkled
his nose as he caught a whiff of her homemade
salve. "Remind me not to get too close next time I
visit," he said with a mock shudder of revulsion.

"Well, how do you think I feel with this obnoxious stuff plastered to me?" Peter demanded indignantly, giving his brother a helpless look.

"Now, ye just lie back and I'll have ye a good
bowl of soup," Dany promised ignoring his request
for a stiff brandy, while she busily fluffed up the pillows behind his shoulders, and straightened the
bedclothes with mother hen admonitions to keep
quiet while she prepared the special healing brew.

After she left, Alex sat down on a small chair he'd
pulled up, and gave his brother a hard look. "Hurts
like hell, doesn't it?" he commiserated sympathetically, but with an undercurrent of anger threaded in
his voice from the concern and shock he had suffered at seeing his brother's condition. "If you do
not feel like talking I'll leave, but I should be interested in what the blazes happened to you. For that
is a gunshot wound, if I'm not mistaken?"

"No, don't go, for I need to talk, Alex," Peter
hesitated, and then blurted out in an anguished
voice, "I've killed a man!"

"Did you?" Alex remarked casually. Masking his surprise, he continued in an undisturbed tone, "I'm sure you had reason."

"Oh, yes, I'm no murderer! It was a question of honor, Alex, but ..." A tortured look entered his eyes as he stared at his brother. "I don't feel good about it. I have always dreamed of defending our honor and name in a duel—but now that I've taken another man's life ... I merely feel sickened by it all." He hung his head in dejection, a flush of embarrassment and fever coloring his face.

Alex leaned forward and grasped Peter's chin with his fingers, pulling his face upwards so he could look directly into his brother's eyes.

"Now listen to me, Peter. No gentleman feels gladness after taking another man's life—regardless of the insult or crime. You would indeed be sick if you rejoiced at killing another human being. You had no other choice. If you had not been the victor—then the other man would have been. Someone must lose, and in a situation such as this—where no other course is open to you—then you fight to win, and to live, Peter," Alex told his brother sternly. "Always fight to win."

"I suppose you are right, Alex, but I never thought I would feel bad about it—like a woman with my feelings—wanting to cry," he admitted feeling more foolish than ever. "You have always seemed so strong and victorious after your duels— you never feel any regrets or remorse. So I thought my feelings were wrong—like those of a coward."

"No, Peter. You have the heart of an honest and compassionate man—and those are the true feelings." He looked at his brother curiously. "Do you really believe that I feel no remorse after I have cut another man down? I feel it, Peter, believe me, I feel it deeply. I am so accustomed to masking my thoughts and feelings, that I show an unmarred countenance to the world. But it hurts inside—it can tear me apart.

"Sometimes though, one finds that one is trapped by the conventions of society, and there is no other method of dealing with a situation. There will always be others who will inevitably force your hand, and at these times it is necessary to defend your name and honor by duelling. Regretful, yes—but necessary I'm afraid. However, I would caution you not to allow that course of action to rule your life. Be the master of your fate, not the victim."

"Well, that is a relief. I thought I'd become a milk-livered, faint heart," Peter said, feeling as if a weight had been lifted from his shoulders. "Yet I would have a word with you. You made me look the laughing stock of London, Alex! Why, I was the last to know you had wed! Every chimney sweep and footman's daughter knew of it before I did!" Peter said in a grieved tone. "Had to read about it in the Gazette. First there were those damnable rumors spreading like the plague about you and some high-born wench in an inn, that really set their tongues a-wagging, and then the news that you had wed! Well, that caught me broadside, I can tell you." He looked doubtfully at Alex. "You are married?"

"Yes. Very much so," Alex answered, an expression of pleased remembrance on his hawk-like features.

"I still can't believe it. You of all people! And you didn't even tell me, Alex. Except for some talk about leaving London because you were fed up with it all—knew that couldn't be true, never believed a word of it—you would've left me in the dark too. Planning all along to marry the girl, weren't you? Do I know her?"

"No you don't, but you shall soon have that pleasure," Alex promised.

"I hear she is a beauty. But that doesn't surprise me, knowing your tastes."

"Yes, Elysia is quite beautiful, in an unusual way. And not in the accepted standard of beauty which is now the rage in London for sweet, blue-eyed, angelic blondes. I find myself married to a real she-devil with emerald-green eyes and wild, red-gold hair—and a temper and tongue to match," he reflected with obvious pleasure at the combination.

"Not too much for you to handle, I'll wager," Peter said confidently, knowing of his brother's somewhat dictatorial and domineering ways, always expecting to get his way. But there was a puzzled look in his blue eyes as he looked at him.

"I sometimes wonder," Alex said ruminatively, shaking his dark head.

"I still feel in the dark about it all. Don't know

how you met, but if you were planning to wed when you left London ... then all those rumors can't be true—despite what the Joker said," Peter commented stoutly. There was still some doubt in his mind as to exactly what had happened, yet he was reluctant to discuss it with Alex, due to the delicacy of the matter. Yet he couldn't seem to stop himself from saying, "But the coloring *is* the same as that other girl ..."

"Beckingham? Now just what did that swine have to impart to you?" Alex asked in a cold voice, his lips curling in distaste at the mere utterance of the name.

"Well, I wasn't going to tell you because I wasn't sure if it was false or true—either way it's a hell of a thing to ask you about. I could see no other way but to challenge him. If what he told me was true then he deserved to die for his infamous trick, and if merely a rumor, then for making slanderous accusations against you."

"You duelled with Beckingham!" Alex was surprised out of his habitual coolness, for once.

"Yes, who else? No reason to shoot anyone else, have I?" Peter asked doubtfully.

"So ... you killed Beckingham!"

"Yes, that's what I've been trying to tell you. He said some pretty inflammatory things to me—in private—and I thought it my duty to deal with him. You know, I think he actually wanted me to challenge him—I couldn't very well not, after what he had told me. He wanted me dead for some reason,"

Peter said in puzzlement. "Never bore him any ill-will, you know, so I don't know why he should have had it in for me."

"He hated me, Peter, and he probably hoped to kill you. Knowing how close we are, he would have known it would hurt me deeply. Unfortunately for him, he failed," Alex explained, seeing for the first time the hatred Sir Jason must have felt towards him.

"Well, he very nearly didn't—he cheated, and shot first. Just luck, and a suspicion he might be up to something kept him from putting a shot through my heart. I owe my life to Charles. If he hadn't warned me, I'd be beyond the grave right now," Peter expostulated grimly.

Alex looked at his brother fondly, knowing how close he had come to losing him. "Well, you've managed to settle the score for me with Beckingham, Peter. I'm grateful, however I regret that it was at the expense of your shoulder."

"Glad to have been of service to you, Alex," Peter replied proudly, some of the throbbing pain in his shoulder lessening under his brother's praise. "When do I meet the new Lady Trevegne?"

"Soon enough. You must rest now, or Dany will have my skin," Alex said as he heard her skirts rustling behind him. She entered the room with a tray upon which sat a bowl of steaming broth.

"But I have a thousand questions to ask you, Alex! Please don't go," Peter beseeched as Alex walked towards the door.

"Ye just sit back now, Master Peter, and ye be getting yesel' out of here, Lord Alex. Ye've already been too long—now get along," she commanded him in a strict voice, reminding him of the schoolroom.

"I can't argue with that disciplinary voice, Peter," he said, making his retreat, leaving Peter struggling ineffectively against Dany's ministrations.

Alex walked slowly down the stairs thinking of Peter's pale face. His fist clenched as he thought of Beckingham's double treachery. He almost wished him from the grave so he could have the pleasure of killing him and sending him back to it again.

He shook his head in disbelief. He'd had no idea that Beckingham had hated him so vehemently. The man must have been insane. He shrugged his shoulders, mentally shaking himself free from the thoughts of Beckingham.

Alex entered the salon where he heard voices. He stood unnoticed just inside the door, silently watching his wife who was avidly listening to young Lackton excitedly retell his tale of adventure. He smiled crookedly as he saw her shocked expressions of disbelief and horror at Charles' vivid recollections. He raised an eyebrow in amusement as he watched a look of rapture finally settle on the young man's face as he continued to stare in ill-disguised admiration at Elysia who was sitting attractively across from him. She gave the impression of being completely untouchable—securely wrapped in her own cocoon of thoughts, and letting none enter—

however close they might have gotten to her physically.

He moved forward into the room, startling the two of them from their conversation. "It would seem that Peter owes you his life, and I owe you a debt of gratitude Charles," Alex said sincerely shaking the young man's hand firmly.

"It was nothing, really," Charles confessed gruffly, feeling a head taller from the unaccustomed warmth from Lord Trevegne. "Just doing what's right and proper for a friend."

"We are proud, and fortunate, to have you as a friend, Charles, and I am confident that I speak for all of us. We are indeed grateful for what you have done. Are we not, Elysia?" He sent a look of innocent inquiry to Elysia, who returned it calmly, without a flicker of emotion on her face.

"Indeed we are, Alex, but tell me of Peter. How is he?"

Alex poured himself a brandy and walked over to the fireplace and leant negligently against it, his arm upon the mantelpiece.

"He will survive," he answered grimly, "but he will need plenty of rest, and this will be the best place for his recuperation. If that madcap journey from London didn't finish him off, then I seriously doubt whether anything could." He shook his head, as if contemplating that painful journey in the coach for Peter, and the frightening journey for Lackton at the reins of the curricle.

Elysia stood up as if to leave the room. Excusing

herself she said, "I shall send our regrets to the Blackmores for this evening, and—"

"No, we might as well attend, since there is little we can do for Peter here. Dany will handle all of his needs. She practically ran me out of his room and he must already be sleeping like a baby. For Dany prepared her special recuperative broth, which she was spooning into his mouth as I left, so I doubt whether we shall hear a sigh from him." He looked at Charles, who was beginning to show the strain from his journey. "Charles, you will stay with us for awhile," Alex said, making it a statement rather than a question.

"Thank you, Your Lordship, it will be a pleasure, but if you will excuse me I must change, for I fear I am indeed offensive, as I am covered with mud," he apologized. He quickly left the room, anxious to clean himself up and rest, and especially to try his hand at tying the intricate folds of the new design of Lord Trevegne's cravat.

Elysia hesitated uncertainly. This was the first time she'd been alone with him since last night. She decided she would make a dignified retreat, and began to walk towards the door.

"M'Lady," he said quietly, moving from his position in front of the fire.

Elysia turned as he approached. "Yes, M'Lord," she replied softly, uncertain of herself.

"I should like a good morning kiss," Alex said taking Elysia into his arms, and placing his firm mouth against her trembling lips. He kissed her deeply and the fires re-kindled instantly as she responded to his caresses. "You see, you need not have feared me. I'm not quite the ogre you would believe of me, M'Lady." He smiled down into her green eyes.

"No, M'Lord. I think perhaps you aren't," Elysia agreed as she gave herself up to his hungry kisses, until a knock on the door and a footman announcing luncheon broke them apart.

"I do not hunger for the tender meat of a pheasant, M'Lady," Alex said softly as he escorted Elysia to the door, his meaning very clear in his passion-darkened golden eyes.

In Xanadu did Kubla Khan
A stately pleasure dome decree:
Where Alph, the sacred river, ran
Through caverns measureless to man
  Down to a sunless sea.

                              Coleridge

Chapter 10

The carriage conveying Elysia, Lord Trevegne and
Charles Lackton, rolled up the tree-bordered drive
to the home of Squire Blackmore. Blackmore Hall
sat in all its glory and ostentatiousness at the head
of the gravelled drive. A combination of all
architectural styles of the day was represented in its
design. Gothic towers loomed over Chinese-styled
cupolas copied from the Prince of Wales Pavilion in
Brighton, and fought with Indian facades and

254

Greek columns. The hall was lighted by what seemed to be thousands of torches placed in front of the entrance illuminating it like a noonday sun.

Elysia gasped aloud in utter disbelief.

"Yes, it's rather overpowering," Alex commented drily. "It really is quite distressing—even worse by day. The original structure was a small manor house which the Squire bought a few years ago and built onto. As you can see, he gave little thought to cost—or apparently to taste. But wait for the *coupe de grâce*, M'Lady."

Charles Lackton was craning his head out the window. He turned and stared at them, his mouth gaping. "I can't believe it! This is fantastic. I've seen the Prince's place in Brighton, but this—this is just like being in China!" Charles exclaimed with excitement.

Alex looked at Elysia in despair. "Spare us the impulsiveness of youth, that any more of these ..." he paused as if searching for an appropriate word to describe Blackmore Hall, " ... atrocities may not be perpetrated on this sacred land of England."

Elysia laughed in agreement. "In fact, M'Lord, it should be against the law, and carry a strict penalty. You will of course, mention it in the House of Lords next time you attend?" Elysia asked innocently, a sparkle of mischief in her eyes.

"Most definitely, M'Lady, for how can I, a peer of the realm, allow such a thing to exist on my very own doorstep?" he mocked, as Charles stared on in confusion at this by-play.

As their carraige halted, the Squire's footmen descended upon them like a swarm of bees, and escorted them into the noisy hall. Dominating the center of it was an elaborately-decorated, bubbling fountain with dolphins spurting water, and mermaids reclining gracefully about the basin, and seats fashioned out of stone into giant shells and lily pads. The whole fountain seemed gilded in gold, and Elysia glanced at Alex's amused expression as he watched her reaction.

"Quite a *tour de force*, M'Lord," she said.

"Quite, M'Lady. Would you like me to build one for you?" the Marquis asked innocently with a wicked gleam in his eyes.

"How did you guess, M'Lord? I quite see it in your study," Elysia retorted with a straight face.

"You wound me deeply, M'Lady," he murmured as they greeted their host.

Squire Blackmore welcomed them with a beaming smile, effusively thanking them for joining the party. He was a jovial host, eager to see to all of his guests' needs, feeling personally responsible for entertaining each and every one. His yellow breeches, red satin coat, and bright-green vest could be spotted everywhere among the crowd—outshining even the elaborate dressings of the Squire's dandified London guests.

What Mrs. Blackmore, the Squire's self-effacing little wife thought, one could not tell, for she said little, and was seen even less. She was small and plain, dressed in mauve with a small, pearl brooch her only adornment. She was a startling contrast to her peacock husband who strutted about in all his finery, diamonds and rubies glittering among his pudgy fingers.

Elysia caught a glimpse of herself and Alex in one of the many floor-to-ceiling mirrors. They looked an attractive couple, she could not help but think, as her eyes wandered proudly over Alex's dark-red coat and white, satin breeches, and silver, brocade vest. A large, blood-red ruby glowed darkly among the folds of his snowy-white cravat.

Elysia's green eyes stared back at her from the glass and seemed to rival the sea-green dress that floated about her with each step. Its interwoven golden threads looked like sprinkled stardust casually thrown by the hand of a playful fairy. Gold ribbons were tied beneath her breasts and threaded behind to disappear beneath the gauzy train falling off her shoulders and down her back. Her hand strayed to the shining green stones encircling her throat.

The Trevegne emeralds—magnificent jewels that hung like a ring of green fire around her neck, adorning her arms like entwining snakes, and winking like cat's eyes in her ears and scattered through her hair.

Alex had brought the jewels, enshrined in a gold-encrusted case, into her bedchamber as she dressed—placing the case carefully in her hands. Her look of astonishment and pleasure when she opened the latched lid and stared speechlessly down at the glowing gems on a bed of white velvet had pleased Alex. Particularly when she admired their settings and disclaiming the idea he suggested of changing them to a modern design—preferring the original design, that had been in his family for generations.

The Marquis had given her an odd look—smiling to himself over her words as if at some private joke. She was unaware of the Trevegne legend, handed down from generation to generation of Trevegne men, predicting a fertile and blissful union for the master and his bride, should the emeralds remain unaltered—retaining their original appearance, as seen in the portrait of the first Lady Trevegne.

Elysia could now see Charles Lackton's bright-blue coat among a group of people reflected in the mirror. She glanced about the crowded room full of chattering people, looking for Louisa Blackmore. But Elysia couldn't see her among the colorful throng of people crowding close to offer their congratulations to the Marquis, and to get a glance of the woman who had finally captured the elusive Lord Trevegne.

She suffered the inquisitive glances, sly and knowing, tinged with a hint of jealousy and malice from the women, and admiring and friendly from the gentlemen. They flirted outrageously with her when Alex was out of hearing. Their glances lingered on her bright hair, magnolia-soft shoulders, and swell of breasts revealed by the décolletage of her gown. Elysia felt half-naked by the cut of bodice and the fragile semi-transparency of the material, until she saw some of the dresses the other ladies were wearing. The transparency of their gowns revealed every curve and line and movement of their perfumed bodies.

Elysia searched around the room for Alex. Finally she saw him in conversation across the room with several gentlemen and a beautiful woman in a glittering gold dress. Diamonds dripped from her neck and arms, while a tiara of diamonds nestled in her dark hair. She was unbelievably alluring and Elysia wondered who she was as she watched her husband laugh at some remark of hers, inclining his head to hear what she was whispering into his ear, her fingers caressing his sleeve intimately.

Elysia abruptly turned away, accepting a goblet of iced champagne from a footman, feeling an unsettling emotion inside of her at seeing Alex with another woman. She took a sip of the bubbly liquid and smiled at the attentive young bucks trying to engage her in conversation, half-listening to them as her eyes constantly strayed to the two people conversing in the corner.

The whole room seemed to be gilded; in fact, it was a mansion of gold glittering against gold, illuminated by the enormous, crystal chandeliers that nearly blinded one with their brightness. Blackmore Hall had none of the aged mellowness and charm of Westerly, with its weathered walls, warmly aged wood, and remembrances of past generations stamped upon it. There the past was a part of the present.

Elysia glanced about her at the garishly-printed wallpaper. Every available space was occupied by tables with vases and busts and priceless *objets d'art*, sofas, cabinets, and chairs of the most outlandish design. Everything bespoke newness, the vivid colors clashing with each other. Blackmore Hall was gaudy in its flamboyance and extravagance—like an overdressed kept-woman, wearing all her trinkets in her insecurity.

Elysia felt a hand on her arm and turned to see Louisa Backmore standing beside her. She was wearing a demure, white, muslin gown, with a single string of pearls clasped about her neck. She looked frail and angelic—like a dove that did not belong among this menagerie of colorful and exotic creatures.

"I'm so glad you've come," Louisa said breathlessly, taking Elysia's arm and guiding her away from the group of surrounding people.

"And I am glad to see you. Yours is the first familiar face I've met," Elysia replied. "I shall commit a *faux pas* soon, for I've been introduced to so many Lord so-and-so's and Sir this-and that, that my head is aswirl with names and faces that do not match."

"I never do know with whom I am conversing, but then they very seldom know who I am either," Louisa said, shrugging without resentment.

"Ah, Lady Trevegne," Squire Blackmore interrupted, "you are indeed looking exquisite, if I may compliment you. Louisa," he said directing a stern look at his daughter, "you must not monopolize our guest of honor. I have warned you repeatedly of this. She is not interested in you—now go see to your duties."

"Yes, Papa," Louisa answered apologetically, drifting off before Elysia could stop her retreat.

"Your daughter had been graciously entertaining me, Squire Blackmore," Elysia defended her friend, resenting the Squire's bullying attitude.

"Yes, yes, but she is a tiresome child at times," he explained, his eyes riveted to Elysia's emeralds. "Those are the Trevegne emeralds are they not?" he said as he gazed covetously at the jewels.

"Darling, aren't you going to introduce *me* to the new Lady Trevegne?" a drawling, feminine voice spoke from behind them.

Elysia turned to face the dark-haired, golden-clad figure she had watched earlier amusing Alex.

"Of course, I had not realized that you had not been introduced. Lady Trevegne, allow me to introduce Lady Mariana Woodley, the toast of London," he said ingratiatingly, in honey-tongued tones.

"Only in London?" Lady Mariana teased the Squire, but her smile was slightly forced as she stared at Elysia's beauty—and the emeralds that she felt should rightfully have belonged to her.

Elysia smiled at the beautiful Lady Woodley, and received a slight smile in return. Then she felt her own smile freeze upon her lips, as she read the blatant hatred and jealousy in the flashing brown eyes—their murderous message obvious. Elysia glanced about—feeling desperate to find Alex. She felt a shiver run up her spine as Lady Woodley flicked her fan in agitation.

"We were all quite surprised to hear that Alex had gotten himself a wife," Lady Mariana said, making it sound like something distasteful. "Alex is—or was—such a *roué*. I wonder if he will change his ways, or have you successfully chained him to your bed?" she demanded brazenly.

Elysia raised her chin higher as she felt a slow anger begin to burn inside her at the other woman's crudeness.

"Alex is quite a man. There will be quite a few cold beds in London now that he is out of circulation," Lady Woodley added maliciously, a sly look in her eyes.

"And will yours be one of the empty ones, Lady Woodley?" Elysia asked sweetly, unable to control her smouldering temper any longer.

Lady Woodley gasped as Elysia's barb scored a hit and she slightly raised her fan as if to strike, when Alex appeared and stepped between them nonchalantly.

"I see you are becoming acquainted with one another," he said smoothly, noticing Elysia's flushed cheeks and flashing green eyes, and the sullen look on Mariana's face. "I want you to meet someone, my dear," he said, guiding Elysia away smoothly. "Lady Woodley, if you will excuse us."

"One of your *amours*, M'Lord?" Elysia asked curiously, forcing her voice to sound casual.

"Possibly. Not jealous are you, M'Lady?"

"Not at all, M'Lord. Although I am told there are a number who will be."

Lord Trevegne laughed heartily, drawing the attention of several people, surprise on their faces at seeing the haughty Marquis laugh. "I seem to recall a line from an unknown poet that expresses my sentiments exactly. Let me see ... how does that go?" he paused thoughtfully, "ah, yes, it begins 'You must sit down, says Love, and taste my meat.' Do you agree?" He looked at her provocatively. "I'm not the one to turn down an invitation to dine—especially if it is well-prepared."

"Are you sure, M'Lord, you did not just happen to think that up one evening in one of your clubs, after boredom and drink had claimed your wits?"

"Ah, you've a genius for making light of my finer accomplishments," he grinned.

"I wasn't aware that you had any, M'Lord."

"I need never fear hearing honeyed words full of cajolery from you, M'Lady—but remind me never to ask you to deliver a eulogy for me, or indeed I shall be damned and sent straight to hell."

With that parting shot he left her with the Squire, who escorted her into dinner. Elysia found herself seated on the right of her host, and Alex opposite her on the Squire's left. The only two people with whom Elysia thought she could have enjoyed the dinner, were lost to her view down the great length of table among the other guests. Charles and Louisa were placed at the end with the less important personages.

Elysia avoided looking across the table where Alex was sitting with Lady Woodley next to him—a smug look on her beautiful face. Like the cat that swallowed the canary—and would choke on it, Elysia thought, as she watched Lady Woodley flirt playfully with Alex. Elysia's eyes narrowed as she stared at the dark-haired woman in speculation. So . . . she was a widow. The Squire had been a fountain of information—especially about the lovely widow who was a favorite of his and was considered a *nonpareil* in London. And, it was obvious even to the casual observer, that the Widow was interested in Alex—and knew him quite well.

"Please to allow me to speak to you. This r-roast beef, *c'est magnifique, n'est-ce pas?*" The Frenchman sitting next to Elysia started a conversation, half in French, half in English. His accent was thick, and he rolled his R's off his tongue in a rhythmic fashion. "*Viola*, Lady Trevegne!" he declared theatrically as he passed her the salt.

"*Merci monsieur, mais je ne sais pas vôtre nom?*" Elysia apologized for not knowing his name, her French accent perfect.

A look of utter delight passed over the young Frenchman's dark features. "Ah, *Madame, vous êtes enchantée,*" he crooned. "*Je suis* Jean-Claude D'Aubergere, Comte de Cantere. To speak to me in my native tongue gives me such pleasure. I feel not so

264

much the foreigner here in this cold land—it warms me as if I were back under the sunny skies of France. For this gesture, Madame, *je suis vôtre servant dévoué*. You are the beautiful Lady Trevegne, of course. We were introduced—but I do not think you remember so insignificant a Frenchman," he said sadly.

"Oh, but I do remember you, Comte, for you most opportunely interrupted a tiresome monologue on the finer points of embroidery by the Vicar's wife."

"Then, it was my pleasure to rescue you from *cette dame formidable*," he grinned engagingly. "It is kind of you, Lady Trevegne, to take pity on this sad Frenchman, who is homesick for the sounds of his homeland. Your enchanting voice reminds me of other *mademoiselles*, laughing and chatting in gaiety. But alas, it is no more," he said shrugging his shoulders in a very Gallic manner. "*C'est un tragédie, et maintenant, je suis un* beggar."

"You are an *émigré*, Count. It must be difficult for you here in England. But you mustn't consider yourself a beggar. Were your estates confiscated?"

"*Vraiment*," he sighed, "that is unfortunately the sad truth for me. And now *Le Petit Corporal* has ruined any hopes I had cherished of returning to my home."

"Napoleon!" a shrill voice echoed from the Comte's other side. "*Monsieur le Comte*, do you believe he will attack London?"

The other guests near them stopped their light chattering to listen to the Count's reply to the question asked by the nervous-looking gentleman with the high, stiff, pointed collar that stood up starchily about his chin, withstanding his futile efforts to turn his head.

"*Non*, this I do not believe. *Je pense qu'il est un rumeur*. He is not strong enough this '*bourgeois Général*' to conquer the strong-hearted *Anglaise*, *non?*"

A loud cheer of stout approval was sent up along with numerous toasts to England and the King, and anything else that entered some guest's mind.

"I doubt whether Napoleon would seriously try it. We've the strongest navy in the world, and you must remember Napoleon is fighting on many fronts. We have only the Channel as a serious threat. He would not dare to attack from the North Sea with winter coming on, if indeed, he is of a right mind—which I sometimes suspect he isn't." Lord Trevegne spoke quietly, in a bored voice, selecting a small pheasant from a platter a footman held.

"But here along the coast we are so unprotected. T-those French could come across the Channel and murder us in our beds before we could even open our eyes!" the Vicar's wife added hysterically, as several voices chimed agreement.

"Nonsense!" Squire Blackmore said vehemently. "The Navy wouldn't allow it. Damn fine bunch of men." He flushed, and glanced about apologetically. "Your pardon, ladies, but it gets my blood to boil to hear us talkin' scared."

"Navy too busy trackin' down smugglers to catch any Froggie sailor that sails up the Thames, even. Probably think they were actors from Covent Garden, putting on a performance," someone from down the table drawled in a bored voice, as loud guffaws followed his comments.

Elysia glanced at the Count, whose lips had tightened at the derogatory reference to French people, his chin lifting higher in arrogance.

"You mustn't allow them to offend you, Count," Elysia spoke sympathetically, placing her hand on his arm, feeling the rigid muscles, "I do believe they hide their fears with laughter."

He stared into her large, green eyes with their softened expression and friendliness, and raised her hand to his lips with a dark glow in his Latin eyes.

"Thank you. *Vous êtes une ange, et je t'adore,*" he breathed softly, passionately under his breath, as his fingers tightened over hers.

Elysia gently loosed her hand from his, and looked away from his amorous gaze with embarrassment straight into Alex's angry, golden eyes as he watched her intently, a frown drawing together his heavy, black brows.

"If it were not for smugglers you'd not be sipping that excellent brandy you have in your cellars," the Marquis commented sarcastically, to no one in particular, "nor that fine tea your lady sips elegantly in her salon."

"I'll wager you've a few renegade bottles tucked away," a dissipated-looking man added slyly.

"Hardly. You insult me, Lord Tanvil, for I only drink what was set down by my father, and my grandfather before him. Can you imagine my drinking anything more recent? You do me an injury," he declared in mock affront.

"Trevegne'd probably have the effrontery to invite Napoleon to sample some of Louis XVI's finest brandy. Wasn't your family given a case from Versailles?"

"Well don't let Prinny know about it, or His Royal Highness will have it for himself," Lord Trevegne said among the laughter, and then added as an afterthought, "and, on the day Napoleon sits down to dine at Carlton House, I'll give everyone here a bottle of that very excellent brandy." A chorus of acceptances followed his offer, and other wagers of ridiculous notions were added to it.

"Well, I think a lot of this talk of invasion and smugglers is a storm in a teacup," the Squire's voice filled the silence when the laughter had died down. "Can't be as many of them rascals smuggling about as people say—about as true as a traveler's tale. The way people talk you'd think everyone was a smuggler. Why, I might even be one," he laughed in disbelief at the absurdity of the idea.

"With your sense of direction you'd probably end up in Marseilles rather than Dover," someone predicted as uproarious laughter engulfed the table.

After that, the conversation changed as often as the many dishes that were brought in. If it had not been for the attentions of the Count and Alex, Elysia doubted whether she would have tasted anything, what with everyone choosing from the main platters of beef, veal and fish, covered in sauces and jellies, as soon as the creamy soups were finished and the plates taken away. Then side dishes of game birds and poultry, and dozens of vegetable dishes and salads were brought in, and the meal was finished off with spongy Genoese cakes with coffee filling and little chocolate souffles. All this was accompanied with various wines for each course. The crystal goblets kept brimming, despite the guests' constant attention to emptying them.

Feeling quite satiated, Elysia retired from the Banqueting Hall with the other ladies, leaving the gentlemen to sit over their port and cigars.

Elysia accepted a small glass of Madeira and sat silently listening to the frivolous chatter of the women as they gossiped and giggled over juicy tid-bits about their friends and, no doubt, about the latest hot item—herself. She felt isolated from the rest. They weren't really the type of people that her parents entertained. They seemed to be a raffish set of people—not the social elite of London, she thought shrewdly. She knew that Alex had only come to introduce her to these ladies and gentlemen from London—assured that the news would get back to London about her, and this time accurately—scotching any false rumors that might have spread about them. The Marquis seldom, if ever, socialized with the Squire and his set of hangers-on.

Elysia glanced about for Louisa, finding her held

captive by a large matronly-looking woman on the far side of the room. Seeing Elysia's glance, Louisa sent her a smile, grimacing as she turned back to the garrulous woman wielding her lorgnette like a rapier. Elysia drifted over to a display of porcelain, feigning an interest as she overheard a conversation between two flashily-dressed young women from London.

"Can you imagine—a redhead! Not at all the fashion," said the young lady with her curly, blonde hair and china-doll features, and catching a reflection of her face in the mirror opposite, smiled smugly.

"I know, and such a surprise," her plump friend said, adding confidentially, "and we had been told to expect an announcement any day between the Marquis and Lady Woodley. Why, John said that no man could resist her—even Lord Trevegne."

"She must be absolutely seething," the blonde chuckled gleefully. "I mean after all, she'd been talking about those emeralds, and how well they'd look on her." She glanced at Elysia who was apparently absorbed by the porcelain figurines, and whispered grudgingly, "I must say, she does wear them well, what with her coloring and all."

"Lady Woodley must be as green as the emeralds with envy," the other added impudently as they laughed, casting a glance at Lady Woodley from behind their fluttering fans.

Elysia moved off, swallowing a smile that became a thoughtful look as she cast a glance at Lady

Woodley. So London had been expecting a match between Alex and Lady Woodley? She now knew why the lovely Widow looked daggers at her—she had expected to become the next Marchioness. What had happened to cause Alex to leave her? Well, she would probably never know, yet she had the uncomfortable feeling that Lady Woodley was not one to lose gracefully, or indeed, to even admit defeat. She had an enemy in the dark-eyed widow.

"I'm so sorry I've not been able to talk with you, Elysia," Louisa said, coming up softly to where Elysia stood alone.

"That's perfectly all right. You must entertain your guests, and I've been admiring these porcelains. It's quite a collection."

"Yes, Mama has a passion for them. I do not really mind talking with the guests—it is just that I do not know how to politely excuse myself when I want to get away.

"Please," Louisa said grasping Elysia's hand and pulling her along with her, "let me show you another display of Mama's—we can talk undisturbed in the library."

They left the room unobserved, and Louisa led Elysia to the library, where a large chiffonier stood, with Oriental vases and plates attractively placed. It was not as large a library as Westerly's, in fact, it offered very little reading matter. Most of the room was taken up with assorted displays—one of which was made up of ornately carved knives and rapiers. Elysia shivered and turned away.

"I am so glad that you and the Marquis came tonight, although I am sorry to know of Peter Trevegne's accident. I do hope he will be quite all right."

"Yes, he will recover. Dany, our housekeeper is magnificent, and has more skill than a doctor. Otherwise, I doubt that Alex would have considered coming tonight and leaving him."

"Yes, well . . ." Louisa's voice trailed off with indecision, hesitating whether or not to continue with what she wanted to say, a shy, worried look on her small face.

"What is it?" Elysia asked helpfully, aware that something was troubling Louisa.

"How do you know when you are in love?" she blurted out breathlessly, taking Elysia completely by surprise. This was hardly the question she would have expected from Louisa.

"Well, I-I don't really know." Elysia was forced to admit.

"But you must know. I mean, you've married Lord Trevegne. When did you realize you were in love with him?" Louisa asked, her eyes taking on a dreamy expression. "It must be wonderful to know your love is returned. I've watched the way the Marquis looks at you—why he was positively mad with jealousy at dinner, when the French Count was holding your hand and flirting with you. He constantly watches you when he thinks you are not watching him."

"He does?" Elysia asked in surprise. For she'd

thought he had been fully occupied with Lady Woodley, who seemed unable to take a bite without asking his advice first—constantly placing her bejeweled fingers on his sleeve.

"Well?" Louisa persisted.

"Well, what?" Elysia answered, her mind elsewhere.

"Well, when did you know you loved the Marquis? Or how did you know that it was *true* love?"

Elysia looked thoughtfully at Louisa's upturned face—expectantly awaiting an answer. How could she tell her that she didn't love Alex, that she knew nothing about love, that Alex didn't love her? Could she destroy Louisa's romantic dreams? Had she the right to tarnish them with her own bitterness? It was apparent that Louisa was very much in love—and for the first time. She had once dreamt the same things as Louisa, but Elysia knew now that they were just an innocent and naïve schoolgirl's dreams.

"To me, love would be when you could no longer think of anyone else but the person you are in love with. You feel bereft when he is not around, and giddy and nervous when he is. You want to please that person, make him happy. You feel jealous of others he might be with. But most important, is that you place his health, happiness, and welfare above your own—no sacrifice is too great to bear for him. You worry about him, fear for him," Elysia continued quickly, almost incoherently with the revelations to herself of her own feelings for Alex which had hidden until now, and were being reluctantly revealed to her. "Nothing must ever happen to him to take him away from you—or your world—or your very existence would be at an end."

Elysia stood silently, breathing hard as the truth emanated from her confused and troubled mind. She loved Alex, she repeated to herself in disbelief. How could it have happened? She had despised him—hated him. She would have escaped from him had she been able. Now she would gladly lock the door to her prison and throw away the key. When she had thought him injured, she had acted like a woman possessed, or a woman very much in love. The truth had been revealed then—but she had been too blind to see it. She thought it had been de- sire—not love. She had believed that love could not exist for her.

She paled as she thought of Alex—what good did these feelings do her? They could only torture her, hers was an unrequited love. He desired her, yes, but he didn't care for her—at least not in the way she wanted to be loved by him. In all of their love- making, he had never said that he loved her. He had whispered endearments that had thrilled her, but never had he mentioned love. She was just one of his many women, the one he was currently fas- cinated with at the moment. He would soon tire of her, as he had done with Lady Woodley and so many other beautiful women. Could she bear to see him turn to another woman—go to London, and leave her at Westerly, alone? No, she could not stand that—but it would be even worse if he knew she loved him. How amusing for him—another broken heart! Elysia wondered if it had been her disdain and obvious dislike for him which had attracted him?—he, who had always received and expected admiration and capitulation to his advances. If she kept up her show of ill-will towards him then possibly he would not tire of her—at least not yet, and she might succeed in capturing his love. But how could she pretend—when she had capitulated so completely to him, and now knew that she loved him beyond all reason. He was so astute—nothing escaped his golden eyes. Although some of the hostility had disappeared in their relationship—she still felt on shaky ground. It was more as if they had entered into an armed neutrality. They teased and traded sarcasms, but with an underlying edge of friendliness. They had entered into a new phase of their relationship—but it could very easily be shattered.

Never would she allow Alex to know that she loved him, Elysia vowed to herself—never—unless he returned that love. She would not let herself be vulnerable to that kind of pain. She would play this game out to whatever its end—and by her own rules.

"Elysia. Elysia," Louisa was staring at her with concern. "Are you quite all right, you're pale. You are not feeling ill are you?"

"No, I'm quite well," Elysia answered dully. Or as

275

well as can be expected with a broken heart, she thought despondently.

"Do you know that what you said is exactly what I believed love to be. Oh, it is precisely how I feel!" Louisa looked over her shoulder to be sure they were alone, and then continued in a confiding tone. "I have met the most wonderful man, Elysia. He is tall and handsome—and has the most beautiful, blue eyes and auburn hair." She looked starry-eyed as she thought of him, her cheeks flushing rosily.

"His name is David Friday, and he is the kindest, most gentle soul on earth. I met him for the first time one day a couple of weeks ago. I was out riding when Dove started to limp. We weren't far from the stable, so the groom went back to fetch another horse, and I was staying with poor little Dove when this young man came out of nowhere and removed the pebble from Dove's hoof. He talked to me so gentlemanly-like, that I'm sure he is one—even though he was dressed as a seaman. I felt so at ease with him, not at all tongue-tied, like I usually am with those London gentlemen."

"A seaman, Louisa?" Elysia asked doubtfully, afraid her friend was sure to be hurt. "Your parents, surely they would not . . ."

"Exactly," Louisa interpreted Elysia's thoughts. "They would not be at all pleased. In fact, if Papa found out that a seaman had dared to talk to me— why, I don't know what he might do in his rage. They have high hopes for my making a successful marriage—even though the Marquis is no longer available," she chuckled, and then bit her lip as tears brightened her gray eyes. "Oh, Elysia I'm sure if you met him you would see that he is indeed a gentleman, and worthy of my love. I only doubt that I am worthy of his."

"What have we here?" Lady Woodley asked amusedly from the doorway. "Schoolroom secrets? Well, you'd better return to the salon, for your Mama is worrying about your whereabouts, and that of her 'Guest of Honor.' Hurry along and tell your Mama that we shall be with her shortly—before she sends you back to the nursery for being rude and spiriting one of her guests away. Luckily I saw you leave, and had to play tattle-tale," she continued maliciously, and laughed cruelly as Louisa hurried past, giving her a resentful look.

"Oh, please do not leave yet, Lady Trevegne," Lady Woodley said, moving towards Elysia, her eyes staring trance-like at the Trevegne emeralds. "I would like the opportunity to speak with you."

"Really," Elysia returned politely, yet not fully trusting the young widow. "I had not thought we would have much to say to one another."

"There you are mistaken, for there are quite a few details of which you should be aware. I would not have you ignorant of the truth, my dear Lady Trevegne," she replied, reluctantly dragging her eyes away from the green stones, only to stare into equally-green eyes. "I would have changed those ancient settings to something more modern," she said, almost to herself, before her eyes narrowed and a thin smile curved her lips. Then she continued, "You do know that you possess a hollow title? It is a title that you did not gain by your own cunning and efforts to ensnare Alex. You are only the Marchioness because *I* turned Alex's offer of marriage down. He married you out of pique—to save his pride. Alex knows I shall be marrying a Duke shortly, and after all the speculation about him and myself, well, you can imagine what people say. Alex would never allow himself to become the laughing stock of London, so naturally, he would have to take drastic steps to appear heartwhole, and show an unconcerned visage to the world. What better way than to take a wife, look the devoted husband. No one could possibly believe that he had been hurt by my refusal. But he still loves me—and I still love him. Just remember that Alex and I shall continue as we have in the past, once he gets over his offended pride, of course. But he always does as I wish." She looked at Elysia venomously. "You did not really imagine that he could be in love with you? I was his mistress for over a year. I know him. And you . . . you've only known him for a fortnight or so. Can that measure up to how long I've known him?"

"Maybe you have known him too long—possibly he became bored with your . . . er, *charms*," Elysia retorted smoothly, yet feeling sick with despair inside. But she would not let this creature know how wounded she felt.

"Bored! Bored with me?" Mariana demanded incredulously. She was enraged all the more because

278

she knew it might be the truth. But she could not accept the remark from this beautiful, younger woman. "How dare you ... you little slut. Do you actually believe that you could hold a man like Alex?" She looked Elysia up and down insultingly, laughing derisively. "He will come back to me—he always does. He still wants me, not you! You have nothing but his name—you don't possess his love."

Lady Woodley turned to leave the room, a smile curving her lips mischievously at the doubt she had planted in Elysia's mind.

"Yes, I possess the title. I bear Alex's name, and I also shall bear his children. You say I hold only the title. Well, the position entitles me to the jewels you have coveted for so long, and the estates, and Westerly, and a place in society that is permanent. Alex married me, and that is *forever*. Yes, I hold all of these," Elysia spoke, halting the other woman in her tracks. "But you deceive yourself, if you imagine I shall not keep Alex—for I shall—and not in name only. You are the one, Lady Woodley, who has nothing. You possess none of the things you so confidently lay claim to—neither Alex, nor that title you covet. I would caution you not to count your chickens before they hatch. Good evening, Lady Woodley," Elysia spoke haughtily as she passed the speechless widow, and returned to the salon where she heard the mingled sound of men's and women's voices.

The carriage returning from Blackmore Hall bounced, as it hit a pothole in the rutted road, and threw Elysia against the Marquis. She pulled back as if burnt, and moved even farther to her side of the seat. She turned her face away from his curious stare, pretending to be absorbed in the darkness beyond the carriage window. Her mind kept returning to Lady Woodley's vicious words, her cruel laughter echoing around her troubled mind. Would Alex return to the Widow? Had he indeed asked her to marry him—and been rejected? From the gossip, it would seem that he had not asked the Widow to marry him. But if what she said was true, his pride would have been salvaged as he planned, marrying her to save himself from looking the fool. She could never let Alex know that she had fallen in love with him—especially now—if he still felt love for Lady Woodley.

She had lied when she told the Widow that the estates and riches of Alex mattered to her. She would gladly have suffered the direst poverty to have but a part of his love. What was wonderful about a grand house if she had to wander through its halls and rooms alone? Who was there to see her dressed in fine silks and satins, bejeweled from head to toe? It was not an empty title she possessed, but an empty heart.

She foolishly thought that given time she could make Alex fall in love with her—eventually he might have, but she had not known that he married her on the rebound. She had believed him when he said he was in the mood to marry—serving his purposes, and saving her reputation. "Lies, lies, lies!" she cried in her heart. Everything was ruined now—now that she knew there was another woman in his life. He would hardly fall in love with her if he was in love with Lady Woodley.

Elysia sighed dispiritedly, half-listening to the conversation between Alex and Charles, their voices taking on a droning quality as she continued to stare out into the blackness of the night. She narrowed her eyes as she thought she saw a flash of light out at sea that quickly disappeared—probably a reflection from the lighted sconces from inside the coach, on the glass of the window. She could see her own face reflected palely, her eyes distorted until they seemed to glow iridescently like white-hot coals in her face. Elysia hugged the warm fur-lined cape about her body, luxuriating in the feel of the soft fur against her bare shoulders and cheeks. Closing her eyes she dreamed of what could have been.

A finger of rock detached itself from the rest and moved silently from its shadowy concealment out onto the road. The man stood statue-like as he watched the big, black coach disappear down the road to become lost in the blackness, the sound of the horses' hooves fading until silence reigned supreme, once again.

He looked out to sea—his eyes alert and searching, until he was rewarded by the flashing of a light three times. Then it disappeared. He glanced along the cliffs of the coast, knowing he would not see the answering flashes from the shielded lantern he knew was signalling the ship at sea from some hidden spot. The ship would now sail into one of the numerous coves along the coast. If he had not had a general idea of the area the ship would venture into, the chances of his locating such a ship—wishing to unobtrusively dock and unload its contraband cargo—would be a million to one. The whole length of Cornish coastline was honeycombed with small secretive coves and deep penetrating ravines where a ship could moor undetected and go about its surreptitious business.

David Friday crossed the road and untethered his horse, where he had left it behind the rocks, and swiftly mounted. He headed down the road in the opposite direction from the coach that had swiftly traveled past only moments before. He rode along the road for several miles until he could see the curve of the coast jut abruptly outwards, forming a natural harbor with a deep ravine. A moorland stream flowed through it to empty into the sea—leaving a rock-carved passage to the high cliffs above, and easy access to the road.

David dismounted and left his horse in the shelter of a group of pines and made his way quietly to the edge of the ravine, carefully lowering himself over the edge—his booted feet seeking footholds among the slippery rocks. Suddenly his foot slipped, and he lunged perilously forward, falling to the floor of the ravine. He landed on an outcropping of rock that formed a narrow ledge just wide enough to stop the descent that would have ended in his death.

He lay still, his breathing heavy, as he tried to regain his breath and listen for any sounds of voices
raised in alarm, followed by searching footsteps. But
no sounds of panic reached him—only the rumble of
the sea. David breathed a sigh of relief. They must
still be at the mouth of the ravine unloading cargo.
The pounding of the waves masked the noise he'd
caused by his fall, and the lookout—posted up on
the road to watch for revenuers—would have been
too far away to hear anything and give the sound of
alarm.

David Friday looked about him from his vantage
point. He could clearly see the little harbor, and the
outline of the lugger anchored beyond the swell of
the waves. A small boat was rowing ashore where a
group of figures were standing in readiness on the
sandy beach.

His ledge overlooked the path, directly beneath
his perch. Yes, this was a perfect spot for observa-
tion. He settled himself more comfortably, in preparation for the loading to be completed and for them
to begin their ascent up the path from the ravine to
the road above. He felt no impatience with this
job—for he wanted to catch this nest of smugglers.
It wasn't so much the smugglers themselves he was
after—men who risked their necks to sail across the
Channel that was patrolled by His Majesty's Navy
and Coast Guard; they were only the arms and legs
of the operation. He wanted the head of the body—
the man who sat safely on British soil, mastermind-

ing everything yet never dirtying his white, uncalloused palms—except with gold guineas.

Every major port, small fishing village, or hamlet, had a gang of smugglers. From the Romney Marsh to as far north as York, smuggling was rampant. It seemed to be an accepted community activity. One could enjoy fine, French brandy after dinner at the Vicar's, or at a local tavern, and fragrant imported tea in the afternoon in an elegant and highly-respected lady's drawing-room.

Taxes were high, shortages of every imported item were prevalent with the continuing of the war, and people had come to enjoy these luxuries—hesitant to give them up. He was not after these people, and their small horde of brandy, silk, tea and chocolate. The village fishermen and farmers who banded together once a month to row across the Channel and bring back a cache of black market goods engaged in small-time smuggling, and were relatively harmless.

He was after the smuggler who brought in 'human cargo,' and dealt in goods on a grand scale—not a bolt of silk and several kegs of brandy, but a cargo of a thousand casks of brandy, and hundreds of pounds of Chinese tea, and a storeroom full of fine silks, velvets, and lace. A great profit was harvested from the sales of these contraband commodities to the fashionable shops on Bond Street and the gentlemen's clubs of St. James. But the highest profit was reaped for ferrying a passenger across the Channel from France to England. The fare was indeed high for the man who wanted to enter England by night, his face unremembered by the silent crewmen, to disappear into the countryside, only to reappear in a crowded street in the heart of London.

David Friday wanted desperately the man who would betray his country by bringing in French spies. Napoleon had eyes and ears in London, thanks to the greed and avariciousness of these traitorous men who dared to call themselves Englishmen. They allowed the enemy to enter England to plot and deceive, and then helped him to sneak away with secret documents and information. But the traitor was far more deadly than the spy who was acting under orders from his country, and at least had a loyalty to it. The English dog who would bring in the enemy had no beliefs. He would act only for the gain and profit he would receive from his actions. He felt no love or loyalty to his country—only an allegiance to the craving for money.

An owl hooted, and within an instant, it was answered by four hoots from the top of the cliff. The lookout had signalled the all-clear, and shortly after the dark horses, loaded down with kegs and casks, and the sturdy wagons with their wide iron-made wheels—to keep the heavily-laden carts from sinking deep into the sandy beach—would begin to move toward the safety of their drops: hiding places in caves and barns, quiet crypts in cemeteries, false-bottomed floors, and hidden closets in the walls of homes in the villages.

David was lying flat, his chest pressed against the rocky ledge, as the pack train moved slowly up the path. He heard smothered curses, as feet slipped and arms were scraped against the rough cliff wall, along the narrow and uneven path.

David watched carefully as the men and beasts trundled by. His eyes were searching for a lone figure in an all-concealing cape and hat. But the men were all dressed similarly in smocks and rough, woolen coats. He knew most of these men from his previous observations. Most were hard-working men from the village. The others were hired men from other parts—vicious and dangerous, with loaded pistols tucked under their wide belts. He could see no new faces. His vigil tonight had been in vain. It was only for cargo, this run—no extra man that would separate from the rest to make his way alone in the night, or return to sea with the unloaded boat.

He waited until the smugglers had got to the road and were well on their way down it before climbing back up the face of the cliff to the top. He mounted and rode off toward the moors, across the road and away from the smugglers' train. He had no need to follow them, for he knew where they would cache the goods. He had watched them seven times in the past as they'd unloaded the ship and prepared the horses, then slowly and quietly moved through the narrow lanes to various drops. But the major part of the load was separated from the rest—this was destined for London, and stored away in a deviously conceived cache—an innocent-appearing summer house. David had watched astounded as cargo after cargo had been unloaded and carried into the small pagoda-like structure—only to disappear. He had searched it in vain after the smugglers left, but found no evidence that contraband had been concealed there. He knew there was a secret panel that must conceal a hidden cave or passage, but he had been unable to find it, despite his thorough searches. It seemed inconceivable that this small structure could hide a cache of contraband—yet it did. The cave probably connected by a subterranean passage to the home of the mastermind—for the summer house stood back from the cliffs, and there was no natural harbor for ships to anchor in. Nor had he found a coastal sea cave in his traversing of the area. So that left one place—Blackmore Hall.

Squire Blackmore was the man he wanted. A man so insidious as to force the villagers and farmers to smuggle for him by enclosure of their lands, and the village common, leaving them no place to raise food or livestock. He closed down the tin mines, putting countless numbers out of work. The village was under his control and with the fishing poor—few men returned with full nets—rather than starve, they smuggled for him.

Yes, David Friday wanted Squire Blackmore. He would enjoy seeing the walls of Blackmore Hall come tumbling down about the Squire's head. But then he thought of two misty gray eyes looking trust-

ingly up into his face. How could he destroy
Louisa Blackmore's world? She was such an innocent—completely unaware of her father's nefarious
villainy. David had never before met such a demure
and lovely young woman. She was still a young girl,
actually, for she could not be more than sixteen or
seventeen.

He would not allow her to become besmirched by
this affair. He must protect her in some way. But
how could he? It was his job—his duty—to catch,
and arrest her father as a traitor. How could she
feel anything but shame and degradation when that
happened—and what would she then feel towards
the man who had brought about her father's downfall? Hatred? Disgust? What a tangle he was involved in, he thought in despair, as he sighted the
small moorland hut directly ahead.

David glanced over his shoulder to ascertain that
he had not been followed, even though he had
taken a circuitous route. He was taking no chances
of being discovered. He dismounted, and knocked
twice on the door before entering the hut.

It was a small hut with one room, and lighted by
a flickering lantern that threw a dim light over the
crude furnishings and the solitary man sitting at the
rough wooden table in the center of the room.

"Good evening, Sir," David saluted smartly.

"Hardly a good evening, Lieutenant," the man answered disgustedly, pulling his coat tighter about
his broad shoulders. Only his bushy, iron-gray
brows and deep-set eyes were visible from behind

the high collar. "Come and sit down, Lieutenant, and relax. You look rather dishevelled. Run into any trouble?" he asked sharply.

"No, Sir, I just missed my step over the edge of a cliff," David explained with a rueful smile lurking in his eyes.

The other man looked startled and then smiled. "I'd hate to lose you, my boy—still got your sea legs? Feel like I'm walking at an angle myself."

"I don't believe I shall ever be able to walk normally again. Still feel the deck beneath my feet."

His commander laughed—a hearty laugh that crinkled his eyes into slits, the myriad lines etching the corners that blended into one crease. He was deeply tanned, his face aged from the sea and weather. He looked at the young man sitting across from him with piercing eyes—eyes that were accustomed to looking far into the distance for land, or the flag of another ship.

"I gather, since you are back so early, that our *friend* did not show up?"

"Right, Sir. It was just a load of brandy and other goods. No sign of any strangers," David answered dejectedly.

"Well, one will show eventually—or our *friend* will decide to travel across the Channel himself. Either way we shall be prepared. And it is absòlutely vital now, more than ever, that we apprehend them. I have received news from London that certain top secret information has been leaked, and certain documents are missing. It is of the utmost importance that we recover this information and put an end to this spy ring," he said in a deadly voice.

"But how could they have gotten hold of such information?"

"We've been fortunate to catch the traitor in the Ministry—an Under-Secretary of small import, yet high up enough to come within contact of important information. He will stand trial. His usefulness is at an end—to all concerned. However we have kept it quiet so as not to panic our quarry. We do not want them to flee and take that information with them—something Napoleon would sell his soul to obtain, if indeed he has not *already* sold his soul to the Devil."

"Do we know who has that information?" David asked, a muscle twitching beside his eye. "Is it Blackmore?"

"No, so far the good Squire has only transported French spies to and from England, along with his other smuggling. He has not dirtied his hands with the actual spying itself," David's superior said with disgust. "Although he might as well have. Giving good English gold for his contraband is the same as putting it in Napoleon's pocket."

"Who is the spy?"

"We were fortunate to get a full confession out of the ex-Under-Secretary. Odd how little courage these spies have when faced with an actual enemy in front of them. They work best in the dark when they can sneak away like a snivelling dog," he spoke sneeringly, distaste curling his lip. "We were informed that he passed the information to a Frenchman posing as an émigré, and is at present a guest of our country. In reality, he is one of Napoleon's top agents. His name is D'Aubergere, and claims to be a Count or something to give him access into society. He is now a guest of the good Squire," he added, looking meaningfully at David. "You realize what that means?"

"Yes. Our Frenchmen will undoubtedly be awaiting his friend from across the Channel, so he can pass on the information and receive new orders. Or he will personally take the information to Napoleon, to receive full recognition for his daring." David pounded his fist on the hard wood table angrily. "Well, what are we waiting for? Let's go in there and arrest him."

"We can't do that, unfortunately. It would give me great pleasure, believe me. However, I doubt whether he has the evidence on his person—it will be well concealed. And we've no proof—except for a frightened traitor's confession that D'Aubergere does indeed have it. Even if we should arrest him, the documents would be in Blackmore Hall. These French are a wily lot—he will have hidden it safely away. Can you imagine the Squire not making use of that? Another spy would be dispatched to retrieve it—at quite a price I should imagine, if I read the Squire correctly. And I am sure he will know the worth of what he holds."

His commander stared thoughtfully at the flickering light as David sat dejectedly, feeling helpless to act.

"No, we must move with caution. They do not know that the hounds have caught scent of the fox," the older man added with a gleam in his eyes. "They feel secure in their cloak of deception. As far as they are concerned they have nothing to fear, and they would not take the risk of causing speculation now, by acting rashly and taking risks. They will play it safe—not chancing discovery. The Count will either wait for a contact, or travel over to France with the information himself. I suspect it might be the latter. Ego has been the downfall of many a man—and this Frenchman is no exception. However, with something as important as this packet . . . well, I am afraid they might send for a French war ship to pick him up. They would not risk being picked up by the Coast Guard with something of such vital importance. So we must wait, as D'Aubergere waits. And under no circumstance can D'Aubergere be allowed to pass on the documents. We will give him enough rope to get them out of concealment and then he will hang himself as we catch him redhanded, along with Blackmore and his smugglers. Although, I'm sure the good Squire will deny all knowledge of D'Aubergere's clandestine activities—claiming he has been duped, and most foully deceived, but we will get him yet," he promised ominously, "for it will be hard to explain why a cache of contraband is hidden in his summer house. Thanks to you we know about this smuggling operation. Just luck you picked up this lead while you were in France. Now, more than ever it is fortunate we know about Blackmore. I think we shall crack this ring yet."

"The villagers are in this against their will, you know," David told him. "They aren't even receiving just pay for their labors. That scoundrel Blackmore has forced them to work for him. They'd starve otherwise. It's abominable that a man like Blackmore could become so powerful. And yet there is a filthy rich Marquis living not more than a few miles west of here, and he does nothing to help the village that is his responsibility. In fact I wouldn't be surprised if he were involved in this too!"

"I shall certainly put in a word for the villagers, never fear," the commander promised. "I know the Marquis of St. Fleur, and although he is rather wild, I do know that he is honorable—he no doubt hasn't the slightest idea of what is amiss."

"Oh, Sir, I should warn you that there are a few nasty customers working with Blackmore that I'd not care to tangle with, unless well-armed. They're from London or thereabouts—not local, and a meaner bunch of characters I've yet to meet," David advised. "It could get messy if there's a fight."

"I've my men. We'll handle that rabble in short work. I'd better be off, the boat will be waiting for me," he said, rising and then looking about the unprepossessing hut. "Sorry you've got to put up here. Couldn't you stay in the village in some decent place?"

"No, I'm afraid not. You know how suspicious the countyfolk are of strangers. I was born and raised in a village up north, and because my parents were not of the district I was always considered an outsider. I'd be as conspicuous as a stableboy in Almack's, if I stayed in St. Fleur," he declared. "I've had less, Sir, and it's a hardship I'll gladly bear, to catch this nest of rats."

"Good boy, I've complete faith in you. Signal me if anything unforseen should crop up. Keep close watch, for I need not stress the importance of this affair."

He buttoned his coat closer about his throat and left the hut, giving a farewell wave to the young man who had to remain within its inhospitable walls.

*Ay, now the plot thickens very much
upon us.*

George Villiers

Chapter 11

The small village of St. Fleur nestled within the
mouth of the bay, the slate-roofed stone cottages
peeking out beneath the surrounding walls of the
red cliffs as the small houses and shops snuggled together against the harsh winds and waves that beat
against the unprotected town.

Elysia rode Ariel along the stony path at the sum-
mit of the cliff and watched as a small boat put out
to sea. The men were hopeful of a big catch to help
feed their families throughout the long, harsh, winter months. Tracings of smoke from countless chim-
neys rose skyward smudging the blue of the sky. A
sky clear, for the first time, of storm clouds and rain,

with a crispness that lingered and promised frost. Elysia breathed deeply of the sparkling air, sniffing the pungent smell of the tall pines and subtle aroma from the wood fires burning in the village homes.

"I say, this part of the country is indeed aptly named—Land's End. It seems like the ends of the earth here," Charles Lackton said wonderingly, as he gazed about. "It's so desolate! Why would anyone want to live way out here?" He shook his head in disbelief.

"Possibly no one new has settled here in the past five hundred years, except the Squire. These villagers can probably trace their origins back to the earliest people who lived here, called the Celts—or at least as far back as the Normans," Elysia explained knowledgeably to Charles as his eyes widened.

"But how do you come to know all of this?"

"I'm an intellectual," she said in an apologetic tone, a twinkle in her eyes, as she noted her admirer's shocked expression, "did you not know?" Elysia felt as if she were confessing to some hideous crime, but she was not about to feign stupidity.

"But you cannot possibly be! Why, you are far too beautiful to be intelligent," Charles exclaimed in bewilderment.

"Oh, and I suppose all I should have is a pretty face and be a shallow-brain—not knowing chalk from cheese?"

"Well I'm no needle-wit either. I just know what I need to. Do me no good to know any more—don't know where I could put it—feel as if I know too much as it is. Reckon I know just enough to get me through each day," Charles speculated.

"Do you not want to know about history and literature? Do you never open a book?" Elysia asked in disbelief.

Charles looked thoughtful for a moment. "No, don't believe I do. Last book I opened was at Eton, and precious few there, either. Don't do me any good. I'm not one to be quoting poetry and such nonsense to the ladies, like some I know," he disclaimed. "And what's the sense in learning about people who died centuries ago? Can't tell me which hand to play—or which vest to wear with my puce coat? Never heard tell of anybody winning at Newhall on a tip from Caesar, or one of those Greek philosophers."

"Well Charles, I suppose you are correct—it probably would not have done you any good," Elysia agreed in resignation, feeling slightly resentful. Charles had access to all the schools of higher learning, yet shunned them—while she and countless other females would relish the opportunity to enter those sacred—yet forbidden—portals of knowledge.

She smiled at Charles. Elysia couldn't help but like him, with his openly boyish face and easy smiles. She didn't feel like she had to be constantly on guard with him. He reminded her slightly of Ian. Only Ian was older, but there was that same boyish look about him, as with Charles. Dear Ian. If only he were here, Elysia thought sadly, glancing out at the great expanse of sea that stretched away to the horizon, blending into one with the sky.

Charles sat silent. She was so exquisite, he thought agonizingly, as he felt a surge of primitive jealousy towards Lord Trevegne. She was the most beautiful woman he had ever seen. He felt tongue-tied while with her, even though she was younger than he was. His ardent gaze lingered on the curve of her mouth, and the long, sweeping, dark lashes that veiled her green eyes. Why, he actually felt like writing a poem to her beauty! He who had scoffed at those other moonstruck Lotharios' idolizings. He continued to stare bemusedly as he composed a poem in his mind—the lines seeming to come like magic out of that vast emptiness. Yes, yes! That was fantastic, he thought proudly. Byron would be insanely jealous of this. It really wasn't so hard. He couldn't understand why there was such a fuss made about nothing—any fool could think up something flashy. Now, if only he could remember it by the time he got back to his room, so he could copy it down. He'd have to get some paper too, and a quill and ink, then ...

"Charles? Charles ..." Elysia spoke softly, waving her fingers before his somewhat glazed-looking eyes. "Is there something amiss?"

"Oh, I do beg your pardon," Charles mumbled in a flustered state.

"Shall we continue our ride?" Elysia asked, hiding a smile as she turned Ariel and headed back towards the road, glancing back over her shoulder to see Charles hurrying his mount to catch up with her. She laughed aloud with pure enjoyment. It felt wonderful to be alive and carefree. For the moment she would only think of clear blue skies and the fun of having a personable young man infatuated with her. She wouldn't think of the hopelessness of her marriage—or what she could possibly do about it.

Elysia jumped Ariel over a low, stone wall and headed up into a thicket, hearing the sound of Charles close upon her heels. She disappeared from sight as she gained the trees, the shadows playing across the narrow path as she continuously ducked and weaved, dodging low-hanging branches.

Suddenly Elysia heard a shot ring out—the sound shattering the quiet of the woods, and then she felt a searing pain in her side and gasped as she saw the blood staining the green velvet of her habit. A branch reaching out into the path caught her and swept Elysia from Ariel's back, knocking the breath out of her as she hit the carpeted floor of the forest— the dead leaves cushioning her fall.

Elysia lay still, as a blackness swirled about her, and she struggled painfully to regain her breath. The earth seemed to vibrate deafeningly and she felt as if she were being shaken to pieces.

Charles dismounted in seconds, and ran to the prostrate figure lying dazed upon the ground. His face was drained of all color as he knelt down next to Elysia and saw the red seeping from her side. "Oh, my God? She's been shot!" he breathed, not daring to touch her. She looked dead, he thought wretchedly, wondering what in the world he was going to do, when her eyelids flickered slowly open and she gazed up into his face with confused eyes.

"Charles?" Elysia gasped out breathlessly.

"Yes, I'm here." He picked up her limp hand—icy cold, and rubbed it comfortingly between his big warm palms. She just couldn't die. She mustn't, he thought in desperation, feeling a knot of sickness churn in his stomach.

Elysia looked into Charles' frightened blue eyes, all amusement wiped from them. She could breathe easier now. She must send Charles for Alex—he would know what to do. Alex, yes Alex would know.

"Listen, Charles. You must go and get Alex," she stated calmly with full confidence in her decision.

"But I couldn't leave you here, alone!" Charles exclaimed in horror.

"You must. You've no other choice, and I can't possibly ride back, Charles."

Charles looked down at her, indecision written across his face. He stood up, having come to a reluctant decision. "Very well, I'll go, but I don't care for it one bit. Leaving you unattended goes against my better judgment—and what will Lord Trevegne think of me going off and leaving you alone and hurt. It ain't gentlemanly." He shook his head in bewilderment. "I shall ride like the wind, Lady Elysia. I shan't be long, that I promise." He stared down at her, his gaze anguished. "Is there anything I can do to make you more comfortable before I go?"

"No, I'll be fine," Elysia managed to whisper as a

shiver shook her. The ground was cold and damp
from the rains, and the woods were cool under the
protection of the trees.

Charles quickly took off his coat and wrapped it
about Elysia's shaking shoulders before he ran to his
horse, mounting and charging off into the trees like
an avenger, barely missing a low-hanging branch.

Elysia managed a grim smile and hoped her rescuer would not also have to be rescued. She closed
her eyes. The sun, peeking through the branches
overhead, found an avenue, and poured its blinding
light down onto her face and into her eyes. She
moved her legs experimentally and bit her lip as she
felt a sharp jab of pain in her ankle. It must have
caught in the stirrup as she had fallen from Ariel.
Ariel? Where was he?

Elysia turned her head worriedly and then
relaxed as she saw him standing nervously a few
yards away, neighing softly, as he glanced at his
mistress lying still on the ground. "Steady boy, it's
all right, fella," Elysia crooned in a soft voice that
steadied and reassured the great beast. He put his
head down and began to crop the grass contentedly.

Elysia had no awareness of the passing of time
as she felt the sun's warmth beat down upon her
face, until the brightness beneath her lids disappeared—as if a shadow had moved across the sun.
Elysia slowly opened her eyes and stared up into a
face bent above her—a familiar face, with the sun
creating a halo behind the head.

It was strange that she did not feel any differently. She had always thought that when she died she would sink down into a darkness, and all pain would disappear. One would just float away—yet she was still feeling pain, and the hard uncomfortable ground beneath her back. But how could she be alive and seeing what she was before her? Elysia groaned in disbelief, whispering almost incoherently, "I don't feel dead—and yet, I must surely be, for I am seeing you, once again." Her words were cut off by a sob rising from deep within, "Oh, Ian, my dear Ian. In death we meet again."

"My dear sweet one," a voice murmured comfortingly, "you are not dead, I'm not dead. Here, touch me, feel me. I'm warm—and alive." He took one of her cold, shaking hands and pressed her fingers to his tanned throat where she could feel the strong pulse beating wildly.

Elysia's eyes filled with tears, and overflowing, they coursed down her pale cheeks. "Ian?" she said tentatively, afraid that he would disappear if she raised her voice any louder.

"Yes, I am here Elysia, my sweet sister. But what are you doing here—and more important, how badly are you injured?" He ran his eyes over her figure searchingly, the blue of his eyes darkening to black as he spotted the blood staining her side. His lips tightened in anger as Elysia moaned softly when his gentle fingers deftly felt her wound.

"I do not believe the shot is still in—it seems to have passed through the fleshy part of your side. Fortunately, it did not damage any internal organs, but you have lost some blood. You fell from Ariel, did you not? That did you no good. I'm going to try to stop the flow—it will hurt, and then I shall have to get you to a doctor, Elysia. I can't leave you here," he spoke in a commanding voice. Elysia absently noticed the new note of authority in her brother's voice, and she winced as he pressed his handkerchief against the wound. He had grown into a man during the last few years, she thought proudly through a haze of pain, seeing his broad shoulders and matured face with its new lines of experience written on it. "Ian, someone has already gone to fetch help," she told him as he finished his bandaging.

"Gone! And left you here? Alone and injured?" he exclaimed wrathfully, expressing Charles' original sentiments.

"We had no other choice. Charles could not get me back to the house alone. Someone will bring a carriage for me, shortly."

"Very well, but, Elysia, you must tell me what happened. And what you are doing down here in Cornwall? Are Mama and Father here too?" he asked, a look of anticipation lighting his eyes momentarily, at the thought of seeing them.

Elysia sighed deeply, and looking up into his eyes, steadied herself for her next task which brought her a pain far more intense than her wound.

"Ian."

"Yes," he frowned, intuitively warned by her tone.

"Ian, Mama and Papa are dead." Elysia took his

big hand into her smaller ones and held it firmly, as she continued chokingly. "They were killed in an accident. Papa's new phaeton overturned—no, Ian please," she said hurriedly, as she watched the spasm of pain and horror flick his features, "they died instantly. They did not suffer—they went together, Ian. They would have wanted it that way. And Ian," Elysia added, "they never knew that you had been reported missing and declared dead. They thought you were still fighting gallantly at sea. We can be thankful for at least that much."

Elysia's hands ached from the pressure of Ian's big hand as it tightened with his grief. His auburn head was bent, and she felt the wetness of his tears as they fell onto their clasped hands.

"When?" he finally managed to ask huskily.

"Over two years ago," Elysia answered, watching him pull himself together.

"You'd better lie still and stay quiet," he told her as she tried to raise herself onto her elbows. A brooding look closed his face as he cut himself off from her. She must not let him bottle up his grief as she had done.

"No, it helps me to talk—takes my mind off of this."

Ian looked at Elysia curiously. "What are you doing down here? I don't recall any acquaintances of ours who lived in Cornwall. Are you visiting?"

Elysia wondered how she could possibly explain her current residence at Westerly, and all that had happened during the last two years.

"You are managing all right, aren't you?" he continued, not noticing her silence, and then demanded sharply, "A chaperone. Who is chaperoning you at Rose Arbor? We've a shocking lack of relatives, if memory serves me correctly. You do have a chaperone, do you not, Elysia?" he asked suspiciously, knowing her inclination for independence and rebelliousness.

"Rose Arbor had to be sold, Ian," she told him bluntly, hating to hurt him again. "Everything is gone. All that we knew, is no more—we've nothing."

"Gone!" Ian exclaimed increduously. "But how? What happened?"

"We were in debt. It all had to be sold to pay off the creditors."

"And you, Elysia. What happened to you? You did not have to seek employment?" he demanded in outraged pride and arrogance, that his sister should be left penniless and destitute. Then he seemed to notice for the first time her elegance, and the fashionable clothes she was wearing. A look of disbelief entered his eyes as he said grimly, "Some man hasn't . . . hasn't become your protector?"

Elysia stared at him uncomprehendingly for a moment, and then as the realization of what he implied came to her, she flushed in a crimson tide of embarrassment, saying reproachfully, "Ian, how could you possibly believe that I would ever sink to such depths?" Elysia looked at him like a wounded animal that had been dealt a cruel blow.

Ian bent forward and kissed her scarlet cheek and explained sadly, "I've seen far too many heart-breaking and tormenting sights, since I left home, to be shocked, or indeed surprised by what may happen. Humanity has made a living Hell of this world. War, death, destruction. I thought never to have seen such cruelty as I have seen," he said with the pain of remembrance shadowing his eyes.

"Ian. This may sound crazed to you—but why aren't you dead? We received a letter from the Ministry stating that you had been killed. It was the day after Mama and Papa died."

"Oh, my poor darling. What you must have gone through, and no one to comfort you. But you see, they did indeed believe I had died. We had engaged in a battle with a couple of Napoleon's big warships. My ship was out-classed, out-gunned and out-manned. We hadn't a chance, but we put up a valiant effort, until we were hit by a volley of big guns that I never want to see the likes of again. We went down like a lead weight—the whole bow on fire. Some of the crew were picked up by the French—destined for prisons, others that had been wounded had no chance at all—they drowned. I was lucky, for I caught hold of a piece of the hull, and drifted off with it concealing me. I was determined not to end up in some French prison—you very seldom leave one alive. I drifted for days—lost count of the time out on that endless sea. I couldn't believe it when I saw a dot far off in the distance. I thought it was a mirage, or worse that I had lost my mind, until I saw that it was an island. It was someplace in the Mediterranean, and it took me close to two years to get through Europe, and back here to England. I was ill for months at a time—that slowed me down. And then 'Boney's finest' kept me under cover. Traveling only at night, I was careful not to run into any of his troops. My French stood me in good stead—never been so thankful for old Jacques' constant drilling of verbs when he was our tutor," he laughed.

"By the time I got to London, I had a pretty good working knowledge of all Napoleon's troop movements and placements on the Continent. The Ministry was quite surprised—and pleased—to have a chat with me. I've only been back for about three months, and due to some of the vital information to which I had access, I was greatly needed by the department to conclude it. I thought it best to finish it before heading north to see you and Mama and Father. I knew a message reporting that I was still alive, after so long, would only disturb them if I wasn't there to prove it. So I just waited until I could go myself. I needn't have worried for the glad tidings would have been sent to strangers," he said bitterly.

"Oh Ian," Elysia spoke softly, her eyes full of pity.

"Where the hell are they," Ian growled and glanced over his shoulder at the empty landscape. "Where did he go, this—what was his name?"

"Charles."

"Where did this Charles go to?" Ian swore, rapping out an oath. "He should have been back from the village long ago."

"He didn't go to the village ..." Elysia took a deep breath. "He went to Westerly."

"Westerly? Why, devil take it, did he go there? It's miles out of the way. Are you staying there?"

"In a way, yes."

"In what way? Are you a governess or something—no, couldn't be that. The Marquis doesn't have children—in fact, he isn't even married. You shouldn't be staying there, Elysia. He has a bad reputation. I'd not trust you with him, my dear. We shall have to plan some other accommodation for you," he said looking at her in puzzlement. "How is it that you come to be there—you are not there alone?"

"Ian, I'm afraid you shall have to trust me with him. You see ... I am married to the Marquis," Elysia told him gravely.

Ian looked incredulous, and for a second was speechless. "Married?" he repeated as if he could not believe it. "My God, Elysia, how could this occur? I feel as if I am in a whirlwind. There is so much that I am in the dark about. I don't—"

Ian cocked his head, listening attentively, then grasping Elysia's hands said, "Listen Elysia. Riders are coming and I hear a carriage in the distance—so they will be here shortly to fetch you. I don't want to leave you, God knows, but I must—no don't speak, I must hurry. This is of the utmost importance. You must speak to no one about me. I am on a mission here, and it would be disastrous if I were discovered, so you must forget you have spoken with me. I must know how you are faring though. Is there a way I can get a message to you, or see you?"

"Jims is managing the stables. He's head trainer!" Elysia remembered suddenly.

"Jims! Here?" Ian said with excitement. "That is marvelous. I shall contact him. But now I must go—time is short. If you only knew how it pains me to abandon you," he said staring down into her pale face. "I am of the inclination to stay," he said hesitating to rise.

"No, you must go! I shall be fine if Alex comes. Please, you must believe me, Ian," Elysia pleaded.

"Very well, my dear, but I feel like a swine. And I promise you I shall find the person who did this to you. Probably some poacher, or other riffraff hanging about these parts." He kissed her cheek and then the sun shone full into her eyes as he moved, blinding her momentarily. When Elysia looked around, he was gone—as if he had never been.

Elysia heard the furiously pounding hooves from a horse being ridden hard, and then felt herself being lifted up into warm strong arms, that held her securely—yet with a curious gentleness. She felt a warm breath on her cheek and opened her eyes to stare up into Alex's worried face, his golden eyes narrowed in concern.

"M'Lady, you seem to have gotten yourself into another mishap," he said in a teasing voice, despite the savage look in his eyes.

"Again I have caused you annoyance, M'Lord," Elysia managed to answer pertly enough before fainting.

Elysia spent the next few days confined to her bed, and under the mothering attentions of Dany. She was a tyrant in the sickroom, and thoroughly enjoyed herself now that she had two patients to cluck over. Peter was still convalescent, but improving rapidly with the recuperative powers of the young and healthy. He was already causing havoc, in his boredom and impatience, to anyone who entered his bedchamber—especially, the young maids.

Elysia received bouquets of flowers and baskets of fruit, with messages from Blackmore Hall and the guests with whom she had dined. All were solicitous of her health, with the exception of Lady Woodley.

Elysia was beginning to tire of her confinement, feeling fretful as the long hours passed slowly. She had only sustained a flesh wound, which was rapidly healing, and her ankle was now less painful, but she had been most stiff and sore from bruises and outraged muscles. She was also worried about Ian. To find out that he was alive and well, was a miracle! She was no longer alone—she had a brother back again. But now not to be able to see him, talk to him, was indeed agony. Elysia had received word from Jims via the stableboy via the footman via the downstairs maid via the upstairs maid, and finally to Lucy—that he had seen Ian and all was well.

Alex divided his time between the two sick rooms with equal attentiveness. Sitting in a chair pulled up to her bed and reading to her and talking to her, making her laugh gaily and forgetting her boredom, Alex played the part of a devoted and loving husband. He could be quite charming when he so desired, and was an accomplished actor, she thought drily. If only she knew what he really felt. He had certainly looked worried when he found her hurt and in pain on the moors, she had to admit. He held her in his arms on the trip back to Westerly, allowing no else to touch her, until Dany had doctored her. He was brazenly angry, wanting to search out the fool who had accidentally shot her—but not a sign of anybody could be found. Elysia had felt a momentary twinge of fear, lest they should find Ian and suspect him of being the poacher.

Elysia pulled distractedly at the lace edging of her robe, and unable to stand it any longer, made a face at the silently mocking faces on the lacquered screen that kept her company.

"It can't make a face back at you but I can," an amused voice spoke from the doorway.

Startled, Elysia looked around at the young man who stood there laughing; his face still bearing the signs of a recent illness as he made a grotesque face at her.

"You will scare those painted faces right off the screen if you continue," Elysia laughed.

"I've the suspicion you are as bored as I am with

being laid up," he said dropping down gratefully onto a cushioned chair before the warm fire.

"Should you really be up and about yet?"

"If I'd stayed in that blasted bed another minute I would have started to grow to it," he declared passionately. "I'm your brother-in-law, by the way, Peter Trevegne."

"I'd surmised that. I'm not accustomed to inviting complete strangers into my salon." Even had she not recognized him at once as the young man who'd been carried in from the carriage that day, she would have known who he was—for he bore a great resemblance to Alex, with that shock of raven-black hair and hawk-like features. Except that his eyes were a soft blue—and friendly.

"Well, I should hope not! And, I hope I shall not remain a stranger to you," he said, his eyes twinkling flirtatiously.

"I don't believe you shall—you are far too forward to allow that to happen," Elysia retorted impishly.

"By God! Alex said you were no simpering little mouse," he laughed in delight.

"Indeed, I'm not! I must apologize for being a complete failure as a hostess. Although this is your home, I should be entertaining you, and seeing to your needs—not the reverse."

"Please don't! I've been 'seen to' enough to last me two lifetimes, what with Dany pouring that wretched witches brew down my throat, and the maids twittering and giggling about me like a nest of sparrows—and all of the time having to dampen my curiosity," Peter said in a grievous tone.

"About me? But as you can see, there is nothing to be curious about me."

"The fact that you are my sister-in-law is enough to cause wonder. If anyone would have told me a month ago that Alex would be married now, I would have suspected rats in their upper story. If I did not know my brother so well, I would suspect you of having accomplished the coup of the century—however, I'm of a mind to believe, now that I've seen you, that you never had a chance to escape Alex—he takes what he wants. I would warn you, if I thought it would do any good, not to cross swords with Alex," Peter warned, "but by the look of you I can see that it won't. I should know—I've been on my beam ends too many times after a confrontation with Alex."

"Your warning comes too late, my fingers have already been burnt—but I'll not be tyrannized," she told Peter emphatically, a light of battle in her green eyes.

"Alex was right. You've a temper. He is certainly going to have his hands full," he laughed, amused by the thought of Alex meeting up with difficulties.

But Elysia did not laugh. Alex would not want to waste his time over her. He had the lovely widow to keep him busy. She had seen him from her window, out riding with Lady Woodley, who had predicted confidently that he would return to her.

"Odd that I never met you in London," Peter was

saying when there were voices from the hall, and the Salon door was opened to admit Charles and Jean-Claude d'Aubergere. The Count was carrying a large bouquet of yellow roses which he presented to Elysia, bowing deeply over her hand as he touched it lingeringly with his lips.

"That you should be so indisposed. I would kill the fiend that dared to do this to you, *ma petite ange*," he exclaimed in a throbbing voice, his dark-brown eyes gazing caressingly on her white shoulders that rose enticingly from the lace about the neck of her green silk robe.

"It is so kind of you to call, Count, and thank you for the beautiful roses." Elysia lifted the fragrant flowers to her nose and breathed appreciatively of their scented loveliness.

"How are you, Peter?" Charles finally asked, taking his eyes from Elysia's reclining figure reluctantly.

"I could have died right here on the spot for all you'd have noticed," Peter complained with resignation, watching Charles' look of infatuation.

Charles flushed and sent him a baleful look. "You're just miffed because the Count didn't bring you any flowers."

The Count looked nonplussed and sent an apologetic look to Peter. "But I am most embarrassed. I did not know that this was the custom—please to forgive me."

Peter scowled fiercely as Charles gave a hoot of

laughter, and repressing a smile, Elysia explained to the chagrined Count that they were just jesting.

The Count's chin lifted higher and he looked haughtily down his thin, aristocratic nose at the two young English gentlemen sitting in the elegant brocade chairs, their long legs outstretched carelessly, and his lips thinned. "It is not polite to make the joke at a guest in my country," he admonished in a stiffly-affronted voice.

Peter had the grace to look slightly ashamed. "Accept my apology, Count, but it was not meant as a slight to you." He sent a quelling look at Charles, who shifted uncomfortably. "He doesn't always think before he speaks."

"That seems to be something that you and Charles have in common, Peter," Alex said, sauntering into the salon still wearing his riding clothes. He glanced about at all the faces turned towards him and smiled his crooked smile. "I leave my wife unattended, and hopefully resting, for a moment, and what do I find when I return? My wife holding court for all of her admirers—and you certainly have collected quite a few."

"Not as many as you, M'Lord, I should imagine," Elysia retorted. He seemed slightly put out at finding her entertaining. She could almost believe he looked jealous—but that was absurd. Had he not just been out riding with the all-too-lovely young widow? If *he* could enjoy the company of others, then *she* would too!—despite the obvious displeasure it caused.

Elysia cast a look at him from under her lowered lashes. He was so handsome in his riding breeches and high boots, as he sat listening politely to the Count. The Count might have dark good looks—his profile reminding her of a Greek god, his eyes smouldering when he gazed at her, his lips sensuous, but she preferred Alex's cool, good looks. He exuded power and strength with every movement of his big, muscular body. The Count seemed to fade into insignificance beside him—looking effeminate with his soft white hands, his gestures seeming theatrical.

"Well, I've lost out on it now. Today was to have been the match—and I'd a winner with my bird, eh, Charles?" Peter was declaring disappointedly.

"Biggest and meanest rooster I've ever seen! Would've wagered my whole allowance on it."

"Never spent so much time on one thing before in my life," Peter said with disgust, "and all for nothing—we'd set this match up to take care of that upstart Peterson's bird—put a stop to his infernal braggings once and for all."

"I did not realize that people trained roosters for cock-fights," Elysia commented ignorantly. "I thought you just found one and let it loose in the ring."

Peter gave her an outraged look and snorted rudely. "Good thing you don't lay wagers or you'd be out of pocket post-haste. It's a science—an art—raising and training a good fighter," he continued ponderously, as if explaining to a small child. "He should be in his prime, about two years old when you start a rigid training program to bring him up to the mark. I trained my rooster for about six weeks, sparring him off with several other birds for practice."

"Wouldn't he get hurt?"

"No, his heels are covered, of course," Peter answered in exasperation. "Don't you know anything, Elysia? They only wear gaffles in the real fight."

"What are gaffles?" Elysia laughed, looking confused. "I am afraid this is completely incomprehensible to me."

"A gaffle, my dear," Alex explained in amusement, "happens to be a spur. It's made of silver and about two inches long, and curved in similar fashion to a surgeon's needle—and quite deadly."

"How perfectly awful!" Elysia protested. "That is cruel and inhumane! And you, of course, enjoy this . . . this sport, although I could think of a more appropriate description for it."

"No, as a matter of fact, I find it rather distasteful. Not at all what I fancy for amusement," Alex commented in a bored voice.

"Well, I do not care for it at all, and think it despicable—even though I've no great love for roosters."

"I would not put in a bird that could not defend himself," Peter said staunchly in defense of his sport. "I go to a great deal of trouble and effort to train him. See to all of his needs myself—even get up early to help fix his feed. Sweated him in a basket of straw after feeding him, too! Then in the evening, you are supposed to take him out of the basket and lick his eyes and head with your tongue," he continued, beginning to warm to his subject until halted by the gasps of dismay from the others.

"Good God! You didn't really lick the damned bird?" Alex asked, astounded.

"Of course not!" Peter exclaimed indignantly. "What do you take me for—a jackdaw in peacock's feathers? I'm no Tom Noddy, had one of the stable-boys do it, of course."

"Ah, *je ne suis pas dupe, cet temps,*" the Count said mockingly. "*Vous plaisantez.*"

"No, I am afraid Count, that this time Peter is serious. He is not fooling, and I am never surprised at the extent to which he will go when he becomes involved in something," Alex said in resignation.

"*Mon Dieu,*" the Court murmured, shaking his curly, brown head with bewilderment. "Ah, you English. But I must take my leave of you," he apologized, casting a regretful glance towards Elysia. "I hope I will have the pleasure of your company soon, when you are completely recovered." He kissed her hand, but his dark eyes were on her mouth. "*Je suis enchanté.*"

"Thank you for the lovely roses, *Monsieur le Comte,*" Elysia thanked him graciously, withdrawing her hand from his tightening grasp when she noticed Alex's eyes narrow as he stood to escort the Count to the door.

"Odd fellow, that," Peter commented after the door closed behind the Count and Alex. "Don't understand all that French gibberish. Fellow ain't got a sense of humor either." Peter got reluctantly to his feet and made for the door. "Better leave, too. Feeling a bit seedy." He looked to Charles. "You coming?"

"Momentarily," Charles answered hesitantly, looking about nervously.

Peter paused in the doorway. "You know, Elysia, you're all right. Didn't think I could get along with anyone Alex married. Had my blood stirred at the thought of who it could possibly be. Didn't know of any I'd care to call a sister-in-law, by God. But you're a thoroughbred," he mumbled shyly, unaccustomed to displaying his feelings, and quickly left the room.

Charles coughed, cleared his throat, and nervously shifted his weight from foot to foot. He pulled a small piece of paper from his coat and dropped it onto Elysia's lap. His color was high as he said haltingly, "Don't hold much for bending the knee to poets and the like—I'm no scholar—no one can accuse me of that, but well . . ." he stopped, not knowing how to continue, ". . . I just had to write this for you. Don't ask me where the words came from, 'cause I don't know. Never happened to me before." He seemed bemused by the experience.

Elysia unfolded the paper and read the hastily scribbled lines of poetry:

Green, green eyes, as green as the grasses,
Red-gold hair as bright as the sun
Soft, soft skin as creamy as molasses,
Our singing hearts shall beat as one.

She looked up at the young man standing uncomfortably before her, anxiously awaiting her reaction. "Charles ... this is the kindest and most thoughtful deed anyone has ever done for me. I shall treasure it forever. Thank you, dear Charles." Elysia stood up and impulsively kissed his scarlet cheek, as the door of the salon opened and Alex walked in, only to abruptly stop at the apparent embrace of Elysia and Charles.

Charles bowed, and hastily made his retreat from the room and the frowning countenance of the Marquis. His heart was indeed singing, as he closed the door and jubilantly made his way down the hall, a wide smile on his face—unaware of the ogling housemaids' giggling looks.

"Well, well, I had no idea you dispensed your kisses so freely—or is it just me you do not care to endow them upon?" Alex asked sarcastically. "I do seem to recall your once saying you were very discriminating in your tastes. I had no idea your taste was for young unfledged and callow youths, barely out of the schoolroom."

He closed the distance between them in a quick fluid movement, until he stood just before Elysia. "I was under the impression, obviously a misconception, that you were fond of a *man's* kisses and caresses."

Alex reached out and pulled her hard against him. "That you responded when he made you feel fire in your blood, your breath coming quickly and unevenly. Didn't you feel hot when he covered your milk white body with his kisses?" he murmured huskily, nibbling about her neck and ears, his lips caressing her throat slowly. Alex's arms tightened about Elysia, pulling her closer into him, hurting her side that was healing.

Elysia shivered as his lips parted hers and he kissed her deeply and passionately, his mouth holding hers possessively as if he could not bear to release it. Then suddenly he picked her up and carried her through the door to his room, laying her down gently on the bed she had lain in only once before. Elysia closed her eyes and waited. She wanted this—even if it was only desire and not love, on his part. She would take what she could—her pride be damned!

Elysia felt his hard hands move over her body, removing her robe and gown with impatient hands until they lay together naked, entwining into one. Alex pressed soft kisses onto her yielding mouth, murmuring lover-like words into her ears. "Do you really need another's kisses? Can Charles or that fawning Frenchman give you this?" he demanded, his lips hardening as he kissed her again, his fingers threading through her hair, forcing her lips hard against his as he kissed her. She struggling for breath.

"It was only gratitude," Elysia spoke, breathlessly. "He wrote a lovely poem to me. It was sweet and I was merely being grateful."

"Charles wrote a poem! You must indeed be a sorceress—weaving your spells like a gossamer web about poor unsuspecting mortals. Well, I will give you more than words penned on paper in response to your sorcery."

Elysia gave herself up completely to his ardent lovemaking. Returning kiss for kiss, caressing him until he groaned with pleasure and desire, taking her swiftly and urgently, until they both lay panting. Still wrapped together, their bodies entwined with her ear against his chest, she could hear the rapid beating of his heart.

"They say I am a devil straight from Hell—but you M'Lady are named for paradise. The ancient Greeks sought Elysium, but I have found it, and hold it here in my arms," Alex whispered thickly, his lips still kissing hers hungrily. "Take me there again, Elysia," he demanded.

Elysia smiled sadly. Heaven and Hell—they both shared a little of each.

Cruelty has a human heart
And Jealousy a Human Face,
Terror, the Human Form Divine,
And Secrecy, the Human Dress.

Blake

Chapter 12

"Lady Trevegne, please wake up. Lady Trevegne!"

Elysia murmured protestingly and snuggled down further beneath the covers, pulling them about her shoulders. But the maddeningly insistent voice persisted, like a buzz in her ear.

"Oh, please, Yer Ladyship, ye've just got to come," the squeaky voice pleaded tearfully, until finally Elysia felt herself being shaken from her sleep. She turned over onto her back and peered into the shad-

323

owy darkness above her bed. "What is it?" she asked drowsily.

"It's me, Yer Ladyship," a small voice spoke weakly from beside the bed.

Elysia reached out her hand and drew back the hangings of the bed, seeing before her a small shivering form vaguely discernible by the light from the fire. "Who is it?"

"I'm the upstairs maid, Annie. I—I sometimes help Lucy."

"Annie?" Elysia yawned sleepily. "Yes, well . . ." she yawned again and sighed. "What is it you could possibly want at this hour? It must be after midnight, at least?"

"After two, Yer Ladyship," Annie answered promptly.

"After two!" Elysia sat up, shaking the sleep from her brain. "Whatever is the matter?"

"I've a note fer ye. It's a matter of life and death I be told te tells ye," she whispered, thrusting the paper forward with a crackling noise.

Elysia took it cautiously, looking suspiciously at the young maid. "Who is it from?"

"Oooooh—I'm never to tell. Seein' how it's a secret an' all. I gave me word of honor, that I did."

Elysia tossed back the bulky covers and slid reluctantly from the warmth of her bed, slipping into her slippers as her feet touched the floor. She walked over to the fire and opened the note, her eyes scanning the contents quickly as the light from the fire threw shadows across her face. "Get my cloak from the wardrobe, Annie. The dark one with the fur hood—and be quick. We must hurry!"

Elysia wrapped herself in the thick cloak, pulling the hood forward over her hair. "Are there some back stairs that will let us out near the stables, Annie?" Elysia questioned the girl.

"Oh yes. There be the side stairs—for the servants."

"Show me quickly—but be quiet. No one must find that we've gone," she cautioned as she swept out of the room, the edge of her cape catching the corner of the table like the snap of a whip, sending the thin sheet of paper floating to the middle of the floor.

Elysia followed the little scurrying maid down seemingly endless darkened corridors, until finally Annie stopped before a plain, narrow door, the flickering light from the candle she held in her shaking hand their only guide.

"This be it, Yer Ladyship. Ye'll be careful, fer it's a might steep. The stables be te yer right."

"Thank you, Annie. Now, I will knock twice," she explained, "and you let me in. I do not know how long I shall be."

"Oh, Yer Ladyship!" Annie exclaimed in a frightened voice. "I don't rightly care to be a-stayin' here in the dark."

"Nothing will harm you here in the house, Annie."

"Well, ye never know what's to be about at night—maybe even one of them Frenchies—cut yer throat they will," she paused apprehensively, "after

325

they've done worse te yer body—if ye knows what I means." She stood nodding her head knowingly as she hunched her shoulders together, hugging her thin arms protectively about herself.

"As long as you remain as quiet as a mouse—not fidgeting about—then you shall be perfectly safe. Sit here and wait for me," Elysia said authoritatively, anxious to be on her way, as she firmly guided the timid girl into a chair near the door. She sat there, perched on the edge, shaking as much as the flickering flame of the candle.

Elysia reached the stables without mishap, entering through a side door that was concealed from the windows of the house. The strong smell of horses and hay struck her nostrils as she moved silently along the stalls, the occasional neighing of a horse in greeting accompanying the swish of her cape, as Elysia made her way towards a faintly-glowing light in a corner of the stable.

"Ian!"

"Shsssh!" Jims cautioned her, placing a warning finger against his lips. "We'll not be wantin' the whole stable to be awakin' up, now do we, Miss Elysia?"

"Ian, what has happened to you?" Elysia demanded, kneeling down beside him on the straw and taking his bruised face gently between her hands.

"I suppose you would not believe me if I told you that I walked into a tree?" he joked feebly.

"No indeed, I would not—more than likely it was

a taproom brawl, by the way you look and smell,"
Elysia declared indignantly, wrinkling her nose with
distaste. She moistened a soft pad of cotton with
water and patted it carefully against his swollen
eye, holding it firmly despite his wincing at the contact.

"Don't know why Jims had to call you in on this.
You're hardly fit to be out of bed. I'll deal with you
later, Jims," he bit off angrily between gritted teeth.

"Now, now, Master Ian," Jims said placatingly,
not at all intimidated by Ian's promise of discipline.
"How was I to know you weren't hurt real bad?
Being covered with blood and all—you looked half
dead. Miss Elysia'd never forgive me if I'd not called
her, and you'd of died or something." He shook his
head worriedly, pursing his lips thoughtfully. "Reckon
these parts around here ain't safe fer Demarices."

"Jims was right to call me, but enough of what
should have been. The important thing is, what
happened to you, Ian? I hardly think a tree deliv-
ered what must have been a fine left hook to your
eye," she said drily, wiping away most of the blood
and dirt that had covered his face.

"Ye'll be havin' a real shiner, Master Ian," Jims
commented.

"I can feel that for myself," he grumbled.

"At least you are beginning to look human again."
Elysia sat back on her heels, handing the soiled rags
to Jims. "Are you in pain anywhere else?"

"My pride has been dealt a mortal blow, along

with a few well-aimed punches into my stomach," he told her as he felt his stomach gently.

"I'll wager a monkey you did some damage before they laid you low," Jims chuckled, relishing the thought of some broken noses and missing teeth.

"Not as much as I'd like to have—but I can guarantee you they will remember the feel of my fists," he added grimly, "and they will be nursing a few bruises before the night is out."

"Ye always could place a punch where it counted," Jims added proudly, as he rinsed out the soiled rags in a bucket of water.

"Well, they certainly made short work of me this evening," Ian admitted ruefully. "Dusted my jacket but good!"

"There were more than one?" Elysia demanded outraged that a gang of cutthroats should accost her brother.

"There were a couple of brawny, ham-fisted fellows that I'd not invite for afternoon tea, sweet sister."

"Oh, Ian, do be serious. You've very nearly had your brains bludgeoned, your face pummelled into a pulp—and you sit here calmly cracking jokes which I do not find in the least bit amusing," Elysia stormed, near to tears.

"I'm sorry, my dear—I only sought to relieve the tension. Sometimes a joke, regardless of its merit, does help."

"No, I am the one who is sorry for snapping at you," Elysia said repentantly, "but if you only knew how worried I have been. I cannot introduce you to my husband, or friends. You skulk about the countryside by night with disreputable types who would kill you—masquerading, as heaven knows what? I know you are involved in something—can't I be of any help?"

"There is too much at stake in this *masquerade* I am playing to take any chances," Ian said, giving Elysia and Jims a hard stare. "The future of England may be in jeopardy."

"Oh," Elysia murmured, dismayed.

"This is far more important than either of us, right now," he explained, "and furthermore, I am not here under my true identity. People know me as David Friday."

"David Friday!" Elysia exclaimed. "But you can't be—you are the one that Louisa was telling me about!"

"Louisa Blackmore . . . she has spoken of me?" Ian asked hesitantly.

"Yes she has," Elysia told him, looking at his flushed face with knowing eyes. "In fact, she is quite enamored of you."

"S-she is? Louisa has some small fondness for me?" he asked with a shining light in his blue eyes.

"Hardly a small one. You made quite an impression on her, I should imagine." Elysia stared at him in puzzlement. "Why must you assume a false name?"

"When you do not know who the enemy is—or what information he has—then you must take all

329

possible steps to safe-guard yourself and your mission. My name might have been mentioned at the Ministry, and as the saying goes, walls have ears. Possibly we are over-reacting, but no precaution is too great, if it insures success."

"I see—it sounds very dangerous," Elysia said thoughtfully, as she stared at Ian's bruised face.

"Yes, these men deal roughly with intruders. I would not care to have you within a mile of them, Elysia—that is why I hate having you even remotely involved."

"How did they discover your identity?"

"They do not know yet who I really am, or I would be fish bait now—not merely suffering from a few bruises."

Elysia shuddered at the horrible thought of what could have happened, taking hold of one of his big hands and holding onto it tightly as if she'd never let go. Ian smiled, knowing she must be frightened, and squeezed it comfortingly.

"They think I'm a no-account sailor—dishonorably booted out of the Royal Navy, and a little too fond of the bottle to be reliable." Ian sniffed distastefully at his clothes, which reeked of cheap whiskey. "I took the precaution of liberally dousing myself with the horrid stuff before venturing too close—just in case I was seen—which, as it so happens, I was," he concluded with self-disgust.

"Too close to what?" Elysia asked anxiously.

"Too close to a vicious smuggling ring."

"Here? But I thought most of those stories were

bombast—and what could a few barrels of brandy and several yards of velvet matter to you—an officer in the Navy?"

"These smugglers do not traffic solely in contraband cargoes—they smuggle in French spies who steal and buy secret information—at great cost to our country and people."

"Treason!" Elysia whispered. "But surely no Englishman would dare to betray his country. Are you quite sure?"

"Yes," Ian answered grimly. "There are men who would sink to the basest of foul deeds in seeing to their own interests. They'd sell their souls for a few gold sovereigns."

Who could possibly be so treacherous to sell out their country, Elysia thought, a frown marring her forehead?

"Squire Blackmore," Ian answered her thoughts.

"The Squire? Oh, no! But that is quite impossible. Why ... he is a ... a puffed-up peacock," Elysia exclaimed in disbelief.

"A peacock, yes, but beneath that brilliant plumage is a greedy, power hungry man—coiled like a snake ready to strike, should someone interfere with his plans. He plays the bountiful host, while he starves his tenants. He shows a benign and affable face to his guests while he tyrannizes the countryside with his cruel ultimatums and threats."

Elysia sat stunned, disbelief written on her face. Squire Blackmore? A smuggler—a traitor! But he acted such a buffoon, an obvious braggart, bloated with pride, obsequious and toadying up to his affluent friends, that she had never imagined he could be dangerous. Elysia remembered how he bullied Louisa though, and he did remind her at times of a jack rabbit—hopping about the place, his nose twitching at the least little thing, aware of every movement in a room—almost as if he were expecting some danger—as if he were on the alert.

She had been fooled, blinded by the flashiness of his dress—not seeing the real man bedecked by the glitter—a glitter that was tarnished.

"We must apprehend this traitorous band of smugglers before they can succeed with their plans," Ian continued in a hard voice. Elysia watched him as he talked. He had changed more than she had realized, for he was a man with a purpose—a determined man who would be a merciless enemy.

"I do not wish to involve you, Elysia, but you could supply me with information. You could be my eyes and ears. You have access to Blackmore Hall, which I do not. You must watch for any new arrivals—anyone you have not met before. I also want you to keep an eye on the Squire, and those with whom he would hold private conversations, although I doubt that he would be so obvious about it. But one can never overlook the obvious, it is sometimes the best form of concealment. The one person I am especially interested in, as to his movements, is the Comte D'Aubergere."

"What has he to do with this?" Elysia asked startled.

"He is our spy."

"Oh, no!"

"You have met him?" Ian asked sharply with interest kindled in his eyes, his left one beginning to close from the swelling.

"Yes I have," Elysia answered sadly. "I cannot believe that he is implicated. I know he is French, but he hates Napoleon. Why, his estates were confiscated, and he is now penniless because of Napoleon. How could he possibly be an agent?"

"He is," Ian replied sternly. "He has secret governmental papers right now which he stole from the Ministry. He will try to get them to France. We've proof of his allegiance to Napoleon. He was lying when he said his estates had been confiscated, if indeed he ever had any estates—probably isn't even a Count. And if he really is what he says, which I doubt seriously, then he is like many of his compatriots who seek to regain their estates by doing Napoleon's bidding."

Elysia sighed heavily. Was no one what they seemed? Were they all playing at deceit—a continuous, never ending game of charades? Even she hid her true feelings from others. How easy it had become for lies to leave her lips.

"The Count has carefully hidden the documents— should you see or hear anything, you must tell Jims, and he will let me know. We have ships watching for the crossing from France, but we cannot allow them to spot us and flee. We have reason to believe they are waiting for a French war ship to transport them—this information is of that great a significance. It will occur within the next few days. Saturday is the first night without a moon, and they could not risk the crossing during the past few nights with it being clear and bright under a full moon."

Ian pulled himself up, and bringing Elysia to her feet gave her an affectionate hug. "You will confine yourself to listening and watching—no snooping. I do not want you to put yourself into any danger. Jims will keep me informed on your recovery—"

"But I am practically fully recovered now, Ian," Elysia interrupted.

"You are still weak and I'll take no risks with your safety, but I know your hot-bloodedness at times, so I caution you, Elysia," Ian warned her, "this is no game we are about. These people are dangerous, and they would not hesitate to remove you from their path should you stand in their way. That is why Jims will know of all that you do, and you shall report everything to him—do you understand me, Elysia?"

"Yes, Ian," Elysia promised reluctantly. "I shall be careful."

Ian seemed satisfied by her answer, but cautioned, "Now you understand why, more than ever, that my identity must remain a secret. No one must know of me, or my mission, for we do not know for sure who are our friends. Now you must go before catching your death of cold. I feel dreadful about your having even the slightest knowledge of this affair—God only knows how much I wish you were back up north, and clear of this situation," Ian added worriedly.

"Do not worry about me, Ian. I shall be fine, for you've far too many thoughts to trouble your mind without adding the worry of my safety to it," Elysia said confidently. "Besides, they wouldn't dare to harm a Marchioness. I shall be quite safe. But what about Louisa?" she added softly. "I have come to like her a great deal, and I am sure she is not involved."

"Of course she isn't—why, she is as innocent as a babe!" Ian looked despondent. "I am worried about her too, but what can I do?" He shook his head with defeat. "She will get hurt no matter what, for there is only one outcome to this, and her name will be blackened by it all." Ian glanced at Elysia as she stood quietly beside him. "Look after her, will you? She will need someone to turn to, to shelter her, and . . ." he stopped, unable to continue, despising the role he would have to play, ". . . she will not desire my presence."

"I shall look after her, Ian, but I think you wrong Louisa. She will understand when she knows the whole truth—she will not hate you."

"Go now, my dear," Ian whispered, resigned to the course he must follow, unable to believe Elysia's words of comfort.

She kissed him quickly, and pulling up her hood,

silently left the stables with Jims insisting upon accompanying her safely back to the house.

"Jims," Elysia implored him as they stood before the small door set into the side of the house, "watch out for him. He will need your help more than I will."

"Now, Miss Elysia. Here ye are a-askin' me to be a-watchin' Master Ian, and he's a-askin' me to be a-watchin' ye, and ye both be a-knowin' that ye never do what I tells ye anyway. Ye always go and do what ye wants to—hardheaded ye both be, and nothin' I'm a goin' to do is goin' to be a-stoppin' ye," he complained.

"Poor Jims, we've always been a trial to you, haven't we?" Elysia asked contritely.

"Well now, I can't rightly deny that." Jims grinned, having wished it no other way. "Ye know I can't abide them tame dispirited un's—like 'em sassy and full o' the devil, that I do."

"Hard as it may be, Jims, do keep an eye on Ian, will you?" she whispered before disappearing behind the narrow door.

Elysia shivered and pulled off her cloak, flinging it upon the bed, and moved to stand before the fire, seeking its warmth, the light silhouetting her slender body beneath the thin, cambric nightgown as she stood rubbing her cold hands together.

Annie had let her in at her knock, with ill-concealed joy at the sight of Elysia—her face pale and eyes round as moons from her solitary vigil in the darkness of the corridor. Annie scurried away gladly to her own bed after hanging onto Elysia's arms with a vise-like grip, as they silently made their way back.

Elysia hugged herself trying to stop her shivers, more from nervousness than from the cold, she suspected, as she stared ruminatively into the flames. She really could not see how she would be of any help to Ian. She did not even know where to begin—or what to watch and listen for. Now that she knew the truth, every action, no matter how innocent, would seem suspicious to her. And what of Louisa? How would she fare after Ian's disclosures? She did not like to think that Ian was correct in his assumption that she would despise him, and turn from their friendship. If only . . .

Elysia turned, startled from her thoughts by the sound of a creaking chair. Alex was sitting quietly in the darkened corner of her room, unobserved by her when she had entered it moments before. How long had he been there?

"Where have you been?" he finally asked, in a deadly quiet voice that was manacing in its intensity.

She could not speak. Her voice felt frozen in her throat, and she could not turn her gaze from the golden eyes that seemed to be burning into her mind—reading her thoughts.

"Well, have you no glib tale to tell me? I do believe that I've some small right to know—after all, I am your husband. Or have you already forgotten that? Maybe you do not believe I've the right to know where my wife sneaks off to, in the middle of the night—a rendezvous of such import, that she braves a cold wind, half-dragging herself to keep her clandestine appointment."

He stood up and came slowly toward her, panther-like—as if stalking his prey. Elysia could feel the barely-restrained violence of his body as he halted before her, blocking any avenue of escape she could have planned, and stared down at her with contempt.

"Was it worth the effort?" he sneered, his lip curling with distaste as his eyes ran over her figure insultingly, mistaking the color in her cheeks from the heat of the fire, and the brightness of her eyes from surprise, as passion. "Did your lover fold you close into his arms and warm your shivering body with the heat from his own?"

He turned from her violently, as if he could not stand the sight of her, pacing back and forth in front of the blazing fire that seemed to feed his anger. Alex paused and looked at Elysia. "Well? Have you no plausible excuses, no honeyed lies to try and deceive me with?" he demanded. "Or are you going to stand there and brazenly admit you have met your lover? Well?"

"I've no lies, or excuses. I've nothing to say. You may believe what you will—although I would caution you that appearances can be deceiving—and what appears to be the truth is not always so," Elysia said quietly, unable to defend herself with the truth without breaking her solemn promise to Ian.

Alex would either have to find it in himself to trust her—or believe her unfaithful.

"You caution me?" he asked in disbelief. "Well, you do speak the truth, Madame—for you are not as you would have people believe!—the innocent young maiden—sweet and gentle, and so honorable." He laughed cruelly. "You were weaned by Eve herself. Deception and intrigue comes naturally to you.

"You are like all women—craving the excitement of stolen kisses—and stolen husbands. You make a mockery of all decent feelings. Your falseness and shamming almost blinded my eyes to your true colors, Madame." He turned from her, a look of self-loathing on his face at his own duplicity, and then abruptly flung a thin sheet of paper at her. "I do not believe I know this Ian—one of your lovers from the North, perhaps—or were you really going to London to meet with him, this story about a wicked and cruel aunt and your seeking a job just another of your lies? Maybe you were even in on Sir Jason's plan, was I that easy a pigeon to trap? I must congratulate you, Madame, for you play the part of the innocent maiden as if born to it."

"You should know better than anyone that you were the first and *only* man that I have ever been intimate with," Elysia finally said in her defense.

Alex's hands clenched, and a muscle twitched in the side of his cheek as if he could no longer control the burning anger inside him. He turned away from Elysia as she stood there with her green eyes accusing *him* of some crime. The cords in his neck were standing out tautly as he glanced about the room, coming face to face with the small porcelain-faced doll that sat taunting him with its painted smile, reminding him of the feminine wiles and treachery that he should never have forgotten. He wanted to smash it into nothingness. His hand reached out, and despite the despair-ridden shriek behind him, grabbed the little figure personifying all that he had come to loathe. He threw it from the table onto the floor where it lay broken—the face shattered.

Elysia pushed past him and sank down upon her knees, oblivious to the sharp pieces of porcelain as she bent over her doll and picked up a piece of the head—she held a blonde curl, odd pieces of face dangling forlornly from the crushed skull. She sank further onto the floor, her body shielding the broken doll in a protective manner, as if from further destruction, sobs of anguish coming from deep within her, shaking her body uncontrollably.

Alex stood dazed, stunned by his own loss of control, until the sounds of Elysia's weeping awakened him from his immobility. He stared bemusedly down at the crumpled figure that shook with each heart-rending sob. Reaching down he placed his hands on her shoulders to lift her up, but she jerked away from his touch as if burned, cowering away from him like a beaten dog.

Alex cursed softly before determinedly placing his arms about her and lifting her from the floor, holding her firmly, even as she struggled to escape him.

"Be still, Elysia. My God, I'll not beat you. You've no reason to pull away from me."

Elysia gave up then, going limp in the arms that still held her tightly to his chest. He put her down gently on the satin coverlet, smoothing back her hair with oddly stiff fingers.

"Elysia, look at me," he commanded, but her eyes stared into space—seeing nothing but her own tortured thoughts. Her face was deathly pale, her eyes red and swollen from her weeping as he reached down and pried loose from her death-like grip a piece of the broken doll.

"I hate you," Elysia finally whispered in an emotionless little voice, as he bathed the scratches on her hands with his handkerchief, moistened from a carafe of water on the bedside table.

Alex stood up when he had finished and said coldly, "The feeling is returned, Madame." With that he left her room. Elysia heard the door close between their rooms—a door that closed off more than just their adjacent bedchambers. She pulled herself up into a half-reclining position, propped up by her elbows and stared down at the mess on the floor. Lying there, broken by an imperious hand, were all of her hopes and dreams, all illusions—beliefs callously destroyed in a second of white-hot anger.

What did she care? If she were honest with herself she would admit that she'd already felt an erosion and corroding of those ideals—she had just not wanted to admit it to herself—possibly because that

was all she had left to hold onto. Even false beliefs
die hard. All she wanted was to be cherished and
loved, wanted and protected, her family about her.
If she lost faith in those dreams, then what indeed,
was there left for her? She would rather die than
have her dreams shattered.

What had she done that was so damning that she
should deserve this cruel blow? Elysia gave a choked
little laugh of despair. To have fallen in love with
that devil—she deserved whatever fate had dealt out
to her.

Latet anguis in herba.
  A snake lurks in the grass!
                   Virgil

Chapter 13

Elysia ran her fingers over the finely-tooled leather of the book she held in her lap, the intricate engravings feeling rough to her touch. Alex was out again—out somewhere riding with Lady Woodley. It was no secret—for Alex let her know exactly where he was going, and with whom, almost relishing in doing it. Apparently, he was unaffected by her cold silences and non-responses to his blatant baiting of her.

She wondered how many times he met with the widow? Did they rendezvous secretly in some secluded spot of their own? He had gone back to her—just as Lady Woodley had predicted. Elysia could not bear to think of the triumphant smile which the widow must be wearing as she gazed seductively up into Alex's golden eyes. Well, she could have him—she despised and loathed Alex for what he had done. No, that was a lie. She could not deceive herself. She was still entrapped by him. Against her better judgment, she was in love with Alex—more than ever, until she burned with desire. It hurt unbearably to be looked at with contempt and loathing by the man she loved—treated with less respect than the lowest scullery maid.

But could she really blame Alex? The evidence had not been in her favor—in fact, it had been damning. However, what could she have done? She had given her word of honor, and could not break it. It was a promise that could have far-reaching and tragic effects upon everyone, if broken—especially Ian.

No, her problem would have to work itself out on its own, and maybe ... one day ... Alex would know the truth about that night. But until then, it was out of her hands. Still, the agony and suspense of waiting through the endless days that followed, seemed almost unendurable. Nothing seemed to be happening that could possibly clear up the misunderstanding that existed between them, and Elysia could only watch helplessly as the gulf between Alex and she widened.

If only something would happen! But all her alert watching and listening gleaned little information for

Jims to pass on to Ian. The Squire sought no private meetings with the Count, at least not while she was there. They kept up a cordial, yet casual, relationship with each other, while in company.

Elysia found it hard to believe that the Squire was a smuggler—and a traitor—as she watched him entertain his guests with amusing stories, smiling benignly like a benevolent saint. And the Count—how easily she had fallen for his flattery and sad tale of woe. He continued to seek her out, pressing his attentions upon her more ardently than ever, with Alex's obvious attentions to Lady Woodley keeping the guests gossiping, while he turned a deaf ear and blind eye to the Frenchman's flirting.

They were all living on the edge of a precipice, she thought one evening in particular, as the laughter rang out around the Banqueting Hall, at one of the many stories the Squire regaled them with. His laughter drowned out the other voices. It seemed to Elysia's somewhat cynical gaze, like the last days of Pompeii—the unsuspecting awaiting their ultimate destruction. Only she was aware of their forthcoming doom.

And what would be the end result, the final act in this charade before the curtain fell? The Squire and Count tried for treason, Louisa and Mrs. Blackmore disgraced—what would they do? Where could they possibly go where the notoriety had not spread?

Mrs. Blackmore. How could she possibly survive such a blow? It was obvious for all to see how heavily she leaned upon the Squire—hanging onto his every word and gesture. She sat in her corner of the opulent salon like a meek little mouse in a room full of sleek cats, peering shyly at everyone, her shawl wrapped tightly about her thin shoulders. Try as she would, Elysia could not engage her in conversation, or even the most casual of pleasantries—but then, neither could anyone else. So after awhile they ignored her, her very existence forgotten.

It seemed prophetic that a storm was brewing, Elysia thought as she watched the angry black clouds gathering to the west. There had been clear skies and calm seas for the past couple of days—an uneasy calm had hung in the air like an axe above their heads.

"Devil of a storm brewing," Peter commented laconically, coming up behind Elysia. A distant roll of thunder rumbled a warning as they stood silent for a moment watching the heavy, rain-laden clouds looming larger with their black lacy edges.

"This is why I prefer London during the winter months," Peter said, jumping, as a bolt of lightning flashed ominously in the distance. "Be awhile yet before it opens up, though. Of course," he added glancing at Elysia's set face, "that storm hasn't a ghost of a chance to beat the one that's been brewing in here. Could cut the air with a knife, it's so thick. What the devil did you do to Alex to put his back up? Never seen him quite so rude and put-offish."

"We had a misunderstanding—a difference of

opinion," Elysia answered off-handedly, with little concern in her voice.

"Some difference! I'd hate to be around when you two had a real falling out, if this is an example of a 'difference of opinion,'" Peter expostulated disbelievingly. "When you enter a room that he's in, it's like waving a red flag at a raging bull. Alex has been going around with a look as black as thunder. I'm afraid to blink when he's with me—or he'll snap my head off. And you—you've been as aloof and estranged from the world as if you were a nun in a convent. It's none of my business, of course," he continued, despite the uncompromising look on Elysia's face, "and I'm not about to bring a hornet's nest down about my ears by asking Alex—but what happened to put you two at each other's throats?"

"A misunderstanding," Elysia repeated, almost as if talking to herself. "One that I am not at liberty to explain—and until I am, then there is no hope of a reconciliation," Elysia explained in a tight voice.

Peter put his arm about her shoulders and smiled sympathetically. This was indeed a new role for him—playing the learned and wise advisor. Why, he felt suddenly a lifetime older than Elysia, and he was only two years her senior, he thought in dismay, as he said encouragingly, "Alex is a proud devil—too proud by half, but proud as Lucifer he is . . . used to getting his own way, too—always has the last word—and certainly not accustomed to being crossed by a female," he laughed. "You've been giving him back word for word. He's so strong-willed and set in his ways that it must go against his grain to have to accept your independence. Why, I couldn't believe my eyes at some of the things that you've pulled off!"

"I am used to having my own way too—and do not take kindly, or give in meekly, to his arrogant, self-imposed authority."

"Well, you've managed to get away with more than I ever could! And I've certainly had more than my share of run-ins with big brother, and that may well be the problem. He is so used to playing the role of big brother to me, and being mother and father to me, that he naturally assumes command of everything, and everyone. He's got a little of the dictator in him, and that is why I'm so astounded by what you've been getting away with. Why, he'd have boxed my ears but good!"

"That is because he doesn't seem to care anymore what I do—if indeed, he ever did. More than likely it was just his ego that had been bruised by my willfulness, not concern for my safety or well-being," Elysia struggled to say calmly as a tear spilled down her cheek.

"Doesn't care!" Peter exclaimed incredulously. "That's absurd. He is mad about you. He's got a fiery nature, and in some way you've managed—as no other woman ever has—to strike a spark off it. And believe me, it's kindled into something big. The fire is there, Elysia, smouldering beneath that cold exterior. He didn't acquire his reputation of being a ..." he paused delicately, a blush spreading over his high cheek bones, ". . . a demon lover for being a cold fish."

"If he is *burning*, then it is for Lady Woodley, not for me."

"Hell!" Peter swore.

"I beg your pardon?" Elysia looked surprised.

"I said Hell, and I meant exactly that," Peter answered unrepentantly, "and you are not offended—I know you better than to think you'd swoon at ungentlemanly language—within reason of course," he added sheepishly.

"And why do you believe Alex doesn't pine after the widow? He has spent enough time with her these last few days."

"Ruse. Just to make you jealous. Doing it out of pique, that's all. Alex can't stand the Blackmores, or that palace they call a Hall. He's just going over there to avoid being alone with you—too mad, I suppose, to trust himself with you. And he is just using Mariana. If he'd have wanted her for a wife he'd have married her back in London—had plenty of opportunity. And he was glad to finish with her too—doesn't like it when they become too possessive, you know."

"Maybe he has changed his mind—realized he has made a mistake by marrying me," Elysia speculated, knowing why he felt the way he did about her—and knowing it was untrue.

"Nope, impossible. Alex doesn't make mistakes like that. Knows his own mind," Peter said with assurance. "Anyway, how could anyone think they'd made a mistake when they look at you? Have to be thick-skulled to believe that."

"All good Trevegne marriages are stormy ones, it's the Arab in us, or so they say," he added devilishly, knowing he'd attracted her attention.

"The Arab? Are you funning me, Peter? An Englishman with Arab blood in his veins?" Elysia asked skeptically. "And admitting to it? I would have imagined it to be the family secret—something to be whispered about—the skeleton in the closet. Most families have one or two hidden away. Of course, I realize that it is desirable to be able to trace one's ancestry back hundreds of years, but hardly advantageous to trace it back to an Arab—no matter how civilized that ancient race may be—when in London it is considered heathenish by proper society. In fact, any foreigner is *outré* nowadays." ·

"Ah, but you forget how society loves mystery and romance. We've already, or at least Alex has, become infamous and rather talked about. Can't you imagine how spicy the rumor of an ancestress who was an Arabian princess would shock and delight their fancy?"

"And is it merely rumor?" Elysia inquired, caught by Peter's intriguing story.

"No, as it so happens, it is indeed the truth; and that, my dear sister-in-law, would really shake the *ton* if they knew it was true—they like it because it adds to the Trevegne legend. It would scare them speechless—which might not be such a bad idea—if they knew all the history of our somewhat adventurous family."

"Well, now that you have succeeded in teasing my interest, it is only fair that you should tell me the story. After all, I can be trusted, since I am a Trevegne, can't I?"

"Ummm, I suppose so, but you're honor-bound now not to breathe a word of our tainted bloodline," he whispered.

"I promise," Elysia said solemnly, a twinkle of humor replacing the tears that had been in her eyes.

Peter smiled with approval and led her over to a chair and settled her comfortably, while sitting down on the rug before the fire, stretching out his long legs to the warmth, and grinned engagingly up at her. "We've quite an unsavory past, you know."

"Yes, I've heard of the freebooter."

"Oh yes, quite a character that," Peter said proudly. "Wouldn't mind going back to those days of adventure—full of swordplay and daring rescues of M'Ladies fair," he dreamed aloud, picturing himself with a cutlass and tri-cornered hat. "Now, this ancestor of ours was quite an adventurer. Must've sailed around the world several times in his travels—set the pattern for generations to follow."

"Including the freebooter who decorated the Great Hall with his loot?" Elysia teased.

"Set a fine example, eh?"

"A fine example for what, one might wonder?"

"Well, one could say that he opened up new horizons, encouraged expanding our knowledge of other people by traveling to far off and distant lands," Peter continued dramatically, enjoying his role as storyteller. "So, back to the first Alexander, my brother's namesake, of course," he grinned.

"Of course. I would have expected nothing less," Elysia agreed.

"He was out exploring when he was engaged in a battle with an Arabian slave ship, riding low with the proceeds from the sale of those poor devils—and with one very special passenger, as yet to have been bargained for—and a very valuable cargo, too—the daughter of a sheik from one of those unbelievably wealthy desert kingdoms. I've heard tell that they live like kings in those tents—put the Prince of Wales to shame it would, what with all their gold and jewels draped about them. These slavers had kidnapped the daughter of one of the desert kings, and was to be ransomed off, and then sold to the highest bidder at auction, no doubt. I'm afraid her fate had been sealed, until my swashbuckling ancestor came long, and claimed her, becoming so enslaved by her dusky hair and golden, desert eyes that he brought her home with him as his bride. That is how we account for the gold eyes which show up every other generation," Peter concluded with satisfaction, feeling like a court storyteller in ancient Baghdad.

"That is quite a story, Peter, yet I doubt in reality that it was as romantic as you have made it sound. Your ancestor was a pirate who took what he wanted, regardless of that poor girl's feelings—she was probably frightened half out of her mind. First, being kidnapped by slavers, and then, by an English pirate from a land she had undoubtedly never heard of, doomed never to see her family again."

"Could be—he was supposed to be quite a rogue—however, the lady in question had eight sons and three or more daughters, and lived to a ripe old age here at Westerly, surrounded by numerous grandchildren, her husband *her* devoted slave, his wandering days over."

"Rogues must run in the family," Elysia commented acidly beneath her breath.

"Are you just now finding out how much of a rogue my brother can be?" Peter asked, hearing her muttered words.

"I've known since first we met," Elysia declared in exasperation.

"Oh? I would have thought you'd have avoided him like the plague then," he commented, wondering if what the Joker had said had indeed been the truth? What a wild scene that must have been, he thought with amusement—and these two fiery-tempered hotbloods at each other's throats.

He didn't know what Alex was playing at, but if he weren't careful he'd lose Elysia, and that indeed would be a shame. Devil take him, why the deuce was he playing the ardent lover to Mariana? He'd only been too glad to get rid of her in London—unless that was all just talk, but somehow he doubted that. Alex was just trying to make Elysia jealous— and that must mean that he was really in love with her. He wouldn't bother otherwise—it just wasn't his style. But something was amiss here; and if Alex weren't careful it could just blow up in his face. He didn't trust that little cat Mariana.

Devil take him, he thought, as he watched a fretful frown settle between Elysia's arched brows as she stared into the fire. No doubt wondering what Alex was doing with Mariana.

Elysia stood up abruptly, and picked up the book she'd been trying to read. "I'm going riding—I can't stand this much longer!" she said defiantly, rushing from the room with a flurry of rose-colored skirts flying out behind her.

Peter started to protest, then shrugged as the door slammed before he could utter a word. He got slowly to his feet and walked over to the window, silently cursing his brother. He glanced out, watching thoughtfully the hazy, white mist beginning to swirl about the rocks, masking the sea in an all-enveloping curtain. Fog—God, what a dismal day. He hoped Elysia saw it and had the good sense to come back in. But then she was in such a reckless, devil-may-care mood she might do anything—better go make sure she hasn't headed into it—just the thing she'd do too. She was so set in her ways—always taking Ariel, that fantastic horse of hers, out for a ride every afternoon, regardless of the climate. No wonder she and Alex struck sparks off one another. Peter shook his head as he poured himself a hefty swig of brandy before braving the cold and Elysia's wrath.

Elysia pushed the thick volume back between the other books on the shelf, mentally noting its place. She'd have to re-read it. Her mind had been so preoccupied by other thoughts that she could not remember half of what she had spent the morning reading.

"Darling, at last we are alone. Must we always be plagued by unwanted eyes and ears?" a petulant voice complained.

Elysia froze as the door to the library closed, and she heard the rustle of skirts move about the room.

"Oh, Alex. Why in here? You know how I do so hate books! And you seem to have an uncommon quantity here."

"You desired to be alone, didn't you, Mariana?" Alex answered with speculation in his deep voice.

"Of course I did, and this is why."

There was silence in the room. Elysia dared not move. From her position on the loft she could have had a panoramic view of the room below, but she stood rigid, pressed into the corner of the loft, her back against the cold glass of the window. She heard a long, indrawn sigh, and then a low, seductive laugh followed. Elysia pressed her knuckles against her mouth, biting into them as she sought to control the cry of agony she felt rising within her.

"I've missed you, my love," Mariana murmured softly in a whisper that carried, in the silence. "I shall make you pay dearly for leaving London—and marrying that creature."

"And I shall be more than willing to pay whatever price you demand," Alex answered lazily, his voice sending a wave of pain and longing through Elysia as she heard it.

"Ummm, I shall have to think of something fiendishly clever, for that will be the only way I will be able to assuage my hurt feelings. You know you were quite brutal to me, and I really should have nothing at all to do with you, Alex."

"If that is what you desire," Alex said coolly, in a bored voice. "It is your decision."

"You know I can't stay away from you—kiss me!" she commanded huskily.

The silence that followed was answer enough, to Elysia, of her husband's compliance to Lady Mariana's wish.

"What are we going to do about *her?*" Mariana finally broke the silence, her voice full of undisguised hate.

"Nothing."

"Nothing? B-but what about us?" Mariana demanded, anger sharpening her voice, its shrillness piercing the quietness of the room like a lance.

"We will continue as before—nothing need alter— we will be in London, and *she,*" he paused as if the thought of Elysia annoyed him, "will remain here. Quite simple, *ma chérie.*"

"You mean she will not be coming to London with you next week?" Mariana asked hopefully, her good humor restored.

"Precisely."

"Well, I suppose it will have to do, but what if she decides to follow you? She could cause trouble—embarrassment," she added, never satisfied until she had caused doubts, making sure her opponent was well out of the running.

"She will not come. I shall leave orders she is to stay here in St. Fleur. If she knows she is not welcome, then I doubt whether even she would care to include herself. Anyway, I think she will be able to 'amuse' herself here—we need not worry about her," he said coldly, his tone striking Elysia like a vicious blow.

"I recall telling you that you should not do something in pique—just because we'd had a small insignificant disagreement. If you'd only done as I'd told you, then we'd have been married now—and I'd be wearing those emeralds—not that red-haired wench. I still want them, Alex. Take them away from her. I know an expert jeweler who can change them into a different setting—something more modern." Mariana sighed, "Can't you get rid of her?"

"I hardly think I'm up to murder, my dear." Alex's laugh cut like a knife through the dull pain pounding in Elysia's temples. "And what of your plans to marry the Duke? Surely you've not forgotten that life-long desire of yours?" He sounded cruel as he added, "Or didn't you dangle the bait long enough, and your noble fish squirmed off the hook?"

"Oh, how horrid—you're so cruel Alex," Mariana reproached him. "I expect the announcement of our engagement shall be in the papers within a fortnight. Lin is quite anxious, as a matter of fact, to marry me. He already calls me his Duchess."

"Good for him—proves he's a man, after all. I wondered if he had any red blood in him at all," Alex commented dryly, apparently unperturbed by her attempt to make him jealous. "Shall we go? It would seem it is going to open up and rain—besides, it looks as though a fog is rolling in."

"This is the most inhospitable part of the world— oh, why did you have to be a Cornishman? Why couldn't you have a nice castle in Somerset or Sussex?" Mariana complained, her voice becoming faint as they moved toward the doors.

"Like Linville I suppose—but of course you needn't . . ." The rest of his words were cut off as the doors closed behind them.

Elysia stood irresolutely, unable to think or act coherently. He was going back to London—alone. She was to stay here in Cornwall—and he would go back to the life he'd lived before, to the woman he'd loved before—and still loved.

She knew now, without a doubt, that she'd lost him. She could no longer fool herself. Peter had been wrong, so very wrong. This was no game of jealousy played out to pique. He was going to leave her, Elysia choked back a laugh. How she would have rejoiced at that thought at one time, when she thought she hated him. Now . . . now she only felt sadness—as if something had died within her. She was like a bud that had begun to open, and flower, half-opened by the first warming rays from the sun and nourishing drop of moisture from the rain, it would now wither and die from neglect.

With tears blinding her eyes, Elysia made her way from the house. She'd already changed into her riding habit and went directly to the stables. No one dared to stop her as she ordered Ariel saddled, her face frozen, without expression. Jims was nowhere to be seen, and despite the groom's worried glances at the sky, Elysia headed out of the stableyard, contemptuous of the clouds.

She rode along the road daring the heavens to open up above her. She felt in no mood for any kind of interference—divine included. The groom lagged behind, becoming a mere speck in the distance as Ariel galloped down the road. Elysia continued to widen the distance, until she saw another horse approaching across the moors, from the direction of Blackmore Hall, with the intention of intercepting her. As the rider drew closer Elysia recognized his livery, a groom of the Squire's. He trotted alongside and pulled up, stopping in front of her.

"Ye be the Lady Trevegne?" he asked, pulling out a sealed note from his pocket.

"Yes."

"This be fer ye from the Hall." He handed it to her, and turning without waiting for an answer rode back the way he'd come, despite Elysia's call to wait. Elysia broke the seal. Probably from Louisa, and read the few words printed neatly on the paper, her hands beginning to shake as the words danced grotesquely before her stunned eyes.

Elysia's face was pale as she looked back to where the groom from Westerly was still an indistinct blur—she could not wait for him.

Alex had been injured, he was hurt. They told her that she must come immediately. The past was forgotten as Elysia raced Ariel faster than she'd ever ridden him before, across the stretch of moorland to the Hall—leaving the path, the dangerous bogs and holes forgotten in her panic. Also forgotten was that last conversation between Mariana and Alex, not meant to be overheard.

All that mattered to Elysia was that she get to Alex in time—all bitterness and anger disappeared as Elysia thought of him lying injured—in pain. That he would not want her solicitude did not phase her—she was still his wife—if in name only now, and she would take her place by his side—regardless.

After reaching the tree-lined drive that led towards Blackmore Hall, Elysia turned Ariel off, heading toward the summerhouse—a pagoda built within a copse of pine some distance from the Hall. It was used for picnics and lawn parties in the warm, spring months, but was now deserted and cold-looking under the darkening skies above.

What had Alex been doing out here? She did not want to admit to herself that Alex and Mariana could not resist stopping—to be alone and undisturbed before joining the others. Their love was so great they must make the most of each stolen moment.

Elysia threw all of these disturbing facts aside as

she dismounted and hurried inside, pushing past the red door with its carved dragon heads grinning menacingly into her face, and entered the octagonal-shaped room. She looked about her at the red, velvet, cushioned benches and large, satin pillows with their tassels dangling undisturbed—they were all empty—Alex was not here!

They must have moved him, she thought wildly, turning to leave just as someone entered silently through the opened door.

"Mrs. Blackmore!" Elysia cried with relief, rushing over to her as Mrs. Blackmore closed the door behind her. "Thank goodness! I'm so relieved to see you. Where is Alex? The note said he was here—and I was to come as quickly as I could. Is he b-badly hurt?"

"He is as well as can be expected," Mrs. Blackmore replied calmly. "We have moved him."

"Yes I know, but where? Up to the Hall?" Elysia demanded, making to move past Mrs. Blackmore, when she put out her hand and grasped Elysia's wrist. Her grip was unusually strong for such a small woman, Elysia noticed, as she gave Mrs. Blackmore's hand an impatient tug. "Please, Mrs. Blackmore. Allow me to pass."

"No. We did not move Lord Trevegne to the Hall." She released Elysia's wrist and walked over to a silk panel set into the wall. Fingering a small carved rose, she turned it. The panel slid open revealing a thick, heavy-looking iron door. Elysia watched in amazement as Mrs. Blackmore took a

361

large key from her reticule and fitted it smoothly into the rusted lock which opened without a protest. Mrs. Blackmore opened the door, revealing a steep flight of stairs descending into blackness.

"Surely he is not down there!" Elysia gasped as she hurried forward toward the yawning opening. "Why has he been taken down these stairs?" She looked at Mrs. Blackmore in confusion. "I do not understand this at all. If he is hurt, then . . ." Elysia's voice trailed off as she looked back into the blackness.

"My dear, should you really go down there?" Mrs. Blackmore asked hesitantly looking at the darkness with a shudder of her small frame. She shook her curly brown head regretfully. "It is not a pretty sight," she warned Elysia, patting her hand sympathetically.

"I have to go to him—don't you understand?" Elysia cried tearfully, pushing past the little woman who seemed nervous, and unable to make a decision.

Elysia stood on the edge of the doorway, peering down into the inky blackness below. "Is there no light, Mrs. Black—" she started to ask when she felt a vicious blow to the back of her head, and felt herself falling as a scream tore from her throat.

Delays have dangerous ends.
                    Shakespeare

Chapter 14

Louisa dallied along the pebbled path, pausing for a moment by a wildflower to stroke its petals, then hurrying along as she glanced apprehensively up at the stormy clouds, then stopping to gaze unseeingly across the moors engrossed in a daydream, the overhanging clouds forgotten in her reverie.

David Friday was avoiding her—he never attempted to see her anymore. He had always seemed to be there before. Every time she turned around, he was there, and she was not blind to the admiring glances she received from him either. But now he was never to be seen—except maybe at a distance, when she caught glimpses of his retreating back, and by the time she reached the spot where she'd seen him—he'd disappeared.

She could not understand it. David had changed from that quiet and attentive, young sailor with whom she'd fallen in love, into a preoccupied and stand-offish stranger who acted as if she bored him. What had occurred to cause this change in attitude? *She* had not changed—she was still the same. She was so confused. She thought she finally had found someone who loved her—and she loved him—yet now it all seemed to be crumbling away.

Louisa sighed dejectedly. Even if David had asked her to marry him it would have been to no avail. She could imagine her parents' reaction to an out-of-work, penniless sailor daring to ask for their daughter's hand in marriage—a daughter for whom they wished to make an advantageous match.

That was another thing that was puzzling her. Her parents still acted as if she would marry the Marquis—even though he was recently wed—and to someone as beautiful and kind as Elysia. How could anyone but a crazed person imagine that the Marquis would desire anyone else—especially someone as nondescript as herself?

But it was indeed an odd situation at Blackmore—Papa, grumpy and cross, drinking heavily, and Mama, edgy and fretful, refusing to leave her room for hours at a time.

Sometimes she felt as if they were strangers to her. Indeed, she had never been close to them. They never displayed any affection for her—she was merely a means to achieve their desires. She was only necessary and important to them as a pawn, to maneuver into a propitious marriage.

Louisa sighed, for she was afraid her parents were bound to be disappointed in that respect. But then, that would be nothing new. She was already a disappointment to them. She was ordinary—a plain and simple girl, with no ambitions to achieve prominence in London society. She was contented to stay in Cornwall. All she ever had hoped for was to fall in love with a respectable man and raise a family, but her parents had always looked higher for her in their grand scheme. Sometimes they frightened her by their single-mindedness—their relentless pursuit of wealth and position. She knew that she would never understand them, nor them her. They were worlds apart in their beliefs and desires. If only . . .

Louisa's attention was distracted from her thoughts as she saw a rider approach the summer house in the distance. She made a moue of distaste. She had never liked the Chinese-style pagoda—it seemed so incongruous and ridiculous to be squatting grotesquely in the English countryside.

As the rider came closer, Louisa saw that it was Lady Trevegne, and she was in a great hurry. Louisa hurried along, anxious to know what was amiss in their pagoda. Elysia had disappeared around the side of the building towards the entrance, by the time Louisa reached it, out of breath from her exertions. She paused a moment, leaning against the red, grilled ironwork decorously shield-

ing the opened windows, and was trying to catch
her breath when she heard voices from within.
Louisa pressed her face against the interwoven,
vine-like designs curiously, as she narrowed her
eyes and peered into the shadowy room.

Two men were just leaving it through a door set
into a panelled wall—a door that couldn't lead anywhere except outside—but they were going down a
stairway that led into the ground!

"We're to get rid o' Her Ladyship—dump the
body into the sea."

The ominous words spoken by one of the men
drifted through the grilling like a poisonous cloud of
gas. The door closed behind them, the panel sliding
closed, leaving a dreadful silence in the empty room.

Had they meant Lady Trevegne? Where was
Elysia? Louisa had seen her enter the pagoda not
more than fifteen minutes ago. She gave a muted cry
and ran back the way she'd come, stopping as she
looked for Elysia's mount. He was still there tethered
to a branch.

Elysia had not left. She must be down in that
ghastly place where the stairs led to—wherever that
was?

Oh, dear God! What was she to do? She must get
help, but she had no horse, and it would take ages
to walk back to the stables—and besides, hadn't
Papa said at luncheon that he would probably be
gone until late evening. Oh, what was she to do?

Ariel neighed nervously, eyeing the small person
making its way determinedly towards him.

There was only one course of action open for her, she must somehow manage to ride that monstrous horse. "Ariel, boy. You must let me ride you," Louisa pleaded softly, stretching out a timid hand to grasp the reins. "Your mistress is in danger. You must help me."

Ariel shied back nervously, nipping at her hand with his big teeth.

"Damn you!" Louisa swore for the first time in her life, before breaking down, tears cascading down her cheeks as she cried in frustration and disgust at her failure. Why must she be so weak?—so helpless that she could not save the only friend she had ever known. Her thin shoulders were shaking when she felt something push her, and Louisa turned around quickly as Ariel nuzzled her neck.

Louisa stared in disbelief, afraid to move as he snorted, not in a threatening manner—but out of curiosity.

"Oh, Ariel. You do understand," Louisa whispered as she once again made to grasp his reins, only this time the big horse made no effort to interfere. Shaking in relief and fright Louisa led him to a fallen log and mounted, not daring to breathe. She urged him forward and before she could catch her breath he was off like a bird taking flight. Louisa swallowed convulsively as she held on for dear life, her chip straw bonnet with its bunch of red cherries bobbing precariously on her brown curls. Louisa was beyond noticing that her blue dress was pulled up above her knees, revealing two stockinged legs and dainty red slippers, as she wondered if this had been a wise plan after all. She had almost decided to brave the hidden stairs and the two murderers when Ariel had consented to allow her to ride him. Now, as she was perched dangerously on his back, she wondered if the other idea would not have been safer.

Louisa had never traveled so fast in her life, the landscape was an indistinct blur in her eyes. Her main problem now was how she could stop him? Ariel was streaking in a direct line for Westerly and his stable, when Louisa saw three riders coming swiftly toward her.

"Please help me!" Louisa screamed, her cry for help capriciously blown back behind her by the wind. She did not think she could hold on a moment longer.

The rider on the larger of the three horses forced Ariel to veer off, and then crowding him as he rode alongside at a swifter pace, the rider leant across Louisa and pulled the reins from her lifeless fingers. Asserting his authority and strength he gently slowed the two horses down until they were brought to a standstill.

Louisa pushed her bonnet back from where it had fallen over her eyes with a hand that shook, seeing for the first time the face of her rescuer.

"Lord Trevegne!" she cried thankfully, never so glad as now at seeing his dark, arrogant features. "Oh, thank God you're here!"

"What in blazes are you doing on this horse,

Louisa!" Alex demanded as he soothed Ariel with a gentle hand as the big horse pulled impatiently at his bit.

"Where is Elysia?" Peter asked, riding up beside them with Jims close behind, and then staring incredulously at little Louisa Blackmore sitting on Ariel's back.

"They're going to k-kill her, and I d-didn't know what to do. I was so f-frightened," she sobbed incoherently.

"Kill her!" the Marquis expostulated, looking astonished. "What the devil are you jabbering about?" First, he had been ridden down by Peter and Jims who were looking for Elysia, who was out riding in this thickening fog—and without a groom. With Peter babbling like a fool, he'd thought, as he caught a whiff of brandy on his breath. Jims was grumbling about trouble and treason, and now Louisa Blackmore riding on Ariel, a horse that even *he* could not mount, was hysterically crying that Elysia was going to be murdered. He must be losing his senses.

He grabbed Louisa by her shaking shoulders to calm her. "Answer me. What is this about murder?" But Louisa continued to shake uncontrollably. Alex lost patience and slapped her across the cheek, in a sudden move, that caught the others off guard.

"Good God, Alex! What the devil—" Peter began.

"This is no time for hysterics, or a fit of the vapors. My God, what if she is telling the truth?" Alex looked at Peter's expression of horror that mirrored

369

his own. "Now," he told a somewhat calmed down Louisa, "tell me exactly what is amiss?"

"It's Elysia," she sniffed, looking at them with tear-filled eyes. "I saw her go into the pagoda—" she stopped, as Jims gasped loudly, swallowing the wad of tobacco he had been chewing, his face turning red as he choked on it.

Alex shot him a penetrating glance that caught the sudden look of fear in his eyes at Louisa's words. "—and what then," he urged Louisa on.

"She seemed very agitated about something, for she was running, and so I followed her, but I was walking and quite a distance, and it took me ten minutes or more to get there, a-and ..." she paused in remembrance as the threatening tears overflowed her eyes.

"And ... come on, Louisa ... you can tell me," Alex prodded gently, but persistently, determined to get the answers he needed.

"And then," Louisa continued, calmed by the Marquis' calmness, "I heard those horrible-looking men say they were going to kill her." She paled as she watched Lord Trevegne's eyes narrow and his lips tighten and draw back in what looked like a snarl.

"She be in real trouble, Yer Lordship," Jims said, his voice trembling.

"Come, we must go at once," Peter said urgently, making to move off.

Alex stared at Jims, knowing that he knew something, but that he could not spend the time to find out what. "Dismount, and await us here, Louisa, it is too dangerous for you to try and handle Ariel any further. It's a miracle you've even mounted him at all," Alex added, as he leant forward to lift her down.

"But they aren't there anymore. They went down the secret passage."

Alex looked dismayed. "Secret passage? Where is it? Quickly! Time is wasting."

"Behind a panel in the pagoda wall."

"Then you will have to accompany us to show us this panel." He lifted her swiftly in front of him and held her tightly in the circle of his arms as they raced back the way she'd come.

"I hope we are not too late," Louisa cried nervously as the ground sped past her frightened eyes. "I-I don't know how to open it, either."

"We will succeed . . . and I pray to God we are in time—for more reasons than you could understand," Louisa heard the Marquis say fervently, as she looked up into his set face—a face that had seemed to age within minutes with an expression of dread foreboding.

"Lieutenant Hargrave reporting, Sir," the young Lieutenant saluted smartly as he greeted his superior.

"Lieutenant," Ian returned the salute. "Glad to see you and your men." He watched as they beached their boat, stowing their oars and sliding the boat up onto the rocky beach in a well-trained, co-ordinated movement.

"The Admiral's compliments, Sir. We spotted the French warship at noon, lying off the point. Just waiting to slip in under this fog, Sir," the Lieutenant reported with rising excitement at the thought of a fight.

"Have they put to shore yet, Lieutenant?"

"The *Valor* will signal Sir, when they do—and we shall be waiting," he explained with anticipation.

"Be sure to conceal the boat," Ian cautioned as he watched every movement with critical eyes. "Yes, we shall indeed be waiting, but now we must act," Ian said—all business as he moved into action. "Get your men under cover—we want our fish well into the net—we don't want any to get back out to sea, nor ..." he paused, sending a speculative look up the narrow ravine, "like a rabbit into its bolt-hole at the scent of danger. And Lieutenant," Ian added, "unless the villagers shoot at you, don't shoot them—we don't want them harmed."

The beach looked deserted as the loaded boat rode the waves into shore, the rocks and crushed shells grating noisily against its hull as it was pulled ashore—the gentle lapping of the waves washing about the struggling men's ankles.

Ian and his men, concealed behind the rocks, stiffened as they heard an owl hoot, and breathlessly watched the emergence of a pack train from the mouth of the ravine where it had awaited the all-clear signal and the beaching of the boat.

"Give your men the word," Ian whispered to the young Lieutenant who was crouched down beside him. "At my signal we move."

Lieutenant Hargrave passed the word along to the anxiously-waiting Marines stationed in key positions along the beach as the pack train laboriously passed by them, heading for the boat where the two parties converged into one.

Ian waited—and then whistled piercingly, the shrill notes activating the waiting men into immediate action.

They formed a circle about the smugglers, making it smaller and smaller, as they closed in upon the astonished French sailors and frightened villagers. Chaos broke loose as the sailors tried to push their beached boat back into the surf, but it was still heavy with its cargo of unloaded contraband, and slow to respond to their futile heavings. The villagers made a break for safety, abandoning the determined efforts of their compatriots, and ran splashing through the shallows, their trouser legs flapping wetly about their heavy shoes as they attempted to flee with a squad of Marines in hot pursuit.

Shots rang out from under cover of the bow of the stranded boat as the French sailors saw the hopelessness of their attempt to escape.

Ian hit the soft sand in a single flying leap, his pistol drawn and primed, but the French were outflanked as the circle closed and surrounded them. Naked to the fire from the right and left of them, they surrendered—leaving several fallen and wounded comrades moaning in the sand.

Ian handed over command to the Lieutenant, whose eyes were shining brightly out of his dirtied face, his once immaculate uniform torn and soiled. Ian looked over the prisoners. He cared little for these French sailors, or for the sullen, frightened villagers being herded back to the boat under guard.

He had not, as yet, found his spy—or the dispatch. He had watched carefully as the pack train of mules and men approached the boat, looking for the Count and Squire among them—but they had not been present. Only the usual village men who unloaded the cargo and transported it up the cliffs to the numerous hiding places were there.

But he was puzzled—the Count and the Squire should have been here. This had been a special trip for the Count, specifically. Usually the French would not venture so close to British guns, but they were taking no chances with the Count—and his information. However, with both parties concerned so greedy, they had slowed themselves down by bringing in an extra cargo for the Squire, a bonus for services rendered, perhaps. Surely, he would have been here, ready to receive his extra booty, and the Count prepared to board at a moment's notice.

Ian swore, and was looking about him in a perplexed, and thoughtful manner when he caught a furtive movement along the cliff face.

"Here, you men, follow me!" he ordered a group of heavily armed men, standing idle now that the fight was over. Ian raced toward the cliff, his eyes trained upon the quickly-disappearing figure high up on the cliff.

"Search for a concealed path!"

They frantically searched the rocks and scrub for the path by which their quarry was fleeing, disappearing into the fog, which was shrouding everything within sight in a veil of white. He would not lose them—not after coming this close, Ian thought savagely.

"Here! I've found it, Sir!" a voice called triumphantly out of the mist.

The path was cleverly concealed between two boulders set back beneath an overhang of the cliff, and winding up through a hollowed-out portion of rock, only to emerge again on another side of the cliff—concealed, from above and below at its entrance, from curious eyes.

Ian and his men moved slowly along the narrow path, the fog hiding the sheer drop over the edge, and the uneven footing of the path. But if it slowed their progress, it also slowed down the fleeing figures up ahead, of which they occasionally caught a glimpse in the blowing fog that swirled about them, hampering each step they took. Ian fired a warning shot above their heads at the next sight of them. One of the figures halted, momentarily with indecision, then turned and continued on.

"The next shot will not be a warning shot," Ian

directed his men who had drawn their pistols in preparation.

The fog drifted about in eddies, fooling and teasing them with false glimpses ahead of the figures.

"Stop, or we shoot!" Ian yelled out as the fleeing figures became visible once again—but they continued, heedless of his warning. "Fire!" Ian ordered, as the fog moved across the figures, shrouding them in whiteness as the round of shots cut through it blindly. "Damn!" Ian muttered as they once more went in pursuit of an enemy just out of reach. Their path was blocked up ahead by a boulder, its black shape sitting squarely in the middle, cutting them off.

Ian bent over it and then gasped in surprise—it was the Squire. His black coat covering him like a tent. Ian carefully turned him over—the Squire was dead—shot through the head.

"Come on, we've more to do before this day is finished," Ian said grimly as he stepped over the dead body of Squire Blackmore, his sightless eyes staring heavenwards.

There is something behind the throne
greater than the King himself.
William Pitt, Earl of Chatham

Chapter 15

Elysia felt waves of pain pounding against her senses as consciousness returned to her with nauseating rapidity. She almost longed for the peaceful blackness of unconsciousness again. She moaned softly as she tried to sit up, but failed, as a sharp pain stabbed piercingly behind her eyes, and she collapsed onto the cold stone floor of the cave in a huddling crouch.

She opened her eyes and looked at her surroundings in disorientation, as the walls spun around and around, the torches wedged into cracks in the walls, flickering hazily before her eyes. In the distance, she could hear the undulating rumblings of the sea, as it surged against the mouth of the cave.

Elysia pulled herself up into a sitting position, leaning against a barrel for support—feeling its hard and steady presence behind her as her vision began to clear and her balance returned, the floor of the cave steadying and righting itself. She put a shaking hand slowly to the back of her head—feeling the sticky, congealed blood matted to her hair, wincing as she touched the tender bump on her skull. It ached unbearably, and closing her eyes she breathed deeply, as her stomach began to heave. She felt sore and stiff all over. Elysia glanced down at her riding outfit—torn and soiled, stained with blood from cuts and bruises covering her body. She nearly laughed hysterically as she thought of the work and careful stitching Dany had done, to mend it from her other accident. It would take more than that to salvage it this time.

Elysia repressed a shudder as she looked up at the steep and narrow steps cut out of the side of the cave, climbing dizzily up to the large, iron door set into the wall of the pagoda.

What had happened? She had fallen down those treacherous steps—and she was still breathing. She remembered the vicious blow to her head, and the emptiness of space before her, as she fell, but then blackness had engulfed her and she was mercifully unaware of her descent into the cave.

And what had happened to Mrs. Blackmore? She remembered that she had been up there with the

Squire's wife when she had fallen. Elysia looked about her—Mrs. Blackmore wasn't down here with her, injured and helpless. Surely they had not killed the Squire's wife, whoever had hit her over the head. No, she couldn't be dead—the Squire wouldn't have his own wife killed. But why did they trick her here to this underground cave, that was filled with their cache of smuggled goods? She wondered if Ian knew about this? What could they possibly want with her?

Elysia struggled to her feet, leaning heavily against the wall of the cave as her knees wobbled beneath her, a giddy feeling running through her. She'd have to get out of here—they must have thought she succumbed to her injuries, and they would soon be coming back to remove her body—probably to dump it into the sea.

She had no idea how long she'd been unconscious, but she felt chilled from lying on the damp stone floor. Elysia began to move slowly and painfully to the steps, when she stopped, startled as the door was flung open, and light streamed down from the flaming torch held high in front of someone coming down.

"Still alive?" an incredulous voice asked. "I am surprised. You certainly are hard to kill—as many lives as a cat," Mrs. Blackmore remarked in a peevish voice as she carefully stepped down the treacherous stairs; slippery from the moisture seeping in.

Elysia stood stupefied, as she stared at the figure of Mrs. Blackmore. That mild and meek little

379

woman—now holding a pistol pointed directly at her heart, a look of dislike in her pale eyes. She seemed to emit an evilness that Elysia had never before noticed.

Mrs. Blackmore's lips were curled back in a snarl as she waved the ominous-looking mouth of the pistol in a threatening gesture at Elysia.

"M-Mrs. Blackmore. What is the meaning of this outrage?" Elysia demanded, stepping forward bravely, as she quelled the fear that shook within her.

"Your pardon, Your Ladyship, for not explaining things more clearly. Will you please forgive me, Your Ladyship? The grand Marchioness—" she laughed unpleasantly, casting a look over Elysia's bedraggled appearance, "you don't look so grand to me, Your Ladyship, eh, boys?" she inquired maliciously of the two men who'd come in behind her, unobserved by Elysia as she'd stared hypnotically at Mrs. Blackmore.

Now she saw for the first time the two men who'd been standing silently behind Mrs. Blackmore. They were big and powerful-looking, with thick shoulders and long muscular arms, menacing as they stood with their bull-like stances, watching Elysia's predicament without a flicker of emotion on their cruel faces. Elysia remembered the men who had beaten up Ian. "They mean business," he'd said, and she'd seen first-hand the punishment they were capable of dealing out—if these were the same two.

"Her still looks mighty good t'us. Yes, indeed," the

smaller of the two, and dirtier one, smirked unpleasantly, giving his companion a knowing nudge with his elbow.

"Surprised?" Mrs. Blackmore asked in amusement.

"Indeed I am, Madame. You wrong yourself by not displaying your talents on the stage. Playing a part seems to come easily to you," Elysia answered flippantly, trying to recover from the surprise of Mrs. Blackmore's metamorphosis.

"I shall accept that as a compliment," she laughed, "for I should be good. After all, I played the boards for more than fifteen years before marrying the Squire—a lucky stroke of luck for me. I was quite a good-looker then—still am—but I'm playing down my looks of course, for this role. It is a role that I have not especially enjoyed but it has served its purpose."

"Which was?"

"To lull you stupid fools into underestimating me. Who would suspect the meek little Mrs. Blackmore as heading one of the biggest smuggling operations in England? No one gave me a thought—laughing and dancing, eating and drinking, enjoying themselves in my home, and never casting a look in my direction. They were too busy being entertained by the Squire—the gullible fools. They ask no questions as long as their bellies are full of food and drink, and they've plenty of games to keep them amused— they're as mindless as a pack of sheep."

"So you are the brains of the smugglers' ring?

And what of the Squire? Is he merely an actor too?" Elysia asked.

"Oh, no, he's quite legitimate. He had a small holding up North, but that's no use for big smuggling—and we needed lots of money. No, that estate had no place in my plans, and the Squire does whatever I want. He knows I'm the one with the brains, who keeps him in brandy and cigars, and surrounded by flunkies," she bragged.

"And what are your plans?"

"Well, I suppose you've the right to know," she deliberated thoughtfully for a moment, building the suspense, "since you play such an important part in them."

"I do?" Elysia exclaimed, startled.

"Oh, yes. You are at the center of the plan—actually, an obstacle, but one that will be removed shortly. Unfortunately, my first attempt failed. You didn't really believe that your accident was caused by an innocently gone astray poacher's bullet?" She seemed pleased by the remembrance. The urge to boast of her accomplishments was too strong to deny, and that streak of cruelty that she usually controlled could not resist tormenting her victim.

"You purposely had me shot? Hired someone to kill me?" Elysia asked in disbelief, feeling a knot of terror rise in her stomach.

"Yes. It was superbly planned—only the fool winged you instead of killing you. Now I shall have to get rid of you with less finesse—but it can't be helped. I am really rather pressed for time—what with my guests, and a new shipment arriving this afternoon. It was luck that this fog moved in this afternoon. We can move ahead of schedule. This is one of my most important loads. Never before have I received such a large payment for one cargo. That is why I shall personally see to it. The Squire is already down there, but I can't trust him not to make a mess of things.

"Do you realize how much inconvenience you have caused me?" Mrs. Blackmore asked conversationally. "You really do owe me an apology—for I have had to worry about getting rid of you, along with all of my other business transactions—which I really need to devote my fullest attention to. When I think of the precious time spent in worrying about you."

Elysia stared incredulously at her. The woman was mad, standing here calmly planning her death while she was expected to admire her brilliance. Had she no conscience? Mrs. Blackmore apparently felt no remorse at all, only slight irritation at being inconvenienced.

"How discourteous of me, Madame. I do beg your pardon," Elysia replied acidly, stalling for time. She clenched her hands into fists as she struggled against the fear she was feeling. She would not show panic in front of these creatures—it would merely add to their pleasure. "A small point of curiosity—if you would be so kind as to enlighten me. Why do you desire my death? I have never done you harm."

"Never done me harm?" Mrs. Blackmore repeated with a sneer. "Cheated me out of my rights, you have."

"That's absurd! I have never taken anything that belonged to you."

"You're Lady Trevegne, the Marchioness of St. Fleur, aren't you?" she demanded belligerently, stepping closer as she waved the loaded pistol wildly.

Elysia nodded her head. "Yes," she said faintly as she backed away from the determined advancing of Mrs. Blackmore.

"You stole that title from me!"

Elysia looked at her in disbelief. What in the world was she talking about? She must be insane.

"Louisa should now be the Marchioness, not you! I would have all of the estates, money, and position—a place in society—not just the insignificant wife of a country squire. But you shall pay for it. You with your lady-like airs. Regardless of your aristocratic blue blood—your veins will drip red blood as you die—and like all others, you will beg me—Clara Blackmore, the little actress that all those fine ladies lifted their noses at, while their husbands kept me on the side—to have mercy and spare that lovely, long, white neck of yours."

"Never!" Elysia spoke imperiously, raising her chin higher. "Since there appears to be little I can do to prevent your murdering me, then I will retain my dignity at least, and not bargain with the likes of you," she said quietly, looking at Mrs. Blackmore contemptuously.

Mrs. Blackmore's hand shook slightly before she shrugged her shoulders, feigning indifference. "Brave words, Lady Trevegne, very brave indeed. But I wonder how long that dignity will last, as death comes closer and closer, until you can breathe it?"

"Dignity is something you will never know—nor will you ever understand. It is beyond you," Elysia said boldly, her eyes glowing like green flames, "and do not think that you will succeed, for you shall not, Mrs. Blackmore. Shall I give you a prediction?"

"Enough! I do not care for this game you play— I'm no fool. Predictions—bah!" Mrs. Blackmore laughed scornfully.

"Oh, but you should. I have been accused on several occasions of being a witch." Elysia laughed as the other woman looked momentarily startled.

"Ah, I can see you *do* believe—if maybe just a little. Well, let me tell you your future. You shall be destroyed, found out, and unmasked, for the traitor that you are—and soon, my dear Mrs. Blackmore, quite soon. All that money and power that you crave will not be yours to enjoy, for my death shall not go unavenged, either," Elysia promised in a soft voice, sounding as if she had placed a curse upon her head.

The two large men behind Mrs. Blackmore shifted uneasily as they stared in fascination at the play of color in Elysia's hair, the flames from the torches seeming to dance within it.

"Kill her!" Mrs. Blackmore screamed as she backed away nervously from Elysia, and the strange, green light that shone from her slanted eyes as she continued to stare at Mrs. Blackmore. There was no fear of dying visible on her beautiful face, only a smile, curving her lips, as she saw the doubt and fear conflicting on Mrs. Blackmore's pinched face. "You're going to die!" Mrs. Blackmore hissed venomously as she made her way down the passage to the mouth of the cave. "Finish her off quickly— we've work to do this afternoon. Good-bye, Lady Trevegne," she added, laughing as she disappeared through the entrance.

Elysia stood silent, facing the two men as they measured her up. Wondering if she would put up a fight, were they? Well, they would soon find out that she was no cowering faint-heart. If she was destined to die, she would go fighting.

But they had other plans for her first. She was not to die immediately, and not with any shred of dignity. Elysia felt her heart stop and start up sickeningly, as she understood what they were planning. She watched them run their tongues over their thick lips and rotting teeth expectantly.

"Ye'll not be givin' ol' Jack any trouble now, eh?" one of them said, noting her clenched fists. "We're to have our way with ye. Ain't nothin' ye can do about it, me pretty—and I reckon we might just enjoy ourselves with ye before we finishes ye off."

"Yeah, I was a-hopin' ye'd be a feelin' that way, Jack me boy," his friend added, making a move forward like a hunter stalking his prey.

"Not so fast there, laddie-buck. She's mine first," Jack warned his smaller companion.

"And who says so?"

"I do—and that should be answer enough, if ye knows whats good fer ye," he threatened in a growl.

Elysia took a step backwards. It was too much to hope that they might kill each other off in a fight over who would rape her first. If there were only some way she could escape—but they were too big and powerful. She didn't have a chance. She couldn't bribe them—what enticement could be great enough for them to risk their necks by hanging. Turning her loose would be endangering themselves with detection as smugglers—even worse, traitors, and possibly murderers. No matter how great a sum she promised, they would not risk it.

The one called Jack made a sudden lunge, grasping Elysia around the waist and pulling her into his arms. Her face was pressed into his shoulder, his shirt smelling of sweat and grime. Elysia gagged as the smell putrefied in her nostrils. He pulled at her dress, already ripped in the seams, revealing her shoulders.

Elysia felt faint, a thousand hammers were beating away in her head and his arms were pressing against her bruised sides. She prayed for unconsciousness to come swiftly and release her from this agony that was far worse than death.

"Oh, no ye don't, me pretty. Come on, fight me," he said thickly as his foul breath hit her nostrils, before his mouth closed down on her lips. She tried to struggle but his arms were like a vise, forcing her into immobility, lifting her off her feet, her half-boots causing little damage to his thickly booted legs.

His large hands pulled at her as he threw her roughly to the ground, following her down, his heavy bulk pressing against her painfully. Tears trickled from beneath her closed lids as she felt his fingers moving along her leg.

The fogginess in Elysia's brain was suddenly shattered by the sharp report of a pistol firing twice, the roar of the shot echoing from wall to wall around the cave until it drowned out the sound of the sea. The man above her gave a surprised cry and rolled from her, a stricken look of astonishment crossing his heavy features.

Elysia stared up into the coal-black eyes of the man standing over the lifeless body of her attacker, the pistol he held negligently in his hand still smoking.

"*Mon Dieu!*" he repeated in a voice of disbelief. "What are you doing here? I would kill the swine a thousand times over for this." He spat on the still form beneath his highly-polished, booted legs.

The Count knelt down and helped Elysia to her feet, removing his coat and placing it about her shaking form, his arms holding her steady as she swayed on her weak legs.

"Here drink this," he offered, drawing a silver flask from his coat and holding it to Elysia's white lips.

She coughed as she breathed the strong fumes of the brandy, but drank deeply of it. Elysia could feel its heat burning through her body, spreading its warmth like a flame. The dizziness passed and her legs no longer felt like quivering jelly. Taking a deep breath she looked at the Count who was staring at her with deep concern in his black eyes.

"I do not know quite how to thank you, *Monsieur le Comte*. I owe you my life," Elysia said humbly, her voice weak and shaken.

"That I could have been of service to you, *c'est un honneur—mais*, I do not think they would have killed you. As a woman of dignity, however, you would have wished it."

"No, you are mistaken—they had orders to kill me."

"Orders? *C'est impossible. Pourquoi?* Why should anyone desire that one so lovely as yourself should die?" the Count asked incredulously, still doubtful. He glanced about him at the stone walls of the cave and the stacks of goods piled up beneath its domed ceiling. "What are you doing here?"

"I was tricked into coming here—by Mrs. Blackmore. She's insane—mad with the lust for power, and she will stop at nothing to get what she wants." Elysia watched the look of disbelief on the Count's face. He may be working with the Blackmores, but he was entirely innocent of Mrs.

Blackmore's murderous plans concerning herself, she thought. He proved that when he killed two of Mrs. Blackmore's hired assassins.

"Why should she want to kill you, Lady Elysia?"

"I am in her way. She had designs on the Marquis. She had hoped for a match between Louisa and Alex, but unfortunately, he chose me instead."

"Ah, *je comprends*. That is a woman to beware of. If it were otherwise ... well," he shrugged, "I would have no dealings with her. It is always safer to know the enemy—then you are prepared—but if you do not think that one is to be feared, then how can you protect yourself from a blow that you do not expect? She is evil, that one, and very dangerous." He looked perturbed. "Even I did not know *how* dangerous."

"Then you know a great deal about Mrs. Blackmore, *Monsieur le Comte*." Elysia's thoughts were beginning to orient themselves once again, despite the aching in her head, and she realized that the Count had no idea that he had been detected, and that she knew the truth of his mission in England.

"*Oui*, this is so," he smiled hesitantly, casting a look over his shoulder expectantly, "and I suppose that you must be wondering what I am doing here. It is true—now that you have seen that woman's true character—that she is a smuggler. My involvement with her is only for the purpose of transportation. You see I must get to France, on occasion," the Count explained sincerely. "You must believe me. I am not a Bonapartist. *Non!* I am a Royalist. I am fighting with the groups who oppose that tyrant, but I also must see to my estates. You do believe me?" he demanded, as if her trust meant something to him. "In fact, I have the sanction of your Prime Minister to do this work," he lied, trying to make her believe him.

If she had not already learned the truth about the Count, then she would have believed every lying word that he had so eloquently spoken just now. He was an accomplished spy, after all, and it was his job to deceive people into trusting him.

"Please, you will believe me?" he entreated. "You do believe me . . . you will not say of what you have seen . . . at least about me?" He seemed so sincere, so anxious for her to believe him, Elysia thought in puzzlement, until she noticed how his fingers were nervously handling the trigger of the pistol tucked into the waistband of his pantaloons. He did not wish to kill her—unless she did not believe him, and denounced him to the authorities. That was the reason for his insistence that she believe him. At least he was giving her a chance—which was more than Mrs. Blackmore had done. Very well Count, you shall receive my complete faith, Elysia thought, and we shall play this charade out.

"Yes I believe you, *Monsieur le Comte*," Eylsia finally answered him, noticing the relief on his face as he seemed to relax.

"You will for once call me Jean?" He lifted her hand and kissed the scratches softly, before glancing over his shoulder nervously again, towards the mouth of the cave, and pulling out his watch to check the time with a worried expression on his face. "I must depart at any moment now," he told her, staring at her with indecision.

What could she do, Elysia thought in confusion? He had saved her life, yet he was a traitor. He was planning to leave England with secret documents—and she could stop him—or could she? Despite his timely interruption that had saved her life, she had no doubt that he was as loyal to France as she was to England. If she tried to stop him, he would kill her without hesitation.

"It is a pity that our paths have crossed—and there it will end. I suppose that is the way of the world. Nothing is the way that I would want it. If you had been French . . . ah! But, alas, it cannot be. Come now, I shall escort you out of here, for I must meet a boat that is coming to collect me." He looked at the suffering in Elysia's eyes, adding, "You had better leave here at once . . . and I shall deal with the Squire's wife in due time." He took Elysia's elbow and begain to guide her to the steep flight of steps.

"Count . . . I must stop you," Elysia began, and would have reached for his pistol, but before she could, there was a disturbance at the mouth of the cave. The Count halted, turning expectantly at the sound. His look changed to anger and watchfulness as he stared at the intruder.

Mrs. Blackmore came to a surprised stand-still in

mid-stride. The sight of the Count and Elysia, and the two prone bodies of her henchmen brought a look of concentrated fury that whitened her already-pale face, tautening the skin painfully across her cheekbones.

"You!" she screamed looking wild-eyed at Elysia. "You should be dead! You deserve to die for what you've done to me with your damed curses," she said panting, a trickle of saliva dripping from the corner of her mouth.

Mrs. Blackmore smiled grotesquely and charged Elysia, snarling like a mad dog, but the Count stepped quickly in front of Elysia, shielding her with his body.

"Stop!" he warned as Mrs. Blackmore's hands reached out, claw-like, the nails looking as lethal as the fangs of a vicious animal. "You are insane. You jeopardize my whole mission! I shall, in future, recommend that we have no further dealings with you."

"You stupid Frenchie. You'll never get out of here alive," she laughed diabolically. "The soldiers are right behind me. You've been betrayed!" she screamed, as she pulled a pistol from her cape, and before the Count could make a move she had fired. There was a look of surprise and disbelief on his face as he fell forward, the blood oozing from his chest.

Elysia stared, mesmerized by the glowing eyes of Mrs. Blackmore, and stunned by the cold-blooded shooting of the Count.

"Now you shall finally die—once and for all," Mrs. Blackmore promised, as she levelled the barrel of the pistol directly at Elysia's head.

Elysia took a deep breath. It would seem that she was really going to die this time. There would be no last minute effort to save her—unless she herself made an attempt—but she was drained of all energy. She could barely stand.

She tensed herself to spring. If she could just knock the gun from Mrs. Blackmore's hand. She was desperate, willing to try anything to save herself, hoping her strength would hold out, when she heard the sound of running feet and voices. They seemed to be surrounding them, from everywhere people suddenly converged upon them. Mrs. Blackmore glanced about wildly, the sounds echoing through the cave without direction, magnified over and over, until it was a confused mass of sound.

Elysia saw Ian come striding through the opening, a look of triumph on his face as he saw the cave and its storage of smuggled treasure. His triumphant look faded abruptly, as he caught sight of Elysia's torn and bloodied figure.

"My God! Elysia!" he gasped in surprise, momentarily taken off balance.

Elysia cried a warning, but Mrs. Blackmore had already turned and fired at Ian. Elysia screamed as she saw Ian grimace with pain and stagger back to fall against the wall of the cave.

Other men had entered the cave now, halting, as

they stood unsure of what to do, as they looked with surprise at the two women standing mute before them—one with a pistol smoking malevolently in her hand.

The opening of the secret door above them broke the spell, as the Marines' eyes were drawn upward to two well-dressed gentlemen entering in a hurry, followed by a small, grizzled man waving a dangerous-looking blunderbuss.

Mrs. Blackmore screamed like a cornered animal, abusing them all with foul language, as she forcibly pushed her way past the bemused Marines, towards the mouth of the cave. Elysia's paralysis seemed to break and she rushed anxiously to Ian, who had slumped down upon his knees. As Elysia knelt down beside him, she was unaware of the sound of the booted feet hurrying down the steps behind her. Her only concern was for Ian.

Mrs. Blackmore had paused at the entrance, her hatred so insane and twisted that she aimed her pistol once more—this time at Elysia's vulnerable back, before the astonished Marines could anticipate her actions. But Alex had been quicker. He grasped the Count's pistol from the dead man's hand and fired it in one quick motion, without stopping to aim.

Mrs. Blackmore screamed as the shot winged her arm, making her drop the pistol. She grabbed her shoulder and turned in panic to escape, but her steps were uncoordinated, as she staggered onto the path. She stumbled as she hurried, losing her balance, and falling forward over the edge, her arms flailing the air futilely.

Inside the cave her blood-curdling scream echoed eerily in the silence, as she fell down the sheer drop, onto the sharp rocks below.

Alex dropped the pistol distastefully as he walked over to where Elysia knelt beside the wounded man. He stared in disbelief at her bruised and bloody appearance. He reached out to pull her to him, and only then did her voice reach him, turning him pale at her words.

"Ian, oh Ian. Are you all right ... oh, please ... don't die. You can't ... now that I've found you again."

Elysia was touching Ian's face with gentle and loving hands, and was completely unaware of all that was going on around her—not seeing the outstretched arms drop, as Alex turned away unnoticed.

'Ah, la belle chose de savoir quelque chose.
  Knowledge is a fine thing.

                                    Moliére

Chapter 16

"Oh, Lady Elysia," Dany scolded lovingly, "I just don't know what's to become of ye?"

She was helping Elysia dress after bathing her and seeing to her wounds, her exclamations of dismay and outrage unable to be contained as she saw the extent of Elysia's injuries. She gently towelled Elysia's long hair, the dust and blood painstakingly washed free from the shining strands.

Dany left Elysia sitting snugly before the fire, its glow spreading a warmth over the room. Elysia gratefully sipped the cup of fragrant, hot tea that Dany had prescribed for her, and wrapped her fingers about the fragile tea cup. The warmth from the hot liquid warmed her fingers as she felt the paper-thin china beneath. How easy it would be to crush it, she mused—and how very easy it was to die. She had seen death happen swiftly and unexpectedly, taking with it something very special and precious, that could never be brought back again. How quickly a life was snuffed out—as simply as the flame of a candle! She had come so close to it herself—yet she had escaped it.

And what would she have left behind her, had she died? All these days of anger and resentment would be her legacy. A bitter taste left in the memory of those she'd lived with. Life was too short not to take what happiness one could.

She would grab at it greedily if it was still within her grasp. Take whatever offer was given her by Alex—even if it meant sharing him with Lady Woodley—even if she only saw him occasionally, when he felt it necessary to visit her from London. She was, after all, still his wife—and he would want an heir. It was one of the reasons why he had married her—to have sons to inherit. And she would have his sons to cherish and love, a small part of him to hold forever. In that sense, she was still necessary—even if he did not love her.

Alex had been very concerned and solicitous of her health, coming back from Blackmore, but she had sensed a wall between them—an indifference and coldness. It was as if he were telling her that he could feel concerned for anyone who had been injured and was in need of care—but not to make anything more of it than that—for that was all it was.

There was a hesitant tap on the door, before it was opened and Louisa entered the room. She was pale, and dark circles of grief accentuated her gray eyes, making them look enormous in her small face. Her hands were nervously clasping a damp handkerchief, wrinkled from constant wringing.

"Louisa," Elysia spoke softly, compassion for the other girl in her eyes. "I'm glad you've come."

"I was not sure of my welcome, a-after ..." she paused as a spasm of pain crossed her face at her words, "what had been done to you."

"You are not to blame!" Elysia was indignant. "Surely you do not believe I could possibly blame you, or bear you any ill-will? Oh, Louisa, you are my dearest friend." Elysia held out her arms to the bewildered girl who looked as if one more blow might snap her in two.

Elysia held Louisa's shaking body, murmuring words of comfort which could not assuage the deep hurt Louisa must be feeling. But they seemed to have a soothing effect, for Louisa's sobs gradually diminished, until she leaned quietly against Elysia, taking deep, ragged breaths.

"Remember when first we met, and I told you we would have need of each other's shoulders to cry on?" Elysia asked, as Louisa mopped at her tears with her ridiculously-inadequate, lace-edged hanky.

"Yes I remember," she replied in a muffled voice, "but never did I dream that it would be under these circumstances. I still find it hard to believe." She looked at Elysia's bruised cheek in mystification. "That Mama would dare to try to kill you ... that she was l-like that ... that they are dead," she whispered struggling to understand the implications of it all.

"I never knew them. It was all a lie that they were living," she sighed with regret. "I was never close to them. Mama and Papa were not ones to show affection—in fact, I sometimes wondered if I was even wanted? I was always in the way as a child. I was with my Nanas more than my parents. It was only when I came of marriageable age that I had any worth or importance to them."

"Louisa, please don't," Elysia pleaded, hating to see the wounded look on her pale face.

"No, please, I'd rather face the truth—it's better this way. I do not feel grief for their death—it is more of a grief of betrayal."

Maybe it was wiser to let Louisa talk. An inner strength was growing within her, maturing her as she faced up to, and accepted what had happened and why. She would be stronger in the end, Elysia thought, as she noticed the new determined light in the soft-gray eyes. She would not be hardened though, for she had a gentleness that would never leave her.

"They wanted too much, Elysia," Louisa was saying sadly. "Their greed corrupted whatever decency they had. But whatever else they might have been, they were my parents, and I shall remember

hem as that—regardless." Louisa stood up reluc-
antly. "Now there are matters to be seen to that I
must deal with, and I do not even know where to
begin." She shook her head hopelessly.

"You can not handle it alone. Please allow our solicitors to take these matters in hand. I don't know
who they are, but I am sure Alex will get in touch
with them on your behalf. After all it is what they
do best and if you have any further difficulties, then
I an my brother will be only too glad to be of assis-
ance."

"Ian? I had not heard that you had a brother,"
Louisa looked puzzled. "I had thought you an only
child. I shall look forward to making his acquaintance."

"Oh, but you have met him," Elysia told her, innocently.

"I have? No," she said with a thoughtful look on
her face. "I do believe you are mistaken, for surely I
would have remembered your brother."

"Possibly you know him under a different name—
David Friday. I do believe he is using that name
hereabouts."

Louisa stared at her as if she were crazed. "David
Friday is your brother! B-but I do not understand
this. He is not a sailor . . . then, who is he?"

"It is a long and incredible story, and one of
which I do not even know all the details, except
that he is Ian Demarice, my older brother, and an
officer in the Royal Navy—and quite a respectable

gentleman. But why not let him answer all of your questions?"

"Oh, dear me ... your brother? Oh, I just couldn't—and besides, if what you say is true ... then he was just doing his duty," she continued flustered. "I always suspected he was more than he said he was. He acted like such a gentleman, always. Everything is so confused downstairs, but I did think that I caught sight of him there. I am so confused. He is an officer, you say?" Elysia nodded, and Louisa's face crumpled as she said, "So it was all an act, e-even his interest in me—a part of the job, which is now over."

"It'll never be over between us, Louisa."

Louisa gave a start of surprise and turned to see Ian striding into the room. His top boots were muddied and there was a rip in the shoulder seam of his jacket where the bullet had torn into it. His arm was in a sling, and he looked tired, but elated. His mission had been a success and all he'd set out to do, he had accomplished.

"Ian, how is your arm? Should you be up and walking about?" Elysia said worriedly, as he came over and kissed her cheek affectionately.

"Now stop mother-henning me—had enough of that from that woman clucking about me downstairs. A Mrs. Duney ... Diney, I don't know, but she sure knows how to wrap a bandage. Could've used her in the Mediterranean, except all the men would've deserted to get away from that horrid stuff she peddles as medicine." He grimaced, still tasting its flavor in his mouth. "All of that for a little scratch."

"That's Dany's special elixir, guaranteed to put you on your feet again," Elysia laughed, delighted to see Ian was not suffering from any aftereffects.

"Nearly put me on my head!" He walked over to where Louisa was standing quietly, intently studying a rather commonplace piece of the mantlepiece, and addressed his next remarks to the smooth curve of neck revealed to him, despite its obstinate set. "I do not believe that we have been properly introduced. I am Ian Demarice." He bowed formally over her limp hand, a smile lurking in his eyes.

"Mr. Demarice," Louisa replied formally. "I'm afraid that I do not know your rank."

"It's Lieutenant." Ian stared down into her gray eyes intently, a muscle twitching in his eye. "I am sorry, Louisa. I would not have had you suffer for anything in the world, but our wishes do not always come first. Believe me when I say I would not have had it end this way."

"Thank you. I know you were only doing your job, and it had to be done. I trust there would have been no other way out of this that could have ended happily. Someone was bound to get hurt."

"I am sorry that it had to be you, Louisa," Ian said softly.

"Yes, well . . . it is all over now."

"Yes it is," Ian agreed gravely, then cast a loving eye on Elysia. "Well, darling sister, you certainly gave me a fright—seeing you in that cave took years

403

off my life. But you were always one to involve yourself in mischief," he reproved her gently. "How are you feeling? I can't honestly say that you look none the worse for wear."

"I feel better than I must look," Elysia declared, catching sight of herself in the mirror. "I shall never be vain of my looks again." She hesitated uncomfortably, then asked, a trifle too casually, "And where are the others?"

"If by others, you mean your husband and brother-in-law, then they are downstairs in the salon with the authorities. There is much to be seen to, and straightened out. I should not like to see the villagers or fishermen punished harshly; they were compelled against their will to join this gang."

"I also would not like to see this happen, and if in any way I can atone for what my parents did to their people—then I would be most sincerely grateful. It is the least that I can do." Louisa looked shyly at Ian, her hands clenched. "I will not presume upon your friendship now that this affair is over. I know that you were only following orders, a-and I truly understand. Now if you will excuse me." She made to leave, but Ian grasped her arm, halting her.

"You are wrong Louisa, for it is I who would not presume upon *your* friendship when you have learned the full extent of my role in this tragedy. If you could find it in your heart to forgive me, then I could ask for no more."

"But I could never hate you, Ian," Louisa cried,

appalled at the thought. "I have nothing to forgive you for; you were only doing your job, and I would not have expected less of you."

Ian smiled into the misty gray eyes, his heart in his eyes as he captured her fluttering hand in his large tanned one, holding onto it possessively as he turned to look at Elysia.

"I shall have to report to my commander, Elysia, but I shall be back within the week, so I will be leaving shortly." His blue eyes caressed Louisa's face as he added sternly. "But Louisa and I have a small matter to see to first, so if you will excuse us, we will try to reach an agreement."

"By all means," Elysia replied smiling, "and Louisa, believe him, for I can vouch for his honesty and ... sincerity. He is also extremely mulish when he wants his own way."

Louisa returned her smile shyly, a becoming blush coloring her cheeks as she left the room with Ian's arm hovering about her shoulders.

"I am afraid that I am sadly out of touch with what has been going on in St. Fleur. I allowed my responsibilities to be assumed by the Squire, who grossly and criminally misused them. But I can promise you gentlemen that I shall take a personal interest in the future of this area and the people who live here," the Marquis promised the Admiral and special envoy from London, who were sitting before him in the salon, a touch of hauteur in his voice.

"Of course it will have to be settled in court, but I feel assured that the villagers will not be dealt with harshly, or suffer unduly, now that all of the circumstances have been revealed. And with your patronage, I feel sure we will no longer have trouble in these parts," the special envoy conceded, but he was still slightly put out that it had been a woman who had led them such a chase, and had been instrumental in his being forced to live aboard ship these past weeks. He felt insulted by the indignity of being outwitted by a woman for so long, although his feelings were smoothed over by the recovery of the secret dispatch, and the end of the spy that had confounded his department so easily.

"Thank you for your confidence, gentlemen. A glass of brandy before you go?" the Marquis inquired politely, as he deftly excused himself. He motioned to Peter to see to it, as he saw Ian and Louisa cross the hall intent upon entering the library. He followed them, catching up with them before they entered the room, and said arrogantly, "Just a moment. I want a word with you."

Ian turned, startled by the command in the cold voice, and faced the hawk-like features of the Marquis. He was momentarily perturbed at the interruption, but how could he refuse his host and brother-in-law, in his own home?

"Certainly, Your Lordship, I am at your service." He pressed Louisa's hand. "I shall be back shortly, so do not disappear," he warned, and spotting a book on a small pier-table, picked it up and smiled

s he noticed its title before placing it in Louisa's
hands. "This will keep you entertained, my love."

Louisa blushed as she stared down at the small
volume of Shakespeare's love sonnets.

Ian followed the stiff-backed Marquis into his
study and glanced at him in bewilderment as the
Marquis closed the door with ill-contained anger,
and turned to glare at him with what seemed to be
enmity. And why should Lord Trevegne be glowering at him? Ian thought in dismay as he stood
uncomfortably for a moment, feeling unnerved before that golden-eyed gaze. He never felt this
tingling feeling of approaching doom when facing a
dozen cannon!

Ian coughed, breaking the silence. "You wished
for a few words with me?"

"More than a few words, Sir," Lord Trevegne retorted sarcastically, "after that charming scene I had
he misfortune to witness."

"I beg your pardon—but what is that supposed to
mean?" Ian demanded, not at all certain he cared
for His Lordship's tone of voice.

"I mean that sickening display of devotion on
your part, while Elysia lies bruised and beaten,
above your very head. I ought to throttle you within
an inch of your life," he threatened ominously.

Ian blanched. Good Lord! What the devil was the
fellow enraged about?

"I say, Elysia will be all right—a trifle bruised yes,
but she's a spirited lass, and I've seen her in worse
scrapes." Ian smiled what he thought was a comfort-

ing smile. Obviously, His Lordship was upset over
Elysia's condition. "I'll admit she's been through a
devil of a time, shocked me, it did, to see her in that
cave. But you can rest assured, Lord Trevegne, for
your housekeeper, a Mrs. uh ... ah yes, a Mrs
Dany, said she would be fine, what with a little
rest."

"Oh, does she now?" Alex asked quietly. "And I
suppose you have been up to see my wife?"

"Of course!" Ian looked at the Marquis oddly
"Naturally, it's my right. What kind of a person do
you think I am?"

"I'll tell you what I think you are, you bloody
bastard," Alex growled, his control snapping in a
wave of outraged fury. He pounced on the startled
young man, carrying him backwards against the
wall where he held him pinned helplessly, oblivious
to the other's bandaged shoulder.

"I could kill you! No one has ever dared to do
what you have dared. What is mine, I keep
Remember that—Elysia is mine, and always will be
No suckling pup with ideas above his station is
going to take her from me! You can clear out, and
don't you set foot on this piece of coast as long as
you live," Alex paused, his breathing ragged, "or
your life will be shortened considerably."

Giving Ian a shake like a dog with a bone, he released him suddenly, throwing him aside, where Ian
stumbled to fall against a large, leather chair
Catching himself, Ian rose to his feet, the blood

rushing into his face as his fists clenched into tight balls of bone and muscle.

"I admit that I was shocked when I discovered Elysia had wed *you*," he spoke with disdain, "and I was, to be frank, dismayed for I have knowledge of your reputation, Your Lordship. And," he paused straightening his shoulders with what dignity he could muster, "you have only confirmed my worst fears regarding this marriage. I know that as a gentleman, I have no other recourse but to remove Elysia from your influence. Divorce is to be looked upon with disfavor, of course, and only as a last resort—but I shall see that you have no more to say or do about her welfare."

"Why you impudent milk-sop. You would dare to cross me!" Alex bellowed, feeling madder than he had ever felt before in the whole of his life. He was beyond all reason. "You would like to have that divorce—a last resort indeed, you lying cheat!" he sneered. Ian's eyes blazed at this final insult. He would take no more from this half-crazed Marquis. He drew his glove to challenge this scurrilous attack of his character, but His Lordship was continuing, not content with his previous insults. It was as if he were purposely goading him into a challenge.

"I will never divorce her. She's mine—a Trevegne—and will remain a Trevegne until she dies. You will never marry her, you snivelling cur!"

Ian stopped, his hand holding the glove in midair. Marry? What the devil? He stared at Lord Trevegne in astonishment. "Marry?" he repeated aloud.

Surely he could not have heard correctly, he thought in bewilderment.

"Yes, marry," Alex enunciated carefully between gritted teeth. "Or had you hoped only for a brief affair? That would be more in your style."

"Marry ... but why in God's name should I want to marry my own sister?" Ian's hand dropped to his side as he continued to stare at the Marquis, who was also now staring, as if he had not heard correctly.

"Elysia is your sister?" he said unbelievingly, his voice barely above a whisper.

"Of course," Ian answered amazed. Then a look of wonder dawned on his features, and he gave a hoot of laughter. "You mean you didn't know?"

"No, by God, I did not! It would seem there is very little I do know about my wife, or my home, or anything else in this damned affair. Master of my castle—indeed!" Alex's eyes blazed. "It would seem I am master of nothing!"

Ian's amusement fled before the burning anger on the Marquis' face. This was no man to trifled with—especially in his present mood.

"But of course!" Ian suddenly exclaimed as he remembered the promise he had exacted from Elysia. "Elysia couldn't tell you—she was sworn to secrecy by me. You must understand that my safety was at stake, if my true identity had been revealed, then all would have been lost. It was not her fault, for I was determined to have my way ... so she gave her oath on it—and that is one thing Elysia will not break. I am Ian Demarice, Your Lordship, Elysia's brother."

Ian stood waiting while Lord Trevegne assimulated this new development in their relationship. Ian watched the harsh features, granite-like and unyielding; a proud and arrogant man, not used to being in the wrong, Ian speculated wisely.

Alex stretched out his hand. "If you will accept my deepest apologies, and my humbly offered friendship, after all that I have said—insulting you unforgiveably—then I would be honored, Lieutenant Demarice," Alex said simply, but sincerely.

Ian clasped the older man's hand, gratefully. He never could abide ill-will existing between himself and others, nor did he intend to be on the outs with his brother-in-law. He had a suspicion of how much it cost this arrogant Marquis to humble himself so. He was also well aware of Lord Trevegne's rather indecent reputation, and had indeed been shocked to find his sister married to the man—a man called a demon, debauchee and devil, among the kinder descriptions he'd heard. But he would reserve judgment until later—after all, the Marquis had been ignorant of all the facts. For now he would accept, without question, this man's friendship. He did not care to have him as an enemy. And what better way to keep an eye on Elysia than to be a member of the family, and welcomed in her husband's home.

"All is forgotten, Lord Trevegne," Ian said in a friendly tone. "After all, you were acting under a misconception."

Alex smiled his crooked smile for the first time. "I should have guessed you were Elysia's brother, you are very much alike in character."

"Well." Ian looked doubtful, not sure whether that was to be taken as a compliment or not. "We've both been accused of stubbornness and willfulness, I suppose."

"I can attest to both of those. But I have kept you too long from Louisa. She will be growing impatient, if I'm not mistaken." He watched in amusement as Ian's face flushed pinkly. "You will both, of course, consider yourselves my guests—my home is yours." It was more of a command than a request, Ian noted sardonically, as he gladly accepted on behalf of Louisa and himself.

"Thank you, Lord Trevegne, I—"

"Alex," he invited with a genuine smile that seemed to change his austere features, warming them like the sun shining on newly-fallen snow. "We can't have formality between brothers-in-law."

"Alex, then," Ian grinned engagingly. "I shall have to report back to my ship, but I shall rest easy knowing Louisa's being cared for while I'm away."

"She is welcome here for as long as she desires. Now, do not keep her waiting any longer," he advised, seeing Ian's longing glance toward the door.

Alex poured himself a large snifter of brandy, downing a good bit of it before replenishing it again. He stared at the closed door, letting his mind roam where it would—uncontrolled by him. He sat down in one of the large red leather chairs, a thin cheroot held indolently between his lean fingers and the snifter of brandy in the other. He leaned back, narrowing his eyes in thought, the heavy lids almost covering the glowing gold of his eyes, as a strange smile curved his lips.

See what delights in sylvan scenes appear!
Descending Gods have found Elysium here.
                                    Alexander Pope

Chapter 17

The Blackmores were given a Christian burial, the Vicar trying his best to deliver a eulogy that would be accepted by all. He could not speak of them as praiseworthy—extolling their virtues would indeed be blasphemous, and subject him to bitter criticism by the villagers; and yet how could he stand before God and condemn them, branding them as the sinners that they were—and beyond God's forgiveness, as the local population would deem fitting?

In the end, the Vicar gave a stirring sermon upon the sin of greed and vice, and the ultimate downfall—illustrated nicely by the dead being laid to rest that day—of those who would follow that un-Christian path. He asked God's forgiveness of those poor souls who had strayed so far from righteousness, and asked the congregation to heed the lesson before them of those whose weaknesses had led them astray.

Elysia, Lord Trevegne, and Peter had accompanied Louisa to the burial, Elysia acutely conscious of the fact that it might very easily have been her they were eulogizing that morning.

Ian had returned to London two days previously, and was expected back within the week. Elysia rather expected he would bring a ring back with him when he returned; also, she suspected he might resign his commission when this war with Napoleon was over—if it ever would end. There was work to do at Blackmore Hall. It could be a profitable estate, if run honestly, and it would benefit the farmers to regain their land, and to have the mines opened again. Yes, there would be plenty to occupy Ian's time when he returned.

The late Squire's guests had swiftly returned to London, not staying for the services, their excuses of urgent business clearly understood. Lady Woodley had left also—a piece of information from Louisa that had interested her extremely; for Alex was still here, and apparently not making plans to leave as yet.

The laying to rest of the Blackmores had been that morning, under clear blue skies with puffy white clouds indolently drifting by overhead, casting their shadows on the countryside below. Now darkness had fallen, and a yellow moon was rising high in the black sky; vying for dominance against the billions of twinkling stars. They looked like brilliant jewels just out of reach, but near enough to tantalize, Elysia thought dreamily. She turned back from the window where she had been staring out into the night, at the sound of two footmen entering the room, and setting up a small table before the fireplace. She watched appreciatively, as they set out the sparkling china and crystal. A small, fluted, bud vase was placed in the center of the now lace-covered table; its faceted curves imprisoning the flames from the fire, as a single red rose was just beginning to open its fragrant petals to the warmth of the flames.

Elysia's heart began to hammer uncomfortably as she noticed the service for two being set, and the silver bucket of iced champagne placed beside the table. She continued to watch in dismay as the tall, slender candles were lit.

Surely Alex was not planning to dine with her alone—in this romantically contrived setting. Elysia dropped down into a chair, her legs refusing to hold her as she slumped forward, feeling her strength ebbing away. How could she fight him any longer? She had not the strength—nor the heart. She had been fooling herself. Now that it came to a confrontation with him, she was a coward. To be mistress of his home, and bear his sons; that was only a dream to occupy her lonely nights.

In the cold revealing light of day she knew that he would not be able to do it—not loving him the way she did. She could not bear to sit across from him in candlelight, knowing he was thinking of another woman—unable to touch him, show him her love. No! She could not endure such Hell.

"Good evening, M'Lady." Alex came into the salon smiling his crooked half-smile that tore at her heart. He casually flicked an imaginary speck of dust from his black velvet sleeve, the white lacy cuffs of his shirt sleeves peeking out provocatively, contrasting vividly with his darkness. All he needed now was a black patch over one eye and he would make a perfect pirate. His white teeth gleamed brightly against his tanned face, as he told her with apparent indifference, "I thought you might prefer to dine upstairs this evening. It has been a rather tiring day." He looked at her critically. "You could use the rest, m'dear. You're looking a bit pale."

"I seriously doubt, M'Lord, whether purple bruises are in fashion at the moment," Elysia was stung into replying sarcastically.

"Ah," he breathed, "I am pleased to hear that your fall did not knock out that wonderful wit of yours. I would sorely miss it. I had begun to wonder if indeed you had misplaced it, M'Lady," he said quizzically with a hawk-like gaze upon her face.

"No indeed, M'Lord, I still possess all of my beloved attributes. They are merely inactive at the moment. I am sure you will understand and excuse me if I have had other and more important things

417

on my mind at the moment than to entertain Your
Lordship with my witticisms."

"Bravo! You are fast returning to form, m'dear," he
laughed, as if thoroughly enjoying himself. His eyes
wandered proprietarily over her figure, clad in a
green velvet robe with a revealing décolletage.

Misunderstanding his look, Elysia explained de-
fensively, "I have just bathed, and had not reckoned
on entertaining before having completed my dressing."

"You need no further dressing on my account,
M'Lady. After all, I am your husband—and have
seen you in less," he said impertinently, watching
her blush at his words. "Shall we dine? I do believe
I've a hunger this evening."

Elysia eyed him suspiciously as he guided her so-
licitously to her chair, dismissing the footmen after
they had placed the silver-covered platters on the
table.

"Allow me to serve you, M'Lady," Alex said pleas-
antly, selecting a platter of poached turbot, covered
with a creamy sauce, for her inspection. "May I
tempt you with this juicy piece?" He forked it expertly onto her plate, adding a slice of ham basted
with Madeira, followed by stuffed lettuce, oysters,
liqueur-flavored jellies, potatoes in Hollandaise
sauce, and lobster. There were countless other platters still covered.

Elysia stared at her loaded plate without appetite.
How could she take a mouthful with him sitting not
two feet from her? Always before, they'd had the

great length of banqueting table between them. This was much too close for comfort.

Alex seemed not in the least bit affected as Elysia watched him expertly open his oysters, forking the soft, succulent fish into his mouth hungrily. He looked up before biting into the shimmering jelly, and gave her a wondering look. "You're not hungry? Antoine has indeed surpassed himself this evening." He ran the tip of his tongue along his upper lip, dabbing at the corner of his mouth gracefully. "Are you sure you are not in the least bit hungry? Here, have a bite of this lobster." He held a forkful out to her, enticing her with its aroma before her nose. "Come now, be a good girl, and take a bite."

Elysia found herself unable to resist him in this mood of gentle raillery, and submitted, taking a bite of the lobster, then surprising herself by eating hungrily of the food on her plate, under the approving gaze of her husband.

Alex kept their wine glasses filled with the darkly-aged red wine. It warmed her within as the heat from the fireplace warmed her skin with a pinkening glow outside.

Elysia was feeling relaxed and pleasingly light-headed as she reclined on the sofa, with the room taking on a rosy glow, as the fire crackled lazily in the grate. Alex handed Elysia a brimming glass of bubbling champagne despite her protestations that she'd had enough, but Alex was insistent and she gave in as before and accepted it, the bubbles tickling her nose as she sipped it.

"Now, we will talk," Alex spoke suddenly, breaking their companionable silence with a hard voice.

Elysia stiffened automatically, struggling to gather her thoughts into some semblance of order. If only Alex hadn't plied her with so much wine. She could hardly think coherently.

"It's no use, m'dear."

Elysia stared at him hazily.

"I intentionally got you relaxed, and slightly drunk," he said bluntly, his eyes never leaving her flushed face.

Elysia's hands shook as she carefully placed the half-empty, golden goblet of champagne down on the table by the sofa. "Why?" she demanded thickly.

"Because, my dear wife, in a slightly besotted state, that sharp mind of yours is not working as quickly as it is accustomed to doing. You will not be able to parry my questions so easily, nor confuse the issue by putting me on the defensive, as you are so capable of doing."

There was a grimness in his determination as he settled himself more comfortably, as if in preparation for a long evening.

She would have gotten up and walked out on him, but she seriously doubted whether she could get to the door—or for that matter, even as far as her feet.

"I owe you an apology," Alex began abruptly. "I should have realized that you, of all people, would not be involved in any kind of intrigue or dalliance.

However, I do not think that I can be wholly to blame for the mistake I made since you were unable to enlighten me otherwise. But that is past, and done with. I can only say that I am sorry for doubting you . . ." he paused and continued with difficulty, "and I regret deeply what I did to your doll. Dany has told me how much it meant to you. That is something that I cannot replace.

"But I can change what has happened between us—we can start anew. I can build something decent, for once in my life, and I want to build it with you, Elysia—you by my side as my wife—and lover."

The fuzziness was rapidly lifting from Elysia's sodden brain. She stared at Alex in disbelief before crying out in a husky voice full of hurt and outrage.

"Is this another of your tormenting games that we are to play? For if it is, then you are no gentleman. Indeed, once before you told me that you were not, but I did not take warning of that as I should have. You do not play by any rules, do you, Alex? You do not care how low you sink to hurt and degrade someone." Elysia felt hot tears on her face as she managed to get to her feet.

Alex's face had paled, and his lips were tightened in a grim line, as he listened to Elysia's rejection of his apology and declaration in disbelief.

"You stand there, after wining and dining me so attentively, brazenly lying to me with your false declarations of husbandly devotion, while your mistress awaits you eagerly in London. How many nights of this new life are we to share before you desert me and run to her?

" 'She will not come where she knows she is not welcome,' you said, or have you forgotten uttering those words to your lady love in the library?" Elysia demanded angrily, her humiliation coming back to her as she remembered painfully those endless moments.

"Oh, God!" Alex laughed harshly, the sound grating on Elysia's ears. "That those words should come back to haunt me. A fine performance, nevertheless, wouldn't you agree my dear?" he said, as if he hated himself, his lip curled in self-loathing.

"What do you mean by performance?" Elysia watched him nervously.

"I hate to disappoint you, but I am not the complete knave that you would believe me to be. Maybe a damned fool, yes, but not quite that despicable. I have done many things in my life of which I am not proud, but I have never lied to anyone. Do you not know that I have always known that you hide yourself away up in the loft, a place where no one can bother you—or torment you."

Elysia looked startled. He knew of her retreat? But how?

"I am aware of a few things that go on around here—not many it would seem, but I have eyes and ears and do see a few things, like you going into the library with a book—and disappearing. It's an apparently empty room until I hear the crackling of a page being turned."

He grimaced. "I would not blame you if you did not believe me, but I knew that you were up in the loft that day. I spoke what I did to Mariana because I knew you would be my audience. I wanted to hurt you, as you'd hurt me—or so I'd thought. Blast my damnable temper, but I'd been mad with jealousy of you—thinking Ian your lover, believing you to be like so many other women I have known, not worthy of trust and love. At first I'd thought you different."

"Y-you knew that I was up there in the loft . . . a-and that I would hear you making love to Lady Woodley?" Elysia asked faintly, scarcely understanding what he was saying to her.

"Yes I did. It was the act of a cruel and selfish man who struck out blindly in his rage—not caring who he injured."

"So you do not really intend to meet Lady Woodley in London? You do not really love her?" Elysia asked hesitantly, almost afraid to voice her thoughts for fear that it was all a hallucination; a cruel trick her mind was playing on her—to hear what she had not dreamed possible from Alex.

"No, I do not love her." His smile was bittersweet. "How could I ever love anyone else after having loved you, held you in my arms and felt your sweet kisses against my mouth?" he jerked out hoarsely. "But I believed that you hated me, were in love with another man. I have nearly wronged you once more by accosting your brother Ian—and a more surprised young man I have yet to meet, when I demanded what his intentions were toward you. thought I had lost you—so once again I acted the madman." A light entered his eyes making them glow like two burning flames. "I had wondered why the devil you were in that cave with Mrs Blackmore," he said softly, eyeing her in speculation. "It would seem that Peter is to be your confidante—but you should know before you confide in him any further, that Peter cannot keep a secret. It is physically impossible for him; he explodes unless he can tell someone."

Alex moved to stand closer to Elysia, his arm outstretched in supplication, as he continued in that quiet tone. "You were placed in unreasonable danger because you thought that I needed you—even though you had just overheard that damned scene in the library. I asked myself why? Why would you do that unless you loved me, despite all that had happened—you loved me. It has given me hope again, that I have not lost you."

Elysia felt tears brimming in her eyes at his words. It could not be true. She shook her head dazedly, letting his words sink in, but she was still thinking so slowly, her reactions dulled by the wine. Alex, alert to her every expression and movement, mistook her actions, and with a groan sank down onto the satin chair, his dark head held in his hands as he stared morosely at the carpet.

"I love you, Elysia. Can that mean anything to you? I've been a fool and a cad; I have been half-crazed since knowing you. I thought myself so clever—making use of you for my own ends. You were so vulnerable for me to exploit. I won't lie to you that I loved you at first; I didn't even know the meaning of the word. But I desired you—as any red-blooded man would desire a beautiful woman. When first I saw you, I didn't realize it at the time, but things were beginning to re-focus in my mind—it wasn't until later that I clearly understood this change. So in the meantime, I ruthlessly made use of our predicament; excusing myself by thinking that what I offered you was far better than what you would have faced in London—and you would have been grateful to me.

"But everything began to get out of control, for you were not like other women I had been involved with—you hated me. That was something new in itself, but even more, I found myself thinking about you, dreaming of you—until you became an obsession with me. I told myself that it was mere physical desire that I was feeling, but even after I had made you mine I still wanted you more than ever—and not *just* your body. I was jealous of every thought of yours that was not mine. When I saw you fallen under those trees in the copse, I died a thousand deaths, thinking you dead. That is when I knew that I loved you beyond my wildest imaginings."

He stood up and walked over to the fire, staring down into the flames. "I am a man who has lived fully, taking what he has wanted—my desires always fulfilled. Now, I want *you*. I could force my will on you—force you to live with me. You are in my home, where I am complete master. You bear my name—and possibly are carrying my child at this moment. Those are hard ties to break. But I will not force you to come to me, nor stay with me—if you desire to live elsewhere. I would like to keep you locked up—imprisoned here, with only me to be in your mind and heart. I am an arrogant and cruel man, and I am a selfish and jealous husband—unwilling to share you with anyone, now that I've found the one woman I love—something I had believed impossible for me.

"But in finding that I love you, I've also lost. For I cannot hurt you in order to have my desires fulfilled." He stood easily before the fire as if he only sought its warmth; the only sign of his agitation were his hands—the knuckles showing white against the tanned skin.

Elysia smiled thoughtfully. He was right, he was an arrogant man—not really cruel, just used to his own way, proud and imperious. But she loved him. She smiled wider, the smile lighting up her green eyes—and he loved her.

A log fell in the fireplace, the sparks flying as it settled and was consumed by the flames. Elysia moved, her immobility broken by the sound. The bonds that had held her, in what she thought must be an enchanted spell, were broken as she made her way to the man she loved.

Alex felt soft arms entwine his waist as Elysia pressed herself against his broad back, hugging him close to her, as if she were afraid he would disappear before she could tell him how much she loved him. He felt the heat rise in his body—a heat not caused by the closeness of the fire. She rubbed her cheek against his shoulder, but he remained still, allowing her to make the first move.

"Alex." Her voice sounded like a contended purr in his ear, as she snuggled against him like a little cat. "I've come to like it here, M'Lord. In fact, I rather fancy myself in the role of Lady of the Manor, and how could I manage to keep my wits sharp if I didn't have such an arrogant, self-opinionated, insufferable—and loveable husband?" she added softly.

Elysia felt Alex's shoulders shake, and heard the deep rumble of laughter as it shook within his chest. He grabbed her arms and released himself. Turning around he swung her up into his arms, holding her tightly against his heart.

"Ah, M'Lady. Was there ever another like you?" he laughed with delight. "You have heard of the Trevegne luck? They say I'm in league with the Devil—well, there'll be no putting an end to the rumor now. Once they've seen my green-eyed witch of a wife, weaving her spells about us all. But," he added warningly, "only I shall master her, and receive her honeyed kisses. No doubt our children will have horns and tails, but we belong to each other as no man or woman have before."

Alex tightened his arms, molding her to him. "Let me hear it again, M'Lady—tell me you love me," he growled, biting her ear as he nuzzled it. "It is something I shall never grow tired of hearing."

"Would you not rather I *showed* you how much I love you?" Elysia inquired, looking up at him with innocent green eyes. "Or if you prefer it, I will just *tell* you how much I love you, M'Lord."

Alex smiled crookedly, a light shining in his golden eyes. "You would play with my affections, M'Lady? Then you must accept the consequences, for I have a man-sized thirst that will not easily be quenched."

He cut off her murmured reply with his lips, kissing her hungrily all over her soft face until his mouth eagerly closed on her parted lips. Elysia wrapped her arms about his neck, pressing her mouth harder against his, opening its sweetness to his demands, as his hands moved searchingly over her body.

He lifted his lips from hers, staring down into Elysia's heavily-lidded eyes, darkened with the passion that his lips had aroused, and with a desire that matched his own.

"Well, M'Lady? Is the price too high?" he asked softly with a devilish glint in his eyes.

"The price is never too high—if it is worthwhile, M'Lord," Elysia answered softly, a look of invitation in her eyes.

THE BLAZING, TUMULTUOUS NOVEL
OF A LOVE AS OLD AS TIME,
AS TIMELESS AS FOREVER ...

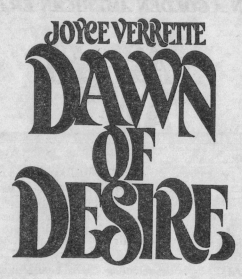

JOYCE VERRETTE
DAWN OF DESIRE

*In a faraway time, by the shores of the ancient River
Nile, they stand, possessed by a single naked desire,
in the dawning light of their eternal love. The unbounded passions of the incomparably beautiful
Princess Nefrytataten and the tawny-skinned Prince
Ameni sweep across the torrid landscape of Egypt
as the two lovers, wrenched asunder by treacherous
events, must brave peril, degradation, and intrigue
before their twin desires can find release once more
in a surging tide of full-blooded joy!*

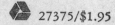 27375/$1.95

DOD 6-76

THE SWEEPING ROMANTIC EPIC
OF A PROUD WOMAN
IN A GOLDEN AMERICAN ERA!

**PATRICIA
GALLAGHER**

Beginning at the close of the Civil War, and sweeping
forward to the end of the last century, CASTLES IN
THE AIR tells of the relentless rise of beautiful, spirited
Devon Marshall from a war-ravaged Virginia landscape
to the glittering stratospheres of New York society and
the upper reaches of power in Washington.

In this American epic of surging power, there unfolds a
brilliant, luminous tapestry of human ambition, success,
lust, and our nation's vibrant past. And in the tempestu-
ous romance of Devon and the dynamic millionaire Keith
Curtis, Patricia Gallagher creates an unforgettable love
story of rare power and rich human scope.

AVON   27649 $1.95

CIA 5-76

From the author of

SWEET SAVAGE LOVE

A BREATHTAKING ROMANCE OF BLAZING UNQUENCHED PASSION...

ROSEMARY ROGERS'

WICKED LOVING LIES

The splendorous saga of beautiful golden-haired Marisa and dashing Dominic Challenger sweeps from the innocence of a sheltered convent, to the intrigues of Napoleon's court and the savage wilderness of Louisiana, in an unforgettable story of soaring wildhearted love!

From the trembling ecstasy of their first silken intertwining, Marisa is plunged into the swirling events of a thrilling age—braving revolution and captivity, wanting Dominic shamelessly, hopelessly, without pride or restraint—in an irresistible novel of unbounded passion!

  30221/$1.95

LIES 10-76